Valkyn shout

Lightning ass

the already cripp

flew into the air,

earth. The area b................... the worst of battlefields.

Cadrio almost expected to hear the cries of the dying.

The bolts continued for one minute, two, then three. Cadrio knew of the power needed to fulfill this spell, but nothing had prepared him for this. It amazed him that the man at his side had managed this much success. Yet it would mean nothing unless the mage followed through to the end.

And then a sound that made even the striking of a hundred bolts seem mute in comparison sent the general sprawling. For a horrible moment, he saw only blackened sky. Somehow, though, Cadrio struggled to his feet and refocused on the castle.

He saw a gaping hole where the citadel had once stood. . . .

DragonLance Classics

THE
CITADEL

Richard A. Knaak

THE CITADEL

©2000 Wizards of the Coast, Inc.
All Rights Reserved.

Cover art by Alan Pollack
First Printing: August 2000
Library of Congress Catalog Card Number: 00-101663

9 8 7 6 5 4 3 2 1

ISBN: 0-7869-1683-4
T21683-620

U.S., CANADA,
ASIA, PACIFIC, & LATIN AMERICA
Wizards of the Coast, Inc.
P.O. Box 707
Renton, WA 98057-0707
+1-800-324-6496

EUROPEAN HEADQUARTERS
Wizards of the Coast, Belgium
P.B. 2031
2600 Berchem
Belgium
+32-70-23-32-77

Visit our web site at **www.wizards.com/dragonlance**

Dedicated to Patty Lee (Beckermann) Perkins.

A young friend lost too soon.

Chapter 1

The Shadows of War

From the deck of the *Harpy*, General Marcus Cadrio, his thinning gray and brown hair plastered to his head and shoulders by the choppy sea, watched as the Northern Ergothian port city of Gwynned appeared tantalizingly at the edge of the horizon. The slim, clean-shaven commander lowered the magical device and stared again. Now he was unable to see even a trace of Gwynned, much less the rest of Northern Ergoth. The weather had turned foul with more vehemence than either he or his staff had anticipated. It was yet another strike against his forces in an already desperate war. He needed a victory soon if he hoped to stake his claim among the survivors of the Dark Queen's commanders.

"Orders, sir?" a subordinate dared to ask.

Cadrio turned toward the fool, briefly eyeing the stylized dragon design on his ebony breastplate. All his officers wore the same design, a fierce five-headed monster that represented a cause now lost. The thought further chilled the already cold tone in his voice. "And what orders would you like, Timinion? Have you some suggestions, perhaps?"

The aide looked away, unable to meet those deathly gray eyes. "N-None, General!"

His officers thought he would call the attack off. He dared not. His rivals were quickly solidifying their forces, preparing to create their own strongholds of power, and so far Cadrio had nothing but defeat to show for his efforts. He had been the chief officer of the Black Dragon Highlord, the most senior officer to survive the debacle when Emperor Ariakas had tried to open the way for their goddess, the great and terrible Takhisis, into the world of Krynn. Had his commander died earlier in the war, Cadrio felt certain that Ariakas would have chosen him to succeed as new Highlord of the Black Dragon Army. Cadrio had been born to lead. He had risen swiftly through the ranks. His destiny had seemed assured. . . .

And then everything had quickly come to ruin.

The War of the Lance, as the victors had recently dubbed it, had been suddenly and decisively won by the forces serving the cursed Platinum Dragon, the god of the Solamnic Knights, Paladine. Cadrio's hand curled into a gloved fist. His dreams, his hopes, his glories, had all vanished with Takhisis and the late emperor. All that remained were scraps.

But from those scraps, the general yet hoped to build his own empire. There were indeed orders he should give, but the lanky general did not do so. Instead, he pondered what had brought him to this desperate plan, commander of an army without a home, seeking to seize a foothold on a rich prize where no one would expect such a bold attack. Perhaps he should have accepted the offer of the Blue Lady. . . . But, no, she knew he stood as one of her rivals in controlling the surviving elements of the dragonarmies. She had only invited him to join her in order to obtain his resources, his soldiers. Then he would have eventually died or disappeared, leaving her in complete command.

Ignoring the harsh spray of the Sirrion Sea, Cadrio looked up. Among the dark clouds, he could make out two massive shapes moving somewhat sluggishly through the sky. Since the Dark Queen's defeat, the fortresses seemed to move with less speed now, as if some of their power had been drained. The clerics insisted that such was not the case, but the wizards questioned the stability of Cadrio's prizes.

"They will suffice, though," he muttered. "They must." The two fortresses had initially served him well after his Highlord's death. He had used them to surprise his nearest rival, to slay him and seize mastery of the opposing army. Then the pair had enabled him to sack the coastal town near Lemish, gaining him the *Harpy* and two other vessels for his fleet. Now his army was packed into a small convoy of ships, awaiting the opening the flying behemoths would give him when they came down upon Gwynned and her sea defenses.

Then he could land his troops, seize the Ergothian strong-hold, and lay claim to the beginning of his own empire.

General Cadrio knew a hint of madness lurked within him, but the brooding veteran saw his madness as yet another weapon at his disposal. He would do what others could not, not the Blue Lady or even Lord Ariakas. He, *Cadrio*, would conquer all. . . .

The general thrust out his empty hand. "My helmet, Zander."

A young but immaculate officer with features like a cat stepped forward with Cadrio's visored helm. Zander never questioned Cadrio but obeyed his orders to the letter. For that reason alone, he served as the commander's chief aide.

Helmet on, Cadrio took up the wizard's device and once more peered at Gwynned. He could make it out more clearly now, and what he noticed made him smile. Only a scant few ships moved about on the sea; the rest had returned to port to wait out the storm. He would be able to sail right in once the city had been softened up a little.

Lowering the device again, he shouted, "Signal the others!"

Two soldiers brought out covered oil lamps from the safety of an overhang and quickly waved the lit lamps in the direction of the nearest vessels. Moments later, identical lights appeared from the sister ships.

Those vessels would signal the rest, Cadrio knew. He looked up and noticed the two hulking fortresses slipping forward into the clouds. Behind them darted a pair of sleek reptilian forms, also part of his force. His allies in the sky had seen the signal and knew their parts. The attack had begun. Soon Gwynned would be his.

"Now let us see what madness can do," he whispered, picturing his twin titans even now descending on the unaware city.

* * * * *

"It seems to be getting darker outside," Leot noted, looking up from his desk. Ink spattered his full beard and the white robe of his order, the effects of the balding wizard's enthusiasm for his work. Leot looked twice his actual age, which had not yet reached three decades, but he appeared as if he had enjoyed that aging.

"It always gets darker around here when the weather turns," Tyros answered with barely concealed annoyance. He hated the changeable weather of this godforsaken port city where he and Leot had spent the past three months. "In fact, it has already begun to rain."

They were a contrast, these two friends. His vanity second only to his ambition, Tyros kept his person immaculate. His light brown hair and his classically styled, mustacheless beard were neatly trimmed. Unlike his companion, no spots marred his crisp red robe. He maintained his quarters with equal precision. His papers and personal items each had its own place.

Leot's personal chamber and his workplace reflected his own appearance, but to the opposite extreme. The ink spots were only the latest additions to the heavy-set wizard's garments, various food stains and chemicals having established homesteads before them. If not for an occasional spell designed to clean his robe, some might have never taken it for white.

Tyros's gaze briefly flitted about the chamber where they worked. It was a circular room, with shelf upon shelf piled high with scrolls, artifacts, and flasks. A skull belonging to some variation of lizard-man no one had been able to identify lay atop one shelf. A round table filled much of the interior. Two writing desks, both facing windows, stood on opposite ends of the room. Tyros preferred the desk that gave him the evening sun, a precious commodity in a port city prone to sudden weather shifts. Oil lamps placed strategically about the chamber kept it lit at night, while six stained-glass windows, a sign of its previous owner's wealth, illuminated the room during the day . . . except when the day grew very overcast. Originally built for a now deceased officer related to one of the seaport's prominent families, the tower had been turned over to the wizards midway through the war.

"Fascinating weather. One minute this, the next that," Leot finally answered in response to Tyros's remark. The rotund wizard always found a bright side to things. His round, almost cherubic features, so different from Tyros's narrow, more angular countenance, broke into a smile. He muttered a spell and the oil lamps burst into life.

Tyros blinked the spots from his eyes. "Warn me next time you do that."

"Sorry."

Tyros knew that Leot would forget. Leot forgot everything except his meals and his work. Tyros admired his focus but wished that same focus included Leot's personal life as well.

He returned to his own task. Deep brown eyes surveyed a scroll written by one Neomidas of Estwilde. Neomidas claimed to have come up with a spell to change gold to steel, an interesting if not particularly useful incantation. Tyros tried to follow the older mage's scratchy writing but failed halfway through. Finally he glanced at the date on which the scroll had been entered into the tower records. Neomidas had lived some two hundred years ago, meaning that if his spell had worked, someone likely would have noticed.

"Futility!" the Red Robe muttered. With barely checked anger, he rerolled the scroll, sealed it, and placed the parchment on the pile of rejected ones.

Since soon after the beginning of the war, Tyros, considered a most promising combat wizard, had taken to using every spare moment to pursue his pet project. Ever since he had first witnessed the use of what some considered the dragonarmies' most potent weapons, the astonishing flying fortresses, he had worked to fathom out their secrets, hoping to redesign one for his own side. Twice he had been fortunate enough to inspect the ruins of downed fortresses, sifting through the rubble and classifying every interesting fragment for later study. Along the way, he had helped formulate several new spells and even developed a strategy to fight the enemy's creations, winning much deserved acclaim among his peers, but as of yet Tyros hadn't unlocked the basis on which they actually functioned. Without that knowledge, he could never repeat the experiment successfully. The realization constantly galled him.

Tyros had requested and, due to his growing reputation, received scrolls and papers from hidden libraries all over Ansalon. The knowledge and spellwork of dozens upon dozens of wizards since the Cataclysm lay available to him, but so far most had fallen into the same category as Neomidas's ridiculous spell. It amazed him how much of the stored history of wizardry consisted of crackpot spells and notions that the authors must have thought they would later come back and revamp into something useful but never did.

"Nothing good?" Leot amicably asked.

"A brilliant deduction." Tyros leaned back. "In the past few weeks, I've seen a mere handful of suggestions that come close to what I seek. A few, such as those of Borlius of Palanthas or Valkyn of Culthairai, actually broach the subject, but their research always lead to ends as dead as they themselves."

"Borlius was a follower of Solinari. I remember his name from my teachings. He died just before I joined the order," Leot mused.

"And Valkyn was a member of my order, now probably as dead as Borlius. Culthairai was overrun early in the war." Tyros shrugged."It hardly matters! From what I have read of their work, neither could have taught me much I didn't know already!"

Leot kept his smile hidden as he listened to his friend's boastful tones. He knew the other's reputed arrogance. Most of the other wizards, not to mention the citizenry, avoided Tyros. Beneath the arrogance, though, Leot recognized a good and sometimes sympathetic man who, unfortunately, did not always understand how he made himself appear to others. The heavyset spellcaster remained one of Tyros's few friends, although Leot himself had many.

If Tyros failed to recognize his faults, he did, however, realize his good looks. More than a few ladies of the Ergothian nobility had dared scandals to approach the foreign wizard sent here under treaty agreement. Northern Ergoth had sought to could keep the dangers of magic to a minimum by housing its wielders in this tower, never suspecting that they would also have to worry about their own women seeking out the wizards.

Well, one wizard, anyway. Leot knew how he looked to the refined ladies.

"What will you do now?" he asked finally.

A bitter smile crept over Tyros's handsome features. "What is there left to do? They made it clear that these scrolls were the last ones I'd receive. The war's all but over, Leot! The Dark Queen herself has been ousted, and most of her commanders are dead or in rout! Imagine! We fight this war, but the credit goes to a ragtag group that includes a half-elf, a couple of barbarians, and a *kender*, of all things! Who are these creatures? I don't even know their names, but in the eyes of the populace, they've apparently saved the world and made my work superfluous!"

"I heard one of them was a wizard," the White Robe commented hopefully. "Our kind will get some credit, at least!"

"Hmmph! Probably turn out to be some wrinkled old illusionist who stayed completely clear of the mess! No wizard's been given due credit since Magius in the last dragon war, and even he's always overshadowed by that knight!"

"Maybe there'll be another war," Leot said, trying to cheer his friend up. What fighting still remained had dwindled considerably, although word of a female Dragon Highlord somewhere to the east gathering together what remained of Takhisis's forces had reached them recently. Still, such rumors tended to be nothing but air once they were investigated. Unfortunately for the ambitions of Tyros, it looked as if peace had broken out all over Ansalon.

A blaze of lightning followed by a crash of thunder startled both mages. Tyros gritted his teeth. "Blasted weather!"

"It helped protect Gwynned from invasion a couple of times."

"Who would ever be crazy enough to attack in such foul conditions anyway?" the crimson mage grumbled.

Thunder boomed again, this time so close that the tower shook.

Horns sounded, but while Gwynned had such signals that alerted its populace to terrible storms, these sounded different. Tyros stiffened, recognizing the call.

"War horns! They're alerting the defenses!"

Leot dropped his quill. "We're under attack?"

Throwing back their chairs, the two wizards rushed to opposite windows. Tyros flung his open and, after cursing the driving rain, peered out. Through the dark storm, at first he noted nothing but the normal appearance of the city, a bustling seaport with numerous docks and, beyond them, the crested buildings typical of the region. Four watchtowers guarded the perimeter of the main portion of Gwynned, and of these Tyros could see two. Yet despite the warning blares and torchlights, he could make out no invasion force. The sea, rough and turbulent, remained empty save for a few hardy ships returning to the docks, but they all bore the flag of Northern Ergoth.

"I don't see anything!" he called to his companion.

"Nor anything on this end!" Leot shouted from behind him. "Could it be a false alarm?"

"I don't know. . . ." Tyros stared up at the heavens, where the clouds had become so thick and dark that water seemed to come down in clumps the size of men.

He suddenly leaned out the window, unmindful of the drenching he received. Those were *figures* drifting down in the storm, figures with wings!

Only one creature came to mind. "Draconians! Dropping through the clouds!"

"What?" Leot appeared at his side. Both humans watched in horror as winged figure after winged figure glided toward the rooftops of Gwynned. They alighted onto some of the taller buildings, immediately trying to secure their hold.

Where did they come from? Fortunately, most draconians could not truly fly, and even if some of these invaders did have the ability, they certainly couldn't carry so many of their lesser brethren with them. Had dragons carried them here? It was a possibility, but for so many draconians, the attackers would have needed a hundred of the leviathans.

Tyros couldn't fathom that being the case, and so that left only one option. He studied the clouds, looking for a telltale shape.

At last he saw it, drifting in and out of the dark clouds, tiny aerial figures diving from its base. An astonishing sight to see, even for one who had seen it before.

A castle in the sky. This one stood tall and narrow, yet even from a distance, Tyros could see that one of its towers had collapsed and another leaned threateningly. Still, despite the damage it had suffered in some past battle, it no doubt filled the hearts of many below with fear.

A flying citadel. The secret of creating such floating castles had been known to mages and clerics of both darkness and light for centuries, only to be lost and then rediscovered from time to time. In this case, the entire castle had been ripped from the surrounding ground, an island of earth coming up with it. The island likely contained the dungeons and under-ground passages that had been built along with the original structure. One ruined citadel that Tyros had investigated had even included the family tombs, resulting in a ghoulish array of skeletal corpses at the scene of the flying castle's crash.

Up in the citadel, Tyros knew, a wizard or a cleric, perhaps both, guided the behemoth. Officers of the dragonarmies would be commanding archers to rain death down upon the city. More draconians would be leaping to the ground below. Of course, to the fortress's human commanders, the draconi-ans were merely fodder, to be used to open the way for their masters.

The flying citadel rocked in the increasingly harsh winds, its operator no doubt having to struggle. Tyros peered at what seemed to be the tallest remaining tower. Inside would be what someone had termed the Wind Captain's Chair, the place where a chosen one would actually pilot the edifice. Tyros strained futilely in an attempt to hear the chanting of the wizards and clerics aboard, an essential part of keeping the citadel afloat. Deep inside, some sort of arcane device would be aiding their task, but the ruined citadels he had studied had not left enough for him to understand just how that device might work.

To be up there now . . . Even with Gwynned under siege, the ambitious spellcaster dreamed of investigating the leviathan. Yet to reach it, he would have needed a castle of his own. A castle or . . .

"Where are they?" he muttered.

"Where are who?" Leot asked. Realization dawned. "Oh! You mean—"

Tyros thrust his hand out into the downpour, pointing to the dark skies. "Sunfire!"

Like a fiery comet soaring through the storm, a great golden dragon raced toward the flying citadel. Sunfire made his home in a cave in the mountains to the east, and since the war, he had made a pact with Gwynned and the surrounding areas to protect the entire region. In return, the people of Northern Ergoth respected his privacy and, on occasion, presented him with food.

"I wouldn't like to be riding him today!" remarked Leot.

Tyros would have traded anything to be astride the golden dragon's back, but that honor this day went to three men more versed in such feats. In combat, the great golden dragon often carried one human rider, generally a knight with a lance. However, against a citadel such as this, three men generally rode, men prepared for what amounted to a suicide mission in many ways. With Sunfire's aid, they would try to board the castle, choosing as their target the highest tower. Tyros himself had determined from past experience that the highest tower inevitably contained the chamber housing the Wind Captain's Chair. The chosen warriors, veterans all, would do their best to seize control of that chamber. At the very least, they would try to destroy it . . . even at the cost of their own lives.

Such had been the plan that Tyros himself had designed and suggested more than a year earlier. It had worked once, although those men had perished in bringing their target down. That in itself had tarnished the Red Robe's vaunted reputation somewhat, but no one could deny that his plan had succeeded. Still, it had irked Tyros that some blamed him more for the three lives lost than the many saved.

Sunfire alone, though, fulfilled only half of Tyros's plan. He scanned the heavens, looking for the other half . . . and spotted what he sought. Glisten, Sunfire's sparkling mate, dived down past the other dragon, two men no doubt on her back. She looked as if she sought to roost on the underside of the citadel, which the female would do if that proved possible, but her true mission also concerned those aboard her. Sunfire's humans had a tactical mission in mind; Glisten's were there to see that they would have the chance to succeed.

Glisten carried mages, veteran war wizards. No youngster such as Tyros, even though he had devised many of the very routines that they would utilize. The dragon himself had vetoed the presence of Tyros, insisting that he would only trust human wizards with robes of white.

"No human who wears robes of blood will battle at my side!" the gold had rumbled, heedless of the insult he had thrown at Tyros. "White follows the light and black the darkness, but red wavers too much in the middle, a friend who might suddenly become a foe!"

The words remained burned in Tyros's memory even now. He knew that members of his order, if they chose a different path, had a tendency to lapse toward the black robes more than the white. Such defections had occurred just before the start of the war and had left a stain on the Order of Lunitari, god of neutral magic. That the dragon would respect the followers of Solinari, god of white magic, Tyros had understood, but Sunfire almost gave the black robes of Nuitari more respect than the red robes, even though the former were the enemy.

"I should be up there," he muttered. He could have proven to Sunfire that some followers of Lunitari could be trusted.

Leot pulled him back into the tower. "Forget such a foolish notion, Tyros! If you want to play a part in this battle, we can do so from down here, and it's time we begin, at that!"

Tyros blinked, staring at the rotund White Robe. He had never seen Leot so possessed. Suddenly the bearded, balding figure no longer looked so clownish. Tyros recalled that some of Leot's own order rode atop Glisten and understood his friend's determination.

Still, thoughts of the flying citadel again pulled Tyros to the window, despite his companion's protests. He looked up but could see neither the dragons nor the castle.

"Tyros!"

"Go on without me!" he finally snapped at Leot. "I'll be there soon. I promise!"

The other spellcaster eyed his friend briefly. Then, with a frustrated expression, Leot turned and left the chamber.

Tyros at last located the flying citadel. Sunfire flew above it, trying to come near enough to land his precious crew. Glisten circled about the fortress, flashes of light occasionally bursting around her as she and her companions kept the mages and archers in the castle occupied.

A dark form moved from the clouds. Tyros's first thought was that an enemy dragon had joined the fray. Then he saw that the invaders had not one but two flying citadels, which helped explain the large number of draconians dropping out of the sky. The invaders had thrown all they could at Gwynned.

Neither dragon had noticed the second citadel, but instead of aiding its counterpart, the newcomer shifted away from the battle. Tyros studied the second fortress and saw why. It looked more battle-worn than the first and wobbled in the high winds. A few winged figures dived from its battlements, but otherwise it seemed almost empty. Against the dragons, it wouldn't have had a chance.

Tyros had just begun to turn his attention back to the first citadel when he noted yet another form lurking in the clouds. A third citadel? He doubted that the invaders could have so many at their command.

A sleek, ebony shape emerged from the clouds above Glisten.

A black dragon. A male, and young, too. Although it was

only two-thirds the size of Sunfire, the black had the advantage of surprise over the massive gold's mate. Tyros pictured savage claws rending the wings of the female. Despite the ludicrousness of his actions, the mage could not help leaning out to shout a warning. "Above! Look out from above!"

Glisten, of course, couldn't hear him. Tyros gripped the frame of the window as he watched the inevitable.

However, Sunfire, who had been hovering over the high tower, suddenly turned from his task, barely managing to come between the treacherous dragon and Glisten. Startled, the black reluctantly grappled with his larger foe, the advantages of both size and surprise now on the side of the defenders. Sunfire snapped at his adversary, barely missing the black dragon's throat. The two males spun in a loop, their great maws snapping, claws raking.

Then, to Tyros's horror, another black dragon, identical to the first, appeared. The second beast fell upon Sunfire's back, sinking talons into the golden male. Sunfire roared in agony, suddenly caught between the black pair.

Glisten immediately came to his rescue, and she wasn't alone. A flash of light, no doubt cast by one of her wizards, burst before the eyes of the dragon grappling with Sunfire, a flash that so startled the black that he lost his grip on the gold. Glisten used that shock to her advantage, barreling into the second attacker with such ferocity that he went tumbling through the air, unable to control his flight.

Realizing that he now faced two golden dragons better versed in aerial combat than he was, the remaining black tried to flee. Sunfire, though, would have none of that. With his talons, he caught the younger leviathan by the tail and pulled. The black let out a howl that reminded Tyros more of a whipped dog than a deadly dragon.

An explosion momentarily lit up the sky. The top of the first citadel had vanished in a flash of white light. Sunfire's riders had managed to drop onto the tower after all. The explosion, no doubt some alchemical liquid or a special spell by one of his fellow wizards, meant that the men had sacrificed themselves, but in doing so they had mortally wounded the flying castle. Devoid of its steering mechanism, it began to spin around crazily, heading in almost madcap fashion toward the sea. Judging by the arc of its flight, it would eventually drop some miles offshore.

Paying no heed to the devastated citadel, Sunfire and Glisten took hold of their hapless foe and, while the black roared in vain, threw the creature end over end toward the second castle.

In that moment of triumph, Tyros heard a thump on the roof. The wizard stiffened at first, then looked up at the ceiling, his hand already forming a fist and his mouth whispering words of power.

Winged forms burst through three of the stained-glass windows. Draconians.

Tyros could read both the determination and desperation in their eyes; they had to know that they would likely die this night, the citadel offering no escape, but they would perform their duties regardless.

That present duty concerned slaying the mage before them.

Two were baaz, draconians known for their sadistic manner, but without any skill at magic. Unfortunately the third appeared to be a bozak, crafty and with a talent for spells of fire and air. All had the same general look of dragons turned halfway into men, but the baaz appeared more brutal, with scales like tarnished, dull brass. The bozak, on the other hand, stood taller and slimmer, more proud, and his eyes blazed with more intelligence than those of his companions. His scales had a more tanned looked to them, like old and faded bronze.

Tyros and the bozak cast spells at the same time. A hand of fire meant to seize Tyros went effortlessly through the wizard, unfortunately setting scrolls on the table afire and singeing the furniture. Where the bozak failed, though, the mage in part succeeded. The smoking table flew at the two baaz, crushing them against the wall.

Tyros grimaced; the spell had been aimed at the bozak, but the creature had anticipated the results and sacrificed his lesser brethren instead. Still, Tyros felt certain that he could handle one bozak if . . .

Through the remaining windows, including the one nearest where the wizard stood, more draconians burst in, two of them colliding with the human from behind. Tyros gasped as the force of the collision pushed the air from his lungs. He and one of the invaders tumbled to the floor. Draconian claws seized him by the wrists and head, dragging him upward again.

"Alive!" a reptilian voice shouted. "Alive!"

The chamber filled with a brilliant light, one that sent the draconians hissing. Those holding onto the Red Robe released him in order to shield their eyes, nearly causing Tyros to crack his skull on the floor. He tried to rise, but his breath had not yet returned to him.

"Tyros! To me!"

"Le-Leot?" Straining, the battered spellcaster looked up to see his rotund friend standing at the door, arms outstretched. Light literally flowed from Leot's hand, a brilliance that seemed to disturb the draconians far more than Tyros.

"Hurry!"

A roar shook the tower just as Tyros managed to rise. Part of the ceiling collapsed. As startled as the draconians seemed by the incident, they did not suffer as much as Leot, who stood just below one of the falling fragments. Wood and plaster struck the White Robe, and with a groan, he dropped to his knees. The light that had so offended the dragon men instantly vanished.

"Leot!" The friend who had saved him now lay injured at the feet of the draconians. Cursing, Tyros struggled to regain his concentration. He couldn't let them take Leot.

Two baaz seized the White Robe, pulling him to his feet. Tyros saw with horror that blood caked Leot's head, and his eyes stared without seeing. The heavy set mage still breathed, but how long that would continue remained debatable.

The two draconians hissed, shock in their reptilian eyes as they released their hold on the stunned mage. In their minds, Leot's arms had become hissing pythons. Tyros immediately cast a second spell in order to keep Leot from crashing to the floor, then took another breath as he readied himself for the bozak's next attack.

Another roar shook the tower. More of the ceiling caved in. One draconian fell, crushed by a beam. Tyros started to rise, then saw the bozak readying his spell.

The room began to break apart.

Animosities were forgotten as everyone sought to escape. One baaz tried for the nearest window, but it crumbled as he leapt through, killing the creature in the process. A second draconian was crushed by a beam.

Tyros started for Leot, only to have strong, clawed hands seize him from behind. He turned, thinking the bozak had attempted some last attack . . . and instead found himself staring into the eyes of a horror the likes of which he couldn't recall ever confronting before.

The monster before him, which seemed to expand in size as it spread its wings, had some resemblance to a draconian, but only in general shape. Red, pupilless eyes flared and a long, beaklike maw opened, revealing row upon row of jagged teeth. Twin horns jutted from the leathery creature's head. The claws that had seized Tyros had only four digits, but its talons were sharper and more hooked than those of a draconian. In build, it more resembled the slim form of the bozak than the baaz, but its taut muscles indicated that, matched one to one, either draconian would have faced an uphill struggle with this horrific intruder.

The creature raised a clawed hand, as if seeking to rip Tyros's face from his head. The frantic spellcaster raised his own hand, magic energy crackling around his fist.

"Fooooolll . . ." the gray abomination hissed.

Tyros struck as the remainder of the tower collapsed.

Chapter 2

Troubled Waters

A debacle. An utter debacle.

General Cadrio stared in the direction of Gwynned, a prize lost. None of his officers dared speak, knowing that in their commander's present mood, it might prove a fatal mistake. Not even Zander dared approach him, even when word came from the lookout that Eclipse and Murk had escaped death and now slunk back to join the invasion force. Just ahead of the ships sailed, rather erratically, the one surviving citadel, battered and nearly unable to fly.

How the Blue Lady would have laughed at the sight of his ignominious defeat. He had thought that attacking when he had would catch Gwynned, fairly untouched by the war, nearly defenseless. The gold dragons should have been far to the northeast, aiding in the Solamnic advance there. So much for military intelligence.

The storm continued to rock the fleet, but Cadrio didn't care. He had given orders to sail until they could make landfall on a tiny uncharted island far to the north of Ergoth, and that meant a journey of several days in rough seas. With Gwynned lost, he had no new plans. There was always that offer made by the mage, but even Cadrio had limits to his madness.

"Hail, General Cadrio!"

Of course, the commander thought with rising fury. One had only to think of the blasted spellcaster and he would appear.

The general spun on his heel to confront a figure who hadn't even been aboard the *Harpy* a second before. "So! Come to gloat, have you?"

The tall, hooded mage spread the arms of his crimson

cloak wide, as if offended by such a remark. Cadrio desired greatly to wipe the wide smile off that goateed face but knew well the danger of even contemplating it.

"General! My friend . . . and you are my friend, aren't you?" When Cadrio didn't reply, the wizard waved off the silence with one neatly gloved hand. "I come to offer my condolences on the fickle workings of fate . . . and renew my proposition to you!"

"This is hardly the time or place."

Narrow, slanted eyes so blue they unnerved even Cadrio cut the frustrated commander off. The hooded mage steepled his fingers and briefly cast his gaze in the direction of the crippled citadel and the two weary dragons. "There could hardly be a better time or place, I should think, my general."

Cadrio began to reach for his sword but thought better of it. The crimson-clad mage took the moment to pull back his hood slightly, revealing short, cropped hair the color of night, save where some gray had intruded at the temple and the goatee. A pronounced widow's peak and narrow, pointed sideburns added to the newcomer's handsome, if demonic, demeanor. The gray contrasted with the youthful features and personality of the man, but the general knew how deceiving age could be where spellcasters were concerned. Dealing with this one made Cadrio feel as if he risked giving up his own soul, although that had long ago been promised to his dark mistress.

The general relaxed slightly. "All right, then. Come to my cabin. We'll discuss this in private."

Still smiling, the mage shook his head. "No, you will come to me, my general! You know where!"

"That miserable province of Atriun?"

"Yes. You know where it is. Five days east of Lemish."

"That's near Solamnic territory."

The smile grew more cold. "Yes, it is. Go there. Where the great castle stands."

General Cadrio needed a straw to grasp after the disaster of Gwynned, and the crimson-clad figure before him had just offered a strong one. Still, he had reservations. "How do I know I can trust you? You serve an enemy, after all."

His visitor gazed down at the crimson robes. "Is this what bothers you? This color?" He muttered a few words of power, then, looking up, added, "Why didn't you just say so?"

A black stain appeared on the chest of the well-tailored robe, a stain that spread swiftly in every direction, devouring the crimson color. The goateed mage stretched his arms wide, the black coursing along until it had reached not only the edges of his voluminous sleeves but somehow had enveloped the tapered gloves as well.

The wizard pulled his hood forward again, revealing that it, too, had changed to black. His smile set Cadrio on edge again. "Is this a color better suited to your tastes? I can wear it as readily as any."

"You mock the gods, Valkyn!"

"Yes, I do. So, will you be coming?"

Despite his reluctance, the general knew he had no choice. The men might fear him, but that wouldn't prevent them from deserting to more victorious rivals. Yet, one problem remained. "Last time you said that if I were to agree, I needed to obtain a certain item for you. Just to be safe, I gave the order the locate it, but—"

Valkyn laughed. "Have no fear, my general! I know you tried to fulfill that need even while you sought Gwynned's rich coffers, but although your pathetic draconians failed, my own servants have dealt with the task! The mage is in my hands. Your mishap proved excellent cover for their own efforts, I must say."

"You were there?" Cadrio felt betrayed, used. Valkyn had turned his defeat into a victory for the mage from the east.

"I am everywhere, my general. You would do well to remember that." As he spoke, Valkyn's form began to grow misty, insubstantial. The wind and rain cut through him, dissolving the wizard as if he had been made of smoke. Despite that, Valkyn seemed unperturbed, and as the last of his form faded, he added, "Atriun, my general. Be there. . . ."

Silence enshrouded the *Harpy*. Cadrio and his men eyed the spot where the unsettling wizard had stood. At last the general broke the quiet, turning swiftly to the helmsman. "Change course! We sail west until we are out of sight of Gwynned, then turn about and head southeast to the New Sea. Now!"

The helmsman quickly obeyed. The general turned to his other officers. "Zander! Timinion! Grako! The rest of you! My quarters in ten minutes. We have plans to make!"

Spirits lifted as Cadrio marched off. If the wizard could deliver what he promised, not even the Blue Lady and her vaunted dragon would be able to match the general. Cadrio would be able to accomplish what Ariakas had not. He would conquer all of Ansalon.

He paused, gazing back momentarily in the direction of Northern Ergoth. "We will meet again, Gwynned," Cadrio whispered.

* * * * *

Dragons. Flying castles. Draconians. All filled Tyros's mind, spinning around again and again in the midst of a strange storm. Now and then Leot's voice called out to him, urging him to safety, but the storm always drew Tyros back in.

And in the midst of that storm, he saw the beaked, toothy visage of the monstrous, fiery-orbed creature. . . .

"Aren't you awake yet, mage?"

His eyes fluttered open. Tyros could feel the sweat soaking his body. He tried to talk, but his first words came out as a hacking cough. Someone gave him water, which finally brought him to his senses.

He remembered where he was now—a healer's temple, along with other victims of the attack. He recalled trying to leave the day before, but he had collapsed on the steps.

For a temple of Mishakal, the place seemed fairly pedestrian. Marble columns rose high, but they were unadorned, unimpressive. Statues of a beautiful woman reaching out a kind hand flanked a set of steps leading to the high-backed chair upon which the priestess of the temple sat. Tyros had seen more impressive work in the courts of nobles. Torches in the walls illuminated paintings showing some of the legends of the goddess's work. On the ceiling was the symbol of Mishakal, a blue infinity sign. The same sign had been repeated in the marble mosaic floor.

The victims of the attack had all been brought to the great chamber where followers of the goddess met. Most of the others regarded the temple with awe, but to a war wizard, the miracles of Mishakal seemed less astonishing than the great spells cast in battle. Still, they had cared for him here, and he was grateful.

At last Tyros turned to his visitor, who had been waiting impatiently for the mage's attention. He was a rough-hewn veteran of many a combat. His chiseled face bore scars on one side, and his black eyes were weary of killing but willing to do it again, a man whose education contrasted to his barbarian look. He had thin hair tied into a ponytail and a short beard. His skin wasn't as dark as that of many Northern Ergothians, but neither was it as light as those from the south. Leon matched him in girth, but whereas the white wizard was fat, what lurked behind the newcomer's silver breastplate was muscle.

The officer frowned at him. "Arrogant mage . . ."

"Captain Bakal."

"Tyros." Bakal had been appointed liaison to the wizards, supposedly because an uncle of his had performed the same function. The more likely reason was as punishment. The captain had a habit of disobeying his superiors' orders in combat and doing what had to be done. That he generally chose the correct course of action mattered not a whit to the military command.

"To what do I owe this visit?"

"I've come to see if you can finally be debriefed today." Bakal's mouth curled up. "Think you've the stamina, boy?"

Bakal had made it plain long ago that he had no use for an arrogant, self-serving wizard such as Tyros. They had sparred a good deal in the past, but today Tyros was in no mood to do battle. He leaned back and idly eyed Mishakal's emblem.

The weary mage blinked, realizing that he had nearly drifted off to sleep. His gaze shifted back to Bakal, who now showed some concern.

"Are you all right, boy?"

"I'm sorry. My head still throbs."

The captain shifted from kneeling to sitting. "Probably shock. It can stay with you for some time."

Tyros tried to straighten again and was pleased with his eventual success. "I'll be better. It's just . . ."

The veteran nodded. "That'll happen."

"Maybe . . . maybe if you tell me how the battle came out, it will help me to focus." Tyros was curious to find out what had happened to the citadels.

"All right." Captain Bakal leaned back. "You deserve as much, I suppose. There's some call you one of the heroes, because the dragons and the lads followed your basic plan. I'd be more inclined to call the brave ones who died in destroying the first castle the true champions."

So they had perished. "Tell me about it."

"You must've been right about the thing's weaknesses, boy. Did the one you helped destroy in the east go the same way?"

"No." In truth, no one actually knew exactly which part of his theory had led to that citadel's collapse. Those at the scene only knew that it had crashed, killing both friend and foe. Yet it had been hailed as a victory, and one that Tyros had readily accepted as time passed.

"Well, anyway, Sunfire tells me that he dropped the men onto the tower. One fell off, but the remaining pair got inside that place where you think the navigation is done." Bakal's tone grew bitter. "They were only supposed to capture it, but something must've happened, and instead they blew the tower to bits—along with themselves." He shook his head. "I never liked your plan, Tyros. Too risky."

"It wasn't mine alone," the mage protested, not wanting to take all the blame for the deaths.

"Well, you've not hesitated to take credit for it in the past." The veteran shook his head. "The point is that they damaged the thing mortally and sent it spinning out of control."

Tyros recalled the sight of the massive castle spinning madly as it headed out to sea. "Did it land in the water?"

"Aye, the sea claimed it. There'll be no salvaging that citadel. It flew out several miles beyond shore before it dropped."

A twinge of regret struck Tyros as he thought of all those secrets, lost forever. "What about the second one?"

A chuckle escaped the captain. "You saw those two black dragons who tried to fool Sunfire and Glisten? The lady, she sent that upstart dragon flying, didn't she?"

Tyros could hear the man's admiration as he spoke of the two golden dragons. It was an admiration Bakal had never shown him or any other mage. He interrupted the soldier's reverie. "The second citadel, Captain?"

"That's what I'm trying to tell you. After the first one went tumbling out of control, the two golds grabbed the other black before he could escape."

"I saw that," the weary spellcaster said, growing impatient.

"Well, they tossed the second black right at the citadel! He hit the castle with such force it rained stone in the harbor. Must've upset something inside, because the citadel wobbled a lot after that, then hightailed it out of there as best it could."

So one of the fortresses had escaped, but not without damage. Tyros wondered if it had been forced to land somewhere nearby. He'd have to listen for news.

"They're sorry about your tower," Bakal added. "They never meant it to happen that way."

"The tower?" A light within dawned. "I heard the dragon cry, and then the tower shook. The draconians . . ."

Not realizing the extent to which Tyros now relived those fateful moments, Captain Bakal nodded. "The young black collided head-on with the citadel. He stayed aloft, but the blow must've addled his senses. Instead of escaping, he flew back into the city. Only he didn't watch too well where he flew, and he sideswiped your tower."

Tyros saw the ceiling come down again. Then Leot fell. The monster loomed before the wizard once more. . . .

"Mage!" Bakal had his thick hands on Tyros's shoulder. He

shook the spellcaster gently. Slowly the wizard recovered.

"The dragon . . . the black . . ." he began. "He hit the tower a second time, didn't he?"

"Aye, after he had regained some sense and saw the two golds coming. As he backed away, he hit the tower again, this time a more direct blow. I saw the whole thing collapse as I battled one of those blasted draconians."

Attempting to avoid another recurrence of his nightmare, Tyros shifted the course of the conversation. "The draconians. The invaders. They're all dead?"

"Or captured. Some had sense enough to surrender. Light casualties on our side. Got the feeling that the draconians knew they'd been tossed into the fire the moment they landed. There are some segments of the city that burned, but overall we came out all right. The storm helped us, too. Bad luck for whoever planned this invasion."

"Which will make him all the more desperate," Tyros mused.

Bakal looked at him in surprise. "You could be right. This may not be the end of things."

"Perhaps not," the tired wizard muttered, feeling light-headed again. "If that's all for now, Captain, I'd like—"

"Hold on, boy. I haven't even asked the questions I came here to ask."

"You probably know more than I do, Captain. A lot of what happened remains a blank to me."

"Such as how you survived." The graying officer eyed him closely. "We're still trying to figure that out. The tower collapsed completely, yet you managed to come out more or less intact."

"Except for my skull."

"We found you unconscious well outside the ruins of the tower. There was no indication how you got there."

Tyros forced himself to a sitting position. "Captain Bakal, I really don't—"

"You haven't asked me whether the White Robe survived."

"Leot?" Belated fear for his friend overwhelmed him. Tyros blurted, "Did he?"

Instead of replying, the veteran rose. "I'd like you to come look at something with me."

Paling, the shaky young wizard pushed himself to his feet. Guilt consumed Tyros. Leot had saved him, yet Tyros had been more concerned with the citadels. "Did you find his body?"

"Just come with me. I'll help you walk if you need it."

Tyros refused his aid. "I have a staff somewhere."

"This it?"

It wasn't the wizard's staff he had carried with him for the last several years. This was a plain wooden one that the healers had given him to use. Tyros's staff lay buried somewhere under the tower.

"Very well," he said finally, accepting the staff and determining that his legs would support him. "Show me what you have."

"It's a bit of a walk. We'll be going to the City Guard's headquarters. The army's secured it for the time being."

Tyros steeled himself, suspecting that whatever Bakal wanted to show him would be unsettling. If it was Leot's body, Tyros would see that the White Robe received proper burial rites. Tyros owed his friend that much.

As they stepped out, Tyros marveled at the bright sunlight. After the fierce storm and the invasion, the day felt tranquil, almost surreal.

Then he saw the damage.

Gwynned had repelled the invaders, but not without cost. The mage could see most of the government quarter, and what he saw shook him. Several of the larger buildings had suffered greatly. In many cases, entire roofs had either caved in or been set ablaze by the draconians. Two structures had been completely gutted, likely with loss of life.

"It appears worse than it is," Bakal remarked, although his tone contradicted his words.

"How many died, Captain?"

"Far fewer than might have."

An unsatisfactory answer, but the only one Tyros would evidently receive. He clutched the staff tightly and concentrated on the path ahead. Captain Bakal marched along as if on parade. Tyros noted the muscles in the veteran's face twitch now and then as they journeyed through the damaged city.

The two paused at last beside a tall domed building surrounded by a high stone gate. Four sentries, wearing the sea-green breastplates of the City Guard, stood at attention, watching the pair with practiced suspicion. The fact that Bakal wore the armor and cape of an officer of the army in no way assuaged them.

"State your business," the nearest guard bellowed.

"You know me, Kelner. Captain Bakal of the First Legion. This is Tyros, the Red Robe."

"Orders are orders, Captain." But the guard signaled entry.

As they entered, Tyros whispered, "I thought the army had commandeered this place, Bakal."

"Yes, but unless we want a civil war with the City Guard, we had to let them retain control of the perimeter." He snorted. "Would-be soldiers, but they think they're our equals."

Tyros had long noted the division between the army and the City Guard, so he knew not to comment. Instead he asked, "Now will you tell me what it is we're here to see?"

"No. I want you to see it with a completely open mind."

Partway down the corridor, they stopped before a huge door. Two helmeted sentries of the army saluted Captain Bakal. The sentries said nothing as they immediately opened the door.

"Any problems tonight?" the captain asked.

"Nothing even the City Guard couldn't handle, sir," one answered with a slight smirk.

"Slow as all that, eh?"

The soldiers shared a chuckle as Bakal and Tyros entered, then closed the door behind them, leaving the captain and wizard alone in near darkness. The windows of the chamber had been covered, leaving only a few oil lamps to light the place.

"Is this all necessary, Bakal?"

"You've fought this war how long, boy?"

Tyros frowned. "The war is over, Captain."

"Not for some. The Dark Queen may be gone, but very few of her puppets have cut their strings. They still dance to her tune, even if they think they're writing their own music now."

"You are somewhat of a poet, Bakal," Tyros said wryly. He looked around and saw table after table piled with objects covered by sheets. Some of the shrouded objects looked uncomfortably like bodies. Tyros thought of Leot and grew unsteady.

"Easy, boy. Didn't think you'd be so touched by this."

"Where—where is he?" Tyros breathed.

"The White Robe's not here, Tyros. Come on."

"Wait a moment!" Tyros called, reaching out for the officer. "You mean Leot isn't dead?"

Bakal replied simply, "I never said that."

Frustrated, Tyros hurried to catch up, only to have the scarred veteran suddenly pause at one of the nearby tables. The mage looked past him, noting with unease the vague shape beneath and torn and stained officer's cloak.

Bakal eyed the shape. "This is what I wanted you to see."

Tyros lifted a corner of the cloak from the corpse, pulled it aside, and gaped. "What in the—"

"Do you know what you've looking at, boy?"

He did, yet he did not. A face from his nightmares confronted Tyros: the long, sharp horns; the hard, leathery beak; the jagged, flesh-tearing teeth. Only the burning, pupilless eyes remained hidden, the monster's lids closed in death.

"You've seen it before, haven't you, mage?"

"The tower . . . I saw it there."

"And we found it near there . . . near where you lay, in fact. Do you know what it is, Tyros?" Bakal watched him closely.

"It reminds me of something from my schooling, but it's not quite as I recall it."

"In Gwynned, we'd call it a gargoyle. 'Course, in Gwynned, we'd only see them in drawings and statues. There shouldn't be any gargoyles in Northern Ergoth, boy."

"A gargoyle . . ." Tyros stared at the taloned monstrosity, shivering at the memory of his encounter.

"I've seen them, Tyros, and they're a savage lot, but this one's not quite the same as those I've seen. Stronger and somehow smarter-looking. I could name a dozen more differences, but the question is why it's here at all. Do you know, perhaps?"

"Why would I know? The first time I ever saw one of these creatures was when it tried to attack me in the tower."

"Attack you . . . or take you prisoner?"

Tyros recalled how the gargoyle could have simply torn out the back of his neck, but had seized him instead. "But why would it want to do that?"

"Why would they take two other wizards?"

"Two other—" The weary mage's mouth grew slack. He stared at the captain, shock turning to anger. "You damned bastard! What do you know? Tyros used his free hand to seize the soldier by the cord of his cape. Bakal stared back. All arrogance had drained from Tyros. "What do you mean by that? You are not certain what's happened to Leot, are you? You think one of these horrors took him, don't you?"

Bakal removed the wizard's hand. "Two of your kind are missing. Leot and Kendilious, of your own order. We don't know what's happened to Leot, but old Kendilious . . . you remember him?"

Kendilious. Tyros remembered a crotchety old mage past his prime who lived to preach to the younger mages that they knew nothing of the sacrifices a true wizard needed to make. In fact, Tyros couldn't recall the man ever talking about anything else. And since they had both followed Lunitari, Kendilious had taken special relish in admonishing his youthful counterpart, who, according to the elder, had more ambition than caution.

"We had us a witness, boy. A member of the guard. Questioned him thoroughly. He and another man were heading for the ruins of your tower, and as they neared, one looked up. Claims he heard fluttering and thought a draconian might be gliding down on them. What he saw instead was a winged form going up, bearing with it a bald figure in red robes. From his description and the fact that there's only a handful of your kind here, we pieced together that it had to be Kendilious."

"And what about Leot? He saw nothing of Leot?"

Bakal shook his head. "Nothing, but a gargoyle like this took the old wizard . . . and since we can't find the body of your friend anywhere, not even in the rubble, I'd venture to say that he's also been captured."

Tyros envisioned Leot being dragged off by such a creature. His friend might still be alive, but headed for what fate? "Why would they want us? Why would gargoyles risk death in the midst of a battle to capture wizards?"

"The command's still debating that one, and so are your superiors, too, boy."

"They know already?"

"Aye, and they're a mite too curious. We finally gleaned from them that some others have gone missing in recent times, the latest being a pair of your crimson lads."

"Two more?"

The captain nodded gravely. "Of course, there's still one more question, one that I was hoping you might answer for me. I'm assuming you didn't kill this beast."

"No. It caught me by surprise. I'm not responsible for its death, if that's what you mean." He frowned. "I just assumed it must have injured itself when it flew me out of the collapsing tower."

"Reasonable assumption." The graying officer removed the old cloak. "Help me roll this thing over."

Tyros stiffened. "The gargoyle?"

"Do it, boy."

With Bakal doing most of the work, they soon had the creature on its back. The technical side of Tyros couldn't help but admire the wingspan of the gargoyle and how those wings were attached. Yet all the while he noticed the gaping wound that had finally killed it, a great gash at the back of the neck.

"You see what I mean?" the captain commented.

"No." One wound looked like another to the wizard. Had something jagged caught the gargoyle as it flew out of the tower?

The soldier sighed. "Save me from school-taught warriors! That gargoyle had its neck *torn out* from behind, probably while it was in flight with you! You're lucky you didn't drop to your death. I'd say the thing lived long enough to flutter to just above the ground, then lost its grip on you. It went a little farther, then died."

"I was fortunate, then."

"More than fortunate; your being here comes just short of a miracle. Don't you understand yet what I'm getting at?"

Tyros despised being talked to as if he were an ignorant child, but he truly did not comprehend yet. "Enlighten me."

"Oh, I will! See those claws? I checked them out myself, boy! They'd be just about right to do such mayhem. Draconians wouldn't leave his kind of mess, even if they did decide to use their talons instead of a good blade. Something either similar or exactly like this gargoyle killed the beast as it tried to make off with you."

"That makes no sense. You're saying that one of its own kind killed it?"

Bakal nodded. "And therein lies the question command and your superiors are going to have fun with. Bad enough we don't know why they'd want you, but who, by the Abyss, saved your worthless hide, Tyros?"

Chapter 3

Atriun

The journey to Atriun had been both tedious and difficult. Sailing the New Sea without being noticed had been trouble enough, but the longer they sailed, the more General Cadrio noted hints of insubordination. Zander had dealt quickly and efficiently with those hints so far, maintaining his commander's power. Still, even Cadrio's second had commented that matters would only grow worse. The mage's plan had to show promise quickly. Otherwise the general would have his head on a lance, magic tricks or not.

Near the southern edge of old Solamnia, they disembarked. Leaving Zander in control, Cadrio and his personal guards, all clad in travel cloaks, rode into obscure Atriun.

Once a part of Solamnia but now virtually unclaimed by any country, Atriun consisted mostly of hills, forest, and the empty ruins of a magnificent estate built by an eccentric knight. The riders passed a few ruined peasant houses overrun by nature and what had once been wheat fields. Some fruit trees clearly imported long, long ago from Ergoth dotted the landscape, but for the most part, only ghosts lived here now.

And they could have found no more appropriate dwelling than the Castle of Atriun.

In the dwindling light of sunset, it took on an even more sinister look. What had urged the Solamnic Knight to build such a structure, General Cadrio could not say. The place seemed better suited to the mind-set of one of the Dragon Highlords, even Ariakas himself.

The massive walled castle stood in stark contrast to its empty surroundings, an imperial fortress in a land that had ever been sparsely populated. Had the entire Solamnic brotherhood chosen to depart Vingaard Keep, they would have had to look no farther than Atriun for an appropriate base. Yet Atriun's wonder had a baleful feel to it that likely would have sent them riding off again, in part because both citadel and surrounding wall had been constructed from a dark, forbidding rock. Cadrio knew of no quarry within five days' ride where such rock could be found, but it wouldn't have surprised him if the insane knight had shipped it from far away.

The outer wall stood two stories tall, much higher than this desolate land dictated. The battlements of the wall had been designed to accommodate a vast array of archers. The only entrance to the castle remained a high wooden drawbridge, surprisingly, still up, that, when lowered, would stretch across the deep, algae-encrusted moat surrounding the shadowy edifice. Cadrio pondered the massive effort it must have taken to dig the impressive moat.

Above the outer wall rose the citadel itself, a gargantuan rectangular structure at least four times the height of the wall and flanked by squat twin towers. Across the uppermost levels of the central building ran several large arched balconies worthy of an imperial palace.

Cadrio could see little more of the castle from his present location save for the third and final tower, this one taller than the flanking pair and positioned over the center of the main castle. The general nearly dismissed it, then noticed a glimmer of light flash from within.

"He couldn't be that ambitious," Cadrio muttered.

"General! What excellent timing!"

The horses spooked. Cadrio forced his mount to calm, then looked over his shoulder to glare at the ebony-cloaked figure who had not been there a moment before.

"Valkyn! The Queen take you! I've killed men for less than that!"

The dark wizard's smile only stretched further, but his voice carried a deadly chill. "The war has made you a little jumpy, my general! Forgive my enthusiasm. I'd not expected you for another day or two! I thought I'd have to put off the event until then, but now everything can proceed as planned."

"I don't like the sound of that," someone in back muttered.

The general ignored the offender. He eyed the mage with suspicion, trying to keep his tone confident. "All well and good, then, Valkyn. I'd like my ships out of the New Sea as soon as possible, so if we can get this done now, I'll be pleased."

The goateed figure shook his head. "Good heavens, no, my general! Not *that* swift. I must still make some adjustments! This will be a marvel such as has never graced Krynn, I promise you! Tomorrow will do well enough."

As if Cadrio had any choice. "I'll be patient . . . for now."

"Of course you will . . . and so will your twin pets."

Valkyn had detected Murk and Eclipse in the vicinity. The commander silently cursed. He wondered if he had inherited the most inept pair of dragons in all of Krynn. First they had allowed their inexperience and overenthusiasm to set them against two gold leviathans; now they couldn't even hide from one wizard. Legend had it that such a rarity among dragon kind as twins heralded creatures of great destiny, but for beings already twice the general's age if not more, the beasts had shown nothing but incompetence.

"They won't cause any trouble."

Valkyn chuckled. "Oh, I know they won't." Turning, the cloaked mage indicated the castle. "Come. Atriun awaits!"

With a rusty groan that set Cadrio's teeth on edge, the drawbridge began to lower. The horses grew uneasy again. The commander immediately urged his mount forward, determined not to weaken himself in the eyes of the others. His personal guards followed reluctantly, more willing to fight sword to sword than against magic. Still, if Valkyn had meant them harm, he would have struck before now, not lured them into his sanctum.

Besides, Cadrio would have almost risked the Abyss for a second chance to conquer Gwynned.

The drawbridge creaked under the heavy hooves of the horses. The general finally exhaled when his mount touched solid ground, an exhalation that faltered as he noticed his surroundings.

Within the walls, the castle and its grounds proved no less imposing. A vast circular courtyard, made from carved gray stone, solemnly welcomed the newcomers. In the center of the floor, lighter stone formed the faded symbol of a glaring kingfisher. Wilted shrubs lined the edges of the courtyard, leading to two massive iron doors through which one could enter the castle.

Cadrio glanced left, where a small group of smoke-colored buildings stood, including a stable. The general started to give the command to dismount when a faint sound made him turn his gaze in the opposite direction. At first he saw nothing beyond the courtyard but the remnants of a once-beautiful sculptured garden with tall fruit trees, but then Cadrio noticed movement among the branches. Suspicious, he urged his steed toward the garden.

The horse snorted, not at all pleased by their nearness to the trees. Cadrio again noticed movement, then caught a glimpse of a winged form the size of a man. The leaves mostly obscured the shape, but the sharp eyes of the general noted an arm, a clawed hand, and the shadow of a muzzled head.

Glaring back at an unperturbed Valkyn, the lanky officer drew his blade. "Draconians, wizard? Thinking of an ambush?"

"I have no use for draconians," the mage returned, his narrow blue eyes staring directly into the general's. "I've seen them in combat too often."

"Then what lurks in those trees?"

"The same thing that lurks all around you, hiding in plain sight atop the walls and roofs, my observant general!"

"What?" Sword ready, Cadrio looked around, studying the castle carefully. Suddenly he spotted stonelike figures perched in the corners, behind battlements, atop towers. They hadn't been there before, despite Valkyn's words. Cadrio and his men would have noticed them . . . and turned to flee for their lives.

There had to be a hundred or more of them, leather-winged terrors with horns and beaklike mouths filled with teeth. They stood as tall as draconians, but moved with a much more savage intensity. Fiery, pupilless eyes glared hungrily at the party below, clearly ready to swoop down and rend the throats of the armored figures upon a signal from their master.

Sesk, the youngest of Cadrio's men, born among the rough mountains of the east, recognized them first. "Gargoyles," he breathed.

"I've never seen gargoyles like those," muttered an older guard.

"But that's what they are!" Sesk insisted. "Bigger than most and a little different in look, but that's—"

"That'll be enough of that!" Cadrio barked. He fixed the point of his sword at Valkyn's throat, ready to carve a second smile on the spellcaster. "Gargoyles or draconians, they may take us, but you'll not live to enjoy it, traitor!"

"Oh, do stop the melodramatics." The general's sword dipped to the left, passing by Valkyn's head despite Cadrio's desires. The Black Robe snapped his fingers and most of the gargoyles faded into the background. "Stone! Crag!"

From the highest tower dived a huge gargoyle, darker than most and with not two but three thick horns. He had a longer snout and narrow eyes almost akin to those of his master. The creature landed scant steps from Valkyn, then fell to one knee in tribute.

At the same time, another, slightly smaller male burst from the nearest tree. Sleeker, grayer, with two sharp horns and watchful eyes, he, too, landed in a kneeling position. Both stared, untrusting, at the newcomers.

"Crag, Stone . . . these men are to be left unharmed. You understand?"

"As you wish . . ." the smaller of the two rumbled in an incredibly deep voice.

Cadrio drew back a little, not having expected to hear anything intelligible. Cautiously he looked the monsters over. Crag, the larger gargoyle, appeared eager for blood. Stone, on the other hand, did not strike Cadrio as entirely pleased with his servitude, as if he would have been as content to slaughter Valkyn as anyone else. The general even thought he saw Stone flash what seemed murderous glances toward Valkyn when he thought no one was looking.

"You know what punishment you will receive if you don't."

Both leathery furies folded their wings around their bodies, clearly cowed.

The mage chuckled. "Good. Now return to your places!"

As Crag and Stone soared off, Cadrio sheathed his blade. "Any more surprises, spellcaster?"

"Only another introduction, a simple one. Lemual! Open the doors for our visitors. Gentlemen, please stable your horses."

The soldiers dismounted, General Cadrio passing the reins of his animal to the nearest man. He followed Valkyn toward the castle doors, which opened as they neared. A ragged bald figure in black cleric's robes hurried out to greet them, looking more like a menial than one who served the Dark Queen.

"I'm sorry, Valkyn! You asked me to make the other preparations, so I couldn't get to—"

"It's quite all right, Lemual."

Although he had only just met the man, Cadrio could hardly believe that this pig-faced groveler served the goddess Takhisis. How could such a thin, fearful soul ever become a wielder of Her Majesty's infernal will? The robes had to belong to another.

Noticing the commander's expression, Lemual's gaze dropped in shame. If he was a true cleric of the Dark Queen, Cadrio couldn't blame him for his embarrassment. What had happened to make him so? Takhisis's failure to extend her will into the mortal plane had struck her priests hard, but could that have affected the man so much?

Determined not to pursue the troubling question any further, the general followed Valkyn into the castle. He had taken but a few steps within when the immensity of the interior struck him. The front hall opened so wide it could have served as a grand ballroom all by itself. The same faded kingfisher pattern appeared in the center of the marble floor.

Above it hung a great elaborate chain. Cadrio assumed the chain had once held a wide, multi-tiered chandelier, but at some point it had either fallen free or simply been removed.

Each side of the vast hall was flanked by three ridged columns. Near them, rising inward from both sides, were twin stairways. On both the ground level and the upper floor on which the stairways met, elegant wooden doors, now faded but still hinting of gilt and heraldic decoration, led to other chambers. High above, open windows allowed for ventilation and some light to enter, but half a dozen torches in wall sconces provided the principal illumination.

An impressive tableau . . . and yet at the same time not. The emptiness of the castle—so far Cadrio had not seen one stick of furniture nor even a tapestry on the walls—simply served to remind one that only memories lived here now.

Memories and Valkyn.

"Each of your men will have a room of his own, my general. You will find things a little austere, but better than you are used to on the battlefield."

"The hall here will be fine."

Valkyn looked disturbed by such a thought. "I wouldn't think of it. You are my guest, my ally, General Cadrio!"

"I'd still prefer—"

Suddenly a howl of pure agony filled the empty corridors of Atriun. Cadrio, in the midst of removing his helm, stood still, thinking of banshees and other undead fiends.

Lemual rushed away, heading to an insignificant wooden door far off to the left, a door so unremarkable that the wary officer hadn't even noticed it before. From the brief glimpse he got before the cleric shut the door behind him, it led to a set of steps descending below ground.

"What by Her Majesty was *that?*" the general asked.

Valkyn had been watching Lemual's retreating form angrily, the first time emotion had slipped onto the mage's visage. However, as he faced the general again, the smile returned. "Just one of the adjustments I still need to make before the grand spell. . . ."

"A man screaming?"

Although he still smiled, Valkyn's expression warned Cadrio not to pursue his questions. The mage put a hand on the commander's arm and turned him back to the stairways. "Tomorrow, all will become clear, General. Tomorrow I will achieve the culmination of my research, and you . . . you will have that which will make you the next Emperor of Ansalon! Long may you reign!"

Caught up by the grand statements, Cadrio forgot the scream. He stared at Valkyn, not actually seeing the wizard, but rather his own legions, all marching to victory under his banner.

Emperor of Ansalon. A fitting title, the product of his years of hard service. Cadrio had been dreaming of such a title, especially prior to the debacle at Gwynned, but to hear another person voice his dream made the notion sound so very possible. He had lost the opportunity to become a Dragon Highlord, but what did such a rank mean in comparison? He would rule as no one other than Ariakas had.

As Valkyn led him upstairs, Cadrio, still thinking of his future glory, corrected himself. He would *not* rule as Ariakas had, for Ariakas hadn't even lived to see the end of the first year of his reign. Cadrio would rule for years . . . even if it meant crushing every bit of resistance, including the Blue Lady.

And the wizard Valkyn would give him the means to crush even her.

* * * * *

The flutter of wings sent Tyros staggering against the wall of the nearest building, soaking his pristine robe with the remnants of the evening's rain.

"A pigeon, boy. Nothing more."

He glared at Captain Bakal. He had not realized the officer was nearby. "Shadowing me, Captain? Come to see if some monster tries to snatch me up into the sky?"

The scarred veteran gave him a wry smile. "Looks to me like you're thinking much the same thing, Tyros. Could it happen?"

"Not if I can help it!"

"Easy, boy! I'm not the enemy! I'm your friend, probably the only one who'd use that term with you now that Leot's gone."

Tyros would not so easily accept his response. "A friend who skulks around corners, trying not to be heard by me?"

"I didn't have to save you from that pigeon, did I?"

The frustrated mage felt his face flush. In the days since Bakal had shown him the gargoyle, Tyros had lived and dreamed a constant nightmare, all of them involving collapsing buildings and toothsome monsters trying to drag him from the ruins. He had been unable to do any work, to research any spells. Worse, Leot's face haunted him whenever the gargoyles did not.

"I understand you spoke with the admiral himself today."

Tyros grimaced. "I spoke to his doorman."

"I could've told you that you'd get nowhere with him, boy."

"Stop calling me that!"

"Gwynned's not interested in pursuing the matter of the surviving invaders. They figure what's done is done. Let someone else pick up the pieces. We won, we survived, and that's that. The war, after all, is over."

The chill wind of the sea did nothing to cool Tyros's temper. "And what do you think, Captain?"

"Me? I always figured that a wounded bear is a dangerous animal. Like you, I think whoever attacked will be back some day."

"Then you should be willing to help me search for them."

Bakal gave him a wry smile. "And how would you suggest I do that, mage? Commandeer the fleet and go sailing off after them?"

In truth, Tyros had no suggestion. He only knew that he had to find both Leot and the flying citadel. So far, though, his attempts had met with utter failure. No one in power would aid his efforts. Not even the suggestion that the city risked further attack had garnered Tyros any support.

Although the rescue of his friend remained his primary

reason for pursuing the matter, Tyros also felt drawn to the citadel and the secrets it might yet reveal to him. He hoped that since the second one had also been damaged, it now stood more vulnerable to capture. Tyros dearly wanted to understand what the wreckage of past citadels had only hinted at . . . how to create one of his own.

Defense of the city, the rescue of Leot, and the creation of flying citadels for his own side. Worthy goals, all of them. Any one reason should have been enough for the lords of Gwynned, and yet had not been. Doors had remained shut, missives unanswered. Appointments had been canceled or rejected outright. Some hints had arisen that part of his failure to gain support might be due to his own past arrogance, but Tyros couldn't believe that. People wouldn't reject a proper course of action simply because they found some minor offense in its sponsor's attitude.

"I want to find that last citadel, Captain. Not just for Leot's sake. Gwynned should realize that it still faces a possible threat. Besides, if we could capture it, think of what it could tell us." His eyes widened at the possibilities. "We might even be able to raise a citadel ourselves!"

The officer looked him in the eye. "Are you doing this for Leot or for your own reputation?"

"I'm doing this for all of us."

"If you say so."

Straightening, the spellcaster turned from his undesired companion. "I should have known not to bother."

"Here now!" Captain Bakal seized his arm, whirling him around. He ignored the brown-haired mage's glare, the way Tyros's hand came up in what might have been the beginnings of a spell. "I do have a thought—maybe one even too radical for the great Tyros!"

"And what is that?"

"Have you asked Sunfire?"

"Sunfire?" He blinked, startled both by the audacity of the notion and the fact that Bakal had thought of it before he had.

Sunfire. The dragon would certainly understand the

urgency. He would see that the flying citadel and its masters had to be hunted down. And with Sunfire's aid, capturing the damaged castle would be considerably easier.

"Sunfire . . ." Tyros murmured. "Of course!"

"You understand how dangerous it might be to see the dragons, don't you? They've been feisty of late, boy! Never saw them so excited as during that last battle. They wouldn't brook—"

"Yes, yes, yes! Captain Bakal, do you know how I might reach their caves?"

Black eyes narrowed. "Are you absolutely certain?"

"You made the suggestion, Captain! What was the point of it unless you thought I might actually do it?"

"All right. I'll talk to someone tomorrow. I know some dragon riders. They'll tell me if it's possible to see Sunfire."

"Excellent!" Tyros felt his spirits rise. The dragons would help him. They wouldn't let puny human dislikes compromise their common sense. They would surely see things his way.

The rain began coming down again, lightly, but enough to warrant moving on to cover. Feeling much more confident now, Tyros thought the least he could do for Bakal was reward him for his able assistance. "Are you off duty, Captain?"

"Depends."

"Care for a drink?"

"I'm off duty."

A few minutes' hurried walk, hastened by an increase in the intensity of the rain, found them at the entrance to the Sea Maiden's Lament, an inn the army officer frequented. The place was dank and smelled of fish, but Tyros suspected that any other inn nearby would be the same. Over the course of the next hour, the captain drank three flagons of strong ale without any visible effect, while Tyros still nursed his first. The contents stung the mage's throat each time he tried to swallow.

With a little ale under his belt, Bakal grew more open with the wizard. For the most part, the graying warrior spoke of his war experiences. Tyros let him talk, only half listening. His gaze drifted around the tavern area, but the mage found little of interest there. The folk were mostly fishermen, sailors, and several unsavory characters who seemed more a part of the scenery than customers. The decor of the tavern itself consisted mainly of nets, spears, fish, and other seafaring items nailed to the walls in what he supposed was the owner's misinformed idea of taste.

While Bakal talked about battles, Tyros contemplated what he would do once he had the dragons to aid him. From what he had gleaned from his companion, the military command believed that the invaders had fled to the southeast, possibly even to the New Sea. The spellcaster wondered at such a choice by the enemy commander. Most of the populated areas of the New Sea were either better fortified than Gwynned or had already been decimated during the war. Farther east, the land consisted of wilderness, hardly worth the effort for any army, yet, perhaps . . .

The door opened. Tyros glanced at the latest newcomer. His gaze froze, for the newcomer was not another grimy dockworker, but rather a young woman who would have been more in place in the finer courts of the city. Even the rain could not suppress her beauty. While others might have looked bedraggled from the downpour, she fairly blossomed. The thick red hair that cascaded down her back seemed nearly untouched by the rain. She had a proud, determined expression, her full lips set as if she found herself on a task of utmost importance. Somewhat obscured by her bangs, bright jade eyes took in everything. She sniffed a little, as if not pleased by her surroundings.

Belatedly he noticed the gleaming yellow robe she wore, simple in design, with only green trim. The combination struck a chord with the mage. A cleric of some kind. The robe couldn't conceal her feminine shape, slim yet curved. Tyros's interests in flying citadels faded as he admired her graceful movements. She nearly floated across the floor.

"Now, what have we here?" Captain Bakal muttered, suddenly all business.

The woman approached the innkeeper, who stood as fascinated as the rest. She leaned forward, whispering. The stout man shook his head, then, grinning, mumbled something back. Whatever he said must have offended her, for her head snapped back and she gave him a fiery glare. The cleric muttered a few sharp words. To Tyros's surprise, the innkeeper blanched and mouthed an apology. Tyros, who had already seen the owner handle two drunks this very evening, found new admiration for the woman.

She turned, and as she did, a small object slipped from a pouch attached to her belt. The clatter echoed through the tavern. The object rolled toward the table next to Tyros. The mage quickly stuck out his staff and steered it to him.

Picking it up, he noticed that it was a ring, a beautifully shaped ring of platinum with tiny markings, an inscription in a tongue he did not recognize.

"I would like my ring back."

Their eyes met, and in that moment, the red-robed spellcaster felt as if his entire life lay out for her to see. Jade orbs snared him, pulled him to his feet. He reached out like a boy with his first crush as he dropped the ring in her hand.

"Your eyes are the color of earth," she whispered, seeming disappointed. "His were the color of the sky."

She floated past him, departing the tavern. Tyros might have simply stood there if not for the low chuckle behind him. He glanced down and saw Captain Bakal studying him with amusement.

"First time I've seen the suave Tyros smitten like a schoolchild! Couldn't think of even one line? Can't really blame you; that one's got enough fire to singe anyone."

Chagrined, Tyros pulled himself together. He noted that none of the other men had dared approach her. Tyros, though, would not so readily give up. So fascinating a woman needed the proper company, and he, having been through so much, needed a diversion, something to take his mind off his failures of late. She obviously sought something; perhaps the mage could offer to help.

Ignoring Bakal's look, Tyros hurried to the door. He

pulled his hood up, then, bracing himself, stepped out into the storm. The wind tried to rip his hood away, but he held it tight with one hand. Wiping moisture from his eyes, Tyros peered around.

He spotted her some distance away, heading toward the business district of Gwynned. Tyros strode purposefully after her, his long steps cutting the distance quickly. The woman walked as if on some quest but did not rush, seeming content to take in everything as she went. Tyros allowed himself a slight smile; he would catch up to her soon.

Part of him knew that he sought the diversion to escape the deep guilt he felt for Leot's disappearance, but Tyros tried to ignore that fact. He had done what little he could for his friend, and until Bakal arranged his meeting with the dragons, the mage could do nothing more. Surely Tyros deserved a little time for his own needs.

Fog drifted over much of the area. Tyros wished that he still had his wizard's staff; a little more light would have been helpful. The woman seemed to see well enough without any aid, moving through the mists and shadows with ease.

He began to formulate bits of conversation that would assure her not only that he could be trusted, but also that it would be in her interest to get to know him. Who or what did she seek? Could he direct her to some place in particular? She was clad as a cleric. Could he direct her to her local temple? Tyros couldn't identify her god, but he knew where most of the major temples were.

The sound of fluttering wings made him pause, but then he noticed the pigeons in his path. Tyros grimaced. Bad enough that Captain Bakal had laughed at him, but he wouldn't embarrass himself in the eyes of this fiery-tressed beauty.

A shadow formed in the fog ahead, a shadow descending from the air.

Tyros swallowed, his eyes widening in utter disbelief.

A gargoyle nearly identical to the creature in the tower landed in the street, its back to the human. Stunned, Tyros lost his grip on the staff, which fell to the ground with a clatter.

The beast turned, glaring at him with red, soulless eyes and hissing in obvious anger at having been discovered.

Fear stirred Tyros to action. In his mind, he relived the horror in the tower. Pointing at the gargoyle, the crimson wizard cast his spell even as the winged fury started toward him, talons out and beaked maw open.

A ring of fire circled the monster, momentarily holding it at bay. The leathery attacker pulled in its singed wings and hissed. Then the gargoyle reached out with one paw, snatching at the flames and snuffing them out.

No one had told Tyros that gargoyles possessed magic.

The creature lunged at him. Tyros retrieved his staff, barely bringing it up in time to jam it hard into the torso of his attacker. Unfortunately, while he managed to knock some of the air from the gargoyle's lungs, the staff cracked in two, leaving Tyros with nothing to protect himself. More furious than injured, the gargoyle reached out toward him.

Tyros blurted out words of magic. The gargoyle recoiled as sparks of lightning burned his fingers. The mage amplified his spell, forcing his adversary to leap back.

"Move aside, boy!"

A massive figure darted past the startled spellcaster. It was Bakal, his sword drawn. Bakal lunged for the monster, which fluttered a few feet in the air, then dropped. Talons sought the veteran's face, but the captain rolled under them, and as the gargoyle passed over him, Bakal thrust up with his blade.

The savage creature hissed, then dropped to the ground, its life fluids mixing with the rain. Captain Bakal rose, and Tyros noticed that a new red scar had been added to the others, this one across the soldier's forehead. Bakal seemed not to notice, intent on dealing with his foe. Any trace of drink had vanished from the veteran's face.

Tyros suddenly realized a golden opportunity was slipping through their fingers. "Wait! Don't kill it!"

"You'd rather he killed us?"

The wounded gargoyle took matters out of their hands

by rising up into the sky. Bakal swung but missed. Tyros tried to keep an eye on the airborne monster, a spell already in mind. If he could cast it before the gargoyle got too far away . . .

Too late. The mists swallowed up his adversary, rewarding Tyros with nothing but a face soaked by the storm.

"You see him?" Bakal demanded, joining Tyros.

"He's gone. Probably a mile up by now. I wanted him alive!"

"And how by Kiri-Jolith was I supposed to know that? Besides, I doubt that thing would've let itself be captured!"

"It doesn't matter now. It's gone."

The captain tried to shake the rain off. "I don't see how it could've even gotten up in the air! Not with that belly wound!"

"How much do you know about gargoyles?"

"Good point."

They were startled by a heavy thud just a few yards from them. The two turned, Bakal's blade ready and Tyros with a spell on his lips.

The mangled form of the gargoyle lay sprawled in the street. Tyros swallowed. Although suffering a gaping wound, it had clearly made it to a considerable altitude before succumbing. The results of the drop were not at all appetizing.

"You can forget about questioning him," Bakal remarked.

Despite the horrific condition of the gargoyle's corpse, Tyros approached the still form, his mind racing. "What do they want of me? If only I could have questioned it."

The drenched soldier joined him. "You might be asking the wrong question, boy."

"What do you mean?"

"I came out just after you, mage. I got a little curious about your intended love there and thought I'd join the pair of you before you made too big of an ass of yourself."

"Your point, Bakal?"

"My point, mage," the graying warrior returned, poking a thick finger in the spellcaster's chest, "is that the gargoyle landed with his back *facing* you. He wasn't after you. See?"

46

"Not after me?" Tyros replayed the moments prior to the leathery beast's appearance in his mind. "He was after her?"

"That would be my guess. Your hot blood got in his way."

Tyros looked in the direction that the woman had gone. If she had heard the struggle, she had chosen to ignore it, and in such weather it would be impossible to find her now.

"I don't know about you, mage, but I'm heading back to the inn. I need to dry my outsides and wet my insides while I think what reason these gargoyles have for trying first to snatch you and then a cleric of a god like Bran!"

"Bran?"

"The woodland god, boy! You know, Branchala. . . ."

Chapter 4

Castle in the Sky

General Cadrio had spent many a night on the battlefield, sleeping to the mournful moans of wounded and dying men. Yet here in the silent walls of Atriun, a sense of unease had assailed him all night. The lanky commander didn't blame the castle for his restlessness; that fault lay with Valkyn. Few people other than Ariakas or the Blue Lady had ever unsettled the vulpine-visaged soldier as much as the deathly cheerful spellcaster did.

Now, dressed and impatient, Cadrio departed his chambers. Two sentries outside his door stood at attention. Even in the sanctum of a so-called ally, Cadrio took no chances.

"The pig was just here, sir," one guard informed him, meaning Lemual. "You left orders not to be disturbed before this hour, so I sent him away, General."

"You did quite right, Syl." Cadrio's alert eyes took in his surroundings. "And what did that poor excuse of a cleric want?"

"To tell you that the wizard wants to see you in the courtyard."

"The courtyard?" The general had expected to finally see what lurked below the castle. "Curious."

His guards flanking him, Cadrio made his way to the courtyard, wondering what Valkyn had in mind. The commander wore his helmet but kept the visor up. Outside, the rest of his men awaited him, weapons at attention. They filed into place as their general passed, creating a small but efficient fighting force ready to react at his command.

As they emerged into the courtyard, Cadrio noted Valkyn at work on a tripod with two small gems at the top. The wizard was being aided by two gargoyles, which had to be

Crag and Stone. The pair reminded him that there were other creatures about, probably watching his group from above.

"Valkyn! Another delay?" He had the satisfaction of seeing that his arrival had slightly startled the robed figure. Good! Let Valkyn see how it felt.

The wizard, of course, recovered quickly. "By no means! You are just in time, my general." He turned his attention to the gargoyles. "This is ready now. Take it out to the spot marked. Position it carefully. Understand?"

The pair nodded. Crag tried to shove Stone aside and take hold of the device, but the other gargoyle would have none of it, snapping at his larger counterpart. The two might have fought, but Valkyn suddenly reached into the confines of his robe and pulled out a dark red wand with a small golden sphere made of crystal set at the end. Stone saw the wand first and immediately subsided. Crag, intent on his rival, yelped in sudden pain as the bearded mage touched one of his wings with the sphere.

"I will brook no more of this. Go!"

Chastised, the two gargoyles quickly lifted the device.

"Gently! Gently!"

Now more cautious, Crag and Stone fluttered into the air, the tripod between them. Cadrio watched the creatures vanish over the wall, curious as to the item's function but determined not to ask.

"Always fighting with one another," Valkyn remarked. "They can be like children."

Children? These monsters? The general recognized deadly rivals. Those atop the castle were a different band than those lurking in the wooded garden. Only the wizard's power kept the groups at bay, but Cadrio wondered if that would someday prove insufficient. As with so many things, Valkyn played a risky game when it came to mastery of the creatures.

"Lemual should be done soon, I think, and then we can all ride out to the safety point and begin."

Interest replaced concern. "You're certain you can deliver what you promised? You can give me the weapon I need?"

Energetic blue eyes gazed his way in amusement. "I would stake my life on it, my general . . . and I do, don't I?"

Some of Cadrio's men shifted uneasily, all too familiar with their commander's preferred method for punishing failure. No doubt they imagined Valkyn's head on a pike. "We're allies, Valkyn, a precious commodity in this war."

"The war is over, my general. This is for our own personal gain. My research and your empire . . ."

The statement led General Cadrio to ask a question that had nagged him since Valkyn had first materialized in his tent shortly after the emperor's death. "Why me, mage? I know why I agreed to this alliance, but why did you choose me? You could've sided with the Blue Lady, Kitiara." Cadrio imagined her lithe body, a tool used to entice so many to her banner. "She would have rewarded you handsomely . . . in more than riches."

Valkyn's countenance momentarily darkened. "I've no interest in such pleasures, General. My work is my life now."

"But still—"

"I chose you, Cadrio, because you once served another general, however briefly. Do you know the name Culthairai?"

Culthairai. It rang a distant bell. A region as obscure as Atriun, overrun early in the war. He had served under a general born in Culthairai . . . a General Krynos, a giant of a man at about seven feet. Ambitious, once thought to be the next Dragon Highlord, Krynos and nearly all his command had been wiped out by a singularly effective plague rumored to have been spread by a dying Solamnic knight. "You speak of Krynos?"

"You survived. He did not."

Cadrio remembered his good fortune. "Ariakas needed to fill a position left by the death of another general. Krynos had recommended me before. I left with three men. The next I heard, he and most of his force had fallen."

"*My brother,* had he lived, would have been my choice, General Cadrio. I've decided that you, who knew his ways, will do."

Krynos's brother . . . Cadrio could see some of the dead

general's manner in the wizard. What sort of land had Culthairai been that it would groom for the world such a pair?

Valkyn clasped his gloved hands together, his tone once more exuberant. He seemed to switch emotions readily, either a sign of madness—in the soldier's opinion, common among wizards—or a hint that the faces he wore were all masks. "And here comes Lemual! We can begin!"

The pig-faced cleric ran toward them. One of the gargoyles perched nearby took a swipe at him as he passed, and although the creature clearly could not reach him, Lemual ducked in terror.

"Come, come, Lemual! Try to put on a brave face in front of General Cadrio!"

"What, by the emperor, is wrong with him? I've never known a cleric to cringe so! What's happened to his backbone?"

"Lemual suffered an accident of faith, or perhaps the lack of it. Happened during one of my earlier experiments. He proves useful, especially now that the grand experiment is at hand."

"Useful . . . as a cleric?"

Instead of answering him, Valkyn turned to the oncoming figure. "Well, Lemual, shall we begin?"

"Yes . . . I suppose so."

Narrow blue eyes shrank to slits. "Are you absolutely certain? Everything must be in place."

Lemual swallowed. "Yes . . . yes, I'm certain, Valkyn!"

"Excellent!" The wizard looked toward the castle, then clapped his hands twice. "Go!"

The gargoyles abandoned Atriun en masse. Cadrio doubled his estimate of the number of gargoyles at Valkyn's beck and call. Two hundred or more.

When the last had flown clear, Valkyn looked up at the central tower. Cadrio expected to see nothing up there save perhaps a lingering gargoyle or two, but instead he noticed a cowled figure, nearly a shadow, gazing down at the party.

The wizard pointed the wand at the murky form. Cadrio

blinked as the mysterious figure drifted back out of sight.

"Who was that? Who else is here, Valkyn?"

"No one of concern, my general. Now, come! Let us get our mounts!"

"But where are the other mages and clerics? Shouldn't they be with us, to chant the proper spells together?"

"I don't require such things."

"But Lord Ariakas's design—"

Valkyn waved off the late emperor's work. "Crude, time-consuming, and inefficient. My design eliminates much of the potential for costly mistakes, my general. Lemual and I will be sufficient for the task. Now, we really must be going!"

Two of Cadrio's men brought forth the soldiers' steeds. Lemual retrieved a pair of mounts for Valkyn and himself. The cleric's horse looked as nondescript as its rider, but the spellcaster's animal proved to be a furious white devil that stood at least a hand taller than even the general's massive stallion. The other horses shied away from the beast, who snorted when anyone other than his master or Lemual drew near.

With Valkyn leading, the band departed for a hilly field to the south. It stood atop a ridge that gave them an excellent view of the entire domain.

Stone and Crag awaited them there. Valkyn dismounted and quickly inspected the tripod. "All is in place. Good."

The wizard pulled his hood up, then brought forth the wand. He looked at General Cadrio and the rest, who remained near their horses. "Come, come, General! Surely you will want to see this!"

"Damon, watch the horses. The rest of you, come with me." The wary commander led his guards to where Valkyn stood.

The cheerful wizard pointed at Atriun. "Watch, my general! Watch as I give you your victory!"

He took the wand and touched the sphere at the end to the ones on the tripod. Beside him, Lemual flinched, almost as if he expected the crystals to explode. Instead, both the one on the wand and those on the tripod began to sparkle with magical energy, growing more golden. Even when Valkyn pulled the wand back, the glow about the spheres increased until it became almost blinding.

Cadrio felt the hairs on his neck rise. His entire body seemed charged. He glanced at his men, saw that they, too, experienced the unsettling sensation.

"Lemual! Do your part!"

"Valkyn! Reconsider what you have in mind."

The dark mage thrust the wand toward the cleric. "Do it!"

To Cadrio's shock, the trembling cleric placed a hand on each of the crackling globes. Lemual screamed, but a single look from the wizard kept him from removing his hands. The general sniffed, noting the all too familiar smell of burning flesh.

"Now, Lemual!"

"She has abandoned me, I tell you!"

"Your faith abandoned her! She'll give you what you want in this case, if only you believe!"

Whether the suffering cleric had truly regained his belief in Takhisis or simply feared Valkyn more, somehow Lemual summoned power. Cadrio saw his lips move, perhaps an incantation or prayer. Pain clearly wracked the man, but he did not stop.

Valkyn began to mutter, his eyes now fixed upon the wand's crystalline sphere. The mage's complexion had grown parchment white, but unlike Lemual, Valkyn's expression was filled with anticipation, not dread.

The general stepped beside the spellcaster, his gaze on the immense castle. From up here, Cadrio could admire its size better, a fortress that spanned the length of several dragons. How massive an army Cadrio could station within the walls, how many months of supplies could he store in its depths . . .

The earth beneath his feet started to tremble.

The horses, all save Valkyn's monstrous beast, struggled against their reins. The two gargoyles took to the air, hovering a few feet above the ground. Even the lanky general had to struggle to keep his footing as the tremor grew stronger.

Only Valkyn and Lemual seemed immune, but the latter lived a terror of his own, his hands black from the heat. Now the cleric looked as if he wanted to remove them from the spheres but could not.

A sound like rolling thunder came from the direction of Atriun.

Valkyn and the cleric continued to mutter. The mage looked more undead than human, his flesh colorless, streaks of gray spreading through his hair. General Cadrio had never personally witnessed so harsh a spell.

The rumble grew to a roar, and cracks began to materialize in the landscape surrounding the castle. The tremor wreaked havoc on the rest of the countryside as trees collapsed and hillsides broke in half. Birds shrieked, and although the day had only been slightly overcast before, a dark, threatening cloud cover now formed above the building. Thunder from those clouds vied with the terrifying roar from the earth below.

"Do it!" the general muttered. "Do it!"

Slowly Castle Atriun and the land directly around it rose. Only a few inches, but it rose.

Valkyn shouted a single word, then returned to his muttering. Lemual, slumped over the tripod, said nothing.

The great fortress rose a little more. A raging storm now spread far beyond the confines of the outer walls, stretching toward Cadrio and the others. Lightning set ablaze a small wooded area to the north. A mad wind drove Cadrio's men back. Even the gargoyles found it impossible to maintain their positions. Only Cadrio, Valkyn, and Lemual remained at the very top of the ridge.

Valkyn shouted once more, his words stolen by the wind.

Lightning assailed the outskirts of Castle Atriun, striking the already crippled ground again and again. Tons of earth flew into the air, moments later bombarding the surrounding earth. The area below resembled the worst of battlefields. Cadrio almost expected to hear the cries of the dying.

The bolts continued for one minute, two, then three. Cadrio knew of the power needed to fulfill this spell, but nothing had prepared him for this. It amazed him that the man at his side had managed this much success. Yet it would mean nothing unless Valkyn followed through to the end.

The ebony-robed mage fell to one knee. Anxious, Cadrio reached for him, but even though Valkyn could not have seen him, the wizard shook his head, clearly rejecting any assistance.

And then a sound that made even the striking of a hundred bolts seem mute in comparison sent the general sprawling. For a horrible moment, he saw only blackened sky. Somehow, though, Cadrio struggled to his feet and refocused on the castle.

He saw a gaping hole where the citadel had once stood. The hole sank some great distance, a chasm vast enough to hold a lake. In fact, he could see some of Atriun's moat draining into the tremendous abyss in a futile attempt to fill it.

Above him, thunder rumbled.

Heart pounding, General Cadrio looked skyward . . . and witnessed the culmination of his voyage to this backwater province.

High above, the storm gathered around it like some mad cloak, floated Castle Atriun. A corona of lightning revealed the full extent of the dark castle, including the massive island of earth attached below. As Cadrio watched, great chunks of rock and dirt broke free, dropping to the ground below with catastrophic consequences. Here and there he could also make out open passages in the earth that no doubt led to some of Atriun's lower levels.

Valkyn had proven as good as his word; he had brought forth unto Ansalon a new and terrible flying citadel. The eager commander had only to gaze up at the unsettling storm raging around the fortress to know that this citadel was different from its predecessors. Surely Valkyn had filled Atriun with many, many surprises.

Recalling his erstwhile ally, Cadrio turned around, only to see a figure in black sprawled nearby. Fear momentarily took hold of the vulpine officer, fear that he would be left with no one to explain to him how to control the flying citadel. Then Cadrio realized that the body belonged to the insipid Lemual.

Valkyn materialized next to the cleric's limp form and bent over him. After a minute's examination, the mage rose. "Poor Lemual. Still, he served his function."

"He's dead?"

"I was fairly certain it would happen, not that I thought to worry him with that knowledge."

The storm had abated somewhat and withdrawn to the near vicinity of the hovering castle. Lemual forgotten, Cadrio eagerly asked, "Will it do as you said it would?"

Valkyn smiled. "Do you still doubt me?"

"No! Only one more question, friend mage. How do we retrieve it? Should I summon Murk and Eclipse to bring us up?"

"If you wish them incinerated. As incompetent as they are, you might yet find some use for them. In fact, I would recommend that any dragon would be better served staying clear of Atriun. As to your first question, I have dealt with that matter already. You see the central tower?"

Cadrio peered up at the aforementioned tower, recalling the shadowy figure within. "He'll bring it down?"

"Well, not exactly."

Valkyn held the wand up, muttering at the same time. The storm all but faded, turning into a few grumbling clouds with occasional flashes of lightning. The flying citadel began to descend toward the ridge. The ominous shadow that covered Cadrio and the rest caused unease among his men, who probably feared the immense structure would suddenly drop on their heads.

Several gargoyles, including Stone and Crag, fluttered over to Valkyn. The general expected them to land, but Crag instead seized his master by the waist, pulling him up. Stone retrieved the tripod, taking less care than earlier. The other gargoyles seized Valkyn's steed and, in a vision both absurd and remarkable, lifted the animal gently from the ground.

Only then did Cadrio realize that they were all heading for the flying citadel, which still floated beyond his grasp.

"Valkyn! Blast you, Valkyn! What about me?"

Crag abruptly turned so that the hooded mage could look down. "You see what I've brought to you, my general! Now return to your waiting vessels and sail toward the western half of the New Sea! Seek out the island seaport of Norwych! Do you know it?"

Furious, Cadrio barely paid attention to the question. The mage had made him sail through hazardous waters to reach this obscure place, then, after revealing this monumental weapon, wanted him to sail back to a city nearly as large as Gwynned and almost as well defended! "You promised me the citadel, Valkyn!"

The wizard had the audacity to look annoyed. "Surely you do not use a weapon before testing its capabilities, my general!" When Cadrio did not answer, Valkyn added, "The seaport of Norwych! I suggest you sail toward it as fast as you can!"

With that, Crag turned and flew Valkyn toward the waiting citadel. Above the soldiers, gargoyle after gargoyle returned to Castle Atriun. Cadrio thought of summoning the two black dragons and taking his prize by force, but then recalled Valkyn's warning.

Exasperated, he whirled on his men. "Mount up! We must return to the ships quickly! Anyone lagging will be whipped!"

As his retinue prepared, Cadrio mounted his own steed, then took a moment to survey the gaping pit and storm-ravaged earth left by the launching of Atriun. "I will look down upon my empire from your creation, Valkyn, my ally," he whispered, "and I will do it whether or not you live to enjoy the fruits of my reign!"

He kicked his mount hard, sending the beast forward at a rapid clip. Behind him frantically rode his personal guard, each man knowing that the general would live up to his threat.

Left in the wake of grand ambitions, the body of Lemual, without whom either the mage or the warrior could have dared continue their respective quests, lay forgotten.

* * * * *

"What is it you want, human?" the gold leviathan grumbled.

Tyros kept his dismay in check, pretending that the thunderous voice of the dragon had not nearly sent him fleeing from the cave. He had come this far and would not be turned back before he had made his request clear. The dragon rider who had led him here had thought the mage a suicidal idiot but had agreed to take him because of Captain Bakal. From there, the man had told Tyros, it would be up to the dragons whether the wizard returned alive.

As a spellcaster, and especially one wearing red robes, Tyros knew that he faced the leviathan already under a cloud of suspicion. Yet despite Sunfire's distrust of the followers of Lunitari, and of a certain proud mage in particular, he had to make the dragon understand the importance of the quest. Surely such an intellect as the gold's would immediately realize it.

"I want you to help me find Leot, the White Robe, and another mage who disappeared during the battle. I want you to help me find the citadel and its masters before they return in force."

A curious and very undragonlike expression graced the giant male's reptilian features as he listened. After a pause, Sunfire laughed.

"I had known of your arrogance prior to this, human," he roared, nearly bringing down part of the ceiling, "but I had never understood its depth until this moment! But a handful of humans ever dare to come to this place, and most come for either our imagined hoard or in response to our summons. I cannot recall the last time one sought to invite us on a quest."

He laughed again, forcing Tyros to cover his ears. It did no good to try to back out of the cave in order to lessen the effect, for the dragons' home had no ledge. To reach the mouth, the determined spellcaster had been forced, with the dragon rider's aid, to climb fifty yards of sheer rock face.

The male gold lay curled up before Tyros, near enough to snap up the human, robes and all. Of Glisten, Tyros had seen no sign, for which he felt disappointed. Females had always been more kindly toward him, and the handsome mage had thought that perhaps Sunfire's mate might be no different.

Still, Tyros didn't give up. "You might also find those two black dragons."

"Them? Upstarts! Honorless lizards!" Dragons considered "lizard" the ultimate insult among their kind. "Twins of darkness, those two! My Glisten still suffers pain in her wings from the wounds they inflicted on her. Look here." He turned his reptilian visage so that Tyros could see his left profile. A series of jagged scars, still fresh and red, left no doubt that the black dragons had not been entirely outclassed.

"Their master must have kidnapped the other wizards," Tyros insisted. "Perhaps we can kill two birds with one stone."

"Or two black dragons with one breath?" returned the gold.

"Or that." All dragons had breath weapons, be they fire, poison gas, or ice. Gold dragons, considered by many, themselves included, to be the most superior, could utilize either flame or deadly chlorine gas. The black beasts, though, had their own weapons, scalding acid chief among them, as Glisten had discovered.

"It would be nice to sink my claws into the throats of those two . . ." the scaled behemoth mused.

Tyros's hopes rose. Perhaps the gold dragon had seen the merit of his plan. "They headed to the southeast. I believe that they may have entered the New Sea and—"

"And I will not be going with you, mage." The male frowned at the human's disbelieving visage. "Did you think me so readily swayed? I have as many reasons to reject your proposition as I do to endorse it, and chief among the former is your own self. I know something of you, Mage Tyros, and what I know I do not like. Your self-serving reputation is matched only by your ego. In addition, you choose to wear the crimson robes of the most waffling of magical orders, those mortals who would claim to follow Lunitari, but, if the whim presented itself, could readily slip into robes of night!"

"I would never do that! I donned these robes because of the freedom of choice they give, but—"

Sunfire snorted, enveloping the human in a puff of smoke. Tyros coughed, nearly suffocating. "Too many of your kind shift to the darkness, little mán! Had you worn the robes of light, such as good Leot, I might have considered your petition."

"But in the end," interrupted a smoother, feminine voice, "we would have rejected it. We *have* to reject it."

From the depths of the cave emerged Glisten. Her scales had been marred by burns, yet still the female dragon presented an awe-inspiring spectacle. Sleeker and slightly smaller than her mate, she moved with grace, while Sunfire moved with muscle.

The male swung his head to look at her. His tone became much more gentle. "You should not be up. This is the most precious of times for you."

"I am not a fragile egg, my love." The moment she finished the statement, though, a strange change came over the coloring of Glisten's face.

Suspicious, Tyros studied her. The female seemed not so sleek as he recalled her from the past. During the battle, his mind had been on the moment, but now Tyros noticed that Glisten looked swollen.

"He knows," she remarked.

The mage hadn't realized she had been watching his inspection of her. "My apologies, fair lady . . . but also my congratulations! Such a wondrous event—"

"The smooth tongue of Tyros Red Robe," Sunfire muttered. "Yes, human, my mate is ready to lay eggs, the first eggs I know of for one of my kind since we awoke!"

"I had . . . I had eggs before that. . . ." Glisten whispered, almost to herself.

"Think not on those, my love!" The male's sudden outburst shook the cave again, forcing Tyros to protect his head. Sunfire focused on the tiny figure. "Perhaps for the safety of our eggs and the pleasure of many in the city, I should devour this intrusive wizard!"

"No!" Glisten swatted her mate on the side, more a gentle tap than an actual strike. Sunfire snarled but acquiesced. The female's gaze met that of Tyros. "He will not tell anyone."

"I swear by Lunitari and my life that I will not, my lady!"

Glisten seemed happier, but Sunfire still looked distrustful. She rubbed her head against his, causing the male to relax. "It probably does not matter. Many know of my condition already."

"The dragon riders we can trust. Elfrim is a man of honor."

"Yes, but some others in the city know, and surely those twin devils we fought will have recognized my condition!"

"Them!" A dangerous look reappeared in Sunfire's eyes. "Perhaps I should risk going with this impetuous fool! I'll tear their throats out for what they did."

"I need you here!" Glisten interjected. "*We* need you here."

The male looked at her swollen form. "So you do." To Tyros, he said, "For your concern for Leot, I commend you. From what I had heard of you, it surprises me that you had even this one friend. Yet I will tell you, as I told the female who came here earlier, this is not the time for quests for either my mate or myself. You must deal with this matter yourself."

Sunfire shifted his attention to Glisten. Tyros felt great disappointment at being turned down, but he could not blame them. Dragon eggs were rare, though only a few people seemed to know why. Tyros had heard rumors but nothing believable.

He started back to the mouth of the cave, hoping that the dragon rider would still be waiting to help with his descent. Yet a question arose, one that the disappointed spellcaster had to ask no matter the danger to him. "Excuse me, great lord!"

Sunfire whirled on him. "I think I have excused you enough, Red Robe! Be off with you!"

"Just one question. The woman who visited you . . . can you tell me anything about her?" Few people would dare to come here unless on a task of great import, which had made Tyros suspicious as to the other adventurer's identity.

"She had better manners than you, that I can say, but one would expect that of a cleric! Now, begone before I forget my mate's condition!"

The golden leviathan puffed a vast cloud of smoke toward him. Tyros immediately departed, knowing that he had reached the end of Sunfire's patience.

He barely noticed the descent, his thoughts on the dragon's refusal and the interesting knowledge that the scarlet-tressed cleric had been there. Tyros wished he could have asked Sunfire more about her request. All the frustrated mage could do now was consider his next move. The trouble was, he *had* no next move. Tyros had made the journey up the mountain with the assumption that Sunfire would agree. Though the dragon had hinted that he wanted to go after the two black beasts, Glisten's condition meant that Tyros had nothing to show for his efforts.

Captain Bakal awaited him as he reached the base. "Brought him back alive, eh, Elfrim?"

The dragon rider, a slim man, possibly with elf blood, eyed Tyros with a cool expression. "Didn't think so for a while. Sunfire didn't like him. Couldn't make out a word from where I was, but I thought I'd be climbing down alone."

"Yeah, I thought the same."

"Well, I am alive, as you can see," the indignant wizard pointed out.

"And no farther with your plan," Bakal returned. "I've got the horses ready. We can still make the gates before nightfall if we leave now . . . unless you'd like to try again up there?"

Tyros felt rather than saw the dragon rider's smirk. Shaking his head, he went to his mount, who seemed to stare at the mage with contempt.

"Why do you ride with me, Bakal?" he asked as they rode off.

"Because you might get lost otherwise?"

"You know what I mean."

The battle-scarred officer rubbed his chin. "Good question. You're arrogant and ambitious and have both qualities in abundance. But I knew Leot, too, and liked the boy even though he was a mage. He was always defending you, only the gods know why. Leot also did me a favor, one that I owe him for. Owe him a lot."

"Leot helped you?"

"Yeah, but don't ask what! I've tried to pull a few strings for you here and there because of him . . . not that it's done much good. Oh, and I do think you're right about Gwynned still being in danger."

"Is there anyone you can still turn to? Any of your superiors?"

Bakal spat to the side. "Don't expect them to do too much for me, either. My reputation isn't much better than yours with some. They'll let me do what I think right so long as it doesn't interfere with the scheme of things!"

"So we're essentially on our own." Tyros stared at the path ahead. Fools ran Gwynned, and if the city fell, it would be their fault, not Tyros's. He considered departing for better climes, leaving the people to their fates.

They arrived in the city at sunset. Bakal bade him a weary farewell, explaining that he had some tasks that he couldn't escape. "Someone claims to have seen a kender within the walls. We've spent manpower and money trying to make certain it's not true. People in the market district are afraid to leave their stalls and shops!"

Tyros had met a kender once and recalled vividly how frantic he had felt after discovering afterward that half his pockets had been emptied by the short, slim creature. Most races considered kender thieves, although Tyros saw them more as magpies, creatures who stole items out of curiosity and habit. That, of course, did not mean that he wanted them in Gwynned.

With the tower gone, the mage had been forced to seek temporary lodgings at a reputable inn. While the owner had not been pleased to have the spellcaster, Tyros's money had changed his mind. Naturally Tyros had been given the darkest, most obscure room, but that had suited him. It gave the wizard the solitude he needed.

In the market, Tyros bought food, simple fare in order to keep his brain sharp. As he entered the inn, the pock-faced, teen-aged son of the owner looked up from his sweeping, his expression shifting from disinterest to knowing grin. Tyros frowned, and the boy return to his task. The mage looked around, noticed one or two men eyeing him with speculation, but they turned their gazes away immediately when he stared back.

Tyros journeyed upstairs, slightly irritated. The rabble below recognized him as a mage, and no doubt rumors had already started as to what he did in his room. He wondered if he would have to begin looking for different lodgings in the morning.

Reaching his door, the tired mage checked to see if his security spell remained intact. Anyone trying to enter would leave an afterimage of himself once Tyros spoke the proper words. It was a spell that had come in handy over the years.

The first image didn't surprise him. The pock-faced boy, his face revealing both fright and excitement. Disappointment had no doubt been his next emotion when he had found the door unyielding. Tyros always made certain to use a second spell to seal both the door and single window.

A second image appeared. One of the men seated downstairs. Tyros had seen him before, a fellow lodger with expensive tastes. Anger filled the bearded man's face. A thief. Tyros made a note to find an appropriate way to teach the miscreant the danger of trying to steal from his betters.

No other images appeared. Satisfied, the tall mage whispered a few words, then safely entered his darkened quarters. He muttered another word, one that should have set the single oil lamp on his table ablaze.

Nothing happened.

"Allow me," a low, feminine voice offered.

Light, soft green light, filled his tiny abode. Tyros blinked, his eyes adjusting quickly. A woman sat on his bed, a woman with cascading red hair and jade eyes, clad in a yellow robe with bright emerald trim that did not at all conceal her shapeliness. The light she had produced came from a sphere that floated an inch or two above her exquisite palm.

Tyros smiled. "Good evening—"

Her look precluded pleasantries. She cut him off, stating in a determined voice, "I understand that Cadrio has been here."

Chapter 5

Serene

Bakal didn't like hunting for kender, but he liked it even less when he had to do it with a squad of men behind him. As he had grown older, the captain had become more independent, which, as his superiors had been wont to state, was the sticking point preventing him from gaining further promotion. Bakal didn't care. He got things done the way he liked; he didn't muck around like so many of his counterparts, who mostly outranked him now.

Night in Gwynned had always been the scarred veteran's favorite time. True, the cutthroats and harlots came out then, but some of them had proven good and interesting people. Better than some of the higher-ups to whom he had to answer.

As he searched, Bakal thought about Tyros's quest. The captain had held vague hopes that the dragons would say yes, but he hadn't been surprised by their refusal. Still, Tyros had one thing right; Gwynned hadn't seen the last of the invaders. The officers of the dragonarmies had always been tenacious and would be worse now, what with everything up for grabs.

A sound like that of a small child running lightly along the moist street made the veteran pause. Although kender much resembled elves, they were no larger than half-grown children. Bakal braced himself and with experienced stealth followed the faint sounds. The other didn't seem in any great hurry, which enabled his pursuer to quickly cut the distance between them. Bakal heard a giggle that no child would have uttered.

"We've enough havoc with the leftover dragonarmies without having to put up with your type of hijinks, boy," he muttered under his breath.

Now he could definitely make out breathing, harsher breathing than he would have expected from the energetic kender, but perhaps the little thief had spent the day wreaking chaos among the townsfolk. Bakal quickened his pace. Another minute, another alley, and he would have his quarry.

He pulled his dagger free. Kender weren't dangerous, but just in case he had accidentally followed a brigand, Captain Bakal wanted to be ready.

His quarry had stepped into what Bakal knew to be a blind alley. The captain took a deep breath, looked to both sides for possible traps, then charged in.

"All right, you little thief! Keep your hands up where I can see—"

A massive beaked head looked down at him. A leonine paw swatted at the officer, barely missing. Behind the menacing avian visage, Bakal made out immense wings and a feline tail.

Unable to speak, the captain stumbled back, trying to stay out of reach of the monstrous animal. His left foot caught on something, though, and Bakal suddenly found himself falling backward. The dagger went flying from his hand.

He was dead, and he knew it.

Nothing happened. He waited for the beast to leap on him and rend his throat, but it did not. Finally, lifting his head, Bakal dared to look into the alley.

Nothing. The alley stood empty. No beast. The scarred veteran found himself shivering as he had not done since nearly being beheaded by an enemy soldier during the height of the war.

Wizards, draconians, gargoyles, clerics, kender, and now . . .

"A griffon!" he gasped. "A griffon!"

This city was getting too crowded.

* * * * *

"Who is Cadrio?" Tyros asked.

"You don't know him?" His beautiful intruder looked surprised. "He tried to sack your city!"

"You mean the attack. Is Cadrio one of the surviving Dragon Highlords?"

"He served under one. Now he's trying to rally what's left of Takhisis's armies to his banner." She gave him a wry smile, which made his heart flutter. "But he hasn't done a very good job of it so far. This debacle will set him back. Unfortunately, from what I've learned, General Marcus Cadrio is more dangerous when he's desperate."

Tyros's brow rose. "You sound as if you know him well."

"In a sense. I've been hunting him for some time." She suddenly rose. The sphere of light remained just above her left hand. "I can see I've wasted my time here. You don't know where I can find Cadrio. I'll be leaving now."

"Wait!" Tyros closed the door behind him. "I didn't say that. Besides, I have some questions for you, too. First, who are you?"

"These robes should tell you well enough, mage. I serve the Bard King, Branchala, and I've no time for your questions. I need to move on."

Tyros didn't want her to leave. "Please!" He put on a smile that had captivated many young ladies of the court. "My lady, please. We have a mutual interest here if you seek those who tried to invade Gwynned. I'd like to know more about this Cadrio. I think there may be a few things I can tell you, too."

She considered his words for a moment, then, with some reluctance, sat back down in the only chair. The glowing sphere drifted to a point near the ceiling and remained there. "Perhaps you have a point. . . ."

"I think so. You know me, I believe, fair lady, but what should I call you?"

"Serene." She glanced about the room. "This place makes me claustrophobic."

As a cleric of a woodland god, Serene no doubt was more accustomed to the outdoors. Tyros sympathized but could do little for her. "I apologize. Would it help to open the window?"

She wrinkled her slightly upturned nose. "This entire city stinks of too many people with too little idea of cleanliness . . . but, yes, the window would probably help."

Tyros gestured. The window flew open. "Yet you sat here in the dark all by yourself."

"I could imagine it was night and I was in my home in the woods, enjoying my privacy."

"I see." The mage recalled the bundle of food held in the crook of his arm. "I've just come from an arduous journey and had planned to eat. Will you join me in a small meal while we talk?"

Again she considered long before reluctantly agreeing. "I would appreciate that. It's been some time since I last ate."

He set the food on the table, then pulled the latter around so that he could sit on the bed while Serene remained in the chair. She inspected his purchases with more disinterest than anything else but accepted whatever he offered her, including some wine.

Tyros took a sip of wine, only to grimace. "Best you don't drink any of this. Tomorrow I will be having a few choice words with the man who sold it to me."

"There's no need for that. Hand it to me, please."

She took the wine flask in one hand. From around her throat, she pulled a medallion upon which had been carved a harp such as a bard would have used. Murmuring what sounded like the first few lines of a song, she touched the flask with the edge of the medallion. The container briefly shimmered, but otherwise seemed no different.

Replacing her medallion, Serene poured wine for both of them. The wary spellcaster took a sip, then brightened as the nectar caressed his tongue. Serene's jade eyes sparkled in amusement.

"This is the best wine I've ever tasted," Tyros admitted.

"Surely with all your vaunted power you can conjure up something better!"

"Nothing like this."

"Humility from a wizard. There's hope for you yet!" She laughed, a sound like crystalline bells, then grew more serious. "Tell me what happened here, Tyros Red Robe. Tell me about Cadrio's assault on Gwynned. I want to know everything you do."

He told her, relating to Serene the shock of discovering the attack, the draconians falling from the sky, and the realization that not one but two castles floated above, raining death upon Gwynned. Serene listened in silence, her eyes narrowing when Tyros mentioned the flying citadels. She hung on his every word, leaning closer and closer as he proceeded. Mention of the gargoyles caused her to sit up straight, but when Tyros sought to question her, the cleric waved for him to continue.

Tyros felt both regret and guilt build up again as he told her about Leot. By the end, the mage found himself sweating and nearly in tears. Serene, though, made no comment about it.

"Gargoyles . . . there were gargoyles, then, too," she muttered. To Tyros she asked, "Do you have any idea where Cadrio's forces went? If you do, please tell me. He's evaded me too long."

The wizard shook his head. "I have told you quite enough. You owe me some information now."

"My story wouldn't interest you."

"But it must be important for you to follow him so . . . or to try to enlist the aid of gold dragons."

She flushed. "So you know of that, too."

"I know that they turned you down." Tyros chose not to mention his own failure.

"For the best of reasons. I'll not risk some things even for army needs!"

"I understand the reason. Glisten's reason."

"Not even all my misery is worth endangering her and her eggs!" The cleric's eyes grew misty.

"I understand." Dragons regarded their young as very precious, even more than many humans did. "But dragons aside, I still want to know why you're pursuing this general."

Serene lowered her gaze. "I might as well tell you. I follow Cadrio because he's stolen something very precious to me, someone I loved!"

Tyros felt a twinge of jealousy. Of course someone as beautiful as she would have suitors.

"I came upon the ruins of his home, destroyed by some terrible, violent force. We'd not seen each other for months, but I thought to visit him to see how he was doing." Her hands tightened into fists. "They'd struck but days before my coming! I searched the ruins but found no trace of him. That was when I prayed to Branchala to grant me knowledge of what had happened and where I might find him. The Bard King sought fit to grant me my wish, although not as I might have liked. I received a vision, a collage of images. A castle that flew, winged creatures with horns—gargoyles, I came to realize—and my love's home torn asunder like so much kindling, all his work laid to ruin or stolen."

"And Cadrio?"

"And Cadrio. I saw his face, the vulture! I also saw a land I knew to be west of where I was, a land I later found the general had used for a temporary base. Unfortunately, Cadrio and his army had already departed." For the first time, some hints of exhaustion showed. "I've chased him from the east of the continent to the west. I've seen his army and even looked the man in the eyes, from a distance, but not once did I ever have the chance to confront him."

"I thought revenge was Sargonnas's domain."

"I don't want revenge; I want only to rescue my beloved!"

Again Tyros felt a twinge of jealousy, which annoyed him. Why should it bother him that Serene loved another? "Did they conscript him into the army?"

She shook her head, sending locks of scarlet flying. "That would've been a waste. They must've wanted his work. You see, he was a mage like you."

Tyros nearly dropped his wine. A flying citadel, gargoyles, and yet another missing wizard. How many had this Cadrio

71

captured? "His work. Why would that be important?"

"He was studying the flying citadels."

The mage stiffened. He knew that others had been attempting the same as him, but still it surprised Tyros to hear that someone else had been researching the devilish castles. Small wonder, then, that this other wizard's work might have been of interest to Takhisis's minions. "But how would they have known about him?"

She shrugged. "He wrote letters, corresponded with others. Word likely reached General Cadrio through one of your order. I'm sorry, but you Red Robes are not known for your undying loyalty to the cause of good, Tyros."

The mage refrained from defending himself. He had nearly given his life to defeat the Dark Queen's warriors, and so whatever slurs fell upon his order, they did not apply personally. Yet still it bothered him to hear it from her. "So you think Cadrio kidnapped him so that he could make use of his knowledge."

The robed woman nodded. "I do, though I've no reason save that Cadrio might be hoping to raise another citadel. In fact, now that he's lost one and his last is crippled, that could be urgent!"

"You may be right. It certainly gives one something to think about." It didn't explain why General Cadrio would need one of Leot's order, though. Admittedly, another red wizard might have been swayed to help, but certainly not a follower of Solinari. Perhaps Leot had been taken by mistake.

Did that mean his friend was dead now?

"I've told you everything," Serene commented, not noticing his darkening expression. "Now I ask you again: Do you know where Cadrio might have gone?"

He nodded. "I think they sailed to the New Sea, but it probably would be a waste of your time to go there now."

"Why is that?"

"Because I believe that he'll be back here before long. He won't accept that Gwynned slipped from his grasp."

"He'd be a fool! Sunfire would be even more eager to bring down his last castle!" The cleric hesitated. "Still, from what I've learned of Cadrio, you might be right. He might come back . . . this time stronger." She frowned. "But I can't wait for him to come back. It might be too late by then. It might *already* be too late. I have to go on and hunt him down!"

"You think they keep them in the remaining citadel?"

"I have to hope! If the prisoners were kept in the one that was destroyed, then both the ones we seek are dead!"

Tyros felt far more concern for Leot than for Serene's paramour, and not simply because the former had been his friend. Trying to remain focused, he looked into her eyes and said, "You went to Sunfire to see if he would fly you to the citadel."

Her cheeks flushed slightly. "Yes . . . that's what I wanted."

"You would have died."

"I didn't know what else to do at the time." Tears threatened to flow.

Truth be told, neither did Tyros. He sat there, watching Serene struggle with her emotions and finding himself wanting to comfort her. It was hardly what his studies had trained him, for and hardly his place, either.

The cleric wiped her eyes, then suddenly rose. "I thank you for your time, Tyros Red Robe. You've told me what I need to know. I won't be bothering you any more."

"I'm sorry," the mage returned, also rising. He didn't want her to leave, but he had no other help to offer her. "If I knew a method other than the dragons, then I'd certainly tell you. As it is . . ."

Serene looked at him. "No need for that. I've another way to get there—not the one I would have chosen, but it will have to do. All I needed from you was Cadrio's whereabouts."

Tyros stared, startled. "You've another way to reach the citadel?"

"Yes, but it's for me alone, wizard."

He refused to accept that, thinking not only of her but of the one chance he might have to rescue Leot. That . . . and the tantalizing opportunity to see a working citadel from the inside. Tyros confronted the cleric. "I have to get up there. I want to come with you."

"You won't like it."

"Why?"

She hesitated, then indicated he should sit back down. Tyros sat reluctantly, awaiting her explanation.

Serene pursed her lips. "I have a friend, Tyros, who has the means to reach the flying citadel. He offered before, but I refused, thinking the dragons would help. Now I see he's my only hope."

"Is it that dangerous?" The wizard envisioned flying on the back of some demon or worse.

Curiously, the beautiful cleric smiled. "Depends on what you call dangerous . . . and I'm referring to my friend, not the transport."

* * * * *

Valkyn stood at the rail of the centermost of the balconied windows, the wind caressing his face. His hair and skin had returned to their normal look, with only a faint bit more gray at the temples. A slight flush of pleasure colored his cheeks. Above him, thunder briefly rumbled, as if acknowledging his greatness. He beamed, genuinely pleased by all that he had accomplished. The thrill of magical discovery touched him as nothing and no one could.

Castle Atriun slowly moved along, so high that few, if any, likely noticed its passing. Down in the courtyard, the battlements, and the garden, the gargoyles, too, savored the wind, their wings outstretched, their beaked muzzles lifted high to catch the scents. Stone, perched atop the tallest tree, looked up at his master, but Valkyn shook his head, desiring nothing. Besides, if the mage thought of a task, he would send Crag first. Stone might be the smarter of the two, but Valkyn trusted the larger gargoyle to obey to the letter. Stone had an independent streak that sometimes proved very useful but occasionally bordered on rebellion.

Valkyn sensed someone behind him. He turned to see

two shadowy figures, vaguely human forms shrouded in cloaks that obscured all but hints of their identity.

"You have something to report?" he asked cheerfully.

One shifted.

"Yes, I thought it might be about time. I'll be with you before long."

They dipped their hooded heads slightly, then backed away, vanishing into the darkness of Castle Atriun's interior.

Valkyn glanced once more into the sky. At the rate the citadel flew, they would arrive at their destination in a matter of days. Cadrio would arrive two, possibly three days later.

Cadrio. Valkyn admired the man's ambitions, if at times the general had too dour a personality. Still, as long as the general did what he was told, the wizard would let him play at being emperor. Cadrio looked to be the sort who would keep everything under control in return for Valkyn's guidance. If the general remained satisfied to rule in earthly matters, then there would be no trouble. Valkyn could expand his research, go about attempting new and wondrous experiments. However, he would brook no insubordination. If Cadrio proved too untrustworthy, he could readily be replaced.

Valkyn's teachers had never understood his thinking. When he had chosen the robes of Lunitari, it had been a simple matter of expediency. White had never suited him, and black, at the time, would have meant that some doors would have remained shut, mostly out of distrust. He wore black now only because it made his ally more comfortable. As far as Valkyn was concerned, one robe meant as little as another. The followers of Nuitari spent too much time bowing and scraping to Takhisis, which made absolutely no sense. The three gods of magic had purposely distanced themselves from the rest, creating a core pantheon devoted entirely to the advancement of their interests, and Valkyn felt that he of all his brethren understood that best. That he now followed the path of Nuitari seemed to him no different; it only meant that he had been forced to adjust his spells a bit to account for a different moon.

Still smiling, the ebony-clad mage entered the castle. A torch set in the wall to his right burst into flame as he strolled past it, another just ahead doing the same. All along his path, the rooms and halls lit up for him, darkening again once he had departed. Had his teachers seen all this, they might have wondered how he could possess such power. Valkyn's gloved hand caressed the wand at his side, the sphere briefly glowing stronger. Limited by their own pre-conceptions, the orders, even his present one, might have found his methods . . . horrifying?

He went not to the lower depths of Castle Atriun, where the two shadows awaited him, but rather to the very top, to where the Wind Captain's Chair stood. Although the way seemed simple and safe enough, Valkyn could sense each of the trap spells installed along the path. Others would find the trek to the tower much more lethal.

The door to the tower opened before him. A figure standing on a platform in the center turned its head to look. Another of his servants, this one slightly more gaunt than the others. The cloaked shadow did not acknowledge him as the rest did because he could not bow or otherwise move. Monstrously thorough, Valkyn had just a few hours before made his servant a very part of the mechanism that controlled the flight of Atriun. Where there might have been feet, the folds of the thick robes melded into two dark circles positioned between a pair of intricately carved pedestals. The ornate silver pedestals, four feet high and with myriad designs and magical symbols traced in gold carved into them, had each been topped with a great gleaming crystal much like the one at the end of the wand. The pedestals, roughly a yard apart, would have been worth a fortune even to those with no magic.

No one would have wanted them as they were, however, for as with the feet, the hands of the servant, in part covered by robes, had become one with the crystals. Even Valkyn couldn't tell where his puppet ended and the device began.

Valkyn felt that his alteration made for smoother, more natural control . . . and certainly his servant could not argue the point.

"All is well?" He expected it to be so, but it always paid to ask, just in case some small fault had come into play.

The hood turned so that the creature looked to the north.

"Yes, I know. They still follow us. Pay them no mind unless they try to enter the cloud cover. Then we shall deal with them."

Cadrio's pet dragons flew far behind, no doubt at the general's request. Valkyn would let them follow so long as they did not interfere. For now, he had Norwych to consider.

The city lay on an island near the opening of the New Sea. Norwych had much in common with Gwynned and, in fact, had been settled by Ergothians just after the First Cataclysm. Not quite as large as the Northern Ergothian seaport, it still remained a viable target with which to test Castle Atriun.

That he felt nothing for those who might die did not make Valkyn evil in his own eyes. Few among those alive did he consider as more than peripheral existences. His brother he had cared for even if Krynos's tendencies for violence had seemed a wasteful use of energy. What mattered to the mage was his work. Norwych would open up new doors for that.

"Keep a steady course," he instructed unnecessarily. The shadow servant could do nothing but obey his directives.

Valkyn left the tower, descending finally into the depths of Castle Atriun. A few gargoyles on sentry duty bowed their heads as he passed, their wings wrapped around them in deference and fear. He ignored them as he ignored the very air he breathed. With each step, anticipation built, just as it always did when he had work of a delicate nature to perform.

One of the shadow servants greeted Valkyn at the door to his innermost sanctum. The hooded creature shifted uneasily, then opened the door for him. A blaze of light shot forth into the darkened corridor, briefly forcing Valkyn to wait for his eyes to adjust. From within the chamber came a muffled groan.

Valkyn clasped his hands together, eagerness rising. "Now, shall we begin?"

Chapter 6

The Gathering

Come meet me at the inn where I now stay.

That was all Tyros's note had said, which did not please Captain Bakal at all. He still had nightmares about the griffon and found himself checking every darkened alley. Of the kender rumor he had discovered nothing, which further soured his mood. He hoped Tyros had a good reason for summoning him.

He entered the inn and walked past the owner without greeting. The officer threw back the hood of his cloak and marched up the steps, quietly cursing the man below for giving Tyros the farthest room. With all he had been through, Bakal did not need to be climbing steps.

At last reaching the mage's door, the captain nearly touched the handle, then recalled Tyros's warning about spells. Bakal knocked instead on the wall next to the door, at the same time calling, "Boy! Mage! Open up!"

The door swung open. What stood before him was not Tyros, but rather a vision of crimson-tressed wonder wearing a very becoming clerical robe.

"There's no reason to shout," she reprimanded.

Bakal gritted his teeth and entered. "Girl, after what I've been through this last couple days, that's the best I can do!"

She closed the door behind him, and only then did the captain see Tyros, who sat on the bed. "Good to see you, Captain. You remember Serene, from the tavern?"

"I do." Bakal had no patience for pleasantries, though. "Now, tell me why you wanted to see me."

"If you will sit down, I will explain."

Bakal noticed that there were now two chairs where there had been only one on his last visit. He grabbed the heftier of the two for himself, then brought the other one to the cleric. "My lady?"

"I don't know if I should even be here," Serene muttered. "I should be on my way after them by now. . . ."

The soldier didn't follow her statement, but Tyros evidently did. He stared at the cleric. "Serene, Captain Bakal may be able to help us, or at least help you."

"I don't need help," she insisted. Nonetheless, the young woman finally sat and told her story to Bakal, who refrained from many obvious questions as he listened. By story's end, he decided that he believed her for the most part, but she had purposely left out details of some import. Whether Tyros realized that or not, Bakal didn't know. For the time being, he chose to keep his thoughts to himself.

"An interesting and tragic affair," the soldier finally commented. "So this General Cadrio is the commander of the invaders. I know that name, mostly from reports in the east during the war."

"You heard what she said about her wizard?" Tyros interrupted. "Taken like the rest! Don't you see? That means Leot is probably alive as well!"

"A presumption, boy." The captain ignored the mage's look. He had offended far more important people. "But I suppose it has some merit." He leaned back on the chair. "Suppose you tell me now what it means to me."

Tyros leaned forward. "Serene has a way to reach the flying citadel."

The weary black eyes became slits. Perhaps he hadn't been wasting his time here after all. "I'm listening."

"I know . . . someone," she began very slowly.

Bakal mentally tensed. Again the omissions.

"He has a way for us to get up there—a risky way, but one that should work."

"And what's this risky way, girl?"

"You'll have to see it for yourself, I'm afraid."

He looked at the mage, who shrugged. "She won't even tell me much, but I believe her."

Bakal wondered if the great Tyros had become too

enamored by this fiery-haired beauty. The captain cared little to take anyone's word on faith, even a cleric's. Still, what other options did he have at the moment? "So what do you want from me, and why should I give it to you, especially considering that you haven't really said much about your transport?"

Tyros had an answer for that at least. "First, I'll remind you why you should help, Bakal. Leot aside, think what secrets we could learn if, even damaged as it is, Gwynned could capture the citadel! Add to that, if it can be properly repaired, which Cadrio may be doing even now, it could serve as just as good a weapon for the cause of light as it has for darkness!"

Since he and Tyros had first spoken on the subject, Bakal had toyed with the idea of capturing the citadel, although in reality he knew that it would be better just to destroy the thing. Had the dragons agreed to Tyros's quest, Bakal would have seen to it that Sunfire and Glisten would send the damned castle plummeting to the ground or into the sea, just as they had its sister ship. If Leot or other prisoners aboard perished, it would be a regrettable consequence. Bakal felt a little guilt and occasionally thought himself no better than Tyros, but he reminded himself that some costs had to be accepted in order to win victory. Even the sacrifice of friends . . .

"I don't suppose you've got some more dragons, do you?" he asked of Serene.

"No."

Still no explanation. He disliked that immensely. What could she possibly have in mind? "All right. You've made one point at least, Tyros. So what do you want from me? I may not even be able to provide it, you know."

Tyros seemed unconcerned on the last point. "Serene tells me she can provide transport for as many as sixteen. Counting us and the one who will provide us with the transport, that's four to start."

"Meaning you want another twelve. So you want volunteers?"

"Or mercenaries, if need be. I have some money, Bakal."

"Better be a lot. Still . . ." He rubbed his chin. A notion formed, one that he quickly decided he had better not yet share with the mage. This would mean some delicate talk with his superiors, and delicacy had never been one of the captain's strong points. "I'll see what can be done, but I still want to know about this transportation. I don't like surprises!"

Tyros eyed Serene, who shook her head. "I can't. A promise was made, and by my pledge to Branchala, I won't go back on it!"

Bakal didn't like that, but he knew better than to press the cleric. "All right. Give me a day or two to arrange things, then I'll contact Tyros."

"Will that be enough?" Tyros asked, startled.

"It'll be enough." Bakal rose. "And unless there's more to talk about, I'll be going now. It's been a long day." He nodded to the cleric, who did likewise. "Make sure you're both ready to leave when I contact you."

"You are really willing to do this, Captain?" the mage asked.

"Just be ready." The officer departed, his mind already racing. The name Cadrio had rung a bell with him and likely would do so with some of his superiors. That would make them more open to his plan, which varied slightly from what Tyros proposed. However, the wizard would just have to understand that not everything could go his way.

Captain Bakal would have the twelve men ready. Those twelve would be handpicked, not mercenaries, and they would answer to the officer, not Tyros or the cleric. It had to be that way, for neither of his companions knew enough about the necessities of war.

Only one thing bothered Bakal. Who, he wondered, was the last member of their party?

* * * * *

Tyros yawned, trying not to think of the sleep he was missing. The sun wouldn't rise for another hour, and the weary mage greatly envied it. He took a sip from the flask he had brought along, a cold tea that one of his teachers had introduced to him long ago. It stimulated the system, revitalized the sleepy mind.

He wished he had brought a second flask . . . with something stronger added.

Tyros sat atop his chestnut mare, gazing at nothing. Oh, he could see the nearby vicinity well enough, as much good as that did him. The problem was that none of his companions had so far shown up, which irritated him. Even Serene, who had chosen this location, had not yet arrived.

This morning found him overly nervous. Since the disaster in the tower, his nerves had never been the same, and in fact he had to fight not to show that. Others could not be allowed to see his weakness. He was *Tyros*, after all.

He had tried to plan well for this journey, assuming that once they reached Serene's transportation, they would continue on. Tyros had brought minimal supplies and only an extra garment or two. He had also strapped a new wizard's staff to the side of his mount. It gave him some comfort, even though for the most part it would best serve for hand-to-hand combat. Given the short amount of time, Tyros had only been able to cast a few useful spells on it.

Tyros wished Serene had at least chosen a site in Gwynned, rather than out here in the desolate countryside. Dark hills greeted him for some distance, eventually changing to mountains far to the east. To the northeast lay the dragons' cave, the only part of the chain that Tyros had ever visited, despite his many months here. He knew that if one went far enough beyond this small chain, one would reach the even more mountainous region of Hylo, but Hylo was the domain of the kender, and few Ergothians ever went there.

From behind came the sound of hooves trampling the dusty landscape. Tyros turned to see a murky form some distance back coalesce into Captain Bakal, followed by several men of so similar a look that the wizard would have almost taken them for brothers. Mercenaries, perhaps, but Tyros suspected that they were regular soldiers, possibly even men who had trained under the captain. He found that interesting, especially in light of Gwynned's supposed disinterest in his proposition.

"Well, good to see you up and bright, mage."

"I've been here about a quarter hour, already, Captain Bakal," Tyros replied, trying to sound fully awake. "Waiting for all of you. I see you found the men after all."

"It took some doing."

When it became clear that the graying officer would not elaborate, Tyros settled back to studying the landscape.

"And where's the cleric, boy?"

"She should be along soon."

"I'm here already," a musical voice interrupted. From out of the darkness Serene materialized, walking gracefully along with a staff of her own. A faint green glow surrounded the cleric. She seemed to smell of morning dew and flowers, and more than one man among Bakal's troop brightened at her presence. "I was waiting until you all arrived."

"You were here already?" Tyros frowned, wondering how she had escaped detection by him. "How long?"

"Long enough. Good morning, Captain."

"Morning to you, my lady."

She looked over his band. "You had little trouble finding men, I see."

"I fulfilled my part." The captain shifted in the saddle. "Now that we're all here, we can get on with it." Bakal squinted. "Where's your horse?"

"I don't need one, Captain."

"I thought we had a journey of some distance."

"Yes, to those mountains there. The nearest ones."

The officer snorted. "You propose to walk all the way there, girl?" He extended his hand. "I'll give you a ride. This old war-horse, he'll carry both of us just fine."

Serene shook her head. "Thank you, but I don't need any help." Again she pointed at the mountains. "Ride directly toward the one with the twisted top. You two know it?"

"I know it," Bakal replied. "A short but jagged peak. Some bad ground there, too. That's where we go?"

"Yes. I'll meet you there."

"Meet us there? You going to cast a spell to fly over there?"

The cleric gave Bakal a frown. "I do not cast spells. I ask for the help of my good patron, and if he deems it worthy, my request is fulfilled."

The captain shrugged. "A spell."

Before she could correct Bakal again, Tyros leapt in. "All right, Serene. We'll meet you there."

"Good. I'll be waiting for you. . . ." The glow around her began to fade, and as it did Serene herself started to vanish. Her gaze fixed on the wizard's and remained there until she had completely disappeared.

"Mages and clerics!" Bakal finally uttered. "Give me swords anytime! At least steel is good, honest, and stays where you put it!" He turned to his men and shouted, "You heard her, lads! Let's ride!"

Tyros noticed that the men only paid attention to the captain, barely even noticing the mage. They had to be soldiers from Gwynned. He had suspected that Bakal would opt for such a choice, but decided to say nothing. In reality, Tyros cared little who the captain chose; he had his own plans for when they reached the citadel. If he could gain access to the Wind Captain's Chair, then he could seize control of the fortress himself. Control it, and he not only rescued Leot, but brought fame to himself. If Bakal helped him, fine.

They rode toward the eastern mountains, the sun rising shortly into their journey. The low hills began to give way to even rockier, sloping landscape, one that forced them to slow down. Tyros knew that the chain of mountains ahead hardly compared to the one bordering Hylo, but it still left an impression. He thought it a shame that most maps beyond Northern Ergoth did not even acknowledge its presence.

Bakal led them to the peak in question, a vicious-looking thing that, while not as tall as Sunfire's home, rose almost vertically on the western face. Tyros hoped that they wouldn't have to climb it.

The veteran officer looked around at the few shrubs. "Well, we're here! You see any sign of the cleric . . . or anyone?"

"I'm right here, Captain."

The redheaded woman stood off to the side, looking as fresh and relaxed as she had earlier. Jade eyes twinkled at the men's startled expressions.

Bakal could only frown and say, "So you are."

"You'll have to dismount if you want to reach where we need to go. You can lead the animals in on foot."

The men dismounted, then followed Serene through a narrow opening leading into the mountain chain. They wended their way along the passage for some time, noting that the rocky walls quickly grew high. Bakal muttered something about ambushes, but Tyros paid him little mind, trying to keep his attention on the uneven path. Serene hadn't been jesting when she had said that they would have to go on foot.

Shadows obscured much of the features of the narrow valley through which they journeyed, but the wizard could see gaps high up in the nearest mountainside, caves suitable for great birds but impossible for any man to reach. As if to verify his notions, a vast winged form suddenly darted out of one, disappearing into the neighboring mountains before Tyros could make any identification.

For what seemed another hour, the group traveled. At last Serene led them to a ridge, more a miniature mountain, that took the better part of their remaining strength to ascend.

"How much farther?" the captain finally grumbled.

"We're nearly there," was Serene's only reply.

Sure enough, only a few minutes later the cleric paused in the midst of a clear gap between peaks and planted her staff in the earth. None of her companions at first believed that they had come to the end of their journey, not until she finally announced the fact out loud.

"This is it?" Bakal's gaze fixed on Serene. "I don't see anything. I don't like that." His men muttered agreement, some keeping their hands by their swords.

"Stay your weapons!" The cleric raised her staff. "This is no trick!"

Having come this far, Tyros did not want to have to turn back to Gwynned empty-handed. "Keep them under control, Captain." To Serene, he asked, "Where is your friend? The sooner he makes himself known, the sooner things will calm down. Is that not correct, Captain Bakal?"

"That depends on—"

"Is it okay to come out, Serene?" a high-pitched voice suddenly interjected. "I mean, I've waited and stayed quiet just like you said, but it's been an awful long time, and they won't like waiting."

Bakal backed away, shaking his head in dismay as the final member of their party emerged from behind a small outcropping. "By the Blue Phoenix!" he sputtered, using the Ergothian title for Habakkuk, god of the sea. "It's a blasted kender!"

Everyone but Serene reached to protect his personal belongings even though the kender stood some distance away. The size of a half-grown child, he looked harmless enough, with his cheerful, elflike face and long, black hair tied in a topknot. He carried no weapon save a dagger and a sling in his belt and wore simple green traveling clothes. Tyros judged him to be relatively young. Belatedly it occurred to him that the race was favored by Branchala, so it stood to reason that of all humans, a cleric of that god would be able to tolerate the mischievous creatures.

Still, what sort of help with transportation could a kender offer? Tyros would have rather accepted the aid of a gnomish machine.

"Behave, Rapp," Serene replied quietly. The kender gave her a hug, which she returned with a smile. The cleric rubbed his head with obvious affection. "Now, it wasn't all that long a wait, was it?"

"No, I suppose not." Rapp's eyes said otherwise. Kender were notorious for their short attention spans. Waiting for Serene must have been agonizing for him.

"Let me get this straight," Bakal snarled. "We've come all

this way to meet this little thief? You're the one people said they saw in the city, aren't you?"

The redheaded woman looked down at her friend. "Did you go into the city after I pleaded with you not to, Rapp?"

"Well, no . . . not much . . . but it was only at night! I'm sure no one saw me, or at least only a few . . ."

"Rapp, what am I going to do with you?" She sighed. "Before we leave, I want to see everything you've got in your pockets and pouches, and, yes, I mean everything. If it doesn't look as if it belongs to you, it goes back to the city. Understood?"

"Yes, Serene, but I don't think I took anything, although I did notice a few pieces that must've fallen in my—"

"Never mind." Serene looked around, as if seeking something. "How are they doing, Rapp?"

"They've fed, Serene! I found them a nice place to hunt fish." He looked at Tyros, who backed away from the suddenly advancing kender. "They like fish. Did you know that? I never did, but I've learned so much from them. My name's Rapp. What's yours?"

The anxious spellcaster found himself shaking hands. He pulled his away, checking at the same time to see if Rapp had somehow gotten into his pockets. "Tyros . . . my name is Tyros."

"Are you a mage? You must be a mage with a robe like that! Can you do a trick for me?"

"Make him disappear," Bakal suggested.

The veteran likely regretted speaking, for now Rapp honed in on him. "Can he really do that? I'd like to see that! My name's Rapp! That's short for Rappskali—"

"Get your hand out of my tinder pouch!"

Serene tapped the stony earth with her staff. "Rapp! Come here! You're bothering Captain Bakal!"

"I'm sorry! Was I bothering you? I didn't mean to!" Mercifully, the spry kender obeyed her, hopping back to her side.

"I'm for leaving," one of the men in back growled, "before that little cutpurse strips us of everything we have!"

"You'll stay where you are!" roared their leader. He turned

on the cleric. "But if he doesn't produce transport . . ."

Tyros could scarcely believe this turn of luck. Had he been made a fool of by this woman? What good was a kender to his quest? Would the creature suddenly sprout wings and carry them?

Serene leaned down, talking kindly to Rapp. "Perhaps you'd better call them now. We haven't much time, and they need to get used to the men."

Rapp nodded, then left her side to climb atop the outcropping. He smiled once at Tyros, then looked up and suddenly called out like a wild beast.

"Why's he spouting like a hawk?" Bakal demanded.

Tyros thought that Rapp's call ended more like that of a lion or some other great cat, but he could see why the captain had taken it for a bird. He looked around, waiting for something to emerge from the rocks.

From above came a deeper, longer version of the call the kender had made. As one, the humans looked up. All but Serene looked startled. Tyros saw birds, huge birds, leave their mountain roosts and begin to descend.

Only they were not birds.

"Gods!" one of the men shouted. "What are those beasts?"

Tyros looked to Bakal for an answer, but the usually fearless soldier stood speechless and pale. He shook his head over and over, his eyes never leaving the oncoming creatures above.

"I knew I'd seen one!" he finally uttered. "I wasn't mad! It was a griffon! It was!"

Tyros had heard of the fantastic animals, even studied them as part of his education, but as with the gargoyles, he had never actually seen one before. Now six of them—no, more like eight—descended upon the party, and at a kender's behest.

Bakal suddenly went into action. "Form a circle! Swords at the ready! Be ready to fight your way out!"

"There's no need for that!" Serene called. "They won't harm you! Rapp, tell the children to land!"

The kender nodded, then gave out a cry with slightly

different tones than the first. The griffons suddenly swerved and, moments later, alighted around the outcropping. Despite their immense size, they landed gently, then folded their wings.

The animals presented a fantastic combination of two other creatures, the proud eagle and the majestic lion. Their tails, although whiplike, had a shock of feathers at the end. The torso mostly resembled that of the feline, golden-furred and very muscular. However, the legs ended in peculiar talons, like a bird of prey's, yet more dexterous. The talons could have easily seized a full-sized man and taken him aloft, not a comforting thought.

The griffons stared at the intruders, their heads almost identical to those of a true eagle. Yet the feathers mixed with fur toward the back and under the beak, the latter giving the winged furies a bearded look. Tyros stared at the eyes and saw far more intelligence in them than in most animals. He wondered if the griffons could actually understand what others said.

"That's our transportation?" Bakal spouted.

"They're really well behaved!" Rapp offered. "I raised them mostly myself! I found them after the parents had been killed by hunters, and even though I was on my way to Solace, which is supposed to be a nice place that I hope to still visit someday, I couldn't very well leave them to die, could I?"

"Of course you couldn't," Serene replied approvingly.

"Well, that's what I thought, and even though it meant having to stay in the woods a lot, I fed them and then found Serene, who taught me more about how to take care of them, and I love them like they're my own children, which they really aren't because they wouldn't look like that, especially the beards."

"I don't know which is worse," the captain said to Tyros. "The griffons themselves or listening to his story about them. You can't be serious about us riding those monsters!"

A couple of the nearer creatures squawked at the last word.

"Be careful, Bakal," Tyros warned. "I think they sense your dislike." To Serene, he added, "but the captain raises a good point. Do you think we can actually make use of the griffons? They seem to obey the kender, but will they let us ride them?"

"They let me ride all the time," she replied with just a hint of mischievousness. "Surely you two will have no trouble."

Bakal took umbrage at the possible slight to his courage. "You tell me what to do and I'll ride one of the beasts," he insisted. "And that goes for the others, too."

While the spellcaster noted some continued unease among Bakal's soldiers, none of them sought to dissuade their leader. The captain had chosen well. Despite their misgivings, these men were still willing to go on.

"It's very simple. Put your leg over the torso, then hold on to either the mane or the rider in front of you."

The wizard studied the huge animals. "They can carry two at a time?"

"They're very strong."

"What about supplies?" Tyros asked.

"They can carry a little, but we won't be able to bring any unnecessary items along." She had made note of Tyros's heavily packed horse.

Thinking of the mounts, Tyros turned to Bakal. "You'll have to leave a man to bring the horses back to Gwynned."

"Already thought of that. Simon there." The captain indicated a tall bearded man about the mage's age. "He'll take them back. Brought him along just for that."

The cleric nodded. "Then it's all settled. Good! The longer we delay, the farther Cadrio and the citadel get. Rapp, you and I need to deal with the griffons before the others mount. They'll be a bit nervous around the men, and I don't want any trouble. Come!"

"Isn't she wonderful?" Rapp asked, gazing up at her with pure devotion. "She can do so much! I thought about becoming a cleric of Branchala—he likes kender more than most, you see—but then I thought that if I were a cleric of the Skylord, then I could talk to all the animals, not just my griffons! Of course, then I might have to go walking around in a robe and pray in temples and—"

Bakal grimaced as the kender went on, then turned to the men. "You heard her! Get everything ready! Hurry!"

As the soldiers obeyed, Tyros studied the beasts, which remained near the outcropping, watching the antics of the people. Serene and the kender talked to each, which seemed to have a relaxing effect on the griffons. Tyros noted that most stared longest at Rapp, their eyes filled with as much devotion as he had shown for Serene.

Returning to Tyros, the cleric commented, "They'll be fine now. By the way, you and I will ride together."

"Me?"

"Rapp and I need to ride different griffons so that we can better maintain control of the entire group. And since you're the one who knows most about these castles, I want you near if there's a question to be asked. The captain will ride with Rapp. Understand?"

"I do." Bakal would be thrilled.

"Fine." She looked past him, to where Bakal and the others had nearly readied themselves. "It's time for them to choose."

"Choose?" Tyros looked over the beasts, trying to pick the best one. "What difference does it make which one we choose?"

Serene grinned. "You misunderstand! You don't choose."

"Then you do it," Tyros said, nodding at the kender.

She tapped her staff, which set the animals moving. Rapp ran over to Bakal, no doubt to give him the good news about their traveling together. "Oh, I don't do it either. They do."

"They?" Tyros stared at the griffons, which now began to circle the humans.

"Tyros! Mage!" the captain called. "What the devil's going on here? Why're they coming toward us?"

Tyros looked back at the captain, trying to keep his voice steady. Serene trusted these animals; surely he could do the same. "Remain calm, Bakal! Nothing to worry about! They're just in the process of—"

A great force landed on the mage's chest, slamming him backward to the ground. Massive talons dug into his chest, hurting him slightly but somehow managing to avoid tearing the cloth of his robe. He stared into an avian face with leonine eyes. The sharp beak opened, and Tyros received a faceful of putrid breath.

"Consider yourself lucky, mage," Serene called from behind the monstrous beast. "I think he likes you."

Chapter 7

Death from Above

General Cadrio eyed distant Norwych, imagining it to be Gwynned. His ships stood ready to sail toward the target, but Valkyn hadn't given permission to strike. Instead, the mage had some other plan in mind and had sent the savage Crag with a note containing instructions.

By an hour before dawn, you must be in position near the Three Sisters. The lanky general briefly looked south, where three tall rocks, vaguely shaped like gossiping women with their heads close together, rose high above the water.

The point will keep you from the eyes of Norwych's watch. Wait there until you notice the skies above you darken. Only then sail closer, but do not enter the harbor of Norwych until given the signal.

Valkyn meant to put on some sort of display before Cadrio would be allowed to attempt landfall. It would have to be impressive if the mage meant to soften up the defenders for the general. Norwych was a formidable island stronghold, one that had resisted the advances of the Dragon Highlords early in the war.

Crumpling the missive, he scanned the clear sky. "So where are you, then, wizard? Where?"

"Sir!" He looked down to see Zander standing at attention, the aide's armor brightly polished as usual, his cloak immaculate. The officer saluted smartly. Zander did everything smartly.

"What is it?"

"Some of the captains have signaled for clearance to sail. They don't like being anchored out here. Apparently the Three Sisters are considered bad luck by seafarers."

"Only if they're stupid enough to wreck their vessels on them!" the vulpine commander snarled. "If any ship breaks rank, I'll hang its officers from the crow's nest! Relay that to them!"

"Aye, General!" Zander quickly retreated.

Again, Cadrio surveyed the sky. He saw a few clouds, but nothing more. Less and less he liked the goateed wizard's attitude. They were supposedly allies, but nothing so far gave credence to that. Cadrio was to be emperor, yet Valkyn gave the commands. What did the mage know of warfare? More important, how dare he think himself the general's superior?

General Cadrio wished he could lay his hands on the citadel. He understood its basic design enough to know that it could be flown by anyone. Valkyn's apparently didn't even need wizards and clerics chanting levitation spells, which meant yet fewer annoyances. If only Cadrio could reach it undetected. . . .

He looked to the rear of the fleet, where the crippled citadel left from the Gwynned raid still floated, awaiting orders. For some reason, Valkyn had insisted that he needed this castle also, but empty of all save those necessary to fly it.

A shadow fell over his flagship. He looked up, expecting Valkyn, but instead two ebony dragons fluttered above.

The first one spoke, its voice low and impatient. "When do we fight? We've waited for your signal, but—"

"Waited much too long!" interrupted the second. "We don't like to wait!"

"Just a little longer, Eclipse, Murk," replied Cadrio, undaunted by their presence. "Hold your positions or you'll give us away!"

"We smell dragon here," Eclipse remarked. "Not gold, likely, but—"

"Likely silver! Yes, silver," added his twin. "Which would be almost as good as gold!"

The general glared at the leviathans. "You'll get your opportunity, but not before I say so! Is that understood? I want no repeat of the last battle! Now, return to your positions!"

Eclipse and Murk reluctantly retreated. They hadn't forgotten their battle with the two golds and sought the chance to redeem themselves. Cadrio swore softly. How he would have preferred a red or blue dragon at his command. They obeyed orders. Instead, all he had was this pair of overly unpredictable black beasts.

The faint sound of thunder erased all thought of dragons.

The wind began to pick up. Clouds suddenly blossomed, swiftly covering the sky. The sea grew choppy, forcing the crew to make sure that everything remained secure.

Cadrio recalled the storm caused by the raising of Castle Atriun, but he had thought that was only a by product of the initial spell. He looked around, yet didn't see Valkyn's prize. Were the winds and clouds simply the whims of the sea?

"Sir!" Zander rushed over to him. "Sir! Up there!"

A speck appeared in the western sky, one that grew larger as it neared the island stronghold.

Valkyn's citadel had arrived.

"Signal the other vessels! We move in when I give the word!" Cadrio glanced back at the other citadel. "Tell him to get that thing underway, too! I want it in position when Valkyn needs it!"

He hurried to the bow of the ship. Like the dragons, Cadrio sought to redeem himself, and now the first step had been taken. Soon he would lead his men to the first of many victories.

The citadel had descended to a height where all could make it out. What must the inhabitants of Norwych be thinking at the moment, seeing death falling upon them?

"What are you planning, Valkyn?" the commander muttered. The gargoyles seemed hardly enough to take a city, even if Cadrio's remaining draconians joined them.

The second citadel joined the first, floating a few hundred yards behind it.

Throughout Norwych, great bells and shrill horns cried out warning to the populace. The general considered Norwych's possible first line of defense. Catapults, perhaps, but Eclipse and Murk had also mentioned the possibility of silver dragons. Had it been Cadrio's decision, he would have sent the dragons in first.

Sure enough, even as the first roar of thunder shook all, from the south came a pair of long, sleek silver forms nearly as large as the golden dragons. Looking at them, Cadrio doubted that his two overanxious beasts would fare any better today than previously. Surely Valkyn had something planned for such powerful threats. . . .

The citadel moved over the city, and with it went the storm. Cadrio marveled at the display. Where did such power erupt from? Surely not from Valkyn himself, even though at times the mage had exhibited hints of great strength. No, Valkyn had discovered some new source of power for his citadel, surely some fantastic force.

Yet despite the harsh wind and rain, the two silver behemoths flew unerringly toward their target. The dark castle moved slowly toward them, as if its master didn't realize the danger.

"Are you mad, Valkyn?" Cadrio shouted. "Do something!"

He expected the gargoyles to fly out, attacking the dragons and trying to take advantage of their smaller size and sharp talons. However, none of the gray monsters showed. Atriun simply floated there, awaiting its doom.

The dragons split up as they neared. They probably intended to pound the citadel from both sides, thinking that a horde of draconians would soon drop from Castle Atriun's walls onto Norwych. The silvers were determined not to let that happen.

Then lightning struck.

Cadrio blinked, not at all certain what he had just witnessed. He leaned forward, squinting.

One of the dragons fluttered awkwardly, one wing ripped and burned by the bolt. A fortunate accident, but one that Cadrio knew could not be repeated. Valkyn had to make his move now or die with his creation.

A second bolt struck the injured leviathan.

Now the dragon could barely fly. The power in one bolt of lightning would have been enough to send any of Cadrio's vessels to the bottom. It amazed the general that the silver dragon still lived, much less flew, but what astonished him more was that two bolts had struck with such accuracy. The odds had to be astronomical!

The second dragon, noting its mate's dire circumstances, suddenly darted toward it, which saved the uninjured beast from a third bolt that shot directly at where it had been.

At last General Cadrio understood. "The storm," he whispered. "Valkyn's harnessed the storm. . . ."

Black clouds surrounded the citadel, but occasionally crimson and yellow flashes highlighted the ominous structure. The winds continued to rock the fleet, but Cadrio didn't care. The mage hadn't lied when he had promised power. Valkyn had created a weapon more deadly than dragons, as the two silvers continued to find out.

Another bolt split the pair apart. The wounded one began to lose altitude. Two more bolts struck it. Its mate roared in horror.

The mortally wounded dragon's wings ceased flapping, and the scarred and burned body plummeted seaward.

An unexpected gust of wind sent everyone aboard the *Harpy* reeling. Cadrio gripped the rail, then looked up. Murk and his twin had disobeyed orders and now flew toward the remaining dragon. They still sought to redeem themselves, despite the risk of the storm.

The second silver hovered over the water where its mate had crashed, completely oblivious to the new threat racing toward it.

Surprisingly, Valkyn didn't finish off the beast. Instead, the castle positioned itself over northern Norwych. At the same time, the crippled citadel moved slowly but inexorably to a location directly above the very center of the city.

The two citadels would keep most of Norwych's defenses occupied. With all eyes skyward, surely it was time for Cadrio to at last marshal his forces and begin landfall. The general seized Timinion with one hand and Zander with the other. "Give the signal to head for Norwych! I—"

A horrific boom sent all three men dropping to the deck. Recovering first, Timinion and Zander immediately helped the general up.

"What happened, you fools? Valkyn's citadel! Has something happened to—"

Cadrio looked up as he spoke and saw that while nothing had happened to Atriun, the same could not be said for the second citadel. A jagged hole remained where once the upper left portion of the castle had been. Smoke billowed from the wrecked area, and fragments continued to drop. The damaged citadel wobbled uncertainly, and Cadrio wondered how much longer it could stay afloat.

He dragged Timinion close. "Did you see what happened? Was it the other dragon?"

"No, sir! Our dragons are dealing with that one! See?"

Murk and Eclipse were indeed dealing with the remaining silver. The twins had it between them, one black ripping a wing to shreds, the other snapping at the silver's throat. They had clearly caught it unaware while it had searched for its mate. The one attacking the throat—Cadrio thought it Eclipse—at last caught his target and held tight. The general imagined the massive fangs biting through scales and sinking into flesh. The silver roared in agony, one set of talons trying uselessly to pull the black from its neck.

The other twin shredded what remained of the wing, then joined his brother at the throat, ripping away. Less and less the opposing leviathan struggled, until finally the head lolled back.

"Excellent!" Cadrio cried. Just then a second boom nearly sent him to the deck again. He turned to the older citadel, which now sported another severe wound, this one at its crumbling base. "What is causing that?"

Zander provided the answer at last. "The lightning from the wizard's storm is destroying the other citadel, sir!"

"That can't be!" Yet Cadrio quickly saw that Zander had spoken the truth. Several bolts burst from the storm, striking hard at the severely devastated citadel. Barely half the castle remained, and a good portion of the earth beneath had broken free, too, creating yet more havoc for the defenders below.

The older fortress tried to move away but could not.

Cadrio felt little concern for the minor mages and clerics aboard, but the man he had chosen to pilot it had been a good officer. "Damn you, Valkyn! You've no right!"

A heavy rumble rose from the storm-enshrouded terror, and a series of bolts worse than anything those aboard the *Harpy* had yet witnessed tore asunder what remained of the other flying citadel. The castle collapsed, the tower with the Wind Captain's Chair falling into the main building. Ship-sized chunks of earth dropped from beneath the ruined structure.

Below the crumbling behemoth, Norwych suffered a horrific torrent. Cadrio could imagine the people screaming, the buildings crushed under the weight of the gigantic missiles, the ruination of a city that had thought itself safe. Not even at the height of the war had he witnessed destruction on this scale; Valkyn's toy threatened to literally level the seaport.

"Bring us in!" he demanded.

"Is that safe, sir?" Timinion asked.

"Don't argue!"

A new wave of lightning pounded the dying edifice, and at last the older citadel started to drop. Earth and stone showered the island city, then what remained intact suddenly fell from the sky. From the general's angle, it looked as if one of the moons had fallen. Certainly to those below, it must have seemed so.

The horrific crash echoed throughout the area, startling even those aboard the *Harpy*. A vast cloud of dust and dirt rose above Norwych, resembling the plume of a volcanic eruption.

"Make certain everyone has his visor down," General Cadrio ordered. That would help keep some of the dust from his men's faces.

Castle Atriun paused now, the storm around it lessening. As Cadrio's vessels neared the chaotic island, he saw gargoyles dive from the edifice, falling upon Norwych like vultures. The general wondered whether Valkyn sought more mages for his mysterious work. That disturbed Cadrio nearly as much as the destruction of his own citadel had. Valkyn did as he pleased, despite their supposed alliance.

The wizard had given him victory, but had made Cadrio more dependent upon him. Matters couldn't remain like this. Valkyn would only tighten control if the general did nothing.

The lanky commander gritted his teeth. First he would deal with the survivors of Norwych, but then . . . then he would see to it that Valkyn remembered that General Marcus Cadrio served no man anymore.

Especially an impudent and expendable wizard.

* * * * *

No word could describe the sensations Serene felt when she soared through the air on the back of the griffon. Even with the stiff form of Tyros in front of her, she could feel the wind, the speed. The massive griffon flew joyfully, completely at home in the sky. Serene envied the creature, wishing she could experience his pleasure.

She felt some sympathy for Tyros, who clearly had never flown like this before. The cleric tightened her hold on him, trying to relay to the mage some comfort. Although at times he had seemed rather arrogant and ambitious, Serene had noted the more human Tyros beneath the surface. He cared for his lost friend and treated her own concerns with nearly as much compassion. In many ways, Tyros reminded her of the one whom she had lost, but with a bit more gentleness and less obsession.

"Where are we?" the wizard suddenly shouted.

She peered down. Water had given way to land. Serene searched her memory. "Somewhere midway between Caergoth and Kayolin, I think," the cleric returned. "And probably the safest place to land. The sun's nearly down, and the griffons should get some rest. We'll still reach the New Sea early tomorrow."

Tyros clearly wanted to go on, but nodded. Serene glanced over to where Rapp and Bakal rode. The captain bore an expression that looked halfway between determination and unease. Some of the unease might have actually been due to the nearness of the kender to his pockets. Bakal no doubt feared to find them emptied out.

She caught Rapp's attention and pointed down. He smiled and nodded. When first Serene had met him and his half-grown orphan cubs, she had doubted that he would be able to tend to them, yet Rapp had cared for the griffons with a single-minded devotion that had startled her. Even now, with the fantastic creatures all but grown, he did not leave them. It made her wonder to what degree other races might have underestimated the worth of Rapp's people.

The party landed in a hilly wooded area that clearly had seen some violence during the war. Although the spot where they camped looked unravaged, in areas beyond it whole copses of trees had been destroyed. In addition, they came across several bits of rusting and twisted metal that might have once been armor and weapons half buried in the earth.

"Some sort of battle took place here," Bakal commented, hands searching his pockets to see if his personal effects remained within. Serene had never seen a man so eager to touch earth again as the captain. "Several months back, at least, I'd say."

"We'll be safe enough," Serene promised. "Rapp and I have brought the griffons here before."

"Good! I need a peaceful night's sleep after that ride. My bones are aching!"

Serene noted the precision with which Bakal's men worked as they organized the camp. Trained soldiers, definitely. It concerned her. The men obeyed him completely, and she wondered how that might affect her quest. Serene knew that Captain Bakal desired to capture the citadel or, failing that, destroy it, regardless of who might be onboard. She couldn't allow that.

While the others dealt with their own arrangements, the redheaded cleric wandered off to be among the trees. Although the woodland was not as thick and lush as her own forest, Serene found the solitude refreshing.

The temptation to remove her robe and commune with her god as nature intended remained in check; the soldiers would have taken her action as an invitation, and even Tyros might have mistaken her devotion for something more base. Instead, Serene finally settled on a soft tuft of grass and folded her legs into a meditation position. She put down her staff, then pulled out her medallion.

Through the medallion she felt the peaceful lives of the trees, the slow spanning of time. The trees lived differently from most other creatures, even their fellow plants. To a tree, a year might seem a day. They saw the world in the grand overall scheme of things, even better than the dragons and elves, who lacked their sturdy patience.

"Branchala," she whispered. "Grant me some of the strength of your ageless children. Give me some of their resolve, their patience. You know that I've been giving you so much of my life of late; please grant me my desire to succeed in this quest. . . ."

She felt a breeze caress her cheek, heard the leaves rustle. Others would have read nothing in those natural acts, but Serene had been trained to hear the words and wishes of her patron. The Bard King promised her strength, but only if she worked to maintain her own resolve.

"Can you not show me any more than you have? Can you not give me some clue as to the future?"

The breeze died. The young cleric shivered, knowing that the wind's cessation had not been natural. Had she offended her god?

She saw that the limbs of one tree still moved, yet no wind guided them. Serene held her breath, watching as the tree underwent a transformation. The ridges in the bark shifted, formed patterns . . . and then a face.

She recognized its avian features. Cadrio. He looked both pleased and envious. His eyes gazed skyward. The image made Serene shiver again.

Cadrio's face vanished, the ridges altering. A new visage formed. Serene almost lost her concentration. It was her love's face, but something looked different about it.

She leaned back, dismayed. He wore another's features, and more and more that other grew dominant.

"What do you mean by this?" she whispered. "What are you trying to tell me?"

The cleric suddenly grew angry. She rose, and as she did, the face began to disappear. Serene rushed forward, reaching for it. She touched the bark just as the last vestiges vanished.

Serene beat her hand against the tree. "Don't play games with me, Father Bran! You know the good of my quest! Tell me what you mean by showing me that face instead—"

"Serene?"

She whirled about to find Tyros. He couldn't have picked a worse time. The cleric reached for her staff, scowling. "Do you think no one's deserving of privacy but yourself? Go away! I'm not one of your court ladies, thrilled by your mysterious power!"

Her words struck him like barbs, sending the spellcaster back several steps. Serene advanced, using her staff as a weapon aimed at his chest.

"I only came to see if you were all right."

"Well, I'm not! Now leave me alone!"

"As you wish." He turned and left in silence, never looking back.

Serene's energy suddenly flagged. What had she done? Her reaction had been uncalled for. Tyros had clearly followed her out of concern. She should go apologize, yet a part of her refused. Perhaps in the morning, if there was time.

The cleric gazed into the darkening woods. "Branchala, what should I do?"

The woods remained silent.

* * * * *

The next morning Tyros suggested that they fly to the mouth of the New Sea before heading east, a detour which, in the end, seemed of little value. He didn't miss the glances of his companions, who had likely begun to doubt his knowledge. The mage, though, had wanted to verify that Cadrio's forces had not yet departed the inland sea, and so he felt some justification.

"We have to land the griffons soon," Serene called to Tyros, her attitude toward him still oddly distant. She acted as if she had to protect herself from the mage. He wondered what he had done.

The young wizard looked down, seeing only water. "There's an island just beyond the horizon with a seaport called Norwych on the eastern side. There are hills and pastures on the west where we can land with little chance of being noticed. Maybe one or more of us could go to Norwych to find out if they know anything!"

Having no better plan, she acquiesced. Tyros still sensed the gap between them but was determined to pay it no mind. All that mattered was Leot . . . and the secrets of the citadel, of course.

The weather had been good, for the most part, but as they headed toward Norwych, the spellcaster noticed clouds forming on the horizon. At the same time, he felt a slight tingle, one both curious and slightly disturbing. It had the taste of magic to it, but nothing he saw hinted at such. Tyros grew more alert.

A shape materialized in the distance. The mage stiffened. "I think I see the island."

Serene leaned forward. "I see it, but it looks as if there's a storm brewing. We'd better ride with care."

Tyros nodded, signaling Bakal. The captain muttered something to Rapp, who leaned forward to talk to his mount. The kender's griffon slowed, followed immediately by the rest. Rapp had a knack with the creatures. Tyros decided it would be good for him to try to befriend the kender. Better to have the griffons in hand if trouble occurred than men who were clearly loyal to Bakal alone.

Closer and closer they flew. The crimson-clad mage noticed several plumes of smoke rising from the distant city, but at first thought nothing of them. Busy ports such as Norwych would have industry. Yet the nearer he flew, the more ominous the plumes seemed, as did the clouds above and around the island.

"Something doesn't seem right," Serene shouted in his ear.

At that moment a massive form flew up from the island, swiftly heading into the clouds. A black dragon.

Bakal called to Tyros, pointing at the darkened sky. The mage nodded. They had all seen the black leviathan and knew that his twin had to be near. Tyros tilted his head back to Serene and asked, "Can you get the griffons to fly just above the water?"

She nodded, then signaled Rapp. Moments later, they were skirting the sea, well below the sight of most observers.

"Cadrio's here," Tyros's companion called, "but I don't see any sign of the citadel!"

He noted a slight trembling in her voice. "It's probably just out of sight, maybe where the dragon flew. We need to get nearer." It would not do, though, for all of them to go flying over Norwych. It made sense for the cleric and him to do so, but the rest were better off waiting in safety. "Get me near enough to shout to Captain Bakal!"

Serene touched the griffon's side gently, and the beast immediately veered toward the officer's mount. From Bakal's expression, he knew that Tyros had something in mind.

"We need to find a place to land!" the Red Robe cried. "Then Serene and I will fly over Norwych to look things over!"

The scarred warrior shook his head. "I should be the one going, mage! This is a battle situation!"

They had no time to argue, and Bakal did have a point. "All right. We go, but your men wait. Rapp! Can you make the griffons understand?"

"They'll listen, Tyros. I'll make them behave and not try to bite the men or drop them or—"

"Just make certain that they behave, please!"

As they neared the island, Tyros saw that the plumes of smoke were thicker than he had imagined. Much of Norwych must have been aflame at some point. He eyed the hills and woods coming up on the west coast. Would even those be safe?

Of the dragons, he could see nothing. Perhaps only one still lived, although Tyros doubted that he could be so fortunate.

The cleric tugged on his sleeve. "That spot looks good. We'll land there."

He stared at where she pointed, unable to see any difference between one wooded hill and another. "Why there?"

"I can sense its tranquility. Cadrio's warriors haven't intruded upon it. I would know!"

Still not quite certain he understood, Tyros nevertheless indicated to Rapp and Bakal where to land. If a cleric of Branchala thought a forest region safe, then he would trust her instinct.

The griffons dropped smoothly among the trees. For such large beasts, they moved with grace whether in the air or on the ground. Tyros would have admired them further, but he and the rest of the party had to remain wary of possible danger. Perhaps the invaders hadn't intruded in this region, but that didn't mean that the group could relax. The wizard looked up, seeking some sign of the dragons. It would take only one glance by either behemoth to turn this quest into a deadly disaster.

The moment the griffons came to a stop, the party immediately dismounted. Bakal's men quickly searched the surrounding area, finding nothing of consequence. While Rapp led the animals to a nearby stream, the wizard and the captain at last went about the task of explaining their intention.

Trained soldiers they might be, but here at last Bakal faced some threat of insubordination. Fighting in battle was one thing; being left with a pride of massive carnivorous animals was another.

"You can't leave us here with those man-eaters!" one snarled.

Returning with the griffons, Rapp immediately jumped to the defense of his flock. "They wouldn't eat a man. At least I don't think so, because I've never seen them do it, although they might have while I was away or sleeping—"

"Hush, Rapp." Serene stepped between the men and the griffons. "They won't harm you. I promise that."

It took more calming words from the cleric and a few

threats from their captain before the men finally gave in. As an added measure, Serene had Rapp move the griffons some distance away and order them to stay there.

"This is strictly reconnaissance," Bakal reminded the men. "We'll be back before long."

Tyros and Serene rode together again, which pleased the wizard. The cleric's distant attitude had faded as anticipation of finally locating the citadel had taken over.

Serene leaned near him as they approached the storm. "Those clouds look even blacker than before!"

The storm had indeed grown worse. Perhaps that explained why they hadn't yet seen the flying citadel. Damaged as it was by the attack on Gwynned, it likely suffered in the fierce winds. Cadrio no doubt had ordered it above the low cloud cover.

They flew within sight of the city walls, already fearful of what they might see below. This close, Tyros could hear the sound of sporadic combat, the clash of arms, the cries of men.

"Do we dare fly over the city?" Serene asked him.

Tyros scanned the sky but still saw no sign of citadel, dragons, or even gargoyles. That and the overcast sky gave him some confidence. "If we make it fast. We'll circle once, maybe twice, then leave."

"No more than that." She shivered. "I have a bad feeling about this place. . . ."

He, too, felt that something out of the ordinary had struck the seaport, and as the griffons raced over the walls, Tyros saw that their fears had been justified.

"What's happened to Norwych?" Serene called out, horrified.

Tyros couldn't answer; he was too busy gaping. He thought about what Gwynned had suffered even in victory and knew that somehow Cadrio had learned from that mistake. Norwych had paid dearly for the lesson.

The seaport had been turned to rubble. Walls and buildings for as far as the eye could see had been crushed. It looked as if someone had dropped another city on top of Norwych, so thorough was the destruction. Few structures over two stories remained standing, and most of those had suffered much damage. Fire and smoke rose up from everywhere, most of the flames clearly left unchecked by the inhabitants.

"It's gone!" the cleric gasped. "Norwych has been utterly destroyed!"

Tyros said nothing, more concerned at the moment with the soldiers he had noticed. Ranks of ebony-armored warriors moved methodically through the ruins, ferreting out all resistance. He saw one local cut down by a pair of the invaders, and although it was too late for the mage to do anything, Tyros still wished he could have burned the soldiers on the spot.

In the distance, the sails of Cadrio's fleet rose high. There would be no escape through the port. Tyros counted at least eight vessels in the invading fleet but expected there were more nearby.

Somewhere below had to be General Cadrio himself. Tyros wondered what would happen if his band managed to capture or kill the enemy commander. He started watching for banners, guards, anything that would indicate the presence of the man.

They finished a circle around Norwych, seeing devastation everywhere but still no evidence of the citadel's presence. Tyros looked for Bakal and finally spotted the other griffon in the growing haze. The captain pointed at something within the city.

"Bakal seems almost frantic," the wary spellcaster informed Serene. "Do you see anything?"

The cleric looked to where the soldier pointed. "All I see is a collapsed building . . . but from the look of the wreckage, it must have been gigantic!"

"He wants us to fly over it."

The cleric had their mount turn, Rapp doing the same with the other. The griffons soared nearer to the huge ruin, which, for reasons Tyros could not yet put his finger on, looked familiar.

"There's something strange about this," Serene called. "It

almost looks as if Cadrio's soldiers destroyed not only the building but the hill it stood upon, too!"

A hill that looked out of place to Tyros. He leaned forward, trying to picture the building whole. A castle of some sort, he finally decided. The design didn't match the rounded structures of Norwych, but it did remind him of something else. . . .

The cleric suddenly gripped him tighter. "Tyros . . . that's not part of the city."

She knew it, too. She knew what they looked down at, what Captain Bakal had been trying to tell them.

The flying citadel, the point of their individual quests, had been destroyed, taking the port city with it.

* * * * *

Stone fluttered through Norwych, doing his part to search for the enemy. He hadn't located any. The dwellers of this place were either dead or gone into hiding. The gargoyle looked around at the ruins as he flew, thinking of all the wasted roofs and overhangs. Norwych had had many fine places upon which to perch, but no longer.

He wasted his time here, just as he wasted so much of it for Valkyn. How he hated the robed one. Crag enjoyed the chaos and destruction that Valkyn brought forth, but Stone preferred the silent solitude of the wilderness, where he and his kindred could live without the interference of humans, dwarves, and other races. And especially where no wizards could force his kind to obedience with the use of fiery spells that left scorched earth and the twisted gargoyle corpses of those who had defied him.

The sleek gray figure paused atop a leaning roof, adjusting himself as best as he could to compensate for its instability. Blood-red eyes gazed around, finding little of interest. This hunt had been played out; it was time to move on. The humans, though, still sought treasures and the like, interests which the gargoyle only vaguely understood. What use were things that could not be eaten?

He yawned, displaying an impressive array of sharp teeth. Stone knew that he couldn't delay his return much longer. Crag would use any excuse to diminish his rival in the eyes of Valkyn.

The gargoyle stretched his wings, preparing to fly. However, something at the very edge of his vision caught his attention. Stone looked up, searching the tempestuous heavens.

And then he saw them, the winged creatures, the four figures. Most of all, he saw the tall one clad in the crimson robe, the same color Valkyn had once worn.

"You . . ." Stone growled.

The gargoyle darted up into the air.

Chapter 8

Deceptions

Cadrio walked through the ruins of Norwych, growing less and less satisfied. Oh, his men were happy enough. Looting always raised morale, but as he partook of the destruction around him, he realized how little this victory could be called his own. Had he been in control of Atriun, the general would have felt different. No, this victory he owed completely to Valkyn . . . and Cadrio disliked owing anyone.

He had to somehow gain control of the flying citadel, of that he had no doubt. At some point, the wizard had to come down, if only to give new orders.

"Caaadriooo . . ."

At first he didn't recognize his own name, since the cry was so drawn out and beastly-sounding. Timinion and Zander, who had been following at a respectful distance, immediately drew their blades and flanked him.

One of the mage's pet gargoyles perched on a broken wall, the savage beast tipping his head as he stared at the humans. From the three horns and immense size, Cadrio deduced the gargoyle to be Crag. Valkyn seemed to prefer to use Crag instead of Stone, a fact that the general filed away for possible later interest. Unlike Crag, who obeyed Valkyn with eagerness, Stone seemed to resent his servitude, something that perhaps Cadrio could make use.

"Swords down." He didn't want the monster to think that Cadrio feared him. "What is it?"

In reply, the gargoyle tossed a scroll toward him. Cadrio casually reached down and picked it up, pretending for the messenger's sake that he cared little what Valkyn wanted to relay. Inside, however, the lanky warrior seethed. Now what did his so-called ally want?

The test is a success. It is time to move on now. Be prepared to set sail at dawn, the message began, an ominous and frustrating command. His men had not yet had time to completely scour Norwych, not to mention the wild lands beyond the city. It never paid to leave things half done. No one liked a vengeful foe suddenly turning up behind him.

Your destination is Northern Ergoth's southern coast. The point is marked on the map I have drawn below. You will wait there until I send further information.

Ignoring the map for the moment, Cadrio turned the paper over, looking for more explanation. Nothing. He confronted the gargoyle. "This is it? This is all he says?"

Crag eyed him like a potential meal. "Will not obey?"

General Cadrio bristled, but otherwise held his temper in check. "Tell Valkyn that we'll sail tomorrow."

Once more Crag's monstrous expression seemed to hint at amusement . . . or mockery. "Will tell Maaaster . . ."

The gargoyle suddenly leaped toward the humans. As his aides rushed forward to defend him, Cadrio ducked, frantically reaching for his own blade. However, instead of falling upon them, the savage gargoyle flew skyward, at the same time emitting a throaty rumble that sounded like laughter.

"I swear I'll have that one skinned and used for boot leather!" the general roared as Zander helped him up.

Zander leaned near. "Sir, how long must we deal with this mage? He and his creatures mock us at every turn, and now we must obey his commands! Surely Valkyn intends himself to be the new Dragon Highlord—nay, the new Emperor of Ansalon—instead of you, despite his words to the contrary!"

Timinion looked around nervously. "Careful, you fool! We've no idea how many more of those beasts might be listening! Do you want them to tell the mage that we plot against him?"

"Better we take what we are due than follow around like lackeys!"

"Strong words until Atriun comes floating over our heads and burns us to a crisp!"

Cadrio came between his two warring officers. "Be still,

both of you, or I'll have your heads!"

Both men immediately quieted down. Cadrio stared at the pair a minute longer, then shifted his gaze skyward, where Crag had dwindled to a speck, at last vanishing into the clouds.

"We'll soon remedy the imbalance," he announced. "I've already had enough of this alliance. In fact, I've something in mind that must be done before we leave Norwych. Meanwhile, we follow the wizard's dictates and make preparations to leave. We'll pretend that all is right in the world and we don't mind being servants instead of the allies he claims us to be. Understood?" Zander and Timinion nodded. "Good! Timinion, sound the call for withdrawal. Go!" Cadrio smiled as the aide departed. "Come with me, Zander. We must speak with the dragons. There's a certain gargoyle who might be useful to us. . . ."

*   *   *   *   *

The citadel lay in ruins, its last task the death of Norwych.

Tyros felt the blood drain from his face as the griffon again circled over the wreckage. Behind him, Serene's body shook as she no doubt thought about her lost love. The stunned mage stared at the fragments, as if somehow he had the power to will the flying castle back into one piece.

What had happened? Had Norwych had dragons protecting it? If so, where had they gone after downing the castle? Surely the twin black dragons had not managed to kill them.

A shape in the distance caught his attention. At first he thought it was one of the griffons. The animals had a fondness for Rapp and more than one had wanted to accompany them. Yet this looked to be a slightly smaller creature, something about the size of a man.

Or a gargoyle.

This one had three horns and looked far uglier than the pair Tyros had confronted in Gwynned. He watched it fly up into the clouds. "Serene! Did you see that? Make the griffon go up! I want to follow that gargoyle . . . from a distance!"

"What about the dragons?"

"Please!"

With much reluctance, she directed the griffon upward. Bakal and Rapp followed, the captain not at all thrilled by the prospect. The winds rocked the riders, but the griffons compensated. Tyros and Serene pulled up their hoods as moisture began to cover them.

"I don't see a thing, Tyros! Shouldn't we turn back?"

"We won't go far."

Bakal and Rapp popped in and out of sight as they ascended. Rapp brought his own griffon nearer so that the pair wouldn't become separated, but even then the others still occasionally vanished. Tyros began to consider turning back.

Without warning, they burst into an open area where thunder roared and lightning flashed. The griffons hesitated. Tyros nearly had Serene make them descend. Then a great flash illuminated the region, and all four travelers beheld a sight that made everything else pale.

Tyros could barely believe his eyes. A second, more astounding citadel floated among the storm clouds, a leviathan compared to the ruined castle below. With its dark stone and high walls, it seemed as much a part of the threatening weather as the lightning and thunder. Occasional flashes of crimson and yellow gave it an ominous appearance, and the mage half-expected to see ghosts haunting its battlements.

Whether or not ghosts haunted it, gargoyles certainly did. Not only did he spot the one that they had shadowed, but scores more fluttered above and around the astonishing fortress. A shiver ran through Tyros. These creatures served the same master responsible for Leot's disappearance and his own near-kidnapping.

"Atriun! By the Bard King's harp, it's Castle Atriun!"

Serene's shocked words caught him by surprise. "You know that fortress?"

"It's the castle of Atriun, a small, secluded province. It was originally built by a mad Solamnic Knight, but it's long been abandoned." She gripped his arm tightly. "Do you see what this means? We still have a chance to find those we sought!"

Tyros had actually been thinking how this gave him the chance to bring back an even greater prize than originally planned. He turned his face from hers, pretending to wipe away moisture. She worried about her love and Leot; he had only been thinking of glory. The mage felt disgust for himself.

He stared at the massive citadel. "I want to get nearer!"

"It's too dangerous. Look at all those gargoyles!"

She had a point. This would require stealth. But what could he do? Tyros hadn't expected so many gargoyles, nor had he thought to confront so deadly a citadel. His entire plan had been based on the crippled older castle, not this imposing edifice.

The winds and rain grew harsher. They couldn't stay here any longer, much less attempt to infiltrate the castle. Bakal waved, clearly wanting to descend. Tyros nodded, bitter to be so near and yet unable to continue. He would be back, though.

The griffons descended, eager to return to better climes. The animals grew even happier when they left the foul clouds; their wings beat faster as they soared in the direction of the camp. Tyros rode in silence, trying to formulate a plan for his next visit. If he could somehow draw the gargoyles away . . .

"Above us!" Serene whispered in his ear. "A dragon!"

A savage black giant flew a few hundred feet above them, surveying the landscape. To their horror, a second monstrosity dropped from the clouds to join the first.

The terrible twins looked left and right, their draconian orbs searching below. Sooner or later one of the beasts would look their direction. Tyros quickly searched his memory for a spell that would help his party but could think of very few. However, one gave him some hope. He began running through it in his mind.

"We'll have to out race them," Serene insisted.

"No! Give me one more moment."

With their far greater wingspan, the dragons readily cut the gap between themselves and the mage's party. The nearer they drew, the more anxious Tyros became. If either beast noticed them, he and his companions were as good as dead. Neither Tyros nor Serene had the power to drive off the pair, and the griffons could certainly not outpace them for long.

Tyros uttered the spell.

For anyone in his party, the only sensation of change would be a slight tingle. For the dragons, however, the spell would do much more.

One of the ebony dragons raised his head, sniffing. He gazed directly at the mage and cleric. "I smell humans!"

The second lifted his face up to test the air. "I smell nothing!"

"There are humans near," said the first, but his gaze turned away from Tyros and the others.

"Humans do not fly," pointed out the other.

Both warily eyed the sky. To Tyros's relief, they now looked away from the griffons' positions. Yet, still the dragons did not move on.

"We are up high," the first mused.

"And as I said, humans do not fly," added the second.

This frustrated his brother. "But I still smell them!"

He turned his head abruptly, gazing almost directly at Tyros and Serene. The black dragon's nostrils flared, and he looked ready to charge forward, possibly discovering the intruders by literally running them down.

A horn sounded in the distance.

Both beasts hesitated. The second twin twisted his head around, listening as the sound repeated. "Cadrio summons us!"

The first appeared reluctant to go. "I smell them near!"

"Cadrio summons! Come!"

Exasperated, the first twin finally gave in, turning in unison with his brother and heading in the direction of the port. Tyros watched them dwindle in the distance, then breathed a sigh of relief.

"That was too close!" Serene gasped.

The mage couldn't reply, more surprised by his success than he dared let her know.

Bakal and Rapp came up beside them. "You cast some sort of spell," the captain shouted. "What was it?"

"A cloak of invisibility. I was afraid it wouldn't be strong enough, stretched as it was over such a distance, but it worked. It won't last much longer, though."

"Then we'd best be getting back to the others."

Encouraged to greater swiftness because of this near disaster, the griffons returned quickly to the waiting soldiers. Tyros's spell faded as the animals descended, startling both Bakal's men and the remaining beasts. The other griffons grew excited at Rapp's return. The kender leaped off his mount, hugged each in turn, then he went around and tried to hug everyone else. While Serene accepted gladly and the mage with some trepidation, neither the captain nor the others would let the small figure near.

Tyros checked his pockets and, after retrieving a couple of items from Rapp, gathered the rest of the party together. With the help of Bakal, Serene, and even the kender, he related all that they had seen, especially the second citadel. The soldiers listened in silence, never betraying fear. Bakal had chosen well.

"The only question now," the captain said, "is what we do about that thing. This is more than I expected. It might be best if we turn back and warn Gwynned instead of trying something foolish."

"You can go back if you want," Serene interjected, "but I've got to go on."

"You can't go alone, girl!"

"She will not be alone." Tyros looked at Serene. He admired her determination. Tyros found himself envying the wizard who had won her heart. Perhaps if they had met at a different time, Tyros might have had the chance to know her better. "I will be going with her."

"The two of you are daft, you know that?" Bakal rubbed his chin, thinking. " 'Course, we've come this far, and one citadel's not much different from another. . . ." He eyed them both. "All right. Let's sleep on this. Tomorrow morning, when things are clearer, we'll settle on what to do."

The captain's words cheered Tyros. Bakal would come with them tomorrow, of that he was certain. Despite the fact that he knew the veteran soldier's intentions did not completely coincide with his own, having Bakal on his side strengthened the wizard's own resolve.

The party began to settle down for the night. At one end of the camp, the griffons huddled together, Rapp in their midst. Tyros considered his own choice for a moment, then located a secluded area on the end opposite the griffons.

Serene started for the woods. "Good night, Tyros."

"It would be safer near the rest of us."

She smiled, suddenly even more beautiful. "The forest will watch over me, but thank you for your concern."

He watched her vanish between the trees, feeling a sudden pang of jealousy. A black thought blossomed. Perhaps if the one she sought had been killed, she might find some interest in Tyros. A moment later, he berated himself for such a foul notion.

Visions of the new citadel drifted through his mind as the tired mage slipped off into slumber. Even from a distance, he had been able to tell that, despite Bakal's opinion, it resembled its predecessors only in superficial terms. A sense of tremendous power radiated from Castle Atriun, as if its creators had found a way to harness magic on a grand scale. Even the storm clouds surrounding it appeared charged with magic.

Tyros slept, dreaming of citadels, Leot, gargoyles, and, for a change, Serene. The dreams were jumbled, yet in all of them the cleric stood by his side, her power complementing his own. No thought, no mention of her lost love disturbed the dreams, and in each the pair triumphed over great odds.

Only in the last dream did matters change for the worse, for as Tyros triumphed over a score of cowardly gargoyles, he suddenly couldn't catch his breath. The wizard fell to his knees. Serene tried to reach him, but she grew faint, a mere shadow whose slim hands went right through him. Tyros bent over, struggling for air . . .

And woke up to find he suffered the very same fate.

"Make no sound," a low, rumbling voice demanded, "or die!"

Tyros opened his eyes, only now realizing that he dangled several feet in the air. A constant beating sound drummed quietly in his ears, the steady flap of wings. Despite the warnings the voice had given him, the mage twisted in momentary panic, reliving the nightmare that had haunted him since the attack on Gwynned.

A gargoyle had him. One clawed hand was over his mouth, the other around his left arm and torso. The creature shifted his talons so that Tyros could breathe, which enabled the wizard to calm down a bit.

His captor brought Tyros not toward Norwych, but rather to a cliff overlooking a wooded region a short distance from the campsite. The gargoyle deposited the spellcaster without ceremony at the edge of a cave in the cliff wall. In the dark of night, the creature looked almost like some tremendous bat as he landed, which only served to reinforce Tyros's old nightmares. Nevertheless, the kidnapped mage prepared a spell to defend himself.

"Fooool," the monster growled. "No spell! Want to talk, not fight!"

His comment made Tyros pause. The gargoyle hadn't killed him, nor had he brought his prisoner to the citadel. What, then, did the creature have in mind?

Seeing that the mage would not immediately attack, the shadowy gargoyle nodded his horned head. "Good! Some sense . . . for once!"

"What—what do you want?"

A rumble of breath escaped the beaked monstrosity. He planted a taloned hand on his chest. "Stone I am. Stone."

Tyros slowly repeated the gargoyle's name, then pointed at himself. "I am Tyros."

"Tyros . . . from the far city and the falling tower."

The wizard started. The falling tower? That sounded

uncomfortably like the events in Gwynned, but how would Stone know about that unless . . . "You were there?"

Stone snorted. "Saved you . . . fought for you."

Saved Tyros? Fought for him? The mage frowned. What did Stone mean?

Then he remembered the gargoyle with the back of its neck torn out. Captain Bakal had thought the dead creature had been slain by something similar to it, possibly even by one of its own kind. Now, if Tyros understood Stone well enough, the gargoyle claimed to be the one who had not only killed the other monster, but had prevented the red mage from joining Leot as a captive.

The notion did not sit well. "I don't believe you. Why save me, and why do it by killing one of your own?"

His companion hissed. "Not one of my own! One of the mountain fliers." He hissed again. "One of Crag's!"

The gargoyle held up three clawed fingers next to his forehead, which at last made Tyros recall the other gargoyle they had seen today, the one with the extra horn.

"Crag is not like you?"

"Not like me! Hissss flock and mine . . ." He slammed his hands together, then twisted them around like two battling serpents. "Understand?"

Stone and Crag belonged to different groups of gargoyles, adversarial flocks who would have ordinarily had nothing to do with one another. "But you both obey another, don't you?"

"Yesss . . ."

"General Cadrio, I assume?"

Stone laughed harshly, a disconcerting sound. "Another fooool! Serve massster of the castle. Wizard like you."

Another wizard. It hardly surprised Tyros and made more sense than a military officer controlling the flying citadel. Such power could not have been wielded by a man with no magical abilities. True, Cadrio could have had some wizards at his command, but would any who could create such a weapon as Castle Atriun be willing to serve rather than lead?

"Why save me? Why go against your master?"

Stone suddenly looked up. Tyros followed his gaze but saw nothing. The gargoyle, though, grew more agitated. "Saved you to slow master. Could not save fat wizard or old one, but saved you . . ." He shook his head. "But fool came back! Fool wizard!" Stone's red, unblinking eyes fixed on the human's own. "Came for castle, yes? Want castle, yes?"

"Yes." He saw no use in lying to the creature, who clearly did not like his own master.

Again Stone shook his head. "Foolish wizards . . ."

Tyros tried to choose his words carefully. "I want to get inside, save my friend, then take control of the citadel and bring it back to Gwynned . . . the far city."

The gargoyle took time to consider this before asking, "And Stone's kind?"

He shrugged. "Leave if you like."

This seemed to decide something for his captor. The gargoyle stretched his wings, then pointed at the human. "Strong magic." Stone pointed up. "But stronger magic there . . ." He leaned forward, his voice quieter, his body tense. "Except when clouds thin . . ."

"What happens when the clouds thin?"

The blood-red eyes came very close. "Castle's magic weakens." He considered. "Tyros could come then . . ." Something beyond the cliff side caught the gargoyle's attention. The earlier agitation returned, only greater. "Must go. Listen, human! Watch when clouds thin. If must come, come then! Will help if can, but . . ."

An unsettling blast of wind rushed into the cave, nearly bowling the wizard over. Tyros sensed movement in the distance.

Again the gargoyle looked skyward. Suddenly he darted up, abandoning his captive without a word. Tyros at first gaped, then realized that not only did he have many questions for the creature, but Stone had also left him stranded in the middle of nowhere.

He heard the flap of wings, but they were those of something far larger than a gargoyle. A moment later, he saw a great shape pass overhead—one of the dragons. Small wonder that Stone had fled, but where did that leave Tyros?

Fortunately for him, the dragon continued on, at last disappearing into the murky darkness. However, that still left the mage lost and alone in the mountain cave. Tyros couldn't be certain that any spell he cast would get him down safely. Still, he had no choice but to try, for any thought of climbing down he dismissed the moment he peered over the edge. Even in the darkness, Tyros could see that the cliff was much too steep.

Again Tyros heard the flapping of wings. He ducked back into the cave, listening to the sound grow. Whatever flew out there now flew toward him.

Carefully leaning forward, the wizard peered out. Only darkness met his gaze. Still the beat grew louder. Had Stone returned for him, or did one of the opposing gargoyles now approach?

A massive animal squawked.

"Shh, Taggi!" a familiar voice reprimanded much too loudly. "Serene says we've got to be as quiet as mice, although I've watched some and they can be pretty noisy, especially if they run across the floor you're trying to sleep on, but I guess they'd be quiet around you, Taggi."

"Hush, Rapp." A globe of dim emerald light materialized in the air several yards from the end of the ledge. Serene's visage, made haunting by the glow, fixed upon Tyros. "We've found him!"

"See? I told you they could track anything just by sniffing a piece of clothing or something! Good thing I found that small pouch he generally keeps on his belt, although how it ended up in my sack, I'll never know!"

Tyros felt by his belt and discovered that he was indeed missing a pouch. For once he was actually grateful for the kender's magpie ways.

The griffon landed in the cave. Serene immediately dismounted, then looked over Tyros with much anxiety. "Are you all right?"

"I am, but thanks for coming for me! I was just trying to figure out how to return."

"Can you do it with magic?" the kender piped up. "Can we watch, or would you like us to go back and wait for you? That might be fun, watching you float down right into the camp. I bet Bakal would find it a real treat, too!"

Serene quieted him down again. "I'm sure that Tyros is too tired."

"Then Taggi'll bring us all back!" Rapp indicated the griffon. "This is Taggi. I named him, and he can carry all three of us. He's real strong, aren't you, Taggi?"

The griffon emitted a peculiar purr as the kender stroked the feathery hair of his mane.

"How did you know I was gone?" the wizard asked Serene.

"One of the griffons woke and told Rapp. At least, that's his story."

The kender's head bobbed up and down. "He said you got taken into the sky, Tyros, and not by a griffon!"

Tyros nodded. "It was a gargoyle."

"A gargoyle? I've never seen one up close. In fact, that big gargoyle we followed today was the first I'd ever even seen!"

Serene looked at Tyros with some suspicion. "What would a gargoyle want with the likes of you, if not to take you to the citadel? Why bring you out here?"

The mage shrugged. "He wanted to talk. Seems to want to help us. He told me when we might best reach the citadel without being caught."

"And you believed him?"

"He apparently saved me once before . . . in Gwynned. So, yes, I believe him." Tyros thought of the storm-enshrouded castle and the intensity of the magic he had sensed emanating from it. "I just hope he knew what he was talking about."

* * * * *

Stone fluttered toward Castle Atriun, already nervous. The dragon alone did not bother him. Rather, Stone knew that he should have been back hours ago. Valkyn kept a strict accounting of the gargoyles. Others had been punished for lesser matters, and if Crag or one of the mountain fliers noted his late return, they would certainly leap at the opportunity to report Stone to the wizard. Valkyn had already begun to question his trustworthiness, and if, in the process of punishing Stone, the master learned of the gargoyle's encounter with Tyros, then Valkyn would certainly see to it that his rebellious servant suffered the ultimate penalty.

The gargoyle hissed, unable to hold back some expression of hatred toward the ebony-clad mage. With one swipe of his talons, one bite, he could end his master's life, but before he had the chance Valkyn would reduce him to ashes with a spell. Gargoyles had some magic, including for defense, but against the master . . . No, cunning was called for now.

His people would be freed somehow.

Caught up in his worries, Stone didn't notice the massive shape above him, not until suddenly a cage of talons snatched him up and a deep chuckle threatened his eardrums.

"Caught you! I caught you! Murk will be so jealous. Cadrio will call me clever and reward me!"

Even as Stone struggled, he wondered what the dragon meant. What did the human, Cadrio, want of him? The gargoyle tried to pry himself free, but the dragon easily held him fast.

"I could crush you, but Cadrio wants you. Be still and you'll suffer little, gnat!"

The dragon soared past the clouds that marked the flying citadel, his destination clearly the remains of what had once been the port of Norwych. Stone watched with a sinking heart as they neared the harbor where the sinister ships of the leviathan's master had anchored. A few minutes later Eclipse settled on the already flattened ruins of a large building near the docks, startling a pair of guards in the process.

"Cadrio!" the dragon rumbled. "I must speak with Cadrio!"

One of the guards hurried away. A few anxious moments later, another armored human came trotting toward them. "What is it, Murk? The general has much to deal with and desires no interruptions!"

The black dragon hissed. "I am not Murk. I am Eclipse! I must speak with Cadrio. I have a prize for him."

At that moment another huge shape descended upon the dark port. Stone didn't have to see the creature up close to know it was Eclipse's twin. The other dragon settled down on a spot near his brother, then glared at the imprisoned gargoyle.

"You found him!" Murk said, sulking.

"Who did you find?" the officer demanded. "What's this about?"

"Never mind, Timinion." A lanky figure joined them, almost seeming to materialize out of the dark. Stone knew the voice too well. "I know who they have."

General Cadrio took an oil lamp from one of the sentries and brought it so close to Eclipse's prisoner that the flames hurt the gargoyle's eyes. The monstrous face of the human filled Stone's vision.

The gargoyle tried to look his fiercest. "Maaaster will strike you down for taking one of hisss servants!"

"Not bad. You certainly talk more civilized than that buffoon, Crag. Aaah, I see you don't like him. You also don't like Valkyn much, do you? That's something I've noticed, too. In fact, I would venture to say that you hate him, eh?"

"Valkyn is maaaster!"

Cadrio gave him a mocking smile. "But what if Valkyn were no longer master? What if you served another who treated you better? A master who would raise you up over all the other gargoyles, especially Crag? Wouldn't that be worth something? I can offer you your proper place as leader of both flocks, Stone, if you cooperate with me. Do you understand?"

The pupilless eyes narrowed. Stone understood. Cadrio planned his own betrayal of Valkyn.

"I know you're clever, Stone. Think about it. If you help me gain access to Atriun, I will kill him. He cares nothing about you, whereas I know your value. You would make an excellent ally!"

Ally. A word not well translated into the gargoyle tongue,

but Stone had heard it used by Valkyn when dealing with this very human. Ally. A creature who one worked with until ready to betray him. Cadrio intended to betray his ally, the wizard, just as the wizard had hinted that he would dispose of the human if necessary.

Ally. Yes, Stone could see Cadrio as an ally . . . temporarily.

"Will help you," he returned, trying not to sound too eager. The humans could fight among themselves, preferably destroy one another. All that mattered was that Stone's flock would be free again.

"Tell me what I need to know, then," the general urged. "There must be a time when Valkyn is vulnerable. Surely when he attacks Gwynned, he'll drain his strength. I have the means to reach Atriun—" he indicated the dragons "—but I need to know when!"

When? The winged creature knew exactly when. "Not have to wait for Gwynned."

Cadrio's eyes widened in eagerness. "No? When, then?"

Stone couldn't help a slight smile, but he doubted that the human could read his visage. Only Valkyn seemed adept at reading such a gargoyle's emotions. "When the clouds thin . . ."

Chapter 9

Storming the Castle

At dawn Castle Atriun began to move.

The first indication to those below came as the clouds shifted to the northwest, even though the wind blew in the opposite direction. Some of the storm clouds drifted off, leaving the flying citadel somewhat visible. Atriun moved faster and faster as it went, quickly leaving Norwych behind.

The ships of General Cadrio departed soon afterward, trying as best they could to keep pace. Aboard the *Harpy*, the commander pondered the future. He had planned to wait until after Gwynned to deal with the wizard, but now, if the gargoyle was correct, a new and better path lay open, one that would hasten the shifting of matters to a more palatable state.

"The southern shore of Northern Ergoth," he whispered to himself. "He'll have to do it then, before Gwynned."

"Aaah, my general! I trust I find you in good spirits?"

Cadrio bit back his startlement and forced himself to turn slowly to the figure now standing just behind him. "Valkyn! I thought you were busy!"

"I can spare the time. I want to make certain that everything is prepared."

With Valkyn's back to several of Cadrio's men, a daring notion suddenly occurred to the general, one that would make it unnecessary to wait any longer. Why trust the gargoyle when Cadrio could deal with the damned wizard now? Several times during his illustrious career the general had taken sudden initiatives like this, always with rewarding results. Surely fate now had dealt him the high card once more.

"I've tried to assure that everything will be ready," the

general returned, making certain to keep his gaze on the mage's. Cadrio's left hand slipped down, just barely grazing the hilt of his sword. The action happened so quickly Valkyn surely would not notice it, but others, trained by the commander, certainly would.

Out of the corner of his eye, General Cadrio noticed Timinion reach cautiously for his blade. Zander, too, started to reach for his weapon. Good! Both men were familiar with the signal, one that Cadrio had utilized for various reasons over the years. Rebellious officers and foolish adversaries had fallen to the swords of his men in the past, and Valkyn would be no different. How pleasant it would be to see that smile wiped off the black mage's face.

Without the wizard, it would be child's play to use the dragons to seize the citadel. The gargoyles would offer little resistance. Stone's creatures would no doubt turn on their rivals. The shadowy servant he had seen in the tower had looked fairly harmless. He was simply there to obey orders.

"You gave us little time," General Cadrio went on, never breaking eye contact, "but the ships are all in order, and we'll be at the rendezvous soon after you."

"I expected nothing else but timeliness from you," Valkyn remarked, ever smiling. "I knew you would serve well."

"Serve well? We're allies, Valkyn."

The dark wizard's gloved hands formed a steeple. "Of course we are, my general, but at this juncture, one of us must guide, and since I can see the greater picture from my citadel, naturally the burden must fall to me. I leave the tactics of ground warfare to you, with only a few simple suggestions, eh?"

Timinion took a step forward, being careful to move in silence. Zander paused, his hand no longer on his sword. Cadrio understood why. Better only one assassin. Two men risked making too much noise. Besides, Timinion now stood but two or three steps from Valkyn.

"What sort of suggestions?" Cadrio asked.

"Just a few directions, a few recommendations of troop movement that I think will better your chances. I know you'll follow them to the letter, won't you, my general?"

Timinion stood within range. Carefully he pulled back his sword, preparing to run the insolent mage through. General Cadrio prayed that Valkyn would not move at the last moment.

"I'll certainly look them over, Valkyn, but why—"

Timinion thrust.

The triumphant smile beginning to form on Cadrio's face twisted into a shocked frown as not only the sword but the officer's hand and arm went right through the wizard. Valkyn stood there, amused as Timinion followed through, the would-be assassin tumbling to the deck.

The general thought fast. "Sir Timinion! Are you mad?"

Valkyn—not the real Valkyn, apparently, but a perfectly cast illusion—smiled at Cadrio, then gave the hapless Timinion a chillier version of the same smile. "A good attempt. A foolish one, but a good attempt."

From the folds of his robe, the illusory Valkyn pulled forth the wand with the crystalline sphere. One hand caressed the sphere, then pointed it at Timinion.

The wood beneath the soldier's left hand suddenly softened, causing his hand to sink in a few inches. Timinion tried to pull free, but not only would the soft plank not release its hold, to Cadrio's horror, it began to spread upward, quickly covering the officer's wrist and continuing on.

Even as Timinion struggled with his hand, his boots, too, began to sink. The entire deck underneath the would-be assassin rippled, more like liquid than solid wood. Timinion fell back and became further mired in the horrific pool. Cadrio realized that the man was truly sinking.

Timinion realized it, too, for he looked frantically at his commander and shouted, "General! Please! In the name of the Queen!"

Cadrio opened his mouth to protest, but a simple glance from Valkyn silenced him.

"There are limits to even my vast patience," the cowled mage announced. "And severe penalties for those who reach those limits."

The helpless soldier reached out with his one free hand, silently beseeching someone to come to his aid. His gaze went to Zander, but although Timinion's rival clearly would not have wished such a fate on the other officer, the latter quickly looked away.

The awful tableau continued to play itself out at the same monstrously slow pace. Timinion could barely keep his head up. All pretense of bravado had slipped away, and now he screamed for anyone to deliver him from the wizard's punishment.

No one dared.

Cadrio studied the doomed warrior and the quagmire sucking him down, only to come to an even more terrible conclusion. He had thought that Timinion sank, but now realized that his officer was being absorbed into the deck, becoming part of it! Already the man's complexion, even his armor, had taken on a semblance of the wooden grain.

"He will serve more efficiently this way," the illusion declared. "As an example . . ."

All but Timinion's face and his one hand had vanished. The officer's mouth moved, but no sound, not even a gasp, escaped it. At last—and much to Cadrio's relief—the tortured visage was completely absorbed into the wood, followed a few seconds later by the last feebly moving fingers.

Timinion's sword rattled to the railing as a wave rocked the *Harpy*, but no one sought to retrieve it.

"And now, my general," Valkyn said, once more hiding the wand. "As to those troop suggestions. I think it would be better if we spoke of them just before you reach Northern Ergoth. They'll be fresher in your mind then. Do you agree?"

Cadrio nodded, not trusting himself to words.

"Good." The Black Robe briefly eyed the deck where Timinion had vanished, then looked up at the general again. "A shame that these lessons must sometimes be taught." The narrow blue eyes narrowed yet more. "I shall be going. We will talk soon."

Valkyn disappeared, simply winking out of existence. Cadrio fell back, gripping the nearest rail. The image of what had happened to the unfortunate Timinion remained burned into his mind, yet if Valkyn thought this would keep Cadrio in line, the wizard was sorely mistaken. If anything, the general was even more determined to end this alliance.

"A few more days, spellcaster," he muttered. "Just a few more days . . ." Cadrio turned to Zander and the others, who still stared at the deck. "Well? What are you gaping at? Every man to his station! All officers with me to my quarters! Now!"

The crew obeyed immediately, relieved to return to normal activities. Zander and the remaining officers waited for Cadrio, who finally released his grip on the rail and, eyes fixed on the door to his quarters, walked silently by.

* * * * *

"Tyros! Wake up! It's leaving." Bakal's gruff voice shattered the peaceful slumber Tyros had finally managed to find. He blinked and realized that the sun had risen at least an hour before. "Why was I not awakened earlier?"

"Orders from the cleric," the veteran warrior replied. "She said you needed it, but when I realized what was happening, I finally had to wake you. The citadel's moving."

The citadel! Tyros rose and looked up in the sky. At first he noticed nothing, but then he caught a glimpse of the castle in the midst of the darkest clouds, clouds that moved contrary to the wind.

"He said nothing about it leaving!" Tyros blurted, referring to Stone, whose story he had mentioned to the officer after his return.

"Maybe he didn't know, or maybe he didn't tell you the entire story." Bakal had been vocal about his distrust of the gargoyle.

"It doesn't matter. We have to follow."

"Rapp has the griffons fed and ready," Serene announced, joining them. "We can leave now, but first . . ." She thrust a small pouch containing fruit and nuts into his hands. "You'll need this while we fly. I picked them myself."

He took them with gratitude, then glanced skyward at their quarry. "It's flying northwest. That's the general direction of Northern Ergoth."

"And Gwynned," the captain pointed out.

"We'll have to ride fast."

More accustomed now to the griffons, the party quickly mounted. In moments, the entire band flew through the skies, carefully trailing the citadel. Tyros pondered Stone's words and wondered just when the clouds would thin. For that matter, did he dare to still trust the leathery creature? Stone might despise his master, but how much was the gargoyle willing to risk?

"Look!" Serene called. "Cadrio's ships are sailing."

The spellcaster looked down to see the dark fleet heading west. They had to be sailing for the same destination as the citadel. That meant that the dragons, too, were in the air.

He doubted that he could enshroud the entire party. Tyros studied the clouds. "Serene, get us higher! Otherwise Cadrio's dragons might see us."

"It'll take some time. Those clouds are high up." The cleric signaled to Rapp, pointing at the clouds. Rapp eagerly nodded, then leaned over and talked with Taggi, who squawked once, then began to lead the others higher.

Tyros breathed a sigh of relief only when they had slipped in among the clouds. He looked down again at the tiny ships . . . and noticed the two black forms winging their way along the New Sea. They had just barely avoided the terrible twins.

"How close do we dare get to Atriun?" Serene asked.

"Not too near. Stone might be on our side, but we don't know which of the other gargoyles follow him. All we can do for the moment is wait and watch."

Yet as the day progressed and the citadel continued on over part of the mainland, not once did Tyros notice any opportunity to secretly alight on the menacing edifice. They had long ago lost sight of the New Sea, and with it not only Cadrio's fleet but also the black dragons. That had at first encouraged the mage, until he had noticed that the gargoyles continued to patrol the outer perimeter of their home.

The griffons began to tire, but the flying castle continued on at a steady clip. Serene finally insisted they land, pointing out that they had a pretty fair idea of the citadel's ultimate destination. "Surely he'll have to wait for Cadrio, who will take days longer with his less direct route."

Reluctantly Tyros agreed, and the party descended to a wooded ridge. Everyone dismounted slowly. Even Rapp needed to stretch tired muscles. Bakal worked some of his shoulder muscles, then took a sip of water. His face readily revealed his dissatisfaction with the day's results.

"All this and nothing to show for it, and that thing is getting nearer to Gwynned! We've done nothing . . . nothing!"

"But the citadel won't do anything until Cadrio catches up," Serene pointed out. "It wouldn't dare move on Gwynned before then. The dragons would take care of it as readily as they did the others."

Tyros had been considering that. "I wonder. That has worried me for some time. You both saw what happened to Norwych."

Bakal snorted. "Of course we did. That other citadel crashed right on top of it. Caused a lot of destruction."

"Yes, but we also saw a lot more destruction that the citadel's collapse could not have caused. Did you notice all the scorching throughout the city?"

"The work of the twins?" the cleric suggested.

"Perhaps to a point, but they don't strike me as being that thorough or energetic. Several of those ruined areas had been hit by a very, very powerful force." Tyros exhaled. "Perhaps I am just imagining things. Maybe the dragons did do it."

Bakal crossed his arms, impatient. "If not them, then what? Did the citadel drop flaming boulders on Norwych? I've heard of that happening a few times, but never on a scale like you're suggesting, mage."

"I don't know, Captain. All I can tell you is that whenever we get near Atriun, I sense immense power, far more magic than should be needed to make that thing fly."

"I see." Contrary to his words, however, Bakal clearly did not see. "Tyros, I've followed your plan so far because I

134

thought it might have a chance, and parts of it still might work. But now that we're nearly back home, I've a suggestion of my own."

"What is it, Captain?"

"They're heading for Gwynned, no doubt about it. My first loyalty is to the city. Since Cadrio has to take the sea route, we've a chance to deal with this flying monstrosity before it can link up with him again. That's why, with the permission of Serene and Rapp, I want to take the fastest griffon, and the kender to guide him, and fly back to Gwynned. Once there, I'll go to Sunfire and Glisten. We all know why they wouldn't come with us before, but now the enemy's coming to them. This threatens their future, too. And with them on our side, we'll be able to bring down the citadel with little or no trouble."

"But what about those aboard?" Serene demanded. "What about possible prisoners? If the dragons are forced to destroy the citadel, then they'll perish!"

The captain shrugged. "I doubt there's much hope there anyway. Besides, girl, more than a handful might die if we don't at least deprive the invaders of this fortress. Probably a regiment of draconians aboard her at the very least, not to mention those gargoyles. I'd like to bring the citadel back as a prize, but as that probably won't happen, better we send it to the ground here rather than over Gwynned."

"You can't do that!" the cleric protested.

"You think there's actually a chance that your man's still alive? Don't be a—"

"Let him go get Sunfire, Serene," Tyros interjected. "But only if he and the dragons give us a chance to try to take Atriun before they destroy it."

Bakal shook his head. "That'd be madness, mage. You'll just get you and the girl killed!"

"No . . . I think he's right!" The cleric met Bakal's gaze, forcing him to look away first. "If Rapp agrees to go with you, I won't raise any objections, but only if you do as Tyros says."

Seeing he had no choice, the captain agreed. "But I think

you're both throwing away your lives!"

Rapp, of course, had no objections about seeking Sunfire and Glisten. "Maybe they'll even let me fly on top of one of them, although they certainly can't be as comfortable as Taggi!"

Bakal nodded grimly. "It's settled, then. Let's be off, kender."

"We'll follow the citadel, but we'll wait until we see you to approach it," Tyros added. He had little doubt that Bakal would convince the dragons to come despite the eggs. By destroying the approaching citadel, they would be defending their own home and future children.

"When we come, we'll be charging in, mage. Rapp, will your animals continue to carry my men without you around?" The kender bobbed his head and tried to reply, but the officer, obviously impatient to start back, quickly cut him off. "Good! Then there's no more time to waste!"

Rapp and Bakal took off on Taggi a few minutes later, but not before the captain had given orders to his men that they were to mount up at first light. Everyone had to be within range and ready the moment the dragons appeared, for certainly those within the flying citadel would see the great leviathans as well.

Captain Bakal had said little to Tyros and even less to Serene, who clearly still did not like the veteran's plan. After the officer's departure, the mage found himself alone, the soldiers busy making their camp, and the cleric, her mood solemn, wandering off into the woods. Tyros thought of going after Serene and talking with her, but then recalled what had happened last time he had done so. Instead, he settled down against a tree and tried to concentrate on the spells he would need for tomorrow.

They would have to be his best, for Tyros suspected that matters would not go as simply as Bakal assumed. This citadel was different from its predecessors. It held some secret, one that Tyros hoped the morrow's events would help him uncover . . . and one that he hoped would not mean the death of him and his companions.

* * * * *

"There it is!" Serene shouted.

They watched Castle Atriun as it neared the western coast of the mainland. Tyros hadn't expected to catch up to it until they were over the sea, but to his good fortune, those in control must have caused it to pause overnight. It seemed that Serene had been correct about those in the citadel not wanting to reach Northern Ergoth's southern coast until Cadrio had also arrived.

"I don't see any sign of Bakal or the dragons," Tyros shouted back.

"They'll be here soon, unless he couldn't convince them after all."

The anxious spellcaster doubted that. An invading citadel would certainly draw the dragons. Captain Bakal would be here, but *when* remained the question. Tyros had expected the veteran to be here already, the wizard having estimated the time needed to fly to Gwynned, convince the golden pair of the necessity of their presence, and then fly back with them. If anything, he had almost expected Bakal to be impatiently waiting for them.

Hoping to keep them out of sight of the citadel, Serene had the griffon descend. However, as the animal obeyed, the wizard caught sight of something on the western horizon. "Wait!"

"What is it, Tyros?"

"Look there! I think I see them!"

She peered in the direction he indicated. "That's a gull or a—"

"It's them!" he insisted. "Look! There are two large forms! It has to be Sunfire and his mate!"

Serene finally agreed, but reminded him, "If we can see them coming, then those in Castle Atriun ought to see them soon, too."

"I know. We have to be ready."

Serene steered their griffon back to the others, seeking out the most senior of Bakal's soldiers, a tall, muscular man named Mirko. Tyros had learned little about him, save that he seemed to give the orders when the captain could not.

"What's happening?" Mirko called. Like the rest, he shared a griffon with another soldier, in this case a very pale soldier.

"The dragons are coming," Serene responded.

"The captain must be with them." The soldier stared in the direction of the golden behemoths. "We need to join him!"

"You'd better go now, then!"

Serene had shown the men how to steer the griffons, knowing that they couldn't always rely on either her or Rapp. Mirko touched his mount's left shoulder, causing the beast to turn. The other soldiers followed.

"They'll make it to Bakal," Tyros's companion assured him. "See there? That speck? That has to be Rapp on Taggi! The other griffons will see them soon and head straight toward them!"

Their own mount wanted to follow the rest, but Serene whispered in his ear and the griffon calmed.

At that moment, Atriun began to move . . . but not toward the dragons.

The two stared. Serene finally blurted, "Tyros! It's coming after us!"

The flying citadel did not turn to face them, but rather simply floated sideways in their direction. Its cloud shawl grew thicker and darker as it neared, and the wind picked up.

Tyros felt his hair rise as energy, both natural and magical, filled the air. Thunder rumbled as the dark fortress edged nearer. Winged forms rose from its battlements, racing toward the pair.

"Get us down! Down!"

Tyros had thought that they were a safe distance away, but either the eyes of those aboard Atriun were sharper than he had imagined, or the citadel had spells of detection much more sensitive than any he could cast. Either way, they were now the target of a hunt.

He leaned toward Serene. "Turn the griffon around! Head back the way we came!"

The citadel increased its speed, closing in on the pair. Gargoyles flew from its battlements, racing ahead of the massive castle. Someone in Atriun considered the pair an important target, possibly because of Tyros's presence.

Despite the animal's swiftness, the gargoyles drew nearer. Tyros thought these were more savage in appearance than Stone. He stared at the foremost of them, concentrating and muttering. With these creatures, Tyros dared not hold back his spells.

A loop of red light snared the leading gargoyle, binding both his wings and arms. Startled, the monster had time only for a growl before plummeting.

To the mage's surprise, a burst of multicolored light flashed before the eyes of the next gargoyles. Two collided, sending them spiraling out of control. Three more fluttered about blindly, trying to regain their sight.

"Praise the Bard King!" Serene gasped. "I didn't know how well that would work up here, away from the strength of the forest!"

Despite both their successes, they were quickly losing the race. Already Castle Atriun loomed near. This close, Tyros could even make out a shadowy figure in the uppermost tower, an almost ethereal form clad in dark robes. Something about that figure made him shiver, even though he also felt with certainty that it could not be the mage who controlled the fortress.

And then, when it seemed Tyros and Serene must be captured, the dragons arrived.

Sunfire came first. Roaring loudly, he soared through the ranks of gargoyles, sending them scattering in every direction. Tyros noticed a human figure atop the male—Captain Bakal. The pair rose up in the air. This time Sunfire appeared ready to wreak havoc on the castle.

Glisten, riderless, came up behind her mate. She appeared slimmer, sleeker. Much sleeker, in fact, than when the wizard had last seen her.

The dragon had laid her eggs and now flew here in order to protect them. Glisten knew that if the citadel reached Gwynned, her young would be at risk.

The female gold dived underneath Atriun, scraping the bottom of the island upon which the castle stood. The entire citadel rocked as parts of its underbelly crumbled away.

With the gargoyles in disarray and the citadel under assault, Tyros's thoughts turned to his original plan. "This is our chance to get aboard! Head toward the uppermost tower of the castle!"

"In all this chaos? It's too dangerous!"

He hated to manipulate the cleric, but nonetheless he did. "It may be the only opportunity to save the ones we seek, Serene!"

Her face paled. The cleric did not respond to him. Instead, she whispered something to the griffon, who banked and headed toward the flying citadel.

The clouds still had not thinned out; if anything, they grew thicker and more foreboding. Not only did it thunder, but lightning flashes cut across the sky. A bolt darted past them, striking the distant ground.

"If the storm gets worse, we may have to turn back, Tyros!"

The wind howled, but so far little rain had come down. The wind made for tougher going for the griffon but did nothing to slow the dragons, who circled the floating edifice once before diving down to begin their assault.

Sunfire opened his mouth, and a stream of fire struck the battlements, ripping apart one section. A few gargoyles scattered from there, one in flames. Still the citadel did nothing to repulse the attacks, which mystified the mage. He had expected it to be more powerful than its predecessors, able to at least attempt to defend itself against the dragons. As they neared the towers, Tyros almost felt disappointed. Other than the gargoyles, the flying citadel had unleashed nothing against them.

Had he been wrong about the magic he sensed?

The griffon flew past the first tower, heading toward the

one where Tyros expected to find the Wind Captain's Chair. If Serene could get him close enough, he would somehow enter.

They passed over a courtyard, complete with outer buildings and an immense wooded garden. An entire army could live in Atriun, almost unaware that they flew over the world. Yet so far Tyros had seen little sign of life other than the gargoyles, who had by this time abandoned the walls. The wizard could scarcely believe his good fortune. If the citadel was all but abandoned, he might reach the tower with no trouble whatsoever.

A flock of gargoyles burst from the treetops.

"Up!" the mage cried. "Bring us up!"

Too late. Tyros managed a spell that sent a pair of the horned beasts crashing against a stone wall, but then a swarm of gargoyles was upon them. Claws grabbed for his arms, legs, robe, anything they could get a hold on.

Serene sang out, her words lost to the wind.

The branches of the tallest trees rose up in response to her prayer, growing until they were able to entangle the attackers.

The griffon brought them out of range of the furious creatures. Gasping, Serene slumped against Tyros, her incantation evidently having taken much out of her.

A horrific crash of thunder shook them. Lightning illuminated everything, stunning the humans and their mount. A dragon's roar of pain echoed in the sky.

Sunfire flew haphazardly about, trying to stay aloft with only one wing. Little of the other wing remained. Most of the membrane had been burned away, and even some of the limb was smoldering.

Of Sunfire's rider, Captain Bakal, they could see no sign.

Tyros swallowed, thinking of the officer. He had come to like the man more than he would have admitted.

At that moment, a bolt of lightning struck one of the other griffons, killing both riders and mount and sending the corpses plunging earthward. The rest of the animals darted off in near panic, the men aboard frantically holding on.

Another bolt shot forth from the black clouds. If Sunfire

had not dipped suddenly, the male surely would have been killed this time.

The mage shook his head, trying not to believe it. The lightning was no coincidence. Castle Atriun was using it to slaughter Tyros's allies.

Glisten abandoned her attack to come to the aid of her mate. She swept away a band of gargoyles seeking to rend his good wing and took hold of her beloved, pulling him up and farther away from the citadel.

She wasn't swift enough.

The full fury of the storm assailed the dragons. The sky grew blinding as bolt after bolt raged down on the leviathans. Sunfire roared in agony, his tail half burned away. Glisten, seeking to protect him, took the brunt of the strikes. Four bolts caught her in rapid succession, literally setting her ablaze.

She lost her grip on her mate. Unable to keep aloft any longer, Sunfire spiraled westward toward the open sea. He continued to flap one wing, trying to slow his deadly descent.

An anguished cry tore Tyros's gaze from the male. Glisten, somehow still aloft after such terrible wounds, forced herself toward Atriun.

"She can barely fly!" Serene called. "Why doesn't she turn?"

"She means to take the citadel with her," Tyros replied soberly. Glisten wouldn't survive her deadly wounds.

Even that heroic effort was denied the brave dragon, for again a rapid succession of bolts caught Glisten. The gold leviathan's form radiated as energy from the sorcerous lightning consumed her.

Glisten let loose with one last pathetic roar . . . and burned away without a trace.

Serene clutched Tyros tightly. "By the Bard King, no! It can't be!"

But it was. Not a trace remained of the valiant creature.

Tearing his gaze away from Glisten's fate, Tyros searched for her mate. Unfortunately no sign could be seen of Sunfire save for a vast ripple just offshore. Tyros thought of the eggs, now left to the elements. There would be no new golden dragons born in the mountains near Gwynned.

Overwhelmed by the likely loss of both dragons, the pair failed to notice the return of the gargoyles. Only when their griffon emitted a leonine roar did Tyros and Serene realize the imminent danger.

The animal swatted at the nearest of the leathery monsters, ripping it open. This sent the gargoyles backing off, which gave the mage a moment to think.

Tyros looked at the central tower. "Get me there, to the tower! It controls the flight of the citadel!"

Charging past several startled gargoyles, the griffon maneuvered close to the windows of the tower. The robed figure within, surely the pilot, paid no mind to their nearby presence.

Unwilling to question such luck, the desperate wizard whispered a spell. Suddenly he began to rise from the griffon's back.

"Tyros! What's happening to you?"

"I've cast a spell! Our only chance is to get inside the tower, but I can only do one person! As soon as I get inside, I'll bring you with a different spell!"

She said something, but the griffon's call drowned out her words. Tyros floated free just as a gargoyle made a grab for his robe. The monster went flying past.

For a few moments, the red-robed wizard flew. His only weapon other than the dagger in his belt remained the small staff, but although he still should have been enough of a threat for the hooded figure to take notice of, the latter did not turn from his duties. Even when Tyros took hold of the edge of the open window and pulled himself half inside, the pilot did not look.

For the first time, Tyros saw the Wind Captain's Chair . . . but not exactly as he had always imagined it. The rune-etched pedestals were there, and so were the circles of dark ebony crystal upon which the feet were placed, but the spheres atop the pedestals were a blinding gold, not black like the circles. They had always been of the same stone in the past. The golden spheres were not only half again as big as their dark predecessors, but even from where he was the mage could sense the tremendous power radiating from them.

Then the shadowy figure shifted, gazing at the intruder from within the folds of his robe, and Tyros realized with horror the reason why the pilot had made no move toward him.

He was part of the mechanism.

The hands and feet melded into the spheres and circles, so that one could not tell where the man ended and the arcane device began. Even had the shrouded figure desired to defend the chamber, he would have been unable to do so. Tyros tried to imagine the sort of mage who would cast such a spell, even among the followers of Nuitari.

The pilot made an adjustment, and as he did, his hood fell back slightly, revealing a more terrible horror. The pale visage, the eyes all white, the ghostly blur of the body shook the desperate mage to the core. What flew the citadel not only did not live, but what life had once been there had been ripped away in some monstrous manner.

Frozen by the dreadful tableau, Tyros stared at that face. He knew it, knew it from Gwynned.

"Kendilious . . ." he whispered in abject fear.

Clawed hands seized Tyros from behind, tearing him free of the tower. His shock at seeing the old Red Robe from Gwynned had cost him precious moments. He tried to struggle, but now two gargoyles had hold of him. Tyros heard Serene scream but could not even turn his head to see what fate befell her.

The sinister pair held the captive wizard tight as a third, larger gargoyle approached him. Three savage horns topped the newcomer's nightmarish head. The leathery beast opened wide his jaws, then raised one hand high with the obvious intent of tearing the human's chest open.

A slightly smaller gargoyle suddenly appeared from above and seized the upraised hand. He and the larger gargoyle glared at one another, nearly coming to blows.

"Master wants!" the latest growled. "Must be taken to Master!"

With a snarl, the three-horned gargoyle pulled free his hand. He glared at Tyros, then reluctantly rumbled, "Take to Maaaster!"

The pair holding Tyros whipped the stunned wizard away, descending toward the main entrance of the castle. Tyros stared in the direction of the tower for as long as possible, but his thoughts were not on the ill-fated Kendilious, nor even Serene. Instead, they focused on the gargoyle who had saved him from immediate death but who might have condemned him to the same terrible fate as the old mage had suffered.

Whose side was Stone truly on?

Chapter 10

Prisoners of the Citadel

Bakal had expected to die in battle, but with both feet planted firmly on the ground, not every limb flailing wildly as he dropped to his death. He would have preferred the bolt that had struck Sunfire to have burned him to ash.

He braced himself, hoping that perhaps his heart, much too strong for his own good now, would stop from fright before he hit the earth.

"Aaaah!" Suddenly he flew up again, both shoulders stinging with pain. It took Bakal a moment to regain his senses, but when he had, the veteran immediately recognized the source of his miraculous ascent.

"Don't you worry, Captain Bakal! Taggi's got a good grip on you, and when he grabs his prey, it never escapes."

Despite the kender's discouraging words of encouragement, Bakal managed to calm himself enough to reassess his situation. It did nothing to assuage his worries, for everywhere he looked he saw only despair. At least one of the griffons had perished, the riders along with the beast. Two more held only one man. He had expected some loss, but not so quickly. Worse, the supposedly defenseless citadel had proven far otherwise.

The captain knew that the lightning strike had been no fluke; some evil spell had sent it soaring directly at Sunfire. Now, at last, Bakal understood what had happened to the other flying castle. For reasons beyond his comprehension, the invaders had chosen to sacrifice the older fortress by destroying it above Norwych. Only that could explain the tremendous devastation.

At that moment, the new citadel struck out at the two golden dragons with a fury that made past assaults appear tame. Glisten tried to aid her stricken mate, only to be assaulted herself. The lightning struck with such force that it momentarily blinded the officer, and when his eyesight cleared, it revealed Glisten's fiery death and Sunfire, now too weak to fly, dropping into the sea.

To Bakal's relief, Sunfire's head burst out of the water a moment later. However, the dragon didn't try to return to the battle. Instead, he swam away, heading in the direction of Gwynned. Captain Bakal knew Sunfire was no coward. The man had been there when Glisten had made her mate swear what had turned out to be a prophetic oath. If one of them perished, the other had to make certain that the eggs survived. Sunfire surely hadn't expected it to fall to him, however. The male would have gladly sacrificed himself for his mate. Now, though, the future of their children rested on him alone.

The maimed dragon could have done very little, anyway. Had he remained, Sunfire would have perished as surely as had Glisten.

All of which did nothing for Bakal's present position. He could think of only one thing to do at this point. "Rapp! Land this beast in the castle, somewhere that isn't swarming with gargoyles!"

The kender obeyed. The griffon soared around Atriun. One gargoyle managed to get close, but Bakal kicked the monster in the jaw, sending his attacker spinning away.

The griffon finally descended behind a building that appeared to have once been used for a smithy and a stable. Taggi released Bakal as soon as possible, the captain immediately racing through a back door of the building.

The remaining griffons landed just outside the entrance. Mirko and the rest of the surviving soldiers leaped off, swords ready, as the griffons quickly took up defensive positions. Rapp pulled out a sling. Several gargoyles hovered overhead, seeking to penetrate the griffons' defenses.

Although the men immediately retreated to the doorway, the animals remained outside, clearly unwilling to enter the unknown structure. Rapp refused to leave them. Standing just behind his children, the kender let loose with the sling, striking a hard blow on the shoulder of one leathery monster. The gargoyles backed away.

Bakal glanced around the interior. "We've got to find a way out of here and into the castle itself!"

"They're bringing nets!" Mirko called from just outside the doorway.

Sure enough, the gargoyles had brought forth great mesh nets. Bakal doubted that they had come up with the plan themselves. Whoever controlled them had likely set the creatures to the task, for Rapp's pets were the only thing truly protecting the small band.

Rapp readied another missile in his sling. To his credit, the spry figure defended his griffons with vigor. Still, the captain believed that he needed the kender's assistance more. "Rapp! Get back here!"

Rapp sent a second missile flying. Its target shifted position, allowing the stone to go past harmlessly.

"Kender!"

The gargoyles had most of their nets in position. Bakal had no certain estimation of a griffon's strength, but judging by the nets, he doubted that the animals would be able to escape.

"They're going to capture Taggi and the others!" Rapp burst out. "I can't let them!"

"You'll have to if you want to save your griffons later, boy! They wouldn't be bothering with nets unless their master wanted the griffons alive. They'll be all right, just caged. We'll get them, I promise you, but right now I need you to come in here and find us a way out before they come after us!"

Rapp looked ready to protest, but at that moment the first of the nets descended upon the griffons. A female tried to rip the mesh, but even with her claws and strength, the net remained intact.

Swallowing, the kender nodded. "All right, Bakal. I'll look around, but we'd better rescue the griffons later."

"We will, boy."

The tiny figure ran past him, disappearing into the shadowy interior. Captain Bakal didn't know what he hoped Rapp would find, only that kender usually managed to locate some way into and out of every structure. If his party had any chance of escape, it relied on Rapp's abilities.

"Corij preserve us," he muttered, calling on Kiri-Jolith, the god of just causes.

Nets now ensnared all of the griffons save Taggi, whom Mirko and another man had managed to keep partially free. A gargoyle got too close to Mirko's long blade, and the huge veteran cut deep into his wing. The other soldier thrust his sword, slaying the monster.

Unfortunately, in doing so, Mirko's companion opened himself up to attack. A massive gargoyle pulled him forward and, with a single slash of his talons, tore open the soldier's throat. With a cry, Mirko moved in and ran his sword through the attacker, but too late to save his comrade.

"Damnation!" Bakal glanced back again into the gloom. "Rapp, you find anything?"

"I found this old horseshoe, but no old horse for it. Do you think they might have flying horses? I've heard they exist, but I've never—"

"Rapp, we can't wait any longer!"

"I'm looking. Honest I am!"

A winged form passed over the officer's head, narrowly missing him. One of the gargoyles had made it inside. Bakal turned as the creature tried for him again, bringing his sword up just as the leathery form swooped down.

The blade sank into its chest. With a cry, the gargoyle crashed to the floor, wrenching the captain's sword out of his hand. Bakal put a foot on the corpse and fought to remove the weapon.

"They're dragging the griffons off, Captain!" Mirko warned.

Bakal pulled his sword free. "They'll be coming for us next. Form a line of defense. Don't let any more get inside!"

Moving to the entrance, he saw several of the gargoyles pulling the struggling griffons away. The animals would be of some use to those controlling this castle, but his small band only represented an obstacle. The gargoyles would not likely let any of them live.

And then, from within: "I found something, Bakal. At least I think I found something."

The captain had no intention of abandoning the defenses without something more concrete. "Have you or haven't you?"

"Oooh! I did find something! You'll like it! It's a shaft, and it's dark and musty and cobwebby and goes down real deep!"

"Wonderful . . ." All he had to do now was stall the monsters while he and the others made their escape down Rapp's dubious shaft. The captain looked around and saw a single oil lamp dangling from a post. Despite the age of the castle, he had already noticed evidence that both the smithy and the stable had been used in the recent past. Perhaps the lamp had some oil in it.

"Mirko! I'm backing away!"

"Aye, Captain!"

Racing over to the lamp, he pulled it free. Still some oil. Bakal studied the building, especially the entrance. Old wooden beams and planks. Very dry. Good.

After a quick search for tinder, Bakal lit the lamp, then headed back to the entrance. He would have only one chance. His aim would have to be perfect.

"Heads down! Prepare for orderly retreat . . . now!"

Bakal threw as hard as he could. Luck was with him, for the lamp flew unerringly toward the upper frame of the doorway, where it shattered. Flaming oil spread over the entire entrance.

The nearest gargoyle drew back, hands burning. The others darted into the sky, expecting more blazing missiles.

With Mirko and the captain covering the retreat, the surviving soldiers rushed back to where Rapp waited.

"This is it. I found it all by myself!" The kender had found a trapdoor and, beneath that, a web-covered hole.

"Looks like a refuse chute of some sort," one man muttered.

"It's not . . . look. It has handles so you can climb down."

They had little choice. The handholds seemed to indicate a tunnel. "All right," Bakal snarled. "Get down there! Which would you rather face, a few spiders or a gargoyle? Go!"

One by one they scrambled down the opening. Four men were inside the tunnel before the winged terrors had gotten over their surprise and darted past the fiery entrance.

"Rapp! You go next!"

As the kender vanished, the first gargoyles reached Captain Bakal and his remaining men. Bakal managed a good slash at one but nearly slipped. A clawed hand closed on his wrist, and a toothy beak snapped perilously close to his nose.

"I've got 'im, Captain!" Mirko brought his sword down, his massive strength enabling him to decapitate the gargoyle.

"Look out, man!"

Intent on saving his superior, Mirko didn't see the savage maw that opened behind him. The soldier turned, but not soon enough to keep the strong jaws from clamping on his throat.

"Damn you!" The older soldier threw himself forward, slashing again and again at the gargoyle. Blood dripping from several wounds, the monster at last retreated from his victim.

Mirko collapsed in Bakal's free arm. The captain started to talk to him, only to see that the big man was already dead.

"Captain!" a soldier called from the shaft. "Come on!"

With one last cut at an approaching gargoyle, the officer leaped for the hole. He slid in just as one of the attackers nearly tore his shoulder off.

A gargoyle thrust his muzzle down the shaft, snapping. Bakal poked up with his sword and the muzzle vanished. Although many of the gargoyles were slightly smaller than humans, their wings prevented them from climbing down the narrow shaft. Yet, despite being unable to reach the men, several gargoyles nevertheless tried, hissing in frustration.

When finally the top of the shaft was a distant sight, Bakal spat some cobwebs from his mouth and called down, "Is there an end to this thing, or do we just fall out the bottom of the citadel to our deaths?"

"Just coming to what looks like a floor, sir."

"Praise the gods . . ." The shaft had to have once been part of an escape route in case the castle was endangered. The captain hoped they would find a usable exit when they reached the end. He didn't want to be trapped in here with only the smithy as a way out. Might as well cut his own throat then.

Bakal wondered if Tyros and Serene still lived. He had briefly seen them heading to the castle before he had begun to fall.

"Can't worry about them now . . ." he muttered. He had his own mission.

The others waited for him at the bottom. Brushing his clothes, the scarred officer noticed that a dim light illuminated the musty corridor for several yards. Looking around, Bakal noticed some emerald crystals in the wall.

"The crystals started glowing when I reached bottom, sir," the first man down the shaft informed him. "They seem to be part of the original design."

"I thought this place was built by a Solamnic Knight," said another. "Solamnics hate magic."

"Only what wasn't their own," Captain Bakal replied, inspecting one of the crystals. They felt slightly warm to the touch. "The Knights of the Rose and some others are supposed to know a few spells, although I think they're more like clerics than mages. Doesn't matter. At least we have some light. Rapp?"

Rapp stood by the shaft, staring up. The expression on the small figure's face looked out of place on one of his kind.

Captain Bakal cautiously put a hand on the kender's shoulder. "The griffons will be okay for now. We'll rescue them when we can."

"Sharpclaw's dead," the kender whispered. "He was Taggi's favorite brother. The lightning got him. I don't want to lose the rest of them, Bakal!"

"You won't, but we've got to keep going if you want to give them any hope, boy! Now, you did a great job up there, but I need you up front with me to look for a way out. Are you up to it?"

Rapp immediately brightened. "I can do it, Bakal! I'll find a way out so that we can rescue the griffons, Tyros, and Serene!"

Not knowing if the last two were already dead, the captain did not contradict his small companion. "Fine. Let's go, then."

The corridor, at the beginning no wider than two men side by side, grew narrower as they left the vicinity of the shaft. Fortunately the crystals in the wall continued to light up, giving them some comfort. However, there were no side corridors nor any rooms. Bakal wondered if they had entered a trap, yet as the minutes passed, nothing confronted them.

"Just how far can this thing go?" someone finally asked. "Are we going to walk the entire width of the castle?"

It seemed that way. Bakal was just about to call for a short rest when Rapp suddenly darted ahead.

"There's another corridor ahead!" the kender called. "It cuts right across this one!"

Catching up, Captain Bakal studied the intersection. The paths left and right looked identical to the one they were already on. He took a few steps into each and saw that the same crystals illuminated them.

Despite the urge to change direction, the officer could think of no good reason to abandon their present course. If it seemed that they were going nowhere, the party could always turn around.

"We'll go straight," he informed the others. "At least for now."

They continued on, and as the minutes passed, Captain Bakal began to regret his decision. The intersection they had left behind had so far been the only one. Ahead of them, the crystals continued to come to life, but all they revealed was more of the same monotonous view. Surely, Bakal thought, there had to be an end to this place.

Soon they noticed that the path ahead remained dark. Bakal paused, thinking perhaps that the crystals here simply reacted more slowly. Yet when still nothing happened after a few moments, the officer decided to check the nearest wall.

There were no crystals, at least as far as he could tell. Perhaps beyond, but definitely not within reach.

Bakal peered into the gloom but could see nothing. He glanced back at the others. "Wait here a moment, all of you. That goes for you, too, Rapp."

Sword ready, the captain took a few tentative steps into the darkness. With his free hand, he reached for the other wall, seeking the crystals there. However, that wall, too, proved bare.

"You all right, Captain?" someone called.

"So far. Looks like we'll have to go back, though. I'll just go a few steps more, but if I don't find anything—"

Bakal heard a slight click as his foot came down.

"Damn!" A trap!

He turned to warn the others to stay back, hoping at least to save their lives . . . and found himself staring at total darkness. The illumination behind him had completely vanished.

Voices rose. "What happened?"

"Captain, are you all right?"

"Be still, all of you," the officer commanded. "I'm coming back."

Feeling his way along, Captain Bakal made his way toward the others. He nearly bumped into Rapp, only missing because of the kender's sudden giggle.

"You did really good, Bakal!"

"Can you see me?"

"Just an outline, and not until you were close."

"Pity." He had hoped the kender's eyes would be better. No sense, then, putting Rapp up front. "All right, listen up. We'll head back to the other corridor, then follow it from there. Who's in front?"

"Garon, Captain!" called a gruff voice.

"Take the lead, Garon, but use caution all the way."

"Aye, Captain."

Garon was a good man. Bakal breathed a little easier. "The rest of you, keep one hand on the right-hand wall and don't get too far from the man in front of you."

Weapons held carefully, they backtracked. Despite having

earlier lit their way, the crystals now stayed dormant. Bakal's eyes grew more accustomed to the dark, but still he couldn't make out much of anything, even Rapp right in front of him.

Frustrated, he called out, "Anything yet, Garon?"

"It's still as black as pitch, Captain," the lead soldier called. "I can't see any sign of the split up—"

There was a sudden hiss. Garon's reply cut off with a brief choking sound.

"What is it?" Bakal roared. "What's happened?"

"Garon" a voice gasped. "Captain . . . I think Garon's dead!"

"Let me through!" Bakal made his way to the front, fearing with each step that he would walk into whatever had slain yet another of his soldiers.

He put his hand out, trying to find the fallen body. Instead, he collided with it. Garon still stood. Cursing under his breath, Bakal felt around the corpse's waist, then the shoulders, at last touching Garon's throat.

A metal shaft had pierced the soldier's neck, passing through one side and out the other.

The shaft extended nearly all the way across the corridor, the needlelike point of the death trap not more than an inch from the opposing wall. The captain's hand came away damp with blood.

"I think we chose the wrong corridor, Bakal," a high-pitched voice piped up.

Swearing, the battle-worn veteran felt around. Enough of a gap existed for them to slide past poor Garon. "All right, I'll go first this time! Everyone stay close and listen carefully for anything out of the ordinary!"

With trepidation, the survivors backtracked once more. Much to Bakal's relief, though, the trek back proved devoid of other traps. Even so, no one relaxed in the least. There was no telling what might lie farther ahead.

The party gathered in the intersection, more than willing to take a pause. While they did, Bakal considered the other corridors again. He still favored the one on his right, but his last choice had resulted in the death of Garon. Of course,

Bakal had no way of knowing if the left corridor were any better.

"Right it is, then." Bakal cursed the eccentric Knight who had built this place and wondered if perhaps the Solamnic had been exiled to Atriun because of his insanity. Certainly that would explain much.

Calling an end to the rest, Bakal led the others single file into the new corridor. He reached out with the intention of again using the wall to guide him and was suddenly greeted by dim emerald light.

"Praise be!" a voice called from among his band.

"Don't get your hopes up," he snapped, then, calmer, "but it could mean we've got the right one this time."

They had journeyed well down the new corridor when Bakal suddenly noticed something different in the gloom ahead. "Rapp! Where are you?"

"Right behind you, Bakal."

"Rapp, peek around me. Is that a door I see at the far end?"

"A door?" The kender shoved forward eagerly. "Where?"

The captain pointed at a dark spot far ahead. "You've got better eyes, I think. Isn't that a door?"

"I think so . . . yes, it is. Do you want me to go open it?"

He had to restrain the wiry figure from racing down the corridor. "Easy, boy. We don't know what other traps might be down this way."

"Traps!" His eyes grew wider. "You really think so?"

"Just . . . let's be careful."

Slowly they edged their way down the hall. Once, Bakal thought he heard a click, but as no one died, he assumed his imagination had just played with him. At last they reached the door, a simple but sturdy wooden thing that looked as if it could withstand the strength of a charging bull.

Disappointed that they hadn't found any new traps along the way, the kender put his hopes now on the door. "Is it locked, Bakal? Do you want me to open it? I'm good with doors, just like Uncle Trapspringer was! Did I tell you how he got that name? You see, he was—"

"Another time, boy." Bakal tested the door. Locked, of course. Nothing could be easy. "All yours."

From out of his topknot, Rapp produced a lockpick. Bakal knew that kender could carry more than two dozen picks on their person and improvise if those were taken from them.

"It's rusted," Rapp murmured. "And it's a Solamnic lock! They're fun! They make different designs that look the same on the outside, and opening one sometimes takes hours, even days."

The thought of staying down here for days while Rapp entertained himself with the lock did not at all suit Bakal. He opened his mouth with the intention of encouraging the kender to speed matters up, but a click from the door halted him in mid breath.

"Oh, that was an easy one! I hoped it would be one of the imperial models! They can take—"

"It's open, then?"

"Oh, sure, Bakal!" Rapp took hold and swung both himself and the door aside. "See?"

The captain did see. He saw that the door opened into a much wider corridor, one that clearly led to the central sections of the castle. He also saw something else, and that something saw him as well.

The gargoyle opened wide his toothy jaws.

Bakal stumbled back, trying to ready his weapon.

The gargoyle shook his head, then raised one clawed hand toward Bakal and rumbled, "I speak for Stooone. . . ."

* * * * *

Tyros woke, nightmares of ghostly mages and his own feet and hands turning to crystal still haunting him. That the first image he saw turned out to be the horrific countenance of the three-horned gargoyle peering at him through strong iron bars did not at all ease his spirits.

Seeing the prisoner was awake, the gargoyle hissed, then hurried off. Tyros tried to move, only to find his hands manacled. Further inspection revealed that he lay in a small, dust-ridden cell that smelled as if it hadn't been aired out since Castle Atriun had been built.

He didn't remember falling unconscious, but clearly it had happened. He also didn't know what had happened to Serene. The thought of her at the mercy of the gargoyles, especially the more brutish, triple-horned one, left him cold. Tyros had to escape so that he could find her.

Clearing his thoughts, the red wizard concentrated on his remaining spells. Finding one that would release him from his confinement would be no trouble whatso—

A horrible throbbing filled Tyros's head, nearly causing him to black out again. Tyros forgot all about spells, Serene, gargoyles, and flying citadels. All he wanted was for the pain to cease.

It did.

The cessation of pain came so suddenly that the captive mage could only blink. He exhaled in relief, praying never to feel such agony again. Now Tyros could begin once more to concentrate on a spell that would—

Again, the pain ripped through his head, this time even worse. Everything pounded, harder and harder. He lost track of his spell, lost track of everything. Tyros's world became agony . . .

And just as quickly reverted to normal.

He groaned, trying to put the pieces of his mind back together. Twice now the throbbing had nearly sent him to oblivion, both times as he had been trying to put together a spell. In fact, even thinking of spells made his head pound a little.

"By the Tower," Tyros muttered. He did not need a third test to know that if he tried a spell, his head would threaten to explode again. Someone had magicked him, made certain that any attempt to use his powers would strike him down. Cunning and not a little sadistic. For a mage not to think of spells was nearly the same as a starving man not allowed to eat food placed around him. Wizards lived and breathed their work.

Tyros suddenly noticed he had company. A shiver ran through him as two murky figures nearly identical to ghostly Kendilious stood before his cage.

They floated—no better word described it—toward him, as if under the robes they no longer had feet. One touched the door to his cell, opening it. The pair flanked him, then each lifted a white, bony hand to his manacles. A simple touch and the bracelets fell away.

He tried to jump up, but despite their emaciated appearance, they gripped his shoulders and held him fast.

"What do you want? Who are you?"

Neither looked at him directly, but one pointed forward, indicating he should leave the cell. The ghastly figures continued to grip his shoulders as he walked. Devoid of his wizard's staff and dagger, Tyros considered his options. In truth, he had only his physical strength left, which seemed little enough against these strong ghouls.

Yet not to try . . .

Acting on instinct, Tyros brought his elbows into his guards' midsections. Unfortunately, striking the phantoms was like striking rock. His elbows felt as if they had shattered. Worse, the ghouls' grip on his shoulders tightened painfully, a punishment for his actions. He fell to his knees, nearly blacking out from agony.

"All right," Tyros gasped. "All right! I'll behave myself!"

The pressure eased, enabling him to stand. They led Tyros down a corridor, then up a lengthy flight of steps. From there, they marched down another long corridor before finally stopping at a brass door with the mark of the kingfisher emblazoned upon it. The captive mage found it ironic that the home of a Solamnic Knight should become a sanctum of destruction.

The door opened. To his astonishment, Tyros found himself in a sumptuous chamber with silken curtains, golden oil lamps, and furniture so skillfully wrought that the richest monarch would have envied them. Tapestries depicting creatures of the forest decorated the walls.

Taking away from the splendor was a pair of savage

gargoyles hunched in the center of the room. They eyed the wizard with dark speculation and perhaps a little hunger.

"Tyros!"

Serene. The cleric stood near open doors leading to a great balcony. She looked untouched, even refreshed. Her face lit up for a moment when she saw him, then grew sad. Curiously the crimson-tressed woman did not attempt to approach Tyros.

"Serene . . ." He thanked Lunitari that she lived but wondered what she was doing in this chamber.

"Are you . . . better now?" the cleric quietly asked.

"Better?"

Her brow arched. "Surely you've not forgotten . . . but you have, I see."

The mage didn't like the sound of that. "Forgotten what?"

Before she could speak, someone behind her interrupted. "A side effect, my Serene, and one that could not be prevented."

From the balcony emerged a hooded, ebony-clad wizard. A little older than Tyros, with black and slightly gray hair and a fancy goatee, the newcomer radiated power on a level that Tyros hadn't experienced in some time. The dark mage gave him a congenial smile, yet one that also hinted of threat. Even the bright, cheerful blue eyes didn't entirely hide some menace.

"Welcome again, Master Tyros," the black wizard called, exuberance in his tone. He clasped gloved hands together.

A flash of memory hit the captive. He remembered those gloved hands reaching for his temples.

"I trust that this time we can speak a little more friendly with one another. After all, your very life depends upon it!"

Both Tyros and Serene started. Tyros noticed the cleric's expression shift momentarily and realized that she tried to keep hidden great misery, as if she had just learned some terrible, heart-wrenching truth. The mage could only imagine that it concerned her imprisoned love.

The dark mage put a hand on Serene's shoulder, caressing it. She did not flinch, but Tyros saw the dismay in her eyes.

"I think, my dear Serene, that once again introductions are in order. After all, I doubt he remembers the first time."

"Tyros." She nearly choked on her words. "This is Valkyn."

Valkyn . . . Tyros knew the name from his research. Valkyn, who had also studied the history of the flying citadels. But that Valkyn had been a member of his own order, not a Black Robe. And yet . . . "Valkyn of Culthairai?"

"Aaah, very good! I feared I might have injured that scholarly brain too soon. Yes, I am Valkyn of Culthairai."

"You wore the robes of the Order of Lunitari."

"The color of a robe hardly dictates our lives, despite what those in the tower might desire." He touched Serene's red locks. "I can be giving just as much as any white-robed follower of Solinari. She knows that. My darling Serene has always known that."

At last he had said it. Had Tyros needed any more verification, he had only to look at the terrible struggle going on within the cleric. Valkyn might not see it, but Tyros could read the turmoil, the battling emotions.

Serene had found her missing love . . . the master of Castle Atriun.

Chapter 11

In the Heart of the Beast

The master remained occupied with the female, a creature he had known from the past. Stone, too, had known of her, at least her existence, although she had never met him nor obviously even realized that her love had trafficked with gargoyles. In fact, Valkyn had seen fit not to mention to his female any of the darker elements of his life, especially his increasingly disturbing experiments. He had realized even then that Serene would not tolerate all of what the spellcaster thought a necessary part of his research.

When the time had come to delve even deeper, he had finally, with some regret, abandoned her and returned to Atriun, where the gargoyles and a few others already prepared for his arrival. Stone had occasionally noticed him wandering the wooded garden, perhaps recalling his time with the fire-tressed woman, but never had Valkyn voiced any notion of seeing her again. His work had been his mistress.

Now she had returned to him, however accidentally, and did not seem pleased by his success. It had occurred to the gargoyle leader that in this there might be some use. Perhaps this female might distract the master, or at least soften him for the kill. The sleek gargoyle had no compunction about slaying Valkyn, not after so many of his people had perished serving the human. Even Crag's people had suffered much.

Thinking of his rival, Stone anxiously moved on. Crag would have dearly loved to catch his rival in such a situation, doing the unthinkable beneath the master's very eyes. If Valkyn discovered his treachery, then Stone could expect a most painful and slow death.

In a darkened part of the castle well below even the chamber housing the secret of Atriun's power, the gargoyle leader reached a thick rock door with an iron handle. Stone grasped the handle and pulled with all his might, the rust of ages adding to the already difficult task of dragging open a rock door almost a foot thick. As he pulled, he hoped that doing so would not leave him a target for those within.

No blade split his gullet. With eyes accustomed to the dark, Stone peered inside, hoping nothing had gone amiss.

"Stand where you are, gargoyle," a human voice within demanded.

"No enemy," the gargoyle hissed. "I am Stone."

A painfully high voice cut through the gloom, echoing far too much for the gargoyle's ears. "It's Stone, Bakal! The one that Tyros spoke to! Remember? He snatched Tyros while the mage was sleeping and could've dropped him or taken him to the citadel, but he didn't—"

To the gargoyle's relief, one of the humans quieted the painful voice. "Be still, boy! You'll give us away."

A figure wielding a lengthy sword stepped forward, an elder warrior with eyes of experience. Stone respected this one, knew that even without a sword this human could very well have defeated many of the gargoyle's people. The warrior eyed him suspiciously, then said, "So you're our savior, eh?"

He didn't quite understand the human's word. It did sound like "save," though, which made some sense. On a hunch, Stone replied, "I . . . saved you."

"For what? To be your dinner?"

The gargoyle quickly shook his head. "No. To help you. To help us!"

"I think he means it, Bakal," the high voice said, this time mercifully quieter.

"Yeah, I think he does," the man before Stone replied.

Stone gazed back in the hall. No one lurked nearby, but he felt uneasy standing in the open. "Please. Must enter!"

The human Bakal considered this for a moment, then finally nodded. The blade lowered a little, and the man stepped back a few paces. "All right, but just enough to close that thing."

With some relief, the gargoyle entered, dragging the heavy door shut behind him. A dim light suddenly filled the room as several of the humans brought forth emerald crystals like those illuminating most of the lower corridors. Stone had seen to it that the humans would have them, knowing that the race disliked living in total darkness. Valkyn would never miss so few, especially since he never traversed the lowest levels.

"Why have you brought us here?" Bakal demanded. "Why do you want to betray your master?"

Was the human daft? Why else? "To be free! We are Valkyn's slaves, human! Slavesss!"

"Some of them looked pretty eager for slaves," another human muttered.

"Aye, they looked like they enjoyed killing for their master," a second added.

The blades focused on him. Stone felt no fear, only resignation. If they charged him now, he would die, his dream of freedom for his people unfulfilled.

"Easy now," snapped Bakal. "Let him speak his mind."

"Stone's flock will not harm you, but cannot speak for Crag's." Stone indicated three horns. When Bakal nodded understanding, the gargoyle continued. "Master very busy. Has female and other mage, Tyros."

"They're alive?"

"For now. Tyros . . ." Stone shrugged. "Maybe not for long."

The scarred warrior nodded. "Then we'd better act soon. Without the mage, it'll be a lot harder to take this place."

A small figure rushed up. Stone hissed. Even the gargoyle felt uneasy around a kender.

"What about Taggi and the others? What about my griffons?"

Annoyed by the seemingly useless question, Stone answered briefly. "Live. Caged near other side of castle."

"A good question, Rapp," Bakal said. "We'll probably need them." He rubbed absently on his scars. "Tell me, Stone. The central tower. That's where this Valkyn directs the citadel's flight from, isn't it?"

"Yesss."

"And the power that makes it fly? Is that there, too?"

The gargoyle shook his head. "No. Below in great room."

"Where is that? We'll have to go there."

"Will show, but not now. Not yet."

The warrior clearly did not like that. "Oh? And when would be a good time?"

Stone repeated what he had said to Tyros. "When clouds thin, human . . . when clouds thin."

"And when, by the gods, does that take place? You told Tyros that, too, but the clouds never thinned while we followed this place!"

The gargoyle summoned his best command of Common, for now he had to explain things that even he did not quite understand. "When clouds thin . . . that is when the master will be most unguarded. . . . Master must work to keep castle in air and will need time. Must use magic of castle for his spells."

Bakal's eyes widened. "Which draws from that unnatural storm outside! That's when the storm fades and the clouds thin!"

"Yesss. Master must work fast. Must think only of spells, not of outside." Stone thumped his chest. "Depends on gargoyles to watch for enemies."

"This will be soon?"

"Soon, human."

The warrior shook his head. "We'll still need Tyros for this. We have to rescue him!"

Stone started to protest, but the kender spoke first. "We have to save Serene, too! We can't just leave her."

The gargoyle hissed in consternation. "Cannot do!"

"He's right, Rapp," the captain agreed, momentarily mollifying Stone's fears that they would go crashing into Valkyn's chambers in the hopes of rescuing a female. "Let's concentrate on getting Tyros. He's the one we need to make this work."

Stone shook his head. "Cannot do. No Tyros!"

"Listen here, friend," Bakal snarled. "If anyone's got a

chance to defeat your master, it's Tyros. We need to rescue him."

The gargoyle's wings stretched as he mulled over the human's words. He had no choice if he wanted them to play their part. Still, it would be risky trying to lead this band to the cell where Tyros had been imprisoned, assuming he even remained there. No, for this to be done properly, it would require only one to do the work, and unfortunately that meant Stone himself.

The gargoyle let out an exasperated sigh. How he longed for the woodland ruins from which Valkyn had plucked him. "Will try . . ."

* * * * *

"I know of you, Tyros. You are not the only one who made use of the conclave's storehouse of knowledge."

Tyros barely paid Valkyn any attention, still reeling at the shock Serene must have felt when she discovered that her lost love had not been kidnapped but had instead been the kidnapper . . . and worse. Already Norwych had suffered dearly because of his creation, this monstrous new flying citadel, and one if not both of the golden dragons guarding Gwynned had also perished. Valkyn had caused more deaths than many commanders in the war, and yet he looked oblivious to it, his demeanor almost constantly cheerful, even inviting. Valkyn cared nothing for anyone save himself.

Yet his eyes lingered on Serene. His hands, though gloved, now and then caressed her neck. Perhaps Valkyn still cared for the cleric, but did he expect her to forgive him for his evils?

"Your efforts showed me some of the particular weaknesses, the errors, involved in the creation of past citadels. All that power invested in something so haphazard! When the war started, Ariakas had at least a dozen flying. Oh, they frightened his foes at first and enabled him to literally drop his forces on the enemy, but the cost to maintain them! The constant chanting by mages and clerics, the lack of defenses against airborne retaliation. To save a citadel, he had to start adding dragons to its defenses, drawing them away from the other parts of his forces. Why create such a marvel if it cannot even sufficiently defend itself?"

The captive mage said nothing, knowing that Valkyn sought no answer to the question but rather simply enjoyed hearing himself talk of his triumph.

Valkyn released Serene and started back to the balcony. "Come join me out here, my friend. I want you to see this."

Tyros had no choice, for the robed shadows thrust him forward, following their master outside.

The wind tossed Tyros's hair around as they stepped out. Valkyn, hair cropped close, seemed not to even notice the gale. He leaned on the rail, staring beyond the castle walls.

The servants shoved Tyros next to him, then stepped back. The crimson mage looked out at the world below, visible in part from the balcony. He felt a brief touch of vertigo as he watched the landscape continually shift.

"A magnificent sight, isn't it? The only other place where you can get this view is from atop a dragon, and there you might find it much less comfortable!"

What did Valkyn hope to achieve? Did he hope to recruit his adversary? Surely not! Tyros could have never been a party to such madness!

"Do you understand anything about where a mage draws his power from, Tyros?"

An elementary question. "From the magic of the world and its moons, as focused to us by the gods Solinari, Lunitari, and Nuitari. Without the three, we would be hard-pressed to perform even the slightest spells."

"But the elements required to first perform magic are the same no matter what order you choose, are they not?"

"I suppose."

"That they are!" Valkyn slapped him on the back. "How else would it be so easy for one to switch robes?" He indicated his own garments. "If it required complete retraining, few would ever shift from one color to the next, would they?"

Tyros didn't know if he followed Valkyn correctly or if he even cared what the mage meant. What did interest him was that not once since he had entered the chamber had thinking about magic caused his head to throb. Could he now perform a spell? If he could catch his captor unaware. . .

Valkyn grinned wider. "Oh, you shouldn't do that!"

The younger mage fell to the rail, his head now feeling as if it was about to split in two. His ebony-clad companion had to pull him back in order to keep Tyros from falling to his death. Tyros collapsed to his knees, holding his head and praying for the agony to end.

"You know how to stop the pain, my young friend. You know what you have to do. . . ."

Tyros forced all thoughts of casting spells from his mind, and as he did, the pain began to lessen. Tears still filling his eyes, he finally managed to look up at his captor. Instead he saw Serene.

"Does it have to hurt so much?" she pleaded with Valkyn.

"Not if he behaves, my Serene. Calm yourself. See? He's almost on his feet again!"

"That . . . was what . . . happened the first time we met!" the stricken mage snarled. "You had me brought here right after my capture, but when I struggled, you put this spell on me. That's what made me black out and forget our first meeting. I still tried to cast . . . to cast a spell . . . but I nearly died!"

Valkyn nodded approval. "An amazing recovery! I am impressed. You've a strong mind, a strong will, my friend."

He didn't like the way his counterpart complimented him, as if measuring Tyros for something in particular. That made the weary spellcaster think of Leot and the others. What had the mad mage needed them for?

"Valkyn," Serene murmured, "at least let him recuperate inside."

"Of course, my love, my serenity."

The shadows dragged Tyros back into the sumptuous chamber, leading their prisoner past the unblinking gargoyles to a well-cushioned chair, where they deposited him. Valkyn walked over to a large decanter, poured a bit of wine in a goblet, then tossed the goblet to Tyros. The captive mage reacted instinctively, then cursed when he saw the wine glass drift gently through the air, not a drop of its contents spilling. He seized it when it drew near, but paused to look at the liquid before drinking.

"You'll enjoy it," the goateed mage urged.

Tyros had to admit that it was excellent, but that in no manner warmed him to his host. He felt like the fatted calf waiting to be slaughtered.

Serene had seated herself on the edge of a couch, her eyes shifting from one man to the other. Valkyn filled two more goblets, then joined her. The cleric drank from hers with as much enthusiasm as had Tyros.

"As you may have guessed, a Solamnic Knight built this castle." Valkyn downed his wine. "A sad sort of fellow, I think, but he controlled great wealth. Have you noticed how few of our kind control great wealth? We generally find it for others, be they emperors, generals, or brigands. A minute share may go to us, but just as often we end up with a blade in our back. Not at all a fate worthy of a mage after so many years of study and effort. We should be the masters, not the lackeys."

"And so you'll conquer Ansalon and turn the world to your liking? You'll do what Ariakas could not?"

"Eventually, although General Cadrio down below will take a more immediate hand in it. Cadrio is a bit unstable, but daring, a trait I like. Of course, if he should become a bit too ambitious, which often happens with military officers, I'll replace him as simply as I can replace this."

The goblet in his hand melted completely.

There was no warning, no slow process. The goblet melted as if suddenly made of warm butter. The softening metal dripped over Valkyn's glove, yet did not burn or stain it. Valkyn opened his palm and let the molten metal fall between his fingers, creating a sizzling puddle on the rich floor. The shining puddle continued to sizzle, rapidly growing smaller. In just a few breaths, it dwindled to nothing.

For the first time, though, Tyros sensed some artifact or

item of power hidden within his captor's robes. It had flared during the spell that melted the goblet, but now had grown all but undetectable. Still, at least it gave him some explanation as to how Valkyn could seemingly perform endless magic.

"Serene thinks that you might be useful to me."

Surprised, Tyros could think of nothing to say. Serene had thought he might ally himself with Valkyn? Surely not! He looked but could read nothing in her face.

"She says that you are ambitious and ever thinking of how to glorify yourself. She acknowledges your intelligence, but believes you use it only to better suit your station. You're no villain, but neither are you a hero, which is why you wear the red, for lack of a more suitable color." Valkyn folded his arms behind him and walked toward his counterpart, eyes very much alive with speculation. "It would be interesting to summon forth a second citadel so quickly. I already have most of what I need to do that." Here he glanced at the cleric, who betrayed no emotion. "It would require one with ambition going beyond the archaic bounds of darkness and light to perform such a spell with me. You would fit the role splendidly, Tyros!"

It occurred to Tyros that Serene had likely suggested him in order to save his life. Certainly it would give the red mage the chance to discover Valkyn's secrets. "I am flattered by your offer and would find it impossible to turn down even if I—"

Valkyn chuckled. "Did I say anything about actually offering you such a chance? I was simply musing about what might have been." His smile turned cold. "Would you care to see how my creation works? How I've taken the design of the flying citadel and enhanced it?"

Tyros tried not to think of the spells involved in Atriun's function out of fear that he would again suffer agony. Very carefully, and with the knowledge that he had no choice anyway, the captive replied, "I would be honored to see it."

"Splendid! Serene, I think you should see this, too."

Valkyn indicated that they should rise. The shadowy

servants brought Tyros over to their master. Serene stepped to Valkyn's side as the goateed mage reached into his robes to retrieve a wand with a crystalline sphere atop it. Tyros recognized the sphere as a smaller version of the ones in the tower.

Valkyn held the wand high and muttered something. Tyros caught one or two words of magic, but no more.

They stood now in a different room.

The shift came with such swiftness that it caught even Tyros unaware. With most teleport spells, one usually felt some sense of displacement, but Valkyn's had brought them to their destination faster than the proverbial blink of an eye. What power did the other spellcaster wield . . . or rather, what power did the wand draw from? Tyros cut the thoughts short as his brain started to pound again.

"Valkyn, remove the spell!" Serene pleaded. "Can't you see that it's hurting him again?"

"Welcome to a place few have had the honor to visit," the dark mage announced, completely ignoring Serene. "Once this housed villains caught in the province, but now it acts as the focal point of my research, my life's work. Here I've turned theory into substance! Here I've taken magic to new directions!"

Tyros looked around. His eyes immediately widened.

Here stood the source of power for both Atriun and its master. Tyros had expected that it would in some ways resemble a Wind Captain's Chair, but on a larger, grander scale. In this Tyros was not disappointed, for before them stood two massive white marble columns that stretched almost to the ceiling, their sides etched from top to bottom with runes. On top of each marble column stood a golden crystalline sphere of gargantuan proportions. Each of the spheres crackled with raw sorcerous energy. Yet more astounding, that energy continually passed between the two crystals, building in intensity.

Tyros's head tingled, but this time he felt no pain. Despite misgivings, he marveled at how Valkyn had harnessed such energy, which clearly then transmitted to the tower above or the wizard's wand. Little wonder that Valkyn had been able to raise a behemoth such as Castle Atriun; with the power that Tyros sensed, the dark wizard might have raised a citadel twice as large.

Yes, Valkyn of Culthairai had indeed created a magical marvel, a flying citadel that did not require the constant chanting and spell casting of several wizards and clerics combined, but one element of his design would forever ensure that in the end Tyros would feel nothing but disgust for it. That element now hung limp between the two high columns, wrists and ankles stretched apart by the manacles holding him in place. Once the tattered cloth the figure wore had been white and the body within had filled it to near capacity. Now the robe hung loose, its wearer only a thin shadow of his former self. He looked dead, but now and then the head moved back and forth.

Tyros had found Leot . . . or what remained of him.

He eyed Serene, who had grown pale. Surely she had never expected Valkyn could be the cause of such evil. Valkyn might have come but late to the robes of Nuitari, but he had earned them well. Tyros doubted that many of the dark order would have dared what this foul mage had.

Valkyn pointed at Leot. Another shadow servant drifted over from the right side of the room. Tyros glanced around and saw that at least four more stood ready. Where had they come from?

The servant reached up and with bony, pale fingers, revealed Leot's face completely to the newcomers.

No pupils stared from the sockets, only the whites. The drawn, dead face looked years older than the man Tyros recalled, as if Leot had aged a hundred years. The soulless whites looked directly at the crimson-clad mage, but Tyros saw no recognition, no sign that Leot still existed in the shell before him.

With a shudder, he eyed the shadow servants again . . . and knew at last their origin. Valkyn might not have needed the chanting of clerics and wizards to keep Atriun in the sky, but he had other uses for his fellow spellcasters. These mages, including old Kendilious, had all suffered so that

Atriun could fly. Now Leot had been added to their unholy list.

The master of the citadel studied Leot's deathly face with the detachment one might have used studying a speck of dust. "As I thought. Not much left. We'll have to remove him soon."

A fury so great that he couldn't control it welled up within Tyros. Again he recalled Leot distracting the gargoyles in the tower in Gwynned. If not for the rotund wizard, it would have been Tyros hanging between these columns, his life burned from him.

Tearing himself free, Tyros lunged at Valkyn. Magic might be beyond the crimson wizard, but his hands were strong enough to throttle his foul counterpart. All he had to do was get them around Valkyn's throat.

Inches from his goal, his hands turned against him. Tyros's fingers snaked for his own throat, trying to squeeze the life from him. He grew more furious and tried to fight back, but his hands inched closer and closer.

"Tyros!" Serene called. "It's just as if you tried magic! Don't think about it! Let the hate go!"

Tyros tried desperately to forget his hatred of the other mage, to forget what Valkyn had done to Leot and others. He found it almost impossible, the image of the White Robe's slack expression still haunting him.

Finally, though, Tyros's hands relaxed, once more under his control. However, the effort he had put into saving himself had cost him, and he fell to one knee, trying to regain his strength.

The exhausted mage turned his thoughts to Serene, imagining the sorrow and horror she must be going through. To find out how horrific Valkyn had become and how oblivious he seemed to his own evil had to have shaken the cleric's faith to the core.

Tyros heard the harsh sound of boots and saw the robe of Valkyn near him. Still gasping, he looked up at the monstrously cheerful countenance of his captor.

"Yes, full of vigor, and more strength than I could have

imagined! You should never have gotten as near as you did!"

Near? Dwelling in his failure, Tyros thought about the futile attempt he had made. Near? He might as well have tried to leap the length of the New Sea!

"I think this charade's gone far enough." Without warning, Valkyn touched the tip of the wand against his adversary's temple.

A shock went through Tyros, and he blacked out.

*　*　*　*　*

For Serene, the day had become an endless horror. She had expected the worst when the gargoyle had snatched her off the griffon and taken her into Castle Atriun, but events had far exceeded even her most terrible nightmares.

When the gargoyle had deposited her in this grand chamber, the cleric had expected to confront some sinister servant of the goddess Takhisis, only to have instead a smiling Valkyn greet her with open arms. She had thrown herself happily into those arms, paying no heed to the change in the color of his robe. Even then Serene had assumed he wore them only because his captors demanded it.

Only when he had commanded the gargoyles to bring him Tyros had she at last admitted to herself that the one for whom she had so long hunted was not a captive, but instead the ruler of the flying citadel.

Even then Serene had tried to convince herself that Valkyn could not be the monster events so far had portrayed him. She could live with his apparent desertion of her, and even his raising of Castle Atriun the cleric could understand. It had always been Valkyn's dream to unlock the secrets of such magic and refine them. But Serene found it impossible to explain away the deaths and devastation in Norwych caused by his citadel.

He had noticed her growing coolness toward him, and although the mage had still smiled, that smile had been tinged by something she had never seen before in him, an emotion dark and unforgiving. Yet all the while Valkyn had treated her as his lost love, caressing her softly with his gloved fingers. Serene, attuned to Branchala's love of nature, had found the gloves unnerving, as if they represented a lack of humanity.

Then, when the gargoyles had finally brought Tyros in, the cleric saw for herself the terrible truth concerning her former love.

Tyros had not recalled this first encounter, not after what Valkyn had done to him, but for Serene it would ever be burned into her memory and her soul.

Valkyn had been very courteous, actually pleased by the presence of a wizard who understood his desire to create such a prize. Despite that, he had never allowed Tyros any semblance of freedom during their conversation, the monstrous Crag and two other gargoyles making certain of that.

Valkyn had talked on and on about the struggles of his research and the sacrifices he had made. He had asked Tyros about his own research, and when the other had not been forthcoming, Valkyn had simply gone on. To the despairing cleric, it seemed the maddening scene would continue forever.

Then Tyros had unleashed the spell he had been patiently working on since being brought to his captor.

The magical flash of light had not harmed the gargoyles much, but it had startled them into releasing their grips. Then, unlike his attempt during their second encounter, Tyros had managed to actually lay his hands on the still smiling Valkyn, grappling with him. Serene had stood there, struggling with old emotions and newer ones concerning Valkyn. That, to her regret, had slowed her reactions. Had Serene joined with Tyros immediately, they could have taken Valkyn and ended this terrible dream. Instead, the cleric had hesitated, pleading silently with the Bard King to tell her what to do.

By then it had been too late. Even the cleric could sense the sudden surge of sorcerous energy erupting from Valkyn. Tyros had been thrown back, shocked by miniature bolts of lightning so intense that they had left the black mage's gloves in burned tatters . . . and thereby revealed yet an even darker secret of the citadel's master.

Valkyn's hands no longer resembled anything human.

Scaled and scabbed, they looked as if they had been burned, flayed, then put together by someone with only a vague concept of their previous appearance. Most frightening, though, had been the glittering fragments speckling the hands from wrist to fingertips, glittering fragments that looked crystalline and gold, just like the tip of the wand Valkyn had pulled out a moment later.

"I had expected more sense, more appreciation from you, Tyros," Valkyn had said. He touched the palm of one of his hands with the wand. An inky black material had formed, spreading quickly over the hand until it covered it completely, a new glove hiding the deformities that Serene could only guess he had willingly given himself. A moment later he had covered the other hand as thoroughly. "We shall have to remedy this impetuousness of yours before we next speak."

Putting the wand away, Valkyn had then reached both hands toward the captive. Tyros had struggled, but now the gargoyles held him tighter.

"Valkyn!" she had called out. "For our love, don't kill him!"

"Oh, you needn't worry, my serenity," he had merrily responded. "I'm only making him a little more manageable."

His fingertips had touched Tyros's temples, immediately causing the latter to scream and scream and scream. This time Valkyn's gloves had not burned away, but she could still make out magical energy flowing from one man to the other.

"There! Required a little delicacy, but that should work!" As the goateed mage had pulled away, Tyros had collapsed in a heap, as if dead. However, Valkyn had pronounced him well but unconscious. "He will wake after a while, but it's possible that he won't remember anything of this meeting. I'll be interested to see if that holds true. The human mind is much more durable in some ways than those of a dwarf or an elf. Did you know that?"

She had not known it, and she didn't want to ask how Valkyn had come to that conclusion. He had always tended to learn through experimentation. "What will you do with him?"

"I haven't decided yet," he replied, his old smile back in place. "Is he a good friend of yours?"

"I've known him for only a short while." Despite saying that, Serene had already realized that Tyros could never have become another Valkyn. Even in the past, the cleric had recognized a reckless side to Valkyn, although at the time she had found it more exciting than potentially evil. Tyros, on the other hand, seemed to care more about life in general and had shown personal concern for her.

Valkyn had summoned two of the disturbing shadow servants, creatures that the cleric realized had once been human. Their arrival had presented yet an even more horrific side to the man she had once thought was her true love.

"Put this in one of the cells for now. You." He had pointed to the largest of the gargoyles. "Go along with them, Crag. Guard him. When he wakes, have them bring him back. He should be more docile then."

Serene watched the hideous creatures drag Tyros off. "What did you do to him?"

"Made him more reasonable, my serenity. If he should cast a spell or even think of magic too much, his head will teach him the consequences of such actions. The same if he tries to attack me physically." He shrugged. "I must protect myself, after all."

With Tyros gone, Valkyn had insisted that she join him on a great couch in the center of the room. The wizard acted as if neither their time apart nor his madness had ever happened. More than once the gloved hands had caressed her or touched her hair, and it had been all she could muster to not cringe or shiver. Serene had called on her training as a cleric of the Bard King, knowing that for a time she had to suffer Valkyn's advances if she hoped to help the others. She had no idea what had happened to Rapp and Captain Bakal, but slowly she had gathered that some of the gargoyles continued to hunt for them in and around the castle grounds. That had, for a time, given her hope.

The second encounter between the two wizards had crushed that hope, though, as first Tyros had unwittingly repeated his attempt on Valkyn, this time failing to even reach his adversary. Then, no longer seeing any use of Tyros as an ally, Valkyn had brought them both to this underground chamber to confront yet another monstrous display of his growing evil.

With this, the last vestiges of the cleric's love for the older spellcaster had died. Serene hadn't had to ask what poor soul hung between the great marble columns; Tyros's reaction had answered that. Leot of the Order of Solinari. So Tyros's search for Leot and hers for Valkyn had both ended in horrible failure, despite the fact that each had found whom he or she sought. At least Tyros hadn't discovered his friend at the heart of the darkness.

"Is he . . . is he dead, Valkyn?"

He misunderstood her, thinking she worried still about Tyros. "Of course not, my serenity! He would be a wasted asset then. No, he'll live." To the shadows, the wizard commanded, "Take him back again, but have him readied. The time nears!"

"What about . . . what about him? Does he . . . does he live?" She pointed at Leot.

Valkyn's eyes brightened, as they always did when he discussed a project of interest to him. How terrible that Serene had once looked into those blue eyes and found them beautiful. "Now, that is an interesting question. At this point, I'd have to say both yes and no, my love. No, the man who used to reside in that head is no more, but, yes, the body functions and an essence of some sort still exists." He indicated the shadow servants. "A very functional, useful essence, I've found."

The cleric shuddered. So her suspicions concerning the robed figures had been well founded. "So they've all been a part of this experiment of yours?"

"An integral part! These subjects were used for the preliminary tests, which proved quite successful, I might add! I dare say I couldn't have done all this without them, my Serene!"

She had to find out more. "What . . . what role do they play?"

He walked up to her and put a gloved hand on her cheek. "Now, my dear serenity, this is something you must not bother yourself with. I know that your role with the Bard King probably makes this entire matter disturbing to you, but in my field of work, some sacrifices must be made. Consider the great mage Fistandantilus! Had he not forced himself to go beyond the accepted boundaries of the magic of his time, a number of astonishing spells would not be available to us in this day and age! I promise you that eventually I'll have the spell work down to the point where such tactics as I've been forced to employ will not be necessary."

To her mind, the most frightening aspect concerning his explanation was his absolute seriousness. Valkyn either believed his own words or hid the truth very well.

"And what about Norwych?"

A flicker of anger escaped him, quickly covered again by his congenial mask. "We'll speak of this another time. I would rather that we dine now and talk of pleasant memories. I've thought of you often."

She had to play along. When at last Valkyn gave her time to herself, then Serene could pray to Branchala, ask him for the power to put an end to her former love's abomination . . . and, if necessary, him as well.

"Oh, one moment, my Serene."

The cleric turned, expecting that Valkyn had some last adjustments to make to his barbaric device. Instead, she found herself staring into his blue eyes, and then at the hand he had brought up to her face.

"A simple precaution, my serenity! I apologize."

He touched her temple.

The shock made her nearly fall over. Valkyn caught her in his other arm, then caressed her throbbing head with the very same hand that he had used to injure her.

"I'm terribly sorry, my Serene! It will pass, I promise you. The spell will keep you from gathering your wits enough to pray to your woodland god. I couldn't take the chance that you might do something misguided . . . say, try to rescue Tyros from his fate! I need him, after all." He looked over at the twin columns and the slumped form between. "Perhaps as early as tomorrow . . ."

Chapter 12

Plots and Counterplots

As the first glimmers of sunlight rose above the horizon, General Cadrio's fleet drifted slowly toward the southern shore of Northern Ergoth, to an area frequented by few other than fishermen. The vessels anchored offshore and began lowering their longboats. By the time the sun had risen, the first soldiers of the invading force had already established a beachhead, not that they feared discovery at this point.

The *Harpy* floated a little farther back, enabling Cadrio to watch the glorious proceedings through the wizard's eyeglass. He had sent Zander ahead to coordinate the landing and see to it that the invasion force remained battle ready. Cadrio himself had other plans to set into motion, plans that would require his absence from the fleet for a time.

"You had better be right, gargoyle," he muttered, lowering the eyeglass. The commander gazed skyward, his vulpine features making it seem he hunted for prey. In essence, Cadrio did, but not the prey most of his men would have expected. The general hunted for Valkyn and his accursed citadel.

Stone had said that there would come a time when the clouds around Atriun would thin so much that the human would be able to make out every detail of the dark castle even from the ground. Then and only then would the citadel and its master truly be vulnerable, and only for a short time. If Cadrio sought to claim Atriun for his own, he would have to strike at that time.

The general hoped to take his prize without the immediate loss of the wizard. Until Cadrio completely understood how to create and control such a fortress, he needed his so-called ally.

"Ally . . . a lackey is what you wanted all the time, wasn't it, mage? Marcus Cadrio is no man's lackey! I'll be no puppet on the throne while you rule from the heavens! This alliance is dead . . . not that it ever lived at all!"

One of his officers stepped up, saluting. "I have him, sir!"

The eager commander looked at the robed figure standing next to the officer. A wizard of the Black Robes, one Rudolpho by name. Young, talented, but manageable. The brightest of the few still left to General Cadrio.

"So, Rudolpho . . ."

The mage bowed his head. "Yes, General?"

Much more polite, much more cognizant of his place in Cadrio's schemes. Yes, he would do. "Rudolpho, you know why I've had you summoned from the *Darksword*?"

In reply, the tall, blond mage glanced up. Rudolpho had a plain but intelligent face and, to Cadrio's further pleasure, was a cousin of loyal Zander. If Rudolpho obeyed his directions half as well as Zander, things would go very well indeed.

"Yes, the citadel. You understand where your loyalties lie?"

The wizard frowned. "Not all the mages who vanished into Valkyn's castle wore white or crimson robes, sir. He knows no loyalty to the orders, whatever color his garments. In my eyes, he is a renegade and so should be squashed like a bug!"

"Excellent! You're the man I want with me!"

Anticipation crept into Rudolpho's expression. "What do you want me to do, sir?"

"You see the dragons?"

Murk and Eclipse perched on a rocky islet just off shore. The pair looked impatient. They had been told their part and looked forward to it. They didn't like Valkyn. Eclipse had asked if he could eat the upstart wizard and had been terribly disappointed when told that Cadrio still had some need for the spellcaster. Still, the general had offered them as many gargoyles as they desired, Stone included. Cadrio wanted nothing of the creatures; he did not trust their kind nor have any military use for them. Stone had been willing to betray one master; he might decide to try it again at some later date.

"Yes, sir. They'll carry the two of us up there?"

"Along with a few carefully picked men . . . and all providing that the storm dies soon and the clouds thin. Supposedly he'll be weakest then."

The mage pondered this. "He must have to recast some spell or replenish some component involved in the device used to control the citadel. That would explain why he would need to focus his magic on that task instead of defenses. General, there is the risk that by interrupting him we will send the citadel falling."

"I'll take that risk, but if you find your blood too thin for this—"

"No, sir, I do not." Rudolpho clearly thought about Atriun's secrets and how they could enhance his reputation.

"We must keep careful watch and wait for the proper moment."

The wizard looked skyward again. "If I may, General, where is the flying citadel now?"

And there lay the one point of frustration for Cadrio. Where, indeed, was the flying citadel? With Atriun able to take a more direct route, Valkyn should have already been here long before. What could have caused the delay?

"My lord!" interrupted the officer who had brought Rudolpho to him. "To the east!"

Cadrio and the wizard looked where he pointed. In the distance, a speck far too dark and far too swift for a cloud moved toward them. Cadrio looked through the eyeglass, verifying the sight. "It's him . . . it's Valkyn!"

He turned the eyeglass back to Northern Ergoth, where his forces continued to land. Zander had everything in order. By the time Valkyn reached the fleet, most of the soldiers would be on dry land, ready to march at a moment's notice.

"Everything moves as planned," he informed the others. "Now we only have to wait—" the commander chuckled, a rare thing from him—"for a break in the weather."

* * * * *

Tyros again woke in the cell, this time feeling worse than ever. Unlike his previous awakening, he remembered everything from his last encounter with the other mage. He remembered how Valkyn's magic had sent him to his knees and how Serene had been unable to do anything to stop it. Most of all, Tyros recalled Leot, poor Leot, whom he had arrived too late to save.

Valkyn would pay for Leot, pay for the other mages he had used, but how? Not only was Tyros manacled again, but with the spell cast upon him, he couldn't perform magic. Valkyn thought so little of Tyros's chances now that he hadn't even left much of a guard, only one of the sinister shadows. Of course, even one was more than he could handle.

Tyros studied the still figure. Had he not known better, Tyros might have thought the shadow was nothing more than a statue.

"Do you talk?" he finally asked.

The figure remained motionless.

"Do you remember who you were?"

Still nothing.

Tyros had no idea why he tried. From what he had seen, nothing human remained. Yet still the captive spellcaster tried. "Did you serve Lunitari? Solinari? Nuitari?"

He received no response. Frustrated, his head beginning to throb, Tyros slumped back. He thought about Serene again. Could she fool Valkyn long enough to do something? He had his doubts. Even as the goateed mage had been caressing her cheek, he had been laying hints that he did not entirely trust his onetime love.

Tyros stared at the wall beyond the cell, trying to think of some nonmagical solution for escape. Nothing, though, would do him any good if he couldn't free his wrists.

Time passed. After what seemed an eternity, Tyros heard someone come near. The weary mage looked and saw only a gargoyle. The creature paid no attention to him, moving past the cell and the ghoulish guard as if on some mission. Tyros looked away, once more absorbed in futile plots of escape.

A sudden, savage hiss startled Tyros and made him look up. Incredibly, the gargoyle had turned and attacked the shadow servant. The creature had one hand on the robed figure's throat, his other hand around one of the ghoul's wrists. Despite the gargoyle's tremendous strength, he immediately began to lose ground. The shadow servant's ice-white fingers closed in on the attacker's throat.

In desperation, the winged creature released his hold on his hooded adversary. Immediately the robed servant sought the gargoyle's neck.

The gargoyle raked his talons across the ghoul's chest, tearing deep into pale flesh.

Tyros hadn't thought such wounds would bother what seemed to be walking dead, but the once-human abomination immediately collapsed. Dark, thick blood slowly oozed from the wounded area.

No longer threatened by his foe's hands, the gargoyle slashed again, this time cutting across the throat.

The shadow servant crumpled, now definitely dead.

Claws still bloody, the winged creature moved to Tyros's cell.

The mage took a chance. "Stone?"

His visitor nodded. "Yes. Am Stone. Must come, Tyros!"

"Only if you can do something with these." The human indicated his manacled wrists.

In response, the sleek gargoyle took hold of the cell door and pulled hard. With a wrenching sound, the lock ripped apart. Stone pushed the ruined door aside and hurried over to the prisoner.

"Impressive," Tyros had to admit. "Can you do the same with these?"

His rescuer inspected the manacles and nodded. "Harder, but can do."

With a delicacy that surprised Tyros, the gargoyle seized one of the manacles near the lock, positioned his thick fingers, and pulled. Every muscle grew taut. The wizard could read the intense effort in his rescuer's inhuman visage.

The manacle tore open.

Stone gasped for breath, then quickly went to the remaining chain. Perhaps encouraged by his previous success, the gargoyle took only a few seconds to break the last manacle. He stepped back, clearly exhausted by his effort but pleased with the results.

Tyros rubbed his freed wrists. "Thank you. Where are we going?"

"Friends." Stone would explain no more. He nearly dragged Tyros from the cell. "Hurry! Little time!"

To Tyros's confusion, the gargoyle did not lead him upward, but rather down into the lower depths of the castle. The corridors they traversed were musty, cobweb-ridden, and looked as if no one had used them in centuries. He would have questioned his guide, but Stone moved with such determination that Tyros had to assume he knew where he was going.

Although a few emerald crystals in the walls illuminated the corridors, it still proved difficult to see where they were heading. Only when they entered a vast chamber and Tyros noticed the first of the massive marble platforms did he realize that Stone had led him to, of all places, the castle's crypt.

Great marble coffins with the names of the interred chiseled on the front end lay atop several of the platforms. Two bore the symbols of the Solamnic Knighthood, the kingfisher with the crown, sword, and rose. Tyros counted six massive coffins in all, with two more open and ready for use. For all its size, this burial chamber had been little used. The rest of the room consisted of empty platforms or unfilled slots in the walls. Apparently the family history of Castle Atriun had been a short, bleak one.

Of the six coffins, the lids of three lay crooked, perhaps the result of the citadel being ripped from the earth. Tyros couldn't resist glancing in the nearest, but saw little other than the armored form of a man, a sword on his breastplate.

Tyros silently cursed his training; wizards were only tutored in the use of daggers and staffs. If he took the weapon and tried to make use of it, he would likely end up cutting his own leg off.

At the far end of the crypt, Stone waited impatiently for him. Tyros quickly rejoined his companion, but instead of moving on, the gargoyle indicated a stone wall to the side. Only after staring close did the mage see that part of the wall was a door.

"Here." Stone tugged on a ringed handle, with effort pulling the immense door open. A sense of dread spread over Tyros. Did Stone intend to hide him here? The mage felt a touch of claustrophobia. To be entombed alive for his own safety?

A cough from within set every nerve on edge.

"Stone?" muttered a voice.

"Yessss . . . with another."

A figure emerged from the gloom, an emerald crystal in his hand illuminating him just enough to reveal his identity.

"Bakal?"

"By Corij's sword! Tyros!"

"Tyros?" popped up a second, higher-pitched voice. Rapp pushed his way forward. "I knew Stone would find you!"

Tyros and the gargoyle joined them in the hidden chamber. Stone closed the door while Tyros finished greeting Bakal and the kender. As pleased as the wizard was with being reunited with his friends, his enthusiasm remained low. Serene was still the unwilling guest of Valkyn, and Tyros had no magic with which to rescue her. Worse, he suspected Bakal and the others, ignorant of the spell cast upon the red wizard, expected Tyros to lead them to victory.

"Bakal, before everyone raises his hopes, I have something I must tell all of you." Without preamble, the weary spellcaster related to them the tale of his encounters with Valkyn and what had resulted from them. Although he made the story short, Tyros left out no horrific detail, especially when explaining the curse under which the citadel's master had left him. Now and then his head throbbed some, but fortunately, because of the swiftness of his tale, never for very long.

The captain glared at Stone. "You didn't tell me any of this!"

The gargoyle shrugged.

"By the Sea Queen! Here we need magic to fight magic, and the only one who can wield it no longer can!" Bakal eyed Tyros. "So if you can't cast a spell, is there anything you can suggest, boy?"

Tyros had mulled over such a question himself and had come up with only one answer. "Even though I cannot cast spells or even think about magic much, I believe that if I can get back into the chamber where Valkyn's device is located, I can do something to stop its foul work!"

"What about his curse on you?"

"I have to try, Bakal. We have no choice."

The Ergothian officer clearly still didn't like his answers, but had none better. "All right. So we go charging into this nightmare of a chamber—"

"No. A large party would be too noticeable. Besides, I need you to find the griffons and send warning to Gwynned in case I don't succeed."

"We're not leaving, mage. We came to either capture this citadel or destroy it. I've just thought of something better. While you go after the heart of this infernal fortress, we'll go after the Wind Captain's Chair. If we seize that, it doesn't matter what Valkyn tries. We'll be in command of the situation!"

Tyros thought Bakal underestimated the black wizard. "Captain—"

"It's settled. Either that or we all come with you, Tyros."

In the wizard's mind, that would be worse. He imagined the soldiers among the delicate yet lethal items in Valkyn's sanctum. "All right."

"What about Serene?" Rapp asked, "or Taggi and the others?"

Tyros drew himself up. "If I succeed, I will go after her."

"But what if you don't? I can go get her."

"No!" Tyros came to a quick decision. "You will serve Serene and the rest of us best by gathering the griffons together. They will listen to you. We need them ready for escape."

The kender still wanted to go rescue Serene, but Tyros felt that was his duty. Only he dared face Valkyn, even if bereft of power. Tyros had faced the madman twice and now believed he knew what to expect. This time, the gods willing, he would see to it that the black wizard paid for his heinous acts.

With Rapp silenced, Tyros turned to Stone. "You've helped us this far. There is no turning back." When the gargoyle nodded his understanding, Tyros continued. "Of all of us, you know Atriun the best. We need to know the safest, swiftest paths to our destinations and what dangers we might come across on the way. You cannot leave out anything. Let's start with the tower. . . ."

Stone nodded again and began to describe as well as he could how Bakal might best hope to reach the Wind Captain's Chair. Tyros also listened, but his thoughts were focused mostly on his quest. Although the mage hoped to save Serene and the others, he had decided that, one way or another, the citadel had to be destroyed. No one could be permitted to reproduce Valkyn's monstrous spellwork and arcane devices. Atriun had to fall, even if Tyros perished with it.

Even if *everyone* had to perish with it.

* * * * *

Valkyn watched Serene's reflection in his goblet, reading her conflicting emotions and knowing that she found his work, and him, horrifying.

She had never truly understood the depths to which his research had taken him, and Valkyn had never bothered to explain. Their first few months together had been sweet, her visits to his lone abode in the woods a welcome interruption. As a cleric of Branchala, she had understood the need for solitude and how it allowed one to clear one's mind and keep one's faculties sharp.

Serene had proven useful for his research. She could read the currents of the world, the forces that bound Krynn together. The cleric had shown how this part of the forest communed with that part and how all lived in harmony unless something was done to disrupt matters. Valkyn had taken all of these concepts and molded them to fit his needs.

Serene had wondered about his disappearances but had been led to believe they had to do with official matters of his order. She had assumed that mages were much like clerics, a mistake he had never rectified. Instead of journeying to the tower to converse with the senior wizards, he had set out to test his more monstrous theories, performing the precursors to the spells she now found so abominable.

She would understand some day, even if he had to make her understand. . . .

"Did you enjoy your meal?" Valkyn asked, trying to remember to keep his voice light. He glanced her way and saw that she now kept her expression neutral.

"It was delicious."

"Thank you. Now I must ask you to remain quiet for a moment." He looked past her, where two of Crag's gargoyles squatted. "See that she does."

Ignoring her anxious look, Valkyn walked to the balcony, taking up a position at the rail. He closed his eyes and concentrated, drawing the magic through his wand. The power came, albeit with more sluggishness. It would soon be time to put Tyros to use. Valkyn suspected that Tyros would last longer than the pathetic white wizard had.

With enough power now at hand, Valkyn's spell took immediate effect. Instead of the balcony, Valkyn suddenly stood on the deck of the *Harpy*. True, it was not the real Valkyn, but an illusion with some substance, as the hapless young Timinion had discovered.

"Mage."

For once he didn't have the pleasure of seeing Cadrio start. This time the general calmly and respectfully awaited his appearance. Evidently Cadrio had finally come to accept this secondary position in the alliance.

"Aaah, my general! So good to see that you've made it!"

"Made it? We were here before you, Valkyn. What kept your precious toy? Is that thing so slow?"

Although he smiled, inside, the black wizard fumed. "Of course not. I simply felt it better to rectify a few matters before crossing to Northern Ergoth. Any capable commander would do the same, wouldn't he?"

"How soon can we march? My men are ready. We've even taken some small outposts in order to cut off warning to Gwynned."

"I imagine that Gwynned has warning already, although it will avail them little!"

"What do you mean?"

The mage let some of his sense of triumph seep through. "Let us just say that you won't have much to fear from the golden dragons, Cadrio. Eclipse and Murk should be able to handle their parts in this battle without looking like fools!"

The general glanced around, almost as if afraid that his two black dragons would hear and be offended. "Something's happened?"

"Gwynned is open to us. That's all you need to know."

He smiled at the commander, aware that his enigmatic words frustrated the man. Cadrio would take out his frustration on Gwynned. In truth, Valkyn didn't care about Gwynned or the rest of Northern Ergoth; his concerns centered around how his citadel would handle the more volatile weather conditions in this region. Norwych had been located in a relatively calm area, where the only storm had been of his own doing. Gwynned's changeable weather would prove just how strong his spell work was, not that Valkyn actually expected any difficulties with it. He had planned long for this moment.

"Expect to meet Gwynned's forces well outside of the city, Cadrio. They'll have some idea of what they face, but not all."

"I wanted the element of surprise. I don't consider heavy losses acceptable, mage."

Valkyn's smile grew colder. "Gwynned's generals will meet you on the field with the assumption that they, so familiar with the land, will have the upper hand. They may have the use of one dragon, but poor use he'll be. Draw them out. With your army, your dragons, and my citadel, your victory over Gwynned—and then the rest of Northern Ergoth—will be assured!"

From his sleeve, Valkyn produced a scroll, which he tossed toward the general. The scroll twinkled in midflight, then fell onto the deck before the startled commander. "The suggestions I mentioned."

Cadrio retrieved the scroll, then looked it over. His avian features took on a darker cast. "This is a complete battle plan!"

"I thought I'd try my hand at it this time."

"I know how to fight wars, Valkyn!"

"Yes, I remember your first attack on Gwynned. I think you'll find this much more promising." The ebony-clad wizard steepled his fingers. "Follow it to the letter."

Cadrio nodded glumly. "As you wish."

Valkyn had expected more argument from the man, but perhaps Cadrio had seen the brilliance of his tactics. "Excellent! Begin the march, then. I shall speak with you when all is in position."

With that, Valkyn ended the spell, his view once more that of the balcony. He exhaled, quite pleased with the way everything had begun to come together. Cadrio knew his part. The citadel would be ready to wreak its full fury upon the Ergothian forces. Serene had returned to him . . . and had also provided Valkyn with the one item he had needed.

Tyros.

He would need much rest for the coming events. Valkyn turned to Serene, who had not dared to move. "My love, I fear that you'll have to entertain yourself for a while."

At his silent command, the gargoyles stirred.

"Valkyn, if we could just speak with one another—"

One of the winged monsters took hold of her arm.

"Take her to her quarters. See that she doesn't leave them." The goateed mage turned away. A moment later he heard Serene and the gargoyles depart.

She would come to love him again; he would see to that. For now, though, Valkyn had no time to think of affairs of the heart. He had glory to achieve, and to do that he had to sleep.

"Come here."

A shadow servant materialized, eager to be commanded. Once bereft of the soul that had occupied their bodies, the robed figures needed him to tell them everything.

"I am not to be disturbed until the eleventh hour."

The servant's head dipped.

"You know how to deal with those who would interrupt my slumber."

Again the head dipped. Valkyn waved off the foul creature, then retired to his bed.

Yes, everything had begun to fall into place.

* * * * *

General Cadrio threw the scroll to the deck. It rolled away, unnoticed by him, but one of his officers had the presence of mind to sweep it up before something happened. . . just in case.

"Alert Zander to begin marching!" he commanded the nearest man. "Inform him that the Ergothians know of our presence and that he should move with caution but still maintain a rapid pace. Tell him that one way or another, the flying citadel will be there."

He glared at the distant edifice, wishing he could pull it down and teach the impudent wizard just who commanded here. "Get Rudolpho. I want him by my side from now on. Where's Eclipse? Where's Murk?"

An aide swallowed. "Still where they perched, sir!"

"Tell them to be ready!" Cadrio began to pace the deck, ever avoiding the spot last occupied by the unfortunate Timinion. "The moment those clouds thin, I want to be in the air!" He pictured the wizard's mocking face. "I want his head!"

Chapter 13

Disaster

Serene sat on the edge of her lavish bed, feeling more confused than she ever had in her entire life. Everything had seemed so simple when she, a woodsman's daughter, had suddenly been offered the role of cleric by the old woman who had for years taught her the ways of the wild. Serene had known of the old gods from her parents, still worshipers of the Bard King despite his absence from Krynn for centuries, but like most had assumed that they and the true clerics would never return. She had accepted the offer, never once since questioning her choice.

She had traveled much of Ansalon during her first few months, then settled in the forest where her family had lived for generations, rarely seeing other people unless they happened to pass through. Her devotion to her calling had helped her with her solitude, guided her through her relationship with Valkyn, then aided her in her search for answers afterward. No matter what had happened, Serene had always had her link to her god.

Now it seemed Valkyn had taken that away.

When she touched her medallion and tried to concentrate, she nearly blacked out. Unlike Tyros, Serene never felt any pain; she simply lost consciousness. A sign of Valkyn's lingering devotion, perhaps, the cleric thought sourly.

Even thinking about Branchala made her light-headed. Serene had always admired Valkyn's skill at his craft, but never once had she thought that those powers would be turned against her.

The gargoyles had left her alone once they had seen her to her chamber. Now was Serene's chance to accomplish something. Tyros and the others needed her. They didn't know Valkyn as she did, although even she had to admit he remained largely an enigma. The man Serene had loved did not exist, possibly never had. Still, the cleric felt she had the best hope of understanding Valkyn's mind and using it to her advantage.

She clutched the medallion, at the same time taking a deep breath to help prevent her from collapsing.

"Branchala," Serene whispered, thinking of Valkyn's powerful magic and what it might do if left unchecked. "Branchala, hear me! Guide my strength again as you've done in the past. Branchala . . ."

The room spun around. Serene tried to rise, but at that moment, the floor chose to do the same.

She fell, only at the last minute managing to twist enough to keep from falling to the hard floor. The cleric landed on the bed. The room continued to spin about.

"Branchala . . ." Serene managed to whisper. She would not black out. She would not!

It seemed the dizziness would never end, but at last the cleric found she could think again . . . but not if those thoughts turned to her god.

"Damn you, Valkyn!" Serene had failed Tyros and the others, failed herself and her god as well. Still, at least this time she had kept herself from blacking out.

A tiny victory, though. Perhaps, given time, she could break his powerful spell, but time was something of which Serene had very little. Gwynned's doom lay but a few hours away, and Tyros's fate even less. Bakal and Rapp might already be dead.

The cleric clutched her medallion, feeling impotent. Without her god, though, what could she do . . . even for herself?

* * * * *

It had been years since Tyros had done anything of consequence without the benefit of magic to make the task easier. At this moment, he would have given nearly everything to regain his abilities. Tyros felt no shame at such thoughts; to wizards, magic meant life. The only things that concerned him more at the moment were the fates of his companions, Serene most of all.

He could only imagine the mental torment she suffered. Tyros had been tempted to go searching for her first, rather than seeking the heart of the citadel. In the end, though, he had known that everyone's best hope, the cleric's included, rode on his sabotage of Valkyn's sinister toy.

Tyros went over Stone's instructions. Stone had given him a fairly detailed description as to how to get to Valkyn's sanctum. The gargoyle had wanted no mistakes made, emphasizing how much this meant to his flock.

That did not mean that all gargoyles could be considered friends. Stone had warned him about Crag's people. They would serve the master no matter what, reveling in the chaos and bloodshed he brought forth. Crag especially sought the good favor of Valkyn, thinking that it would make him look even stronger in the eyes of the other gargoyles.

A slight clink of metal made Tyros curse. He had done the unthinkable, the unforgivable. In his left hand he carried the sword of the Solamnic Knight. Mages were forbidden such weapons. All the covenants spelled this out in black and white.

Tyros didn't care. He had wanted—no, *needed*—that sword, oaths and laws be damned.

He started down a new corridor, then immediately backtracked. Pressing against the nearest wall, Tyros held his breath as a large gargoyle stalked past. The powerless mage remained frozen, uncertain whether even with the sword he could kill the monster before it tore him to pieces.

Fortunately the gargoyle, clearly not one of Stone's folk, continued on. When at last the monster had vanished down the hall, Tyros hurried on his own way. If Stone's directions held true, the wizard couldn't be far from the chamber where Valkyn kept his horrific device.

Sure enough, he came across the doors but a few minutes later. Although Tyros's own memories of this area consisted mostly of the chamber's interior, he knew that this had to be the place he sought. Not only did it fit with the gargoyle's directions, but even from out here Tyros could sense the awesome power within the chamber.

No guards stood at the doors, but that didn't mean that none waited inside. Still, from what Tyros knew of his counterpart, Valkyn's arrogance might lead the black mage to believe that nothing could harm him from within his own abode. Cautiously the mage crept to the entrance, sword ready. Tyros touched one door gingerly, then with more force when no spell attacked him.

The door swung open with a loud squeak.

Gritting his teeth, he leaped inside, the sword wobbling in his grip. Tyros had assumed correctly; in the center of the great chamber stood the massive marble columns with the huge golden crystals, from which pulsated pure magical energy. Here stood Valkyn's infernal marvel, the secret not only to keeping Atriun afloat, but also to powering the deadly storm surrounding the citadel.

And here also hung what remained of Leot.

Head throbbing slightly, Tyros started for the columns with the intention of cutting his friend free, only to pause halfway there and look uneasily to his side. Not one but four of the ghostly servants of Valkyn stood nearby, staring in his direction.

Turning his weapon toward the nearest, Tyros waited for them to attack. Yet not one so much as raised a bony hand toward him. When Tyros moved, he saw that they continued to look past his prior position. The servants stood as if statues, their will nonexistent without Valkyn to guide them.

Breathing a little easier, the crimson-clad mage made his way to the columns. He lowered the sword to the ground, then moved closer to the still figure.

"Leot . . ." Tyros cupped the other wizard's head in one hand. Up close, the damage the spell work had wrought on the white-robed spellcaster looked even more terrible. Little flesh remained on the man; Leot looked as if he had died long ago. His hair had turned pale, and the robes draped over him, now several sizes too large for what had once been a massive frame. "Leot?"

No response. Valkyn's hellish mechanism had burned away all that had been the once cheerful mage.

In some ways it made Tyros's task a little easier. With no need to worry about Leot, he could press ahead with what he truly needed to do. Taking hold of one of the manacles, he inspected the lock. Without magic, Tyros needed either a key or a way to smash it open. He looked around, deciding at last to inspect the several large tables and benches where the dark wizard evidently kept much of his equipment. Perhaps there he would find a key.

Moving closer, he quickly looked over various objects, trying not to think of their possible uses. Each time he did, his head throbbed, throwing his concentration off. Nothing on the first tables he surveyed resembled a key, but surely Valkyn had to have one somewhere in case of emergency.

Tyros surveyed the entire chamber again. At last his eyes alighted on a ring on the far side of the room. Two keys hung from the ring, which had been looped around a knob in the wall. Could it be so simple? Tyros shook his head and started for the keys. He had to try them.

The keys were in good condition, not rusted as they might have been if left over from the days of the castle's initial construction. Surely these were the ones Tyros sought.

He had taken only a few steps back when he realized that the shadow servants had begun to close on him.

Three were nearly upon him, the fourth still several steps behind. Taking the keys had done it. Until then they hadn't seen Tyros as a threat. Now, though, he endangered their master's work. How terrible, Tyros thought, that these victims of Valkyn's evil would now defend his monstrous device.

Tyros threw himself toward the columns just as pale, bony hands groped for him. He slid against one column, hitting his shoulder then colliding with the sword. Desperate, Tyros seized the blade and rose just as the first of the servants came at him. More out of luck than any hint of skill, the wizard shoved the tip of the blade into the torso of the murky figure.

With a raspy gasp, the cloaked form fell to the floor. Tyros stared at the black, thick substance dripping from his sword, momentarily feeling sick to his stomach.

One of the other ghouls seized his right arm. Tyros brought the sword's edge down on the elbow of his attacker and watched in shock as the blade cut through, leaving the lower part of the limb still clutching him. Undaunted, the servant tried to grapple with his remaining hand.

Tyros managed to bring the sword across his foe's neck. Black fluid, akin to molasses, dripped from the creature's throat, some of it spattering Tyros. At last the shadow servant collapsed, still trying to maintain a hold on him.

Tyros shook off the limb still attached to him, then backed to the columns. He had been lucky so far, but the remaining pair would surely not fall so easy. Measuring the gap still between the hooded figures and him, the mage worked anxiously to unlock the manacles that held Leot's feet.

His head throbbed dangerously as he worked, for Tyros couldn't help thinking about what he hoped to accomplish. Leot was part of the mechanism. Without him, surely it couldn't function properly. Valkyn's spell would cease. All Tyros had to do was free the white mage's body and remove it from the area of the columns.

Or so he hoped.

Finished with the lower manacles, the red wizard finally undid one wrist. Tyros caught Leot's limp form as it tipped to the side. The energy passing between the two huge crystalline spheres seemed to lessen. Tyros tried pulling the corpse out from between the columns but couldn't. He would have to undo the last manacle.

Caught up in his efforts, Tyros miscalculated the time he had remaining. He realized too late that one of Valkyn's horrific minions had reached him. The macabre figure seized the hand that held the keys, turning the mage about. Tyros tried to attack, but the hooded ghoul knocked his sword away. As they struggled, the pair twisted around in front of the columns, Tyros's situation quickly becoming more desperate.

He tried to push the shadow servant into one of the marble columns, but the creature was too powerful.

Then a white arm wearing the remnants of a pale garment fell forward, wrapping around the shadow servant's neck and pulling Tyros's attacker back. Caught by surprise, the servant released his hold. Tyros stepped back, staring in shock as Leot held the guard tight, his arm squeezing. His friend stared sightlessly ahead, only the whites of his eyes showing. The drawn, wrinkled face bore no expression. Nothing indicated that anything of Leot remained, and yet Tyros could find no explanation as to why the seemingly limp corpse had moved to save him. Perhaps Tyros had just been fortunate. Leot's reaction might have been the same if he had come too close.

And yet . . .

He had no more time in which to ponder his second rescue by the White Robe, for the last of the guards still sought him. Encouraged by what had happened, Tyros retrieved the Solamnic Knight's blade and charged, thrusting with all his might. The hooded servant caught the blade with his pale hands, but momentum kept it going. Tyros pushed the blade into his adversary's chest up to the hilt.

His foe dropped, trapping the sword in death. At the same time, Tyros heard a harsh cracking sound from behind him. He quickly turned, thinking the last of the shadow servants had freed himself, only to watch the ghoul slump, his neck broken by Leot.

Leot, too, slumped, as if this last effort had used up whatever hint of life remained. Tyros rushed to the other mage's side, undoing the last of the manacles. He dragged Leot free, noticing only peripherally that the energy flowing between the columns had completely ceased. The spheres still glowed, but with less intensity than before. Still, the link had obviously been broken.

Not at all concerned at the moment with the consequences of what he had wrought, Tyros turned Leot over. The other wizard continued to stare without seeing. His chest did not rise and Tyros could feel no pulse.

"Leot? Can you hear me at all?" He knew the answer already but prayed he might be wrong. "Leot . . ."

The figure in white exhaled. The eyelids fluttered closed.

Tyros wished that he could bury or burn Leot's body in order to keep it from any foul use Valkyn might think of. Yet the frustrated mage could do nothing for his friend now, especially considering that others still needed his aid.

With much reluctance, Tyros abandoned Leot in order to inspect the columns. The spheres glowed dimmer, but so far nothing else had changed. He had expected the citadel to continue to fly for a time, assuming that its creator would have thought of such a need. Even though Tyros despised the other mage's handiwork, he had to admit that Valkyn had performed wonders.

One question of great importance remained for the red mage to answer. Now that he had disrupted the source of Valkyn's great power, had he regained his own ability to cast spells? Tyros's head throbbed, but that could be the results of his earlier efforts.

Tyros began to mutter the basic words to create an illusion of fire . . . and nearly fell to the floor as raging pain filled his head. Only by forcing himself instead to think of other matters—Serene's safety, Bakal's dangerous trek—did he keep from losing consciousness.

So Valkyn's curse held, although it seemed weaker. Still, if Tyros couldn't perform spells, that weakness hardly mattered. His only hope lay in Serene, who, as a cleric, might be able to overcome Valkyn's sinister curse with a prayer to her god.

The sword remained embedded in the shadow servant's chest. A search of the chamber revealed nothing worthwhile until the mage discovered what seemed to be another wizard's staff, left almost without thought against the edge of one of the tables. Tyros hefted it, pleased to have the weapon but wondering if it would serve him. He didn't have time to study what spells had been imbued in it, much less if they would work for him. Nevertheless, the unknown staff gave him something of a chance.

Weapon in hand, Tyros finally left the chamber. No one waited in the halls. Tyros listened but heard no sounds of alarm. Captain Bakal had not yet made his move, then.

The mage continued on, certain that at any moment he would confront a foe. Yet after several anxious minutes, he had seen only two gargoyles, and both of those were perched outside a window, their attention fixed on something beyond his view. Tyros hurried away from them, not caring what interested them as long as it kept the pair from noticing him.

He again followed Stone's directions. The gargoyle hadn't been absolutely certain which quarters Serene had been given, but he had believed that Valkyn would only assign her to one of two. Much to Tyros's relief, both chambers lay near one another, which meant he wouldn't have to search an entire section of the immense castle.

His good fortune seemed to end at last at the intersection of two wide corridors. There a figure shrouded in dark robes stepped around the corner just as he came from the other direction. Tyros managed to fall back immediately but felt certain that he had been discovered. Thinking quickly, the powerless spellcaster slipped into a nearby alcove, then waited, with staff ready, for the shadow servant to come.

A minute passed, then another, and still no one came.

Peering out, Tyros saw nothing. Curious, he returned to the intersection. A quick glance revealed no evidence of the shadow's passing. The macabre figure had simply vanished.

With some trepidation, he moved on again. Moments later Tyros came upon a staircase that Stone had described, one that led not only up to where Valkyn kept Serene but also to the dark mage's own private chambers. Gripping the staff tighter, Tyros ascended.

He reached the top undetected, but now the mage risked an encounter with Valkyn himself, and that forced him to move slowly, eyes ever shifting back and forth. He had been fortunate so far, but in addition to the possible presence of the black mage, Stone had warned him that a guard might stand duty outside of Serene's chambers. Valkyn didn't even trust the woman he had once loved.

Sure enough, down the hall where he had expected to find Serene's chambers stood a huge brown gargoyle. The creature didn't look at all pleased with his task. He watched the hall with fiery eyes, ready to pounce on any who did not have the master's permission to pass this way.

Tyros remained out of sight around a corner, wondering what to do. He had originally assumed that disrupting Valkyn's grand device would give him back his powers, but that hadn't been the case. He could try using the magic of the staff, but he didn't know whether the spells would work or if doing so might trigger Valkyn's curse, leaving him at the mercy of the gargoyle.

That left his physical skill with the staff. While many mages soon forgot the lessons of hand-to-hand combat they had learned as apprentices, Tyros remembered his. Whether those lessons would work against such a creature, though . . .

Taking a deep breath, Tyros started around the corner again.

The warning cries of a host of gargoyles suddenly echoed through the citadel. The guard turned away from Tyros, peering toward the nearest window. Seizing the opportunity, Tyros raced toward him, staff held high. The cries of the other gargoyles continued to reverberate through the corridor, drowning out his footfalls.

At the last moment, the massive creature started to turn back. Tyros brought the tip of his weapon forward, slamming it into one of the monster's most sensitive regions, his throat.

He had hoped at best to stun the leathery beast, having assumed that with such a tough hide even the throat would be well protected, but to Tyros's astonishment, the great monster fell to his knees, choking. The mage immediately swung the staff with all his might, bringing it across the stricken gargoyle's face.

The monster collapsed, motionless, at the mage's feet.

Certain that he faced some trick, Tyros stood over the creature, tempted to bring down his weapon again. Taking a breath, the untrusting spellcaster finally prodded his foe. The monstrous guard remained prone.

Richard A. Knaak

More confident now, Tyros turned to the door. With a guard stationed, surely Valkyn had cast no spell to keep the door protected. Still, as a precaution, Tyros touched the handle with the tip of the staff. When nothing happened, he tried the door and not only found it unenchanted but unlocked as well.

Staff before him, he slipped into the room. "Serene!"

At first he thought he had guessed wrong, that Valkyn had set the gargoyle to watch this chamber for some other reason, but then the cleric came running from the direction of the balcony, eyes wide in both surprise and concern.

"Tyros! It's you! Are you mad? Don't you realize what you've done?"

Caught by surprise, the mage managed to blurt, "Come to rescue you, of course! Listen to me. I'm still under Valkyn's spell, but you might have a chance to remove it. We need to—"

"Tyros, I can't help you!"

He noticed something strange in her expression. Had he been wrong? Had Serene returned to the arms of her former love?

She read his expression. "No, it's not that. Never! I can't help you because Valkyn's put me under a spell!"

"But you're a cleric. You commune directly with Branchala. Valkyn's power cannot be that strong, unless your faith has been weakened because of the past you two share."

She might have answered him, but the renewed cries of the gargoyles outside caught the attention of them both. Tyros raced to the balcony.

Bright sunlight momentarily blinded him. As his eyes adjusted, the crimson-clad mage realized that he hadn't seen the sun since the party had arrived at Castle Atriun. Gazing up, Tyros noted that not only had the sun broken through, but that most of the cloud cover had, in fact, dissipated.

A time when the clouds will thin . . .

"Come on, Bakal!" Tyros muttered. "You have to hurry!"

"Bakal?" Serene joined him, looking confused. "They're not acting up because of Bakal! Don't you see what's out there?"

Going to the rail, Tyros searched the sky, looking for a

reason that would draw the attention of every gargoyle in sight.

He found not one reason but two . . . and both were black dragons.

Someone else had apparently taken advantage of his handiwork, someone with an entirely different agenda. On the back of each behemoth rode at least five men, all but one armored. The other looked to be a mage of the Black Robes.

Twin black dragons meant General Cadrio, yet somehow Tyros doubted that the general had come to confer with his supposed ally. No, from what Tyros already knew of Valkyn and the sinister manner in which the dragons raced toward the castle, Cadrio had not come to visit but to conquer.

The dragons circled the citadel, then quickly dived toward the courtyard. Tyros saw tiny figures leap off the moment one of the leviathans landed, then the beast returned to the air.

Airborne gargoyles hovered about the heads of the dragons, trying to harass the invaders. One of the dragons unleashed a spray of acid, forcing the gargoyles to retreat. The two leviathans turned in opposite directions and then flew upward.

One apparently grazed the tower above as it departed. Bits of mortar and rock began to rain down on the balcony.

Tyros pulled Serene back inside. "Bakal and Rapp were supposed to head up there. I hope nothing's happened to them."

"They're likely prisoners at this point," a blithe voice answered, "or they may be dead."

Valkyn stood at the doorway, wand held in his left hand like a sword. It still glowed, however faintly.

The smile that Tyros had come to loathe spread as Valkyn went on. "I am as prepared for their mischief as I am for the dear general's. I fear General Marcus Cadrio has been a terrible disappointment. I expected him to at least wait until Gwynned lay in ruins before trying once more to end our alliance. Well, I forgave him once, but his usefulness is at an end. His forces will still march on Gwynned, but under my command. Of course, I only need them to be on the field. Nothing else matters after that."

"And why is that?" Tyros had to ask.

"Because that will draw out Gwynned's forces, and I can then study the full effect of my creation in an actual battle. Norwych was interesting but far too easy a target. To fully understand the potential of Atriun, I need Gwynned."

Tyros's eyes flickered to the wand, which seemed dimmer. He tried to stall Valkyn. "And then what happens? You conquer the rest of the world, Valkyn? Become the new emperor?"

The goateed spellcaster smirked. "I suppose I'll have to carve out some kingdom of my own, if only to allow myself the freedom for my experiments. I already have the plans in motion to create more citadels such as this one, citadels that, with a bit of work, will make even Atriun seem clumsy and pathetic."

Tyros recalled Leot. "But you will need more wizards, won't you? Your foul device can't function without them."

"Very good. Almost correct, just as you were almost correct in assuming that without your friend chained to it, Castle Atriun would lose its abilities."

The crystal on the wand had definitely grown dimmer. Tyros gripped his staff, ready to charge. Valkyn still no doubt had magic of his own, but how powerful would he be without his toy?

"As you and others have already noted, Atriun is weakening, but it's hardly ready to plummet to the earth." Valkyn held up the wand, the crystalline sphere suddenly ablaze. He chuckled at Tyros's disconcerted expression. "I've cast the spells so that the castle itself stores some of the magic, giving me a reserve." The sinister smile grew wide. "And once you're chained in your friend's place, I shall be able to draw more power than ever."

He pointed the wand at Tyros.

In desperation, Tyros raised the staff, already feeling his skin tingle. To his surprise, however, the tingling ceased and the piece of wood in his hands began to glow slightly of its own accord.

For one of the few times the crimson mage could recall, Valkyn frowned. "You found that staff in my sanctum, didn't you? Here I thought you'd managed to retrieve your own pathetic staff." The elder wizard shrugged. "A temporary measure at best."

"Stop this!" Serene ran between them. "Valkyn, if you ever loved me, don't harm him!"

The dark mage pursed his lips. His brow furrowed. "No, I don't think so."

Valkyn gave the wand a turn. Tyros felt the floor beneath him dissolve. His legs sank down to his knees.

Tyros brought Valkyn's staff down on the floor, trying to use the magical artifact to pull himself up. Instead, the staff sparked and the floor partially solidified, enabling the younger spellcaster to push himself free.

His head began to throb. Even the use of the staff's magical properties activated Valkyn's dark curse.

Serene seized the older wizard by the arms. "Don't do this!"

"I'm tired of your begging, my sweet serenity," Valkyn said, almost sadly, "and since it seems that's all you can do now, you should go elsewhere."

The cleric vanished, her mouth still open in protest.

"What did you do to her?" Rage drove Tyros. Had Valkyn killed Serene?

"She's in another, more secure chamber, where she can mull over her indiscretions. Now, shall we put an end to this?"

Valkyn reached out with one gloved hand, fingers spread wide. He began to make a fist, and as he did, bonds of pure shadow formed around Tyros, squeezing him as if he stood in his foe's palm.

The embattled wizard raised the staff, touching it to the shadowy fingers. This time, though, Valkyn's tool did not save Tyros. Instead, the staff fell from his constricted grip, clattering to the floor. Tyros could barely breathe.

"Much better," murmured the ebony-clad figure. Blue eyes sparkled with amusement. "It might have been interesting to see what you would have done against me if not for my spell."

"You like experiments. Find out!"

The castle shook. Valkyn spread his arms. "Alas, we have no time. Cadrio is making himself something of a nuisance, and I have an army to take control of." The smile came again. "And you must now take on the role I've reserved for you, since as I understand it now, you escaped my gargoyles in Gwynned. Time, Tyros, to take your friend Leot's place. I trust you'll last a little longer. . . ."

* * * * *

The clouds had thinned.

"Stand ready!" Captain Bakal ordered. This had to be the moment on which the gargoyle had been harping all this time. If Stone's explanation made sense, then Tyros had accomplished at least some of his work, and now Bakal and his men had to begin their part.

Stone had guided them to the stairs that led to the Wind Captain's Chair but had left it in the humans' hands from there. The gargoyle had said only that he had another task.

No one met them for the first half of the climb, which surprised the scarred soldier. Where were all the guards? He had heard some commotion outside, but surely at least one of the robed creatures would have remained to protect this tower.

Bakal looked around for the kender. "Rapp!"

"I'm trying to keep up, Bakal, but these steps are big!"

Despite his energy, the kender had fallen behind more than once, the high steps forcing the tiny figure to climb at twice the pace of the humans. That wouldn't do. Bakal needed the kender up front, in case the entrance to the Wind Captain's Chair was locked.

"Frankel! Take the lead!" Bakal slowed, allowing the man to pass. The captain reached for Rapp, intending to carry the kender under his arm if necessary.

Rapp reached for the officer's outstretched hand, then looked past him, eyes wide. "Bakal! Behind you! He's—"

Captain Bakal turned, but it was too late. Frankel put his

foot down on a seemingly chipped step, a step that suddenly glowed brightly.

"Frankel! Get ba—"

A flash of light enveloped the lead man. One second Frankel stood in front of them, arm raised to shield his eyes. The next second the light faded, and with it, the man. No sign of the soldier remained, not even his weapon.

Magic. Black Valkyn's magic. Bakal had yet to see the man, but he hated him. Twice now good soldiers who had taken the veteran's place at the point had perished. Given the chance, Bakal would have been willing to pay with his life if only he could cut Valkyn to little ribbons and feed him to his pet gargoyles.

"Probably poison all of 'em," he muttered. The officer studied the next few steps. Determined not to risk his small party, he stretched his sword over the step where Frankel had perished. When nothing happened, Bakal reached up and gently tapped the next step. Still nothing.

"From now on, each step gets tested first, and I stay at the point." The veteran glanced at Rapp. "Keep behind me, with one step between us. Got it?"

He studied the stairs again. If he was wrong, there would be no second chance. Taking a deep breath, the captain judged the distance over the trap and leaped up.

Bakal landed squarely on the step above the trap. "All right," he called, looking back. "Just keep your eye on me."

A roar shook the staircase, the entire building. Bakal had to fall against the wall or risk dropping back onto the deadly step. Bits of masonry pelted the soldiers.

"What in the name of the gods was that?" someone shouted.

"Sounded like a dragon!" came the reply.

"Captain!" the first man called. "Gargoyles!"

Two of the creatures flitted through windows near the top of the staircase. In their hands they carried nets similar to the ones used on the griffons. Bakal's heart sank. In such tight quarters, the nets would prove extremely effective.

"Gargoyles at the rear!" a soldier called.

"We've been trapped!" the captain snarled. Bakal kept his sword pointed at the monsters above as he gingerly leaped over the trap again.

"The gargoyle tricked us!" one of the others shouted. "He led us into this!"

Bakal doubted that. If Stone had wanted to turn them over to Valkyn, he could have done it at any time. He had even risked his own life to free Tyros. No, somehow Valkyn had discovered their plan, which meant that Tyros, too, likely walked into a trap.

More gargoyles entered from above, one of them with three horns and a malicious grin. The savage Crag.

"Here come the nets!"

The first net fell short; the second Bakal managed to shove aside with his blade. The gargoyles reached to retrieve their nets. Acting on instinct, Bakal used the sword to snag the nearest snare. Then, with his free hand, he pulled it toward him just as one of the monsters took hold of the other end.

Caught off-balance, the leathery horror rolled over once, then landed awkwardly on the step that had claimed Frankel.

The step glowed, and the flash of light enveloped the gargoyle.

"Well, that's one down," murmured the officer as the light faded. He waited for the creatures to try again, but now they acted with more care.

Someone bumped Bakal from behind. He looked over his shoulder. The gargoyles below pressed forward, the ones in front armed, much to the captain's consternation, with spears. The captain and his men were being herded.

The nets came at them, this time thrown with more precision. One landed over Bakal, who sliced at it desperately. He realized instantly why the griffons had been unable to rip their way free. The nets had been interlaced with metallic thread, making them difficult to tear or cut. Given enough time, Bakal could have freed himself, but the gargoyles would not permit him that.

Cries broke out among his men. The gargoyles rushed in but instead of using their spears and claws, they began to pummel the soldiers with their fists. One man screamed, a sound that was quickly cut off. Bakal heard Rapp shout. He tried to look for the kender, but a huge hand seized the captain by the collar.

Crag flashed the captain what could only be a mocking smile. The hardened veteran paled, expecting to have his throat ripped out, but instead Crag slapped him hard across the face.

Still in the lead gargoyle's grip, Bakal fell back, barely conscious from the vicious blow. He heard Crag's deep, gravelly voice, sounding frustrated. "Kender! Where kender? Find kender!"

So Rapp had escaped. Bakal took no pleasure from that, wondering, just before he blacked out from pain, what a lone kender could possibly do at this point. He already knew the answer.

Nothing.

Chapter 14

The Power of Atriun

The gargoyle had spoken the truth. Cadrio, helm on and visor down, had watched in anticipation as the last of the clouds broke up. The time had come. Murk and Eclipse, each burdened with five men, flew upward, beating their wings hard to make up for the added weight.

He waited for Valkyn's magic to bring them down, just as it had the gold and silver dragons, but no lightning struck, no wind tossed the black leviathans and their riders about. Only the gargoyles came to the citadel's defense, and to Cadrio, they were little but flies. The dragons would deal with them. The twins were eager to prove their mastery of the sky over these tiny intruders.

As for the gargoyles' master, Valkyn had only two options: bow before Cadrio or get his head lopped off. Cadrio savored the second scenario, but still wanted to make certain that he had gleaned all the information he could from his arrogant ally first. Then, one way or the other, he would rid himself of Valkyn. The black wizard would ever be a danger while he lived.

The dragons skirted around the flying citadel, seeking out any possible danger. Without the storm, though, it seemed that Atriun was nearly defenseless. Eclipse finally dropped to the courtyard so his riders could dismount. Rudolpho and the four soldiers leaped off, immediately seeking shelter.

Cadrio, on Murk, leaned forward. "Go to the main doors of the castle! I want them burned away!"

The massive black nodded. Given the honor of carrying the commander, Murk was determined to prove that he deserved the honor. He stretched his wings and began his descent.

As they neared, Cadrio noticed that several of the gargoyles ignored the dragons entirely. They seemed more interested in some incident within the tower containing the Wind Captain's Chair. Cadrio didn't care what kept the defenders occupied, so long as it did not interfere with his plans.

Murk alighted just before the tall doorway of Castle Atriun. The dragon positioned himself so that he faced the bolted entrance.

"Best to dismount behind me!" Murk roared.

The men slid down the length of the behemoth just as Murk inhaled. As the general's boots touched the stone courtyard, the black dragon let forth with a hard blast of pure acid. The deadly torrent struck the great doors, completely scalding them. Even the dark stone around the frame sizzled and smoked.

Despite his grand effort, Murk had failed to open the way. The doors had been damaged but not destroyed.

"They've been treated with some protective substance!" Cadrio snarled. Whether it had been the work of the Solamnic Knight or Valkyn, the general did not care. He would brook no delays. "Do it again!"

This time, Murk drew in as much air as he could, then unleashed a burning storm that ravaged Atriun's entrance. The doors at last crumbled, the remnants smoking, pockmarked. Bits of the arched frame collapsed.

"Return to the *Harpy*! Bring up the reinforcements!"

The dragon nodded, leaping into the sky. Cadrio gathered Rudolpho and the others together, then made for the devastated doorway. A pair of gargoyles landed among them, one seizing the man next to the general. Cadrio wasted no time, thrusting his blade through the monster's neck. As he pulled it free, another soldier helped the first man up.

Rudolpho stood in front of the remaining creature, the black mage's hand raised. The gargoyle froze in place, then toppled over like a statue. Rudolpho brought his foot down, shattering his petrified victim.

"Save your magic!" the commander shouted. "You'll need it for Valkyn!"

As he said the other wizard's name, thunder crashed.

"By her infernal majesty!" The vulpine commander paused at the ruined entrance, peering up at a sky that had darkened so suddenly that his eyes needed a moment to adjust to the gloom. The wind picked up, blowing with such strength that the men could barely stand. Cadrio felt his skin burn where droplets of acid, flung up by the gusts, splattered against his cheek.

"No . . ." he whispered. "Too soon! Too soon!"

Eclipse had already flown off, but his brother could still be seen from the courtyard. Cadrio started to call the dragon to him, then noticed that Murk also struggled with the wind. Even as Cadrio watched, the black leviathan was pushed back toward Atriun.

"Fly, you miserable wyvern! Fly!"

Murk tried but lost more distance. Now he flew nearly directly above the enchanted fortress, tossed about like a leaf.

Lightning crackled. Thunder roared again.

A crimson bolt struck Murk.

The black dragon roared in agony. He tried to fly in one direction, but a fearsome wind tossed him to the side, sending the helpless leviathan away from the citadel.

A second bolt ripped through the dragon's left wing; another scorched his tail. A sickly sensation spread through the commander.

Valkyn had control of the storm again and now demonstrated to Cadrio the folly of having dared to betray him.

Scorched in a score of places, his wings half-tattered, Murk roared in agony and once more tried desperately to flee. At first Cadrio thought the dragon would make good his escape, but then he noticed the black clouds swirling just over the beast.

Twin bolts caught Murk between them.

The black dragon let out a howl of agony, a howl cut off by a final bolt so powerful the behemoth's form shook uncontrollably.

One eye burned away, Murk's head slumped. The wings ceased beating. Cadrio had witnessed the deaths of the silver and gold dragons, but found this no less stunning. Now limp, the immense body of Murk should have immediately dropped toward distant Krynn, but for several seconds it bounced around in the sky, tossed by turbulent and highly unnatural winds.

Then, when Valkyn apparently thought the lesson had been burned into Cadrio's mind, the winds slowed. The ebony dragon's great corpse vanished from sight as it fell beyond the walls of the citadel.

The storm intensified once more. Wind tossed loose objects about like a child's toys, and even the gargoyles, who should have been under the protection of their master, could barely reach safe perches. Buckets of rain poured down, driving Cadrio's squad into the castle. Thunder shook Atriun.

A lone figure, clad in dark, shadowy robes, awaited them in the front hall, not the ghostly shape from the tower, but almost identical. Within the confines of the black robe, different from that worn by Valkyn, Cadrio noted the lower half of a sallow, emotionless countenance with thin, almost nonexistent lips.

The specter raised a bony hand and uttered a single word: "Waaait . . ."

The voice put the general's already taut nerves on edge, but he wouldn't let any walking corpse tell him what to do. "Where's Valkyn? Where's your master, ghoul?"

When the lone guardian did not reply, Cadrio marched forward, his sword at the ready. Behind him, slightly more reluctant, came Rudolpho and the others.

The shadow servant pointed at the floor just before Cadrio.

A flash of fire drove the men back. The fire traced after them, almost as if it were alive . . . and hungry.

Only Rudolpho stood his ground, already casting a spell. "Simple fireworks, General! I'll have them countered in just—"

What looked like a wide, toothy mouth formed in the flames. Suddenly it snapped forward, growing ten times larger in an instant.

The fiery mouth swallowed Rudolpho whole before the mage even had time to realize his fate.

Cadrio and the soldiers stumbled back, each certain that he would be next. The mouth vanished, but the fire advanced, driving them farther back. The invaders tried to retreat to the ruined doorway, but the flames were faster.

A wall of blazing heat surrounded Marcus Cadrio and his men, imprisoning them. The flames burned so close that the general felt as if he were going to be boiled alive in his armor.

And once more the ghastly guardian repeated: "Waaait . . ."

Sweat pouring down his body, his armor like a tight-fitting oven, General Cadrio knew he had no choice now but to comply.

*   *   *   *   *

Tyros screamed.

"The pain should eventually numb you," Valkyn remarked calmly from somewhere beyond the other mage's tear-filled gaze. "They all cease screaming eventually."

A sensation such as Tyros had never thought to experience coursed through him. He felt as if his body burned, although no flame could sear him from the inside as this agony did. The fair-haired wizard knew what assailed his body, knew what caused him such pain, and that knowledge only made his situation that much more terrible.

Magic—the elemental force that had, since his first teachings, grown to be so much a part of Tyros—filled him, touched him each passing moment, became anathema. It ripped the mage apart from within, entering his body, coursing through his very being and flowing out into Valkyn's arcane device. Tyros drew magic into him, more magic than he could ever use, and then gave it to his captor. He could not do otherwise. The spells the black wizard had utilized to create his diabolic mechanism demanded it.

The arcane device and the spells with which it had been imbued forced Tyros to repeat the process without pause. So much magic entering, filling, then leaving his body in a rush took a toll on him, both physically and mentally. The pain threatened to drive him mad, and the tremendous magical forces, more than a mortal body should have to accept, ate away at his imperfect human form. Given time, the process would drain Tyros completely, leaving behind a burned-out husk.

Tyros stood with arms and legs stretched to the side, manacles holding him securely in place. Only now did he notice that the manacles had not been forged from iron, but rather some more conductive metal, perhaps copper. Tyros realized that, in addition to keeping him chained, they served also to transmit the magic to the columns, where the great crystalline spheres then stored or discharged it as needed.

Above the trapped mage, the twin spheres crackled with renewed vigor. Obviously Tyros was a more useful component to the mad device than burned-out Leot. Even deep within the castle, Tyros could hear the thundering of the sorcerous storm as it grew to new life.

This, then, was how the spellcaster had chosen to work around the cumbersome design of previous citadels. Although Valkyn did not see it so, his powerful spellwork demanded at least as much, if not more, power. Leot had lasted only a matter of days; Tyros might last that long, but little longer. Valkyn would have to constantly capture new wizards to keep his creation afloat.

The mad mage had turned from the teachings of the orders, even those of Nuitari. Valkyn had chosen to make himself a renegade, one who served his own evil, not that of any god.

Yet Valkyn clearly did not see himself as evil . . . just determined in his research.

"Gwynned will be the final test for my castle, Tyros. I will need the city and its resources to further my experiments. The choice could not be better! Do you know that the mountains of Northern Ergoth are where these crystals were originally mined? I'll be needing more of them, both to replace these eventually and to ready citadels still to come!"

Tyros had always been ambitious, even to the point of

arrogance, but clearly Valkyn had outdone him. Gritting his teeth and blinking away tears, Tyros forced out, "And how do you . . . hope to keep them all . . . afloat?"

Valkyn smiled. "There will always be magic and those taught to wield it."

"But who . . . can you trust to fly your demented creations? Cadrio? The gargoyles?"

"No. My shadow servants are more loyal. Give them a command and they obey it to the letter. They will serve as my captains."

Tyros tried to sneer, but his pain no doubt made the expression a pathetic one. "As no one else can be trusted? You will become . . . a very lonely, very nervous emperor of Ansalon if you can trust no others to serve you."

The smiling figure did not reply at first, instead going to the column on Tyros's right and inspecting the symbols carved into it. A frown briefly replaced the smile as Valkyn touched his gloved hands to the column and started mumbling. The symbols suddenly shifted and changed. New patterns appeared.

Valkyn pulled back, mulling over his work. "There! That's better. That should regulate the flow better and keep you alive a little longer." Seeing no gratitude in the prisoner's expression, Valkyn shrugged, finally replying to Tyros's remark. "A tiresome role, Emperor of Ansalon. Ariakas would have been welcome to it had he lived. I thought Cadrio would do well so long as he understood his place, but I've been forced to rethink that alliance." He clasped his hands together. "And speaking of the general, as he, too, has made his way so diligently to Castle Atriun, it behooves me to greet him and perhaps admonish him properly. If you will excuse me?"

A flash of light burst forth where Valkyn had stood. At the same time, new, sharper pain ripped through Tyros. He screamed and did not stop screaming for more than a minute. When at last he could keep himself from crying out, the ragged wizard looked around. Valkyn had completely disappeared. The shock that Tyros had felt had been due to the mad mage's latest spell, which had drawn upon the device.

So each time Valkyn cast a spell of strength, the magic would course through Tyros.

"What a fool I've been. . . ." He had dreamed of capturing the citadel and flying it back, creating a legend that would rival that of the motley band that had somehow managed to defeat Lord Ariakas and drive Takhisis back. Instead, he would be a minor part of another legend, Black Valkyn's Death Citadel. Tyros had witnessed what Atriun could do against gold dragons; surely nothing else could match it so long as its master kept the foul edifice powered.

As for that, as Valkyn had said, there would always be magic and those taught to wield it.

Another surge caught him unaware. The helpless spell-caster let loose a roar of agony, at the same time feeling a slight shift in the castle. Atriun had begun moving toward Gwynned, and Tyros could do nothing to stop it. Nothing.

Again the devilish device flared. Tyros cried out, tears streaming down his cheeks.

Nothing . . .

* * * * *

Serene lay atop the immense, soft bed, staring, without seeing, at the gilded decor of the sumptuous chamber Valkyn had provided her. Love had truly blinded her, for how could she not have noticed his dark ambition? He had played her for a fool the whole time. Serene had thought him a kindred spirit, one fascinated by the wonders of the natural world. Instead, he was the foulest of monsters. She did not quite know what her former love's spellwork entailed, but in the process, it turned his fellow mages into soulless puppets, animated husks who existed only to obey Valkyn's will.

And now Tyros suffered the same fate.

Tyros. The cleric had at first found him insulting, arrogant, but that had changed, in part because of him, in part because of her. He reminded her of Valkyn, but Valkyn before the evil had revealed itself. Beneath the arrogance, though, Tyros cared more than he often revealed. True, he had his ambitions, but so far she had noticed that his ambitions stepped aside when lives were at stake.

In her mind, Serene imagined the faces of both men. She saw the Valkyn she had loved, the Tyros she had come to know. Already the cleric had a better idea of what the second mage was like. Tyros was a man she could look up to, could trust . . . possibly even some day love?

Serene remembered the face in the tree. The final face. The one that Branchala had shown to her when she had wanted to find Valkyn.

The Bard King had shown her Tyros's visage instead.

It was too soon to say what might lie in her future where Tyros was concerned, assuming that the two of them had a future. The Bard King might have simply been trying to save his cleric from the horrible truth about Valkyn, yet Serene would never have the opportunity to find out if they didn't escape. Tyros, though, could do nothing. He was chained to the magical device, tortured every second that Valkyn made use of him.

It was all up to Serene.

She sat up. A brief sense of vertigo nearly forced her down again, but she fought it back. Valkyn's damned spell still held her in check, still prevented Serene from calling upon her god.

A sorry cleric she made. Her own regrets about Valkyn worked against her. Serene rose from the bed and headed toward the balcony, trying to clear her head.

Outside, the storm clouds rumbled. The cleric stepped back as a gust of wind tried to pull her from the balcony. Branchala watched over weather, and so Serene usually reveled in displays of nature, but as with everything else in and around Atriun, she felt nothing but revulsion for the elemental forces that parodied a true storm. This weather existed only because of Valkyn.

She stepped out again, daring the magical storm. Amongst the black clouds, crimson and gold lightning flashed. Serene felt a tingle and knew it to be magic. Trying to calm herself, she looked down at the wooded garden, the only location in the castle that gave her comfort. How she longed for her woodland home . . .

Out of the treetops burst three ferocious gargoyles. They quickly flew skyward, clearly anxious about something. One glanced her way as he rose, his beaked maw opening in warning.

Serene fled back into the chamber, not afraid but no longer comforted by the outside. Her entire world seemed to be of Valkyn's design, and try as she might, Serene could find no escape from it.

Caught up in such turmoil, the cleric didn't notice at first that she was no longer alone.

"Serene! Is this your room? This is much nicer than where Captain Bakal and I had to stay and probably better than where the captain is now if he's still alive."

"Rapp!" She flung herself on the kender, holding him close. To see a familiar face now briefly erased some of the pain she felt. "How did you get here?"

"The door was locked, but I had my best picks, and it—"

"That's not what I mean." Given a chance, the kender would go into great detail about his lockpicking skills. Serene had no time for that. "I meant how did you get past the guards?"

"Oh. They found something down the hall to investigate." Rapp put a finger to his lips. "You shouldn't talk so loud. They may be coming back soon."

That the small figure's own voice carried far more than hers did not, of course, occur to him. The cleric nodded, though, knowing that if she spoke more quietly, so would Rapp. "You mentioned the captain. Where is now? Can he help us?"

Rapp momentarily grew serious. "I . . . I don't know where Bakal is, Serene. Tyros wanted us to go to the tower where the controls are supposed to be to fly this castle." He brightened again. "Can you imagine that? I'd like to try to fly a castle! Do you think that if we'd gotten up there, Bakal might have let me have a hand at the wheel?"

"Rapp!" Forcing herself more to be calm, Serene asked,

"Where did you last see Bakal? Did he ever reach the top of the tower?"

Again the tiny figure lost much of his usual cheerfulness. "No . . . there were magical traps and gargoyles everywhere. Not like Stone, but bigger, nastier ones! They came at us from all sides, and they had nets, too! I slipped under one gargoyle and got away. I couldn't help the captain. I hope he's not mad at me!"

She squeezed his shoulder. "I doubt it. So they didn't kill them?"

"I don't know, Serene. I saw them dragging Bakal and three others away. They were beaten bad, but not dead . . . I think."

Valkyn could have only one reason for leaving any of the remaining soldiers alive. He was interested in what Bakal might know about Gwynned's defenders.

So that left only the kender and herself. Not what Serene would have preferred, for in truth, without her link to her god, Serene had nothing to offer. Even Rapp could offer more.

"Serene, do you know where Tyros is? He said he was going to do something to make the clouds go away, but the clouds only went away for a few minutes, then came back real fast and even killed one of the black dragons. You should've seen it! I almost felt sorry for the dragon, even though I really don't like black ones because they try to eat griffons, not to mention kender!"

"Rapp." The cleric kneeled down on one knee and looked him in the eye. "Rapp, Tyros is a prisoner, too. Of Valkyn. You remember Valkyn, don't you?"

Rapp's eyes narrowed, as close as the kender ever got to anger. "I don't think I like Valkyn, Serene, even if you did love him. He destroyed Norwych and hurt my griffons."

"I've no more love for him than you do," Serene promptly returned. In truth, only loathing remained for the mage. He had betrayed everything she believed in. "He's using Tyros to keep the citadel flying, but the longer Tyros is part of the spellwork, the more likely he'll die!"

The kender thought about this. "We have to help him, then! I like Tyros. Taggi likes him, too, I think, and Taggi's a good judge. He liked you, didn't he?" Rapp rubbed his chin. "Maybe you can pray to Branchala to stop the storm; he'd be real good at that! When that happens, Valkyn will want to investigate, and I can find Tyros and release him! I'll bet he's down deep inside the castle! I remember which way he went originally, and I can—"

"Rapp, I can't call on Branchala. Valkyn's seen to that. He's cast a powerful spell on me. I'm cut off from the Bard King."

Instead of dismay, puzzlement dominated the kender's expression. "But how can that be? Valkyn isn't stronger than Branchala. Does he make you not believe in the Bard King?"

"No, I still believe in him."

Rapp shook his head. "Then I don't understand, Serene. Valkyn's just a wizard. I mean, he's a strong wizard, but just a wizard! Branchala's a god, and you talk to him all the time! How can Valkyn's spell stop you from doing that?"

"It's not that simple," the cleric snapped, recalling how Tyros had said much the same. Even though she had managed to keep herself conscious after her earlier attempts, Serene had made no further progress. The harsh headaches still plagued her. If she pushed herself too far, she felt certain that she would again collapse. "I can't be of any help in that way, Rapp."

She had never seen a kender look so disappointed. Rapp hid the emotion almost as quickly as he had displayed it, but the expression remained burned in Serene's mind and heart.

"It's all right, Serene," he finally murmured. "Don't you worry. I'll get Tyros on my own!"

Disgust for her own uselessness filled her. "But you can't do that. I'm going along with you. I can handle a staff, at least."

Rapp crossed his arms, trying to look stern. The cleric had seen him assume such a stance when he had admonished the griffons for breaking into some farmer's chicken coop. "I really better go alone, Serene. You humans are big and clumsy when it comes to sneaking around. You better wait here. I'll find Tyros and rescue him. He'll know what to do then!"

Before she could argue with him further, Rapp hurried toward the hallway door, eager to be off on his adventure. However, as he reached for the handle, he suddenly paused, his head cocking slightly to the side. Serene realized that the kender was listening.

Shaking his head, Rapp returned to her.

"What is it?"

"Your guards are back. I'll have to go out the balcony. Doesn't that sound exciting?"

"You can't. You'll be blown away."

Despite her anxiety, Rapp raced to the balcony, taking cover only when he stepped outside. Serene went as far as the balcony doors, watching her small friend. Rapp slipped to the rail, then, after peering through it, started to climb over it.

"I'm going with you!" Serene stepped out just as a hard gust struck. She had to keep hold of a door to prevent herself from crashing into the rail.

Rapp hugged the rail tightly. He finished climbing over the moment the wind died down, pausing only to stare at Serene through the columns of the rail. "Go inside, Serene. I promise you that I'll be safe. You just go talk to Branchala, all right?"

He dropped out of sight before she could reply. Rapp's words stung her. Abandoning the windblown balcony, the cleric returned to the bed, trying to convince herself that the kender just didn't understand. She well knew Valkyn's power. His magic had brought Tyros to his knees. His magic had raised Atriun, and with that magic, the sinister flying castle had torn Norwych apart. What hope did she have of overcoming Valkyn's spell?

"Listen to yourself!" she murmured. "Maybe Rapp's right. You never let such thoughts bother you even during the worst of the war. Why now? You've fought terrible evil, and the Bard King has always been with you. Why would he abandon you now?"

Something stirred within Serene. She knew Valkyn too well, knew his power, knew his mind. She wouldn't let Valkyn's trickery and betrayal be her downfall. His love might have grown twisted, but for her, there would always be one whose love for her would remain pure and compassionate. Despite her doubts, he would be there for her. He had to be.

"Branchala," the cleric began, her head already feeling light. "Bard King, forgive me for my lack of faith, my lack of love. . . ."

The room began to swim. Serene fought against it. She had not only Valkyn's spell to defeat, but her own misgivings as well, which gave that spell more strength over her.

"Branchala, hear my song. Hear my call." Her hands shaped themselves, as if holding a lyre or a Bard's harp. Serene's fingers began to move as if she played that instrument. No sound came, of course, but the movement soothed her, pushed back the vertigo.

Emboldened, the cleric opened her mouth to sing. The words were not in the Common tongue, nor even that of the elves, who had served Branchala longer than humankind. The words came from the Age of Dreams and had been passed down to the faithful from Branchala himself. They evoked the beauty of the forest, the caress of the wind, the gentle might of nature. The first time she had learned to properly sing those words, Serene had found herself filled with such bliss that she had known no other calling would ever suit her more. She had been certain that she would ever be a cleric to the woodland god.

Again a wave of vertigo nearly overwhelmed Serene. Her fingers faltered and she missed a word. Summoning her resolve, the cleric picked up the song again, letting the words come louder, more free. The rumble of the storm without helped mask her singing, but Serene knew that she risked discovery. Still, she didn't care, at last feeling as if she had rediscovered herself.

On and on her fingers strummed, playing the silent notes in accompaniment to her voice. Serene sang, picturing the forest in which she had lived, the animals she had known, the people whose lives she had touched. The cleric imagined the faces of her present companions, Rapp, Bakal, and, most of all, Tyros. They needed her and the strength and love of her god. Serene looked to Branchala, asking him in song to give her the chance to fulfill that need and help them all put an end to Valkyn's abomination.

And as her fingers continued to play the air, notes began to resound through the chamber.

Chapter 15

The Approaching Battle

Cadrio's forces under Zander had moved swiftly toward their ultimate destination. The scouts had chosen well. The path was an open yet barely populated stretch that offered little in the way of resistance. Thus far they had over-whelmed a few tiny outposts with minimal effort. Soon they would reach their true prey, the defenders of Gwynned. Even now Zander could make out the rolling landscape that opened into the great city's territory.

And in those rolling hills, the true battle would be fought.

Zander felt quite comfortable in the role of commander. Zander respected his general, but thought himself the better tactician. He had already deployed his forces for combat, knowing that each passing moment meant a more likely chance of coming across the first resistance.

It was possible that he had already inherited the mantle of command. Zander glanced behind him, where Eclipse, wings folded, still stared, unblinking, at the heavens. Zander had never seen a befuddled dragon before. In halting words, Eclipse had told him what had happened to Murk, a tale that had left even Zander unnerved. The ebony beast seemed at a complete loss without his twin, constantly rubbing his fore-paws together and missing half of what the younger officer told him.

Cadrio had told his second about the black cleric who had served Valkyn, the fearful fool who had evidently died in the making of the floating edifice. Eclipse reminded Zander of that cleric and pointed out once again the folly of defying the mage. If Valkyn offered the young officer the position of general, and perhaps later puppet emperor, then Zander would gladly accept it. The riches and power would certainly assuage his feelings at being at the beck and call of the spellcaster.

To his dismay, however, it proved to be Cadrio rather than Valkyn who suddenly appeared in the midst of battle preparations. The tall, vulpine commander was oddly subdued as he materialized.

Zander quickly saluted the illusion of his commander. "Sir, I took the liberty of advancing as per the mage's instructions, but we dare go no farther, for the defenders' troops have been spotted just beyond the hills. They mean to take us when we approach the high ground, keeping the battle far from Gwynned. I have a plan to draw their right flank out and eat away at their lines from there."

Cadrio blinked, at first not responding. After a moment, he sighed, then said, "You'll march the men straight ahead, Zander. Keep everything according to Valkyn's battle plan. No deviations."

Zander, who had tried to keep his deviations within reason in order not to anger Valkyn, frowned, then nodded. "I understand."

The general hesitated, as if listening to something. The young officer swallowed. Now that he had been able to study his superior, he saw that Cadrio looked haggard, beaten.

"Hold your lines and keep advancing regardless of the forces you face. Draw out their cavalry if you can, but remain in the open."

"Sir?" This hadn't been a part of the black mage's original battle plan. Zander didn't like the thought of placing his troops in such a precarious position. With the defenders already settled in, his men would suffer heavy casualties.

From what Zander read in Cadrio's eyes, the veteran commander clearly thought much the same. Zander finally realized that Cadrio spoke Valkyn's words, not his own. All pretenses of an alliance had been flung aside. The general lived only with the wizard's permission.

"When dark clouds cover the battlefield, Zander, you must be prepared. Atriun will strike, but you must be there to purge the land of any remaining resistance. Is that understood?"

Zander swallowed. Saluting, he shouted, "Yes, General!"

"That is all."

The lanky figure vanished in the same unsettling manner that Valkyn always had.

Putting on his helm, Zander turned to the other officers. "You heard the general! Regroup all forces! Alert all subcommanders of their new instructions. See to it that order is maintained so that this adjustment doesn't turn into a rout before we've even begun to fight. Go!"

The men scattered to obey. Zander, his anxiety and fury masked by his helm, stormed past two minor officers who served as his own aides. He did not stop until he came face-to-face with Eclipse. The dragon eyed him, then looked away, clearly lost again in some inner world.

"Eclipse! Damn you, dragon! Look down here!"

Slowly the behemoth acknowledged him. "Go away, human."

"I have orders for you and you'll obey them!"

"I don't listen to you. I don't listen to Cadrio anymore." Eclipse puffed some smoke his way. "Murk is dead."

Zander bristled. "You'll be dead, too, if you don't obey!"

The dragon snorted. "And will you kill me, puny human?"

"No, but if you do not follow Valkyn's plan, then Valkyn will have no use for you, and you know what the wizard does with those he has no more use for."

Now he saw fear in the dragon's eyes, fear drawn from Eclipse's vision of his twin dropping lifelessly from the sky. The leviathan might be mourning his brother, but he still cared something for his own scaly skin.

"I will obey! I will!" The sight of the black dragon cringing from the distant citadel looked so pitiful that Zander lost some of his fury. Neither he nor Eclipse desired Valkyn's wrath, even if it meant marching everyone straight into Gwynned's bristling defenses.

"All right, then. Stick by me. You will be my mount. We'll coordinate matters with the general and the citadel."

As he spoke to the dragon, Zander mentally prepared himself for the upcoming battle. Though alive, Cadrio clearly did not have Valkyn's favor. If Zander could prove himself, then surely the wizard would see who could serve him best, who could be the most useful commander. Why keep untrustworthy Cadrio around when loyal and earnest Zander would do better? Perhaps he could still convince the wizard that he was worthy of the same offer that Valkyn had originally given to the general.

Emperor Zander . . . he liked the sound of that.

* * * * *

"Now that's better, isn't it, my general?"

"Yes, Valkyn."

The mage smiled at his companion. "Don't be so sullen, General Cadrio. After all, I did let you live, didn't I?"

He saw the soldier shiver and knew that he had made his point. The executions of some of Cadrio's men had been necessary and, at the same time, had allowed Valkyn to test the level of power of Castle Atriun. Yes, Tyros would do well, outlasting not only the taking of Gwynned but also perhaps the next Northern Ergothian city as well. By that time, Valkyn would have made more adjustments in his spellwork and kidnapped another wizard, ensuring that the massive citadel would continue to fly.

The people of Gwynned could have saved themselves much horror if they had surrendered rather than resisted. It would have saved the mage some time. Still, Valkyn looked forward to the upcoming battle, eager to see how Atriun would fare.

At some point, Valkyn would have to turn on his former masters. The Orders of Sorcery would move against him in force, as much out of jealousy as fear, the renegade mage believed. For that, he would need at least two more citadels, one of which he knew he could find in Gwynned.

Valkyn and Cadrio now stood upon the outer wall of Atriun, peering down at the tableau opening up before them. Cadrio's men—now Valkyn's—moved with the swiftness and efficiency that had been the essential reasons the wizard had chosen them in the first place. The officer in charge, Zander, seemed particularly adept in his role as ground commander. Perhaps Cadrio would need to be demoted after this battle. . . .

Ahead, they could make out the defenders' movements. Valkyn knew that the male gold dragon lived, and because of him, Gwynned would have some notion of the might arrayed against them. In addition to their previous positions, Ergoth's soldiers had spread out into the hills and valleys, choosing locations wherever they thought they might escape the fury of Valkyn's castle.

Those new positions would work against them. Where Valkyn could not strike the foe, he would strike at the ground around them. Hills could be turned into weapons, especially when shattered by lightning.

"The regions to the north are hard rock," Cadrio suddenly commented. "Can your bolts break them up?"

Valkyn's smile grew genuine. Cadrio had seen what he had in mind. "Of course."

"That will wreak some havoc on the northern lines," the commander conceded. He pointed south. "But the soldiers there are entrenched in that rift, and I don't think your magical lightning will give them much to worry about."

"You have a suggestion?"

"Use the gargoyles. They fly better than draconians, and their hides are much tougher. Even if they're hit, there'll be less damage, less loss. Give them something scalding or heavy to drop on the enemy."

The wizard looked over the region in question. "And you open up a hole in a very vulnerable part of the defenses! Of course, I could just sail over everything and attack Gwynned myself. That would save time."

Cadrio grew more bold. "This isn't Norwych. The city will be harder to take without you destroying what you want. Besides, the Ergothian soldiers will fight on even if Gwynned falls. You'll be dealing with small but steady battles long after taking the city if you don't eliminate the vast majority of the army first."

"You may be emperor yet," Valkyn commented with a chuckle.

"I'm trying to save my hide." The general considered further. "The officer. Have you questioned him yet?"

"The opportunity has not yet arisen. Present matters and past interruptions have kept me too busy, as you should know."

"He knows more about the defenses than either of us. Those catapults, for one thing. Have you considered their range and what they might toss at you? I saw a citadel set aflame by some sort of alchemical soup. Burned the very stone."

Valkyn congratulated himself on not disposing of his ally as he had originally intended. "You raise a good point, my general."

The wizard snapped his fingers, and although the glove should have muffled the tone, one creature evidently heard it. Crag fluttered down from the highest point of the castle, alighting near his master.

"Crag, loyal Crag, I've a simple task for you."

"I obey always . . ." the gargoyle rumbled.

"Bring me the remaining soldiers, Crag—alive and in one piece, please." The cheerful mage steepled his fingers. In capturing the Ergothian officer and his band, Crag had not held his fellow gargoyles in check, the result being that some of the prisoners had been pummeled to death. Only Captain Bakal and two others survived, and all three sported wounds. Valkyn generally admired enthusiasm, but not in this particular case.

Crag bobbed his head up and down. "As Maaaster says."

As the winged monster flew away, Valkyn said, "He is simple, but loyal . . . unlike poor Stone." He saw that his remark touched a nerve in Cadrio. "When one crosses me, my general, one must be prepared to be punished, as you know."

"What have you done with the beast?"

Valkyn's smile grew. "Clipped his wings."

"Clipped his wings? What do you mean by that?"

"Exactly what I said. Exactly."

"But that would mean . . ." Cadrio clamped his mouth shut, understanding having dawned at last.

Valkyn's gaze returned to the shifting armies below. Soon, very soon, the battle would be joined. From here, the soldiers looked like tiny pieces in a game of strategy, pieces that the wizard looked forward to moving.

"Yes, a shame, really, that gargoyles have no feathers. A shame for Stone, anyway . . ."

* * * * *

The gargoyle did not scream, nor did he even snarl. Instead, he lay in a miserable heap, neck and limbs secured by glowing manacles clearly resistant to both his strength and his meager magic. It was questionable whether bonds were really needed, as the gargoyle seemed to no longer have any will. The red orbs had lost their fire, and the claws scratched absently at the stone floor. Even the arrival of an unexpected visitor did not arouse him from his stupor.

In such a condition did Rapp come across Stone.

He hadn't searched for the gargoyle, but his path, after a couple of very interesting but hardly useful detours, had led him past this area. At first his discovery of the gargoyle had cheered him, for Stone surely knew where to find Tyros, but then Rapp had realized that something terrible bothered the creature, something worse than just captivity.

"Stone!" Rapp whispered. "Stone, it's me, Rapp. I knew you didn't betray us. I knew something happened to you. Don't you worry, though, I'll get you out of there!"

The gargoyle slowly lifted his head. He blinked once, then quietly hissed, "Go away."

"But I want to rescue you! Then you can help me find Tyros, and after that Taggi and my other griffons."

Stone looked away. "Want to die . . ."

"If you help me, we can all get out of here, and then Valkyn won't have anything to power his castle, and it'll drop in the sea or on some mountain peak!"

Some bit of life returned to the gargoyle as his rage took over. "Go away! Want to die!"

"Why would you want to—"

The leathery creature rose, snarling. The crimson eyes flashed. The massive wings stretched—or would have if anything remained of them.

"Oh . . . Oh!" For once, Rapp had been struck speechless.

"Seeee? Seeee?" Stone twisted around, the better to show the kender what had been done to him. Of his once proud wings, only sore, red stubs, about a foot in length, remained. The rest had been seared away.

"Oh, my!" Rapp finally managed. "Did Valkyn do that?. . . Of course he did. What a stupid question! Does it hurt much?"

Stone chuckled, a somber, defeated sound. "Pain is nothing. Master knows that. That is why Master took wings. . . ."

The small figure swallowed. To gargoyles, flight was considered as much a natural part of their existence as eating or sleeping. Rapp tried to imagine not having the nimble hands that enabled him to open locks or investigate interesting containers or pockets. What a horrible existence that would be!

"I'm sorry, Stone." The gargoyle paid him no more mind having returned to a sitting position. Rapp remained silent for a moment, then asked, "Stone, if you don't want my help, could you at least answer a question for me? It's real *important*. Do you know where Tyros is being held?"

With little interest, the gargoyle pointed down the corridor in the direction that the kender had been heading. "There."

"Thank you." Rapp stepped away, then hesitated, unwilling to leave Stone in such a condition. Even if the creature no longer cared what happened to himself, Rapp had to do something.

The lock on the cell door opened easily. Rapp approached Stone, who paid him no attention. Even when the kender looked over the glowing manacles, Stone only glanced up once in disinterest.

The manacles themselves were simple, but what surprised Rapp was that the spell on them seemed to be no impediment against lock picking. Valkyn had evidently only worried about the gargoyle's magic, not the fact that someone might simply unlock the bonds. Even when Rapp toyed with the mechanism, nothing happened. It was almost disappointing.

With practiced skill, the kender opened the first manacle, then watched in frustration as Stone simply let the freed limb drop to the floor. Undaunted, Rapp worked on the rest. Stone sat still through the entire process, looking as miserable as ever and not a bit grateful.

"Come on, Stone! You can't stay here. If they find you, they'll just lock you up again."

"Cannot fly . . ."

"You could ride one of the griffons . . . I think." Rapp didn't know if they would accept a gargoyle as a rider, but he could think of nothing else. If not for what had happened to Serene, he might have suggested Stone go to the cleric for help. "After all, she's a cleric of Branchala, who watches over animals, and I suppose a gargoyle might count for that," he mused out loud. "Maybe she could have even made him new wings."

Stone suddenly stirred. "New wings?"

"Well, as a cleric, she probably could have, but—"

"New wings!" The leathery monster jumped up, all trace of his earlier lethargy gone. "Yesss . . ."

"Now, just a minute! I said she could have, but Valkyn cast a spell on her that—"

Stone no longer listened. The fiery orbs blazed. The gargoyle's claws flexed in anticipation. Even the two burned stubs twitched, as if he already sought to test the new wings he hoped to receive. "Yesss . . . the cleric . . ."

"Stone!" Rapp chased after him, but the gargoyle moved with incredible speed, rushing out of the cell and down the corridor in the opposite direction the kender needed to go. Rapp paused, unwilling to follow any farther. He had a more important mission. The kender only prayed that by releasing Stone he hadn't ruined that mission. Somehow Rapp doubted that the gargoyle would be able to keep his escape secret long if he went charging down every hall searching for Serene.

What would Stone do once he discovered that the cleric couldn't even help herself, let alone the gargoyle?

Rapp had no time to ponder that. He hurried on down the corridor the opposite way, following Stone's vague direction and hoping he would discover Tyros soon.

The halls here were not lit by glowing crystals, but rather a few torches spread intermittently along the walls. For humans, the hallways would have been dark and gloomy. Not only could the kender see well, but he also enjoyed the spooky effect given off by the flickering flames. Rapp imagined wonderfully scary ghosts and creatures inhabiting the castle, perhaps even the spirit of the Solamnic Knight who had built Atriun in the first—

A figure seemingly made of shadow loomed over him, reaching out with one bony but strong-looking hand.

Rapp backed away just in time. Under the heavy robe, vacant eyes stared at the kender, sending an exciting chill through the tiny intruder. Rapp knew that he had to be close to his goal; otherwise, this unliving sentry would not have appeared so suddenly. Some invisible spell must have alerted the creature . . . at least, that would have been how the kender would have designed the trap.

Pulling his slingshot free, Rapp thrust a round stone into the sling, then let loose. His aim proved true. The missile scored a direct hit on the forehead of the ghoulish servant. Unfortunately, it bounced off without any noticeable effect.

"Oh, dear." Backing away farther, the kender drew a dagger . . . not his own, but one that somehow had slipped from Bakal's belt into his. For the smaller Rapp, the dagger nearly served as a short sword. He waved the weapon at the shadow servant, who hesitated. So, blades did worry them. Feeling more daring, Rapp thrust it forward, trying to drive the unliving guardian back.

A hand seized the dagger by the blade. Thick black fluid spread from where the blade cut into dead flesh, but the ghoulish sentry remained undeterred. With strength belying its emaciated form, the creature tore the dagger from Rapp's grip, dropping it on the floor. The other hand again sought the kender's throat.

Rapp looked around for a weapon and noticed the torch nearest him. Whoever mounted it had been ignorant of kender needs and so had set the torches too high. That left the annoyed kender with nothing more to do but keep retreating, not at all a proper course of action.

And even that course of action vanished as another of the grotesque undead came at him from behind.

"Now, this really isn't fair!" The shadow servants, though, didn't care about fairness. The second one reached out skeletal fingers, seeking Rapp's topknot. The kender pulled away, wincing as a few strands of hair were torn free.

Flattening himself against the wall, Rapp again looked at the torch. A metal ring also held the torch in its niche, which meant that the odds of knocking one free with his sling were minimal. For Rapp to reach the torch, he would have had to grow another two feet.

Or . . .

Rapp studied the two approaching undead, trying to judge which was most suitable for his plan. While neither much appealed to him, the one to his right was positioned best. All the kender had to do was wait a second or two more . . . and hope his plan worked as well as it sounded to him.

One step. Another step.

His chance came at last.

The small figure suddenly charged the nearest hooded ghoul, leaping at the last moment. Caught unaware, the pale horror reacted slowly, enabling Rapp to use his adversary's arms to climb up. As the shadow servant's grip tightened around Rapp's torso, the inventive kender took hold of the torch.

He gasped as thin, bony limbs tried to crush his breath from him. Rapp brought the torch down toward the drawn countenance of his foe, setting the hood on fire. The dead face revealed no shock, but the shadow servant released him and tried to put the flames out. Instead, the sleeves of his robe caught fire.

The other attacker paid little heed to his companion's troubles, reaching again for the kender's topknot. Rapp twisted and thrust the torch at the groping hand. The shadow servant pulled back singed fingers. Although they had some sense of self-preservation, they clearly did not feel pain, for despite the blackened appendage, the ghoul lunged forward once more.

Stepping away, Rapp nearly collided with his first adversary, who, even though his entire form was now ablaze, seemed more concerned with seizing the kender. Rapp ducked under fiery arms, then rolled past. He came up behind the burning figure and, with careful aim, kicked.

The blazing ghoul stumbled forward, falling into the arms of the other creature. Flames spread over the hands and sleeves of the second. The first tried to rise but collapsed again. This time it remained still.

With effort, the remaining ghoul abandoned the other and tried to pursue Rapp. However, the shadow servant's steps were ragged, undirected. The hooded figure collided with one wall, then the other. Rapp used the confusion to further set the creature aflame, and in moments the second servant had turned into a fiery inferno.

Still reaching for the kender, the robed horror dropped to the floor. Flames quickly consumed what was left.

Rapp wrinkled his nose at the stench. Despite his victory, the kender felt a bit sad. These had once been men, albeit men who had died long ago. He had not killed men, only the abominations someone else had made of their corpses.

And that brought his attention back to Tyros.

A short distance down the corridor, Rapp at last came across two large doors that surely had to be the ones leading to the mage. As if to verify that, a cry from within shook the kender to his very being. He recognized Tyros's voice and recognized also the intense agony the human suffered.

To Rapp's surprise, the doors weren't locked. With some caution, he pushed one open and peered inside.

The kender's eyes widened.

Valkyn's creation towered over Rapp, nearly touching the high ceiling of the chamber. The twin marble columns were thicker than the trunks of the mightiest trees, and upon them were etched symbols and words of magic that seemed to squirm with life of their own. Above each was positioned a huge crystal that blazed like a miniature sun.

To his surprise, Rapp discovered that he was not so fascinated by the arcane device as he was repulsed. It felt *evil*. Rapp had never come across anything that actually felt evil, and he would have expected such a discovery to fill him with excitement. Instead, just looking at it made the kender shiver, especially seeing what it had done to the helpless wizard chained to it.

Tyros looked haggard, his skin pale and drawn. The mage's hair had turned partially gray. He was thinner, too, his robe hanging loose. Tyros slumped as low as his chains would allow.

The great crystals suddenly flared. Raw energy crackled between them. Tyros screamed.

A bolt of energy shot toward the ceiling, flowing through it as if the stone and wood did not exist.

The glow around the crystals subsided again. The captive mage groaned, falling forward. He looked older, more worn.

Rapp surveyed the chamber and saw that other than Tyros and himself, it was empty. The kender noted a stool near one table. Finding a place to put the torch, Rapp grabbed the stool and rushed over to the captive. Tyros looked up as he neared, and although surprise momentarily flashed in his eyes, he didn't look at all hopeful.

"Don't worry. I'll set you free!"

The mage started to say something, but his words twisted suddenly into renewed screaming. The sound hurt Rapp's ears. He couldn't let Tyros suffer any longer. His best lockpick in hand, the kender positioned the stool, and climbed up so that he could reach the glowing manacle binding Tyros's left wrist. The manacle looked identical to the ones that had secured Stone, which gave Rapp every confidence that he would soon have his friend released.

Tyros suddenly jerked his wrist away, at the same time blurting, "N-No!"

He screamed again, leaving the kender to stand there, frustrated. How could he help the mage if Tyros did contrary things like that? Didn't he realize that Rapp had to work fast to rescue him?

Once more Rapp reached for the manacle, Tyros again pulled his wrist out of reach.

Confused and annoyed, the small figure glared at his friend. "Tyros, it's me, Rapp. Stop doing that so I can get you free!"

Gritting his teeth, his eyes tearing, Tyros forced the words out: "Manacles . . . magic! If you touch . . . you'll die!"

The mage slumped forward. Rapp stared at Tyros, then at the manacle. He had opened the ones holding the gargoyle without incident, but the mage said these were different. Valkyn must have put a potent spell on them, not wanting to take any chance of someone removing his fellow wizard.

Rapp swallowed, feeling uncommonly dismayed. If he couldn't unlock the manacles, then how could he free Tyros? And if he couldn't free Tyros, how could any of them hope to escape?

Chapter 16

A Prayer Answered

From the battlements of Atriun, Bakal watched the defenders and invaders maneuver themselves in preparation for the battle. He tried his best to keep his despair hidden from his captors. With Castle Atriun at full strength and no dragons to protect the city, Gwynned would surely fall. First, though, the wizard and the general wanted to make certain that no outside resistance remained. Those defenders that survived the citadel's attack from above would be annihilated, driven into the swords of their foes.

"Many will die," Cadrio reminded him. "The longer the battle, the more deaths. You can save a number of lives, Captain. Give us specifics on Gwynned's strengths, and we can end this battle swiftly. Minimal losses. Men can go back to their wives and children . . . if they also acknowledge their new master, of course."

The general seemed very eager for results, and from the glances the man gave the wizard, Bakal gathered that Cadrio wanted desperately to please Valkyn. However, the scarred veteran would be damned if he would help the villain do that. "There's nothing I can tell you."

"If not you, then perhaps one of them." He pointed at the two remaining soldiers. Galan, the younger of the pair, leaned heavily against Korbius, a veteran like Bakal. As with Bakal, the two men had been released from their bonds, but their captors hardly feared that they would try anything. Korbius's leg had been torn open by the gargoyles, leaving him unable to run. As for young Galan, he could barely stand and, if the captain were any judge of neck wounds, slipped nearer to death with each passing moment.

"We'll not betray our home and our kin," dark-skinned

Korbius muttered. Galan nodded agreement, unable to say anything.

"Then we've no use for either of you," the wizard suddenly announced. He had been quiet for the most part, letting Cadrio do the questioning. Now, despite his disinterested expression, he had evidently run out of patience. "Crag, eliminate them."

The monstrous gargoyle turned toward Korbius and Galan.

"No! Wait!" Bakal started for the beast, but two sentries in black, men as nervous as Cadrio seemed, held him in place.

The winged beast hissed. Korbius put young Galan behind him, then brought up both fists, but Bakal knew how little good those hands would be against the hard hide of Crag.

The soldier swung, striking the gargoyle in the beak. Korbius grimaced at the pain, but Crag easily shrugged off the blow. With fiendish glee, the eager gargoyle fluttered high above the pair, then quickly dropped down on them, talons extended.

Korbius put his hands up, trying to hold the murderous creature off, but Crag's sheer weight brought the humans to the ground. Galan struck his head and lay still. The older soldier struggled in vain to keep the toothy jaws from his throat.

Bakal turned his gaze away as Crag's claws and teeth swiftly ended the horrible, one-sided struggle.

"That'll be enough, Crag," Valkyn finally commanded. To the human guards holding Bakal, he added, "Show him the price for not cooperating."

They forced his gaze back to the mangled bodies. Bakal barely managed to keep the contents of his stomach down. Crag had clearly thrown himself into his task. Even now the horrific gargoyle perched nearby, licking his blood-soaked paws clean. The creature looked up at him and gave what seemed a macabre imitation of the wizard's own mocking smile.

"This is what fate awaits your kin below," Valkyn calmly stated. "I'd rather not see such bloodshed if we can do this properly. You could save lives by cutting short the battle. Tell us about the catapults, the intentions of the commanders, and where the weakest links in the lines likely are."

Bakal couldn't betray his people. "You must be joking. You'll have to fight to win your prize, spellcaster."

Cadrio reached for his knife. "Let me begin on him, Valkyn."

Before the goateed wizard could decide, a noise from below caught the attention of everyone.

"What was that?" Valkyn demanded.

The general turned from Bakal, gazing over the edge. "It's the Ergothians. They've decided not to wait. They're on the move!"

Sure enough, the defenders had decided not to wait any longer for Valkyn's forces. The noise those in Atriun had heard were the sounds of catapults launching their deadly missiles. Even as Bakal and the others watched, the first missiles struck.

Massive boulders flew through the sky. Simple but very deadly, they shot unerringly toward the enemy. With the catapults positioned on higher ground, the defenders gained even more distance on their shots. The stone missiles dropped into the first ranks of the invaders, wreaking havoc.

Even as the enemy struggled to maintain position, a huge form emerged from the hills, wending its way toward Gwynned's foes.

Sunfire.

Initially cheered by the sight, Bakal realized quickly that the dragon had suffered greatly from his previous encounter with the citadel. Sunfire moved more slowly than usual and, with one wing in tatters, clearly would never fly again. Still, a dragon on the ground, especially a gold one, could spell disaster for the enemy soldiers.

"Our men will be decimated unless something is done!" Cadrio snapped.

"And do something we will, General." Pulling out the crystal wand, Valkyn turned his gaze toward the central tower.

At that moment, an incredible force shook Atriun.

The fortress moved as if struck by an earthquake. Atriun tipped forward, forcing everyone to grab hold of whatever was handy or be tossed over the side. One of Bakal's guards lost his grip and fell over the battlements, screaming. Crag abandoned his roost, opting for the safety of the sky.

All but forgotten in the chaos, Bakal saw his one chance. As the citadel began to right itself, he pushed his remaining guard at Cadrio. Bakal had hoped to send both of them over the wall, but the general threw himself to the side. As the second guard tumbled to his death, Captain Bakal raced to the inner edge of the walkway.

The steps were too far away, but not so the flat roof of the stables. Taking a deep breath, Bakal jumped.

The roof creaked ominously but held his weight. Bakal ran along the roof even as a shadow swept over him—Crag, come to reclaim the Ergothian for his master.

The boards beneath Bakal's feet suddenly cracked. Before the captain knew what was happening, he fell through, dropping into the old building. Above him, he heard the flutter of wings and knew that Crag had just barely missed catching his prey.

Bakal landed on some old sacks, which split apart, spilling dried feed grain. Coughing from the dust, the soldier pushed himself up and looked around. A few rusted implements caught his expert eye, especially a hand scythe.

A manic force crashed against the doors. Bakal heard a roar that could only have come from Crag.

Both doors went flying as the huge gargoyle threw himself at them again. The captain took hold of the hand scythe.

With a savage roar, the gargoyle flew at Bakal.

The soldier brought the scythe around just as Crag fell upon him. The curved blade caught the monster across the muzzle. Only Captain Bakal's experience and strength enabled the rusting blade to dig into the hard, leathery skin.

Dark blood splattered Bakal, and he had the satisfaction of hearing Crag howl in pain. The soldier kicked with all the force he could muster, sending the gargoyle falling backward into a pile of rotting bridles and wagon gear.

Knowing that the scythe wouldn't serve him well enough to slay the monster, Captain Bakal dashed past the gargoyle and out the doors. Even though he knew that Crag would soon be on his trail again, Bakal had only one thing on his mind. With Valkyn occupied with the battle and most of the gargoyles in flight, the Wind Captain's Chair would be less defended. This time Bakal would be ready for the traps on the stairs.

This time Bakal would make it to the top even if it killed him.

* * * * *

Cadrio glanced back and saw the desperate figure racing into the castle. "Your pet gargoyle hasn't done a very good job, Valkyn. The Ergothian's inside the castle!"

"He's probably heading to the tower again." To the wizard, one soldier meant nothing. He saw Bakal as no threat; what could the man do? Still, best not to leave anything to chance. "Deal with him, then, General. I prefer to keep matters tidy, which seems at the moment beyond Crag's capabilities."

Even as he said it, the gargoyle flew into sight, searching for his prey. He headed toward the castle, but at the last moment turned right, vanishing into the wooded garden.

"Fool of a beast!" the general said with some satisfaction. Cadrio drew his sword, then turned to the mage. "What about Crag? Will he attack me, too?"

"Crag knows I suffer you to live for now, General Cadrio. He'll not touch a hair on your head if he knows what serves him best. If necessary, slay him. I'm growing less fond of gargoyles; they either turn incompetent or traitorous. Perhaps I could capture some kyrie next time and turn them to my purposes. For avians, they've always seemed an intelligent race."

"You want the Ergothian alive?"

Valkyn pursed his lips. "No . . . we're past needing him." A sound from below, one that both men knew to be that of a catapult launching its missile, made the black mage smile.

"Run along now. I must concentrate my full efforts on Gwynned, so you'll need to rely on your own resources and ingenuity. Be quick about it, though. I may have need for you here shortly."

As Cadrio dashed toward the steps, Valkyn returned his attention to the battle below. More catapults had gone into action, and from where he stood, the wizard could see that they would strike his own forces with tremendous accuracy. The defenders were good—very good. The quake that had shaken Atriun and allowed the prisoner to flee had been the result of an exceptional shot that had struck the underside of the citadel. Valkyn had taken the citadel higher now, so there would be no repeat of that incident.

Now it was his turn.

Still holding the wand, he clasped his gloved hands together almost gleefully. "Well, then!" he whispered to the unknowing masses below. "Shall we show you true power?"

He held up the wand, briefly caressing the crystal on top. So much magic, and all his to control . . .

The clouds rumbled and spread. A flash of lightning paid homage to its master. Valkyn smiled at the quickly darkening sky, then peered down at the hills where the enemy catapults stood.

"Yes. You'll make a most suitable first target. . . ."

The wand glowed.

* * * * *

Music from thin air.

Serene's heart leaped at the heavenly sounds. Her prayers had been answered. The Bard King had not abandoned her. Serene sang and played, rejoicing in the sensation of goodness that filled her.

The doors to her chamber flew open. Serene's song faltered as a gargoyle leaped inside, eyes burning bright. She rose from the bed, certain that Valkyn had sent this creature to stop her.

Then Serene noticed that the gargoyle had no wings, only two burned stubs.

"Cleric!" he growled. "Help me fly!"

Why would one of Valkyn's monsters ask for her aid, knowing that their master wouldn't approve? Suddenly a thought struck her.

"Stone?"

The gargoyle's head dipped. "Stone . . . yes . . ."

What had happened to his wings? Had he been in some terrible accident? "Did Valkyn do that to you?"

The head dipped again. "The master . . ."

Her role as cleric took over. "Come to me."

He obeyed, falling to one knee so that she could inspect the damage. Valkyn had been monstrously thorough, of course. He could always be trusted for that. Serene couldn't believe the callousness with which he treated life. How had he kept such darkness hidden from her . . . or had she kept it hidden from herself?

"Can make better?" the gargoyle asked.

Serene had healed the wounds and injuries of animals several times, but none this severe. Could she grow Stone new wings? Could any cleric perform such a miracle?

There was only one way to find out. If Branchala willed it so, it would happen.

She placed her hands on the burned stubs. In the past, her prayers for such efforts had been in the form of soft, nurturing melodies, songs that urged growth and renewal. Best that she keep with what had worked best for her.

"Branchala, hear my plea for this unfortunate creature," Serene began. Outside, thunder and lightning punctuated her request, sending a shiver through her. The ungodly storm reminded her that others faced terrible danger. Yet, for now, Serene didn't know what to do for them. She couldn't very well face down Valkyn's storm.

Her hands felt pleasantly warm, like a wonderful spring day. Again the cleric became caught up in her song, in her devotion to her god. Branchala would aid her if he saw the right of her task; if not, then he had his reasons. She would not question them.

Stone suddenly bent over and began moaning. Serene

forced herself to continue, her words accompanied by music that flowed from within her. She hoped her deity would see Stone not as a monster, but rather a poor creature who had tried not only to free his own people, but to aid her and her companions as well. Surely he deserved a better fate.

Stone hissed. Serene stepped away. The gargoyle's stubs glowed green, the green of the forest. They also looked much larger, with small areas of leathery skin growing from them. The appendages twisted, spread, taking on a familiar form.

Stone had *wings* again.

Pathetically small, they looked nonetheless fit. Still, Serene did not cease her efforts. She threw herself more into her devotions, already thanking Branchala for what he had done but asking if, in his heart, he could do a bit more.

And the wings grew. . . .

In a heartbeat, they doubled in size, then doubled again. Stone continued to groan, but not with pain. He seemed to be putting forth an effort of his own, as if the Bard King insisted that the gargoyle, too, be responsible for what he had asked of the cleric.

At last the leathery creature rose, stretching new, magnificent wings. Not only did they look larger, more grand, but so did the gargoyle himself. Serene marveled at what she had accomplished. Stone extended his claws and tested his wings again. The pupilless orbs flared bright red.

He turned to the cleric, who briefly wondered whether she had made a fatal mistake in judgment. However, Stone fell to his knees, placing his muzzle on the floor just before her feet. He folded his wings and extended the back of his neck for her to see, a sign of deference.

"Mistress, thank you."

"Please don't thank me," she returned, although a slight bit of pride touched her. "I'm but a vessel for the Bard King."

Stone clearly did not see the distinction. If the power came through Serene, then she had to be the one to thank.

"Cleric is greater than Master," he replied.

Greater? If true, then she would not be trapped here, helpless, while Valkyn and his citadel literally rained down destruction upon the Ergothians. Even Rapp had seen her as less than an asset when it had come to mounting a rescue of Tyros.

And yet she had helped Stone gain his new wings. Of course, that had been in great part due to the Bard King, who, though his greatest spheres of influence lay over the forest and weather, also watched over animals, which apparently included gargoyles. If only . . .

"The weather . . ." Serene suddenly murmured. "The weather . . ."

The cleric glanced outside, where the unnatural storm had begun to blow in earnest. If Valkyn had not already struck at the defenders of Gwynned, he would in the next few moments.

"Branchala, please forgive me for the madness I'm about to ask of you." She considered the gargoyle. "Stone, please close the hallway doors." Serene couldn't afford to be disturbed. "Stone, is your flock willing to fight for their freedom?"

A look of great anticipation spread across the monstrous features. "Yes . . . oh, yesss . . ."

"If I succeed at what I'm about to attempt, they must be ready to do so. However, I must first make you promise that they'll also watch out for my friends."

"Will do that."

Serene looked around. She hated sending the gargoyle away, but he needed to spread the word. Still, with Valkyn busy, the cleric hoped to have time to complete her plan before anyone realized she was responsible. "You'd better go now. May the blessing of the Bard King be with you, Stone."

"Have wings again," the creature replied. He gave the cleric one last appreciative look, then trotted out to the balcony. Serene watched in admiration as the gargoyle spread his new wings. Stone dived from the rail, then soared into the air.

"And now it's up to you and me, Branchala." Seating herself on the bed once more, Serene took up the same position she had earlier. If the music came when her fingers played, the cleric would know that she had a chance to succeed . . . which did not mean that she would. Even the Bard King would only do so much for her. "But this is for more than just me, my lord."

Serene began to strum the air, at first hearing nothing. Yet when she started to sing softly, tender notes accompanied her. As her voice found strength, those notes increased in strength, too. The woodland god was with her . . . so far.

The cleric turned her gaze to the baleful storm and sang louder.

* * * * *

"Hold your ranks, damn it!" Zander roared as the first missiles struck. "Hold them together!"

The officers did their best to keep the lines intact and in position, but the wizard's primitive battle plan kept the frontlines too much in the open and too large a target. Zander would have realigned most of the left flank, but any alteration had been forbidden. He had to make do with what Valkyn allowed, however murderous that turned out to be.

"Can we fly now?" Eclipse snapped. "They come too close!"

For once, Zander had to agree with him. "All right. Take to the air!"

With clear relief, the black leviathan leaped into the sky, nearly unseating Zander from his back in the process. The young officer made no remark, though, more interested in what happened below. From the sky, the situation looked more bleak than he had thought. Gwynned's forces had arranged themselves to the best tactical advantage, with catapults positioned on well-defended hills that gave them a view of his entire army. Archers set lower down on the hills made certain that those who avoided the missiles ran straight into their deadly fire, after which cavalry harassed the survivors. Zander's men were open targets no matter where they were, and it was a wonder he had managed to keep them from routing. It looked like certain victory for the Ergothians.

Thunder rumbled, causing Zander to smile for the first time. Certain victory . . . if not for the flying citadel.

Those manning the two catapults situated on a hill to the southwest likely never knew what hit them. The first bolt, a massive, jagged monster, flew unerringly toward its unwitting target. One moment, the men and their weapons stood untouched. The next . . . nothing but shattered bits and smoke remained.

Zander laughed, admiring the mage's handiwork. Eclipse joined in the mirth, ever pleased to see others suffer.

"We attack?" the dragon cried.

"No, we hold back. This hour belongs to Valkyn!" And he was welcome to it. There would be plenty for Zander's men to do once Castle Atriun had destroyed the defenders.

"I see the gold!" hissed Eclipse. "Look there!"

The gold dragon moved along the ground just beyond the hills, harrying the advance troops still caught out in the open. Zander studied the beast, noticing the ruined wings. "He can't fly."

"Good! The better to kill. I want to kill!" Battle would keep the ebony dragon from thinking about his twin.

A second and third bolt struck.

The first of the pair tore apart more of the catapults, leaving a blackened hole and mangled bodies. The second wreaked still more havoc on the Ergothian troops. As Zander watched, a fourth lightning bolt struck behind the defenders' front lines, forcing many of the Ergothians out into the open. Two more quick and deadly strikes behind them sent the startled warriors directly into the waiting arms of the invaders.

"Now!" Zander shouted. "Now!"

His men couldn't hear him, of course, but the officers on the ground nonetheless took advantage of the chaos, setting their troops loose on the desperate defenders. Valkyn's plan had worked. Already Gwynned's front lines were in disarray. Zander nodded in satisfaction as the first swords of both armies met, the clash audible even from this high vantage point.

Only Eclipse found no satisfaction with events. A thousand men might die, but the dragon only had eyes for one thing.

"I want the gold male!"

Zander considered. With Atriun striking with the power of the storm, nothing could stand in the way of the invaders. Yes, it was time for a little glory of his own.

"All right," Zander shouted, drawing his sword. "We'll take the golden male, but I command the attack!"

"So long as I taste his blood and feel his death!"

The black dragon dived, roaring. Sunfire looked skyward, saw the danger, and roared his own challenge.

The battle began in earnest.

Chapter 17

~

Turning the Storm

Rapp heard thunder again, followed by the renewed screams of Tyros. The kender paced the area before the infernal device, frantic with frustration.

From Tyros, he had learned that, unlike the manacles holding Stone, Valkyn had set these to kill anyone who tried to open them without his authority. After Tyros had so readily freed his friend Leot, the other wizard had decided not to take any more chances.

Despite all his lockpicks, Rapp could do nothing. Even Tyros himself didn't have an answer.

The screaming subsided. The captive mage shook his head and, with tears streaming down, shouted, "Rapp, listen to me! One choice!"

"You've thought of something?" The kender's eyes widened in hope.

"K-Kill me, Rapp. It's the . . . the only way!"

Rapp looked at him in shock. "But I can't do that!" It was one thing to hunt an animal for food or fight one of Valkyn's undead servants, but to slay a friend, even for the sake of others . . . "I can't!"

"Y-You have to! Valkyn . . . using me . . . to help kill others. Without m-me . . . loses way to power. Otherwise," Tyros gritted his teeth and blurted out, "too many more will d-die!"

Not since he had found the orphan griffon cubs had Rapp been confronted by such a monumental decision. Of course, that choice had been easier. Rapp might have been a kender, one of a race with the inborn urge to wander, but he also had a sense of caring. The griffons would not have lived without him. Now, though, the small adventurer had to choose between one life and many.

"There must be another way." Rapp turned once more to survey the chamber, finally focusing on the tables. With renewed hope, the kender rushed over and began studying the contents of each, looking for anything that might help.

There were rocks and crystals of all shapes, colors, and clarity. A few resembled the great crystals, and these Rapp marked for possible later perusal. Several jars held fascinating specimens of creatures or organs, but none of those seemed appropriate for the task at hand. Valkyn also kept a vast array of tools for crystal work, and while a few of these accidentally ended up in Rapp's pouches, none would serve to free Tyros.

The imprisoned mage cried out more than once, which urged Rapp on. Yet nothing seemed right. The kender searched the rest of the chamber and found no sign of the original keys. Valkyn no doubt now carried those on his person, but Rapp could certainly not go hunting for the black mage. Yet without a key . . .

And then a very unkenderlike notion occurred to him. He had constantly been thinking of lockpicks and keys, believing the manacles the focus of his efforts despite the deadly spell on them. However, if he couldn't even touch, much less open them, what if he concentrated elsewhere? Maybe Valkyn hadn't thought about that.

Rapp looked around for anything that might do the trick. Of course, wizards were not very physical, and so the kender could not immediately find what he sought. Still, Rapp felt encouraged.

"Give . . . give up, Rapp! K-Killing me is . . . is the only way!"

"No. I think I know how to free you!"

"I told y-you. Manacles . . . enchanted."

Rapp had no time to explain. He needed a good, strong edge, something he could lift and swing.

And there, seemingly forgotten in one remote end of the chamber, lay a sword. Rapp recognized the sword from the catacombs. Tyros had taken it with him, despite the fact that mages were not allowed to use any edged weapon larger than a dagger. A foul-looking black crust covered a good third of the blade. Still, the Solamnic weapon would serve well enough for what the kender had in mind.

Tyros misunderstood his intentions. "Good . . . S-Strike true . . . please! And hurry! No telling what . . . what carnage Valkyn's caused."

"Don't you worry, Tyros. I know what to do."

The mage closed his eyes, preparing himself. Rapp shrugged, then dragged the stool he had used earlier to one of the great marble columns. Hefting the sword with both hands, the kender stepped up. With the stool, he could readily reach the chain, which had been bolted into the column roughly level with the wizard's shoulder.

Tyros finally opened his eyes, no doubt curious as to why he still lived. When he saw what Rapp intended, his expression grew more horrified. "Rapp! Don't!"

"But don't you see, Tyros? I'm not going to try the manacles at all. I'm going to break the chain off at the base."

"I-Insane! Rapp, l-listen to me!"

The kender readied the sword. It felt heavier than he had first thought. "There isn't time, Tyros! You said so yourself!"

As if to punctuate his words, the device flared and the mage screamed again.

Rapp stared at where the chain was bolted to the column. Perhaps he had been mistaken and all he would achieve would be death. It would be an interesting, if rather final, experience.

"Oh, well . . ." He swung the heavy sword like an axe.

The edge of the blade struck true. Rapp felt every bone in his body rattle, but no spell turned him to ash. The clatter echoed throughout the chamber.

Again he swung, nearly losing his balance in the process.

"Anything?" Tyros asked, now hopeful, since the kender had not been obliterated.

"Let me try again." This time the miniature warrior inhaled, then swung. His bones did not rattle so hard this time, and at last he had the satisfaction of seeing part of the marble at the bolt break away. "It's working!"

"P-Praise Lunitari!" the captive spellcaster gasped.

Rapp continued his efforts. The sword chipped more of the marble away. The kender only prayed that the sword would hold up. The edge was already badly chipped.

Tyros tugged on the chain. "I think . . . I f-felt it give a little."

Again Rapp attacked, and this time a crack appeared in the column. A small crack, but near where the chain began.

Tyros pulled. The kender marveled that the mage had strength after his ordeal, but the prospect of release clearly urged the human on.

Rapp stumbled off the stool as bits of marble and the heavy chain suddenly rained down on his head.

The pair looked at one another for a few seconds, drinking in the realization that one hand had been freed. Tyros flexed his hand, the chain dragging behind it as he swung his arm around. "Gods, that . . . f-feels good!"

"Is it over, then? Will it stop funneling magic through you?"

The captive mage suddenly gritted his teeth, which more than answered Rapp's question. "No . . . not until . . . completely free!"

Kicking the stool aside, Rapp studied the chain that held Tyros's ankle. "Then I guess I better get started on this one."

"Hurry . . . before it's too l-late."

Once more they saw the flash of lightning and heard the rumble of thunder . . . the sound of death for the defenders of Gwynned.

* * * * *

The Ergothians fought with desperation as even the very elements seemed to turn against them. Lightning bolts assailed the defenders. A good number of the catapults had been reduced to cinders, the bodies of the soldiers manning them scattered like leaves in the wind. The cavalry, which had managed to push back the invaders in several places, was suddenly decimated by a series of strikes in their very midst. Those that survived faced the blades of Valkyn's warriors. The defenders' lines wavered, broken in many places, but nothing could be done about the cause of their despair.

Castle Atriun drifted in the center of the ungodly storm, a monstrous, untouchable nemesis. It stayed well out of the range of the catapults, and the only defender who might have been able to face it not only could no longer fly but also had troubles of his own.

Sunfire snapped and slashed at the foul black, but Eclipse hovered just out of range, moving in only when the gold left himself open. Both had tried unsuccessfully to use their breath weapons, but even though Sunfire held his own, he knew he was at a great disadvantage. The human riding Eclipse knew well how to direct the black's battle and even when to use his own tiny sword to distract the injured leviathan.

The gold dragon knew he would die, and that with his death would come the death of the eggs, but Sunfire couldn't abandon the land he had chosen to protect. Glisten would have understood. The evil citadel and its master were a far worse menace than either of them had believed. If Sunfire could even slow it, he would buy others precious time. Yet to reach it, he would have to fly, and not only did his wings not work, but he doubted that he would even survive the battle with this upstart black beast.

Eclipse mocked him from above. "Old crippled wyrm! You should have died with your mate instead of running like a coward. No better than a wyvern, old one!"

"Better at my worst than you at your best, foul one!" Sunfire slashed at Eclipse and had the satisfaction of watching the other leviathan dart back in momentary retreat.

Eclipse, though, immediately dropped down, catching his adversary by surprise. The black's claws dug into Sunfire's hide, drawing blood. Before the gold could take a bite out of him, Eclipse quickly released his murderous hold and flew back out of reach.

The human's doing! The younger dragon had neither the cunning nor the experience for such maneuvers. His rider had directed the last attack, knowing that each blow would weaken Sunfire more and more until he proved an easy kill.

It would only be a matter of time. Still, Sunfire would do what he could to avenge his family. If he could at least badly wound Eclipse, it would give him great satisfaction.

A horrendous bolt ripped into the earth, startling the two dragons. Sunfire blinked, realizing that the lightning had nearly hit his adversary. Previous bolts had struck their targets with unerring accuracy. Why this mistake now?

An ear-shattering rumble made both behemoths look up. To their mutual astonishment, the storm had abruptly shifted. Even as they watched, a lightning bolt struck the front lines of the invaders. Caught off guard, scores of men perished. Confusion rose on both sides of the conflict.

"What goes on?" muttered the great gold. "Is the citadel's master mad? Does he plan to destroy everyone but himself?"

And then the storm turned on the castle itself. . . .

* * * * *

The smile upon Valkyn's face utterly vanished as his precious creation suddenly went mad. The misdirected bolts attacking his soldiers he could have forgiven as some sort of accidental discharge of pent-up magical forces, but now one had shattered a good portion of the outer wall to his right. In fact, only his own intervention had turned the lightning enough to miss the castle. Unfortunately, while Valkyn had been busy with that blast, a second had ripped through the sky, battering one of the lower towers.

"Impossible! Utterly impossible!" He had worked so hard to create this new flying citadel, and now someone else had the arrogance to think he could turn it against the dark mage. The source of his ire had to actually be aboard the castle. Only one other, in Valkyn's estimation, could have managed such a feat.

"Tyros . . ."

* * * * *

Had Valkyn thought further, he might have considered that one other had the capabilities. That other now sat in her chamber, singing and praying as her fingers created note after heavenly note without the aid of an actual instrument. The magic of Branchala was with her. Serene felt her god hear her plea, felt him grant what she asked. Yet to keep the storm from returning to the control of Valkyn, the cleric had to keep singing and playing.

She had shifted the emphasis of her song. Even if Serene and the others could not escape, she would see to it that her former love's mad creation never harmed anyone else. Given enough time, she would make the storm tear Castle Atriun to pieces.

A shadow loomed over her, a shadow with wings. Still singing, the cleric looked up, thinking that Stone had returned.

Only the gargoyle before her stood more massive than Stone and had three wicked horns jutting from his head. He glared at the bright surroundings, as if looking for someone else; then his gaze shifted to her. Hot, fetid breath struck her face, and her view filled with the toothy maw of the large gargoyle.

Crag.

Despite her growing apprehension, Serene ceased neither her playing nor her singing, fearful that to do so would reverse her success. The cleric tried to pretend that she sang without care, as if what she did should be of no consequence to the gargoyle.

Crag growled. Though not as quick-thinking as Stone, he knew that something didn't look right. Certainly the winged fury did not trust this woman. He moved forward, reaching out with one taloned hand to touch where the harp should have been, frustrated when that did not stop the music, which seemingly came from nowhere.

The beast pulled back. His expression darkened further. "Stop muuuusic!"

Serene kept on playing, trying to decide how to deal with the intruder. Crag looked dangerously near to forgetting his master's authority and attacking her.

"Where maaan? Where?"

She had no idea what man he spoke of, although Tyros came to mind. Had Rapp managed to free him?

When the human didn't answer, Crag grew even more incensed. He leaned very close, causing the cleric to falter. The gargoyle suddenly reached out, snaring her right hand and putting a jarring end to her music.

"Let go of me! Valkyn will not be pleased!"

"Nooo . . ." Crag gave her an evil look. "Maaaster will be pleased."

He pulled her to her feet. Serene didn't fear so much for herself as for her work. The storm would revert to Valkyn's control. Gwynned's defenders would once more be crushed from above.

A second winged form fluttered through the window. Serene's heart sank further until the newcomer, instead of joining Crag, snarled at the larger gargoyle.

"Release human . . . now!"

"Stooone . . ." Crag seemed to forget all about Serene. His fiery eyes blazed with anticipation. "Traitor to Maaaster!"

The smaller gargoyle said nothing but simply flared his wings. The action startled Crag, who must have momentarily forgotten what Valkyn had done to his rival.

"Wingsss?"

Stone nodded. "Wings . . ." He extended his talons and puffed himself up. Now he looked nearly as ferocious as the other creature. "Claws, too."

Crag tossed Serene aside carelessly and started for the other gargoyle. Only then did the cleric realize that Stone had challenged Crag to combat.

She leaped up, intending to help the smaller gargoyle, but Stone shook his head. "No! Play music!"

He knew as well as she that only her song and playing could keep the storm under control, yet still Serene hesitated. Crag was so huge. . . .

"Play! Sing, mistress!"

Taking opportunity of his foe's distraction, Crag roared and charged Stone. The two rolled across the floor, hissing and snarling as they fought.

With reluctance, the scarlet-tressed cleric seated herself and once more took up her song to her god. To her relief, the words and music came back immediately. Serene could feel the storm suddenly bend to her needs again. Now, though, she had to press the attack, increase the intensity, and hope that Tyros escaped so that she wouldn't kill him in the process.

And before her, Stone and Crag engaged in battle. Stone kept the pair rolling until he lay on top, but Crag used his greater weight to push the other gargoyle off of him. The larger beast snapped at the throat of his rival, barely missing. As Stone pulled away, though, Crag slashed with one set of talons, raking Stone's chest and leaving a trail of crimson.

A tremendous crash shook Atriun, the tremors sending both gargoyles tumbling to the corner of the room.

Crag recovered first, and before Stone could stop him, he seized the smaller creature by the throat. Stone made an attempt to pull free, but Crag shook him. The larger gargoyle raised his rival high, then hurled him across the chamber. Stone smashed against one of the walls, then dropped to the floor, dazed.

With a triumphant roar, Crag flew to finish off his adversary.

* * * * *

Captain Bakal hurried toward the steps leading to the Wind Captain's Chair, knowing that he had to be cautious. He had managed to escape the gargoyle, and the way ahead seemed clear, but the veteran knew that appearances could be deceiving. Not only did Bakal have to worry about the steps, but he had to do it with someone still in pursuit. The captain had caught a glimpse of General Cadrio, sword in hand, racing down from the battlements. Bakal considered himself a good swordsman, but he doubted his skills would long match Cadrio's, especially armed only with the scythe.

Already inside the castle, Bakal did not at first realize what happened beyond the walls. The first violent shockwave sent him to his knees, but he assumed that the defenders had simply managed a second hit with their catapults. Only when the captain reached a window did he realize that he might have been wrong.

The gargoyles fought among themselves. Bakal blinked, not at first willing to believe it. Despite the terrible storm and their master's wishes, the two factions fought tooth and claw with one another. Why would Stone risk his people so?

Then lightning struck one of the side towers, ripping off a section of wall and laying waste to part of the roof. Bakal would have marked it down as an errant strike if not for a second bolt, which tore apart one section of the outer wall.

The storm had turned on Valkyn.

It hardly seemed possible, unless someone had purposely done it. Tyros, perhaps, but then Bakal recalled that clerics of Branchala had some effect on the weather. Could it be possible that Serene had taken control of the storm? If so, could she maintain her hold? The black mage would certainly investigate, and even his past relationship with Serene wouldn't keep him from punishing her.

Whatever the reason, it made Bakal's task more essential. If he could take over, or at least damage, the Wind Captain's Chair, then certainly that would give everyone more hope.

He started up the steps to the tower, only to see one of the shadow servants descending. Bakal dropped back down and hid around a corner. The hooded figure paused at the bottom of the steps, but to the captain's great fortune, it turned the opposite direction and soon disappeared down a hallway.

Once more ascending, Bakal watched the steps carefully. Although the shadow servant had moved unhindered, that didn't mean the way was clear. From a pouch, Bakal pulled out a handful of small pebbles he had scooped up on his way into the castle for just this moment. The veteran didn't know if what he planned would work, but he couldn't think of anything else.

With careful aim, Bakal threw the pebbles on the steps before him.

He waited for a flash, a bolt, something. The steps remained normal. Bakal exhaled, both disappointed and relieved.

Knowing that he could wait no longer, the captain carefully scooped up as many of the pebbles he could, then proceeded up, repeating the process.

On the tenth step, the pebbles vanished in a familiar flash of blinding light.

Swearing, Bakal let his eyes adjust, then studied the stairway. He had been certain that the tenth step would be safe and the twelfth the deadly one. The captain cursed his aging memory. Either he had miscounted or the spell had shifted position.

Carefully crossing the magical trap, he pushed on. Even though the next few steps proved harmless, Bakal's nerves were on edge. It would take only one mistake, one lapse, to finish him. Valkyn surely had at least one more vicious trap set; wizards, after all, held a morbid fascination for such things.

Five steps from the top, Captain Bakal found another trap . . . and almost too late.

The step itself looked innocent, and even when he tossed the pebbles on it, nothing happened. Bakal even reached up and tapped the step with his scythe, quickly drawing back in order to avoid any surprise.

Still suspicious of his luck but unwilling to hesitate anymore, Bakal put a foot on the step.

A slight hiss sent him dropping.

Razor-sharp sheets of metal sprouted from the opposing walls, slicing across the step. Less than an inch separated the vile pair. If Bakal had stood there, the top half of his body would no longer have been attached to the bottom.

As quickly as they had appeared, the huge blades retracted. The devilish device had clearly been set into place by the dark mage, for as the sheets retreated, they vanished into seamless blank walls.

"Draco Paladin!" uttered the scarred veteran, for the moment unable to rise. His body shook as he thought of his near death. The captain had always been ready to give his life on the field of battle, but that hardly compared to this. Better a sword thrust through the heart than severed in half like a fish prepared for supper.

Despite the blades, Bakal knew he could not rest. Estimating the height at which they had materialized, the captain started crawling up the stairs. When the blades did not shoot out, he grew encouraged. Only two steps remained.

Two steps that he had not yet tested.

Still lying down, Bakal took the scythe and tapped the nearest. Nothing. Then, recalling that it had taken the weight of his foot to set off the blades, the Ergothian officer took a chance and used his free hand to push down.

Again nothing.

Only one step left.

Sweating, Bakal used the scythe again. When that failed to bring about any result, he touched the step himself.

And two more blades shot out of the walls, this time just above knee level.

Bakal flattened himself on the stairs, not daring to look up until the blades had vanished again.

"B-Blasted spellcasters!" Bakal didn't let the new trap slow him, though. Taking a deep breath, he pushed himself up the final few feet. The second set of metal blades forced the Ergothian to practically slither.

It was with some relief that he reached the entrance to the tower chamber. The captain gingerly touched the door. To his amazement, it opened readily, with no further surprises. Bakal entered, scythe held before him.

Windows lined the circular room, a different touch from what the veteran recalled from previous flying citadels. In those, the chamber had been sealed off from the outside save for a single inner entrance. Reports had indicated that the one who flew the castle had some magical means of viewing his destination. One had claimed that a spell on the ceiling created some sort of window to the outside world. Bakal actually thought Valkyn's approach made more sense; let a man see where he's going and be done with all the mystical nonsense.

At that moment, Bakal caught sight of Valkyn's steersman, a thing more shadow than man. No matter how many times he had seen the creatures, the cloaked ghouls still unnerved him, more so because he knew that they had once been living men just like himself.

Steeling himself, Captain Bakal shouted, "You there! Away from that thing! Do it now!"

The shadow servant did not obey. Instead, he simply turned his sightless gaze toward the soldier, revealing the pale, drawn face.

Bakal shivered. Something about that face struck a memory. He quickly dismissed the thought. Bad enough to confront the creature without the added knowledge of who he once had been.

Still the robed figure did not move. Bakal exhaled. If the shadow servant wouldn't listen to his demand, then the captain would have to use force. Holding the scythe high, Bakal marched up and took hold of the ghoul's sleeve, which slid back . . . and revealed the awful truth.

There were no hands—or rather, what little that remained of them simply melded into the controls of the misnamed Wind Captain's Chair. Glancing down, Captain Bakal saw that the feet, too, had become part of the mechanism. In fact, it was impossible to tell where the steersman ended and the Wind Captain's Chair began.

"By the gods!" Captain Bakal murmured, overwhelmed by revulsion.

"Disgustingly efficient, isn't it?" came a voice from behind him. "He told me about it, but seeing it is certainly something else. Typical of Valkyn to come up with something like this."

General Cadrio stood at the entrance. The vulpine general had his sword drawn, its point leveled at the Ergothian's gut.

Bakal realized that he had been a fool. Cadrio had allowed him to show the way. The general had likely watched from the bottom of the steps, marking each trap or action.

"You can offer to surrender, Ergothian, but I just want you to know that Valkyn doesn't see much need for you."

"You, either, from what I've seen."

Cadrio's expression darkened. "He's been more clever than I would have thought, but I'm working my way back into his graces. Better a puppet emperor of Ansalon than dead."

"Until you can cut the strings, I suppose."

The lanky villain smiled slightly. "Until then, yes . . ."

The captain doubted that Valkyn would prove as foolish as General Cadrio believed. From what Bakal had seen so far, the wizard would let Cadrio hang himself when the time came. "It will be interesting to see which one of you proves wrong. . . ."

"Does that mean you're surrendering?"

Now Bakal smiled. "No, I don't think I'll be doing that."

"Probably not the best idea, but the result will be the same whether you accept your death willingly or not."

Bakal readied the hand scythe. "I'll take that chance."

Cadrio suddenly thrust. The general moved even swifter than Bakal expected. He barely parried the blade with the more awkward scythe, then quickly backed away before his adversary could follow through. The Ergothian veteran skirted around the shadow servant, assuming that General Cadrio wouldn't slay the creature.

The dark warrior nearly did just that, so eagerly did he want Bakal. The sword went past the face of the servant, who paid it as much mind as he did the air. Cadrio backed away, then started around the robed figure. The captain kept pace, trying to assess his chances. Not only did Cadrio move fast, but his sword far outreached the curving scythe. Bakal needed to get well within range of the skilled swordsman to do any good with his own weapon.

"Stop dancing and fight . . . or is this how the Ergothians lost their vast empire?"

If he expected taunts to get to Bakal, Cadrio was sorely mistaken. The captain had not lived this long by falling prey to words. "Trade weapons with me and we'll see how you dance."

Again Cadrio thrust, and again he nearly skewered the shadow servant. The general seemed not to care if he killed the only one keeping the castle on course. If anything happened to the robed creature, then Atriun would go flying out of control and . . .

Bakal had made many quick but difficult decisions in his

career, but this one he found the worst. Castle Atriun needed to be destroyed. No one, not even the Whitestone Council, had the right to the knowledge needed to create such an ungodly craft.

He held the scythe ready, as if preparing to meet Cadrio head-on. The general smiled, poising himself for the Ergothian's attack.

"I'll make it quick for you, Captain."

"Just what I was thinking . . ."

Bakal swung with all his might, but his target was not General Cadrio. As the commander moved to defend himself, Bakal suddenly turned in a different direction. Cadrio finally realized what his adversary intended and let out a cry of outrage.

The scythe bit into the neck of the shadow servant.

Black bile spurted from the open wound. The shadow servant shivered, then grew still. The Ergothian muttered a quick prayer to the gods, feeling remorse for slaying a creature that could not even defend himself.

The corpse slumped forward . . . and the castle suddenly dipped sharply.

Both Bakal and his foe tumbled to the wall. The two soldiers lost their weapons, but that didn't stop Cadrio. Rising to one knee, he twisted the captain's arm behind him, then pushed Bakal hard against the wall again. Out of the corner of his eye, Bakal saw the general draw his dagger.

The citadel dipped a different direction, throwing Cadrio off-balance. Captain Bakal managed to pull free but couldn't drag himself out of his adversary's reach.

Cadrio spun the captain around. The two men grappled, the taller Cadrio pressing Bakal against the open window. The general brought his dagger up . . .

And again Castle Atriun twisted in a different direction. The pair went flying into the Wind Captain's Chair, shattering it and sending the corpse sprawling.

Even as he rolled free of the wreckage, Bakal wondered how long the chaos could continue. Atriun flew out of control, turning and dipping in random directions, and now the only method by which to control its flight had been destroyed. In truth, what did the outcome of the fight matter when surely the citadel would eventually destroy itself?

At that moment, General Cadrio rose over Bakal, dagger high.

Finding himself eager to live despite Atriun's certain doom, the Ergothian reached blindly for anything he could use for a weapon. His hand touched something hard and crystalline.

With a practiced arm, Captain Bakal threw the object at his looming foe.

The fragment from the Wind Captain's Chair struck Cadrio hard in the temple. The general dropped his weapon and staggered backward. Bakal threw himself at Cadrio, catching the general at the waist even as Atriun lurched wildly.

Both men fell toward one of the open windows. Bakal, facing it, saw the danger and released his hold, tumbling to the floor.

The general couldn't stop his momentum. As he fell through the window, he tried to grab the edge of it, but his fingers slipped free.

With a cry, Marcus Cadrio plummeted from sight.

Pulling himself up, Bakal peered out. General Cadrio lay in the courtyard below, his tall, slim form now jumbled like a scarecrow cut loose from its pole. The commander's battered face wore a bitter expression.

Lightning struck so near that it momentarily blinded Bakal. He blinked, then looked up and noticed that not only did Atriun seem lower in the sky, but the mountains in the distance no longer appeared so distant. They were, in fact, getting much, much closer.

The flying citadel had become a victim of the whims of the magical storm. Now it floated to the north, away from the battle and toward the nearest of the mountains . . . with no way to turn it back.

Chapter 18

❦

Victory and Sacrifice

"There! I did it!"

"Good, Rapp. B-But hurry! Still . . . still need my . . . other arm free." Tyros stretched his leg, trying to work the cramps out of it. It kept his mind from the pain that still coursed through his body each time Valkyn's foul device drew raw magic through him. Until Rapp had him completely freed, Tyros remained a living part of the arcane spell.

Tyros hoped Valkyn wouldn't discover what they were doing, at least not until the red mage was ready to face him. He needed a chance to rest a little and recoup from what he had suffered.

The wizard's entire body vibrated as Rapp struck the base of the last chain with the badly beaten sword. Rapp had a keen eye, but the massive weapon had tired the generally energetic kender to such a point that he had to pause for a breath after each swing.

"I'll get it, Tyros. I promise!"

Another wave of horrific pain sent Tyros to his knees, and the tall mage couldn't answer. Each time Tyros was forced to funnel magic through him, it felt as if some part of his soul was ripped away.

Again Rapp struck the base of the chain. Tyros steadied himself, then leaned away from the column in order to keep the chain as taut as possible. He tugged over and over, trying to see if any of Rapp's blows had managed to loosen it.

The entire chamber suddenly dipped. Benches slid from the walls, spilling flasks, tools, jars, and other items on the floor. A cloud of yellow smoke rose over one table and slowly began to spread.

Rapp lost his balance. His sword slid past Tyros. Even the mage had to steady himself or else risk pulling his chained arm out of its socket.

"Tyros, did you feel that? How come the room is at an angle? I mean, it's fascinating and all, but it doesn't seem very practical, what with things dropping all over the place."

"I . . . don't know. Perhaps . . . a change of c-course." A violent change of course, to be certain. Had he believed it possible, Tyros almost would have thought that Valkyn had lost control of his flying citadel.

Whatever the reason, it made no difference to Valkyn's monstrous device. Still it forced Tyros to draw power for spellwork, then drew that power from him, once more sending Tyros down on one knee.

As the mage fought the pain, Rapp dragged the stool and battered sword back to the column. The kender looked pale and tired, but hardly vanquished. Tyros praised the gods for a kender's tenacity; he freely admitted to himself that he would have been hard-pressed to keep up such a pace.

Once more Rapp swung at the chain's base, chipping away at the marble but further chipping his blade. Tyros thought at last he felt the chain give a little. He tugged hard, trying to help. "A little . . . little more, Rapp. I think it's l-loosening!"

"Now, we can't have that, can we?"

A shiver ran through Tyros, but it wasn't caused by the foul spell. Near the door stood Valkyn, his damnable smile in place and his wand held high in one gloved hand. The smile seemed a little forced, as if the black mage barely held himself in check.

Rapp took one quick, desperate glance at the hooded wizard, then swung at the column again.

"You were warned, kender."

Tyros saw the wand glitter. "Rapp! Watch out for—"

A miniature bolt of green lightning flashed from the wand, heading for the kender. Rapp tried to leap out of the way, but moved just a little too late. The bolt struck kender, chair, and sword, tossing all three violently across the chamber.

"Rapp!"

The small figure dropped to the floor. Much of Rapp's skin had been burned and his clothes smoked.

"Rapp!"

"Such energy . . ." Valkyn commented as he approached. "Still such life within you. I believe you'll last far longer than any of the others did, even that hefty white-robed friend of yours."

"You . . . killed him!" Tyros's pulse pounded. "You killed Rapp!"

"I sincerely doubt the world will weep over one less kender, my friend. They have no practical use, serving only to create disorder. I do Ansalon a favor, in fact."

Tyros tried to spit at his counterpart but couldn't draw up enough moisture. "Small wonder," he finally gasped, "that s-so many fear and . . . and hate our kind. . . ."

"And well they should. We are more intelligent, advanced, and capable than most of the rabble. I more than any." Valkyn looked over Tyros. "But I seem to be capable of a mistake now and then. You didn't do anything to the storm after all, did you?"

"I don't know what you're talk—"

The sinister mage waved off his reply. "No, you don't. It seems I overestimated you and underestimated another."

Tyros tried to reach for him, but his adversary remained just out of range. Frustrated, he pulled hard on the last chain.

Valkyn smiled more broadly, bringing up the wand. "You seem secure enough, and as long as you are, I can make use of you. However, it wouldn't do to take anymore—"

The chain broke loose of the column.

More from a lack of balance than because he planned it, Tyros's arm swung forward, the chain with it. Where previously his reach had been limited, it now extended more than twice as far because of the chain.

The metal base struck Valkyn in the head, part of the chain wrapping around his hood. Valkyn lost his hold on the wand and fell. Blood dripped from his forehead where the base had cut into it.

Forcing himself up to nearly a sitting position, the black mage rasped, "You dare to strike me?"

Valkyn retrieved the wand. The expression on his face had no trace whatsoever of a smile, and he didn't even seem to notice the blood dripping down his cheek.

"I won't kill you—oh, no—but I will see to it that you remain more pliable for the short future you still have."

Tendrils grew from thin air, reaching immediately for the crimson-clad wizard. Tyros reacted instinctively, the words to create a magical shield springing to mind.

And to his surprise, the shield materialized.

The gleaming shield of light not only deflected Valkyn's tendrils, but flung both them and their creator back to the doors. Valkyn collided with the doors, grunting. Tyros stared at his hands. The spell put on him by the Black Robe had vanished, possibly because of stored power from Valkyn's device.

Whatever the cause of his freedom, Tyros dared not concern himself long with it. Glaring at the manacles still attached to his wrists and ankles, he muttered another spell. Immediately all four manacles clattered to the floor.

Despite his past suffering, despite the tortures he had barely survived, Tyros readied himself to face Valkyn and the wand. He looked up, certain to see his rival already preparing a deadly counterattack . . .

And found that Valkyn and the wand had vanished.

Tyros felt more relieved than frustrated. Even with magic once more at his command, he would have preferred to meet the other wizard under better circumstances. Besides, Valkyn could wait. The others needed Tyros's help.

One, though, he could no longer help. Tyros hurried to the kender's side, doubtful that his small companion even lived. Yet when he touched Rapp on the shoulder, the kender tried to open his eyes. He only succeeded with one, the other bloody and swollen shut.

"T-Tyros . . ."

"Easy, Rapp. I'll find you some water."

Rapp didn't seem to hear him. "Tyros . . . I got you free. . . ."

"You did."

The kender stared off somewhere. "Taggi . . . my griffons . . . I hope they're okay."

The mage sighed. "We'll find them and set them free, Rapp. You don't have to worry about them."

He stopped. The kender's face had grown nearly as pale as that of the shadow servants. Rapp stared, but clearly no longer saw anything.

Hand trembling, Tyros touched the kender's cheek and felt the skin grow cool. The mage swallowed, then put his hand on Rapp's chest. He felt no heartbeat, no breathing.

For a brief time, Tyros remained there, staring in frustration at what even his magic could not rectify. Rapp had saved him, had done so much to get them this far. The wizard felt guilty for not having gotten to know the kender better.

The others still needed Tyros, yet it frustrated him that he had to leave Rapp's body in this place. Rapp should have lain in the woods or mountains, where he had made his home while caring for his beloved griffons.

Tyros dared not expend too much energy, but he knew a minor spell that would at least place the kender's body in a safe place where the wizard might retrieve it later on. Tyros whispered the words, then watched as Rapp's body vanished.

The kender would lie in the wooded garden of the castle, hidden from the gargoyles. Tyros would see what he could do later on for his companion, but for now this would have to do. Serene and Bakal still needed him.

Thinking of the others, Tyros recalled Valkyn's earlier words. Valkyn had believed the captive spellcaster responsible for a dramatic change in the storm, but had realized that it had to be someone else. Tyros could think of only one other person with such potential.

Serene.

* * * * *

The cleric continued to sing despite the terrible tableau before her. As Crag leaped at Stone, she fully expected this to be the end of the smaller gargoyle. Serene nearly stopped singing, intent on doing something to save Stone's life, but then the gargoyle suddenly burst into action.

His feet came up as Crag dropped on him. Caught off guard, the larger gargoyle left his midsection open. Stone kicked with both taloned feet, not only throwing his startled rival backward, but leaving a trail of bleeding scars across Crag's torso.

Stone didn't wait for Crag to land. He darted after the larger creature, catching Crag before he could recover. Stone slashed at his foe's chest twice, turning the other gargoyle's torso into a crimson field.

Breathing heavily, Crag managed a strong blow against the side of Stone's head. The smaller gargoyle wobbled back. Unfortunately for Crag, he couldn't pursue his advantage. Still winded and dripping his life fluids, he moved sluggishly, enabling Stone to recover.

Taking flight, the smaller gargoyle maneuvered over his slowing rival, avoiding the sharp horns and grasping claws. Crag tried to keep Stone before him but could not. Stone waited until he had gotten completely behind his more massive opponent, then dropped on top of him.

Stone sank his talons deep into the larger gargoyle's back. Crag tried to shake him off but could not. The badly wounded monster fell to his knees.

Stone leaned forward and sank his jaws into Crag's neck.

Crag howled. The massive gargoyle's struggles grew weaker and his breathing turned ragged. He tried to roll over onto Stone, but the other gargoyle refused to let him.

The toll was too much. Crag finally slumped forward. He hissed once . . . and then lay still.

The triumphant gargoyle let out a cry that chilled Serene even as she silently cheered his victory. Stone then took hold of the massive corpse by the feet and dragged it to the balcony. As the cleric watched, ever mindful of her own task, he hefted Crag's body over his head and roared again.

Despite the storm, the wind, and her own song and music, the cleric of Branchala heard other cries as gargoyles beyond the balcony replied. They honored his victory, Serene finally realized.

With a last roar, Stone hurled his foe over the rail.

The gargoyle folded his wings and turned back toward her. As he did, however, the entire citadel suddenly dipped at a steep angle. Stone took to the air, but all Serene could do was momentarily pause in her song in order to keep from falling.

Serene recovered her balance as quickly as she could, not wanting to give Valkyn any time to regain control over his creation. The cleric tried to make sense of what had happened. Surely Valkyn had not directed Atriun to turn at such an angle. Serene had expected the fortress to be buffeted by the unnatural storm, but now it flew about as if under no control whatsoever.

A second gargoyle suddenly alighted on the balcony. Stone turned to face the newcomer, his breath still rapid. The cleric feared that he would now have to do battle with a new foe, but instead the second gargoyle dropped before him, muzzle to the ground.

The newcomer said something to Stone, who growled back. The other gargoyle glanced at Serene, nodded, then flew off again.

Stone returned to her. "Castle flies to mountains . . . mussst come!"

She didn't quite understand but feared to stop and ask him to explain. Stone's claws scratched impatiently at the floor as the gargoyle sought to make himself clear. "Castle flies blind! Will strike mountains!"

Now the cleric understood. She ceased her song. "I have to find Tyros and the others before that happens."

"No!" The gargoyle vehemently shook his head. He stretched his wings to their fullest. "Come with Stone, mistress. Now!"

"But I cannot leave the others."

"Stone's people will—" The gargoyle broke off, suddenly

275

staring at the center of the room in consternation. "Come quick!"

He seized her wrist, pulling her from the bed just as a tall figure in black robes materialized at the very point where the creature had been staring. Stone tried to rush to the balcony, but the doors suddenly swung shut, sealing the pair inside.

Hissing in anger, the gargoyle quickly released her and, with a roar, leaped at the new intruder.

An ebony-gloved hand reached out, fingers twisting like claws. Stone suddenly reeled, clutching at his chest. The gargoyle stumbled back, nearly colliding with Serene.

"I see that your first lesson did not hold," Valkyn quietly commented. "There will be no second."

Serene tried to throw herself in front of Stone. "Valkyn, no!"

The black wizard gave a twist of his wrist.

An incredible wave of heat forced Serene away from her winged companion. She turned to see Stone howl in agony as a brilliant sunburst formed on his chest. The sunburst spread swiftly, enveloping the struggling gargoyle.

Knowing that he was lost, Stone lunged at his tormentor. However, even as his wings launched him into the air, the gargoyle simply faded, his roar cut off midway through.

Although tears streamed down Serene's cheeks, anger had command of her now. She glared at Valkyn, wondering how she had ever thought she would love him forever. "You've killed him!"

"It was only a gargoyle, and not a very good one at that. Not worth any more than a kender, which is why we're better rid of them both, my dear serenity."

"A . . . a kender?" Not Rapp, too, she thought.

"Yes." Valkyn's tone became brusque. He stretched forth the same hand toward her, but instead of feeling tremendous heat burning her from within, the cleric found herself floating to the mage. "Now come to me. I've had enough of these irritations. My house must be put back in order."

He took her wrist. Up close, Serene noticed for the first

time the blood and the injury to his forehead. Someone had struck Valkyn a damaging blow. It gave her the encouragement she needed.

"I'll go nowhere with you, you monster!" Serene murmured a prayer and had the satisfaction of seeing him release her wrist in sudden pain. The area around his hand glowed a soft emerald color.

"Damn you!" Valkyn swung his other hand at her face. The wand caught Serene across her jaw and sent the cleric reeling.

She fell to the floor, stunned. Valkyn's menacing shadow loomed over her, a spectre of death. The glow around his other hand faded.

"What a fool I was to think so little of you," he murmured. "The young cleric of a woodland god just returned." The wizard's smile had turned decidedly grim. "I thought Tyros had turned my storm against me. I never even considered you in that equation. A sloppy bit of calculation on my part."

He pointed the wand at her. Serene noticed that it didn't glow as strongly as it had when he had first materialized. "And so you'll kill me now, dear Valkyn?"

"Kill you? Perhaps temper you. Bend you. Break you. Not kill you, though. You mean far too much to me."

"Once that would have been flattering, but now I feel nothing but loathing for you."

The dark wizard's smile widened, never a good sign. "As if that mattered. You're going to give me back my citadel, my dear, and you're going to help me make it stronger, more efficient. But first you're going to help me deal with one loose end."

The hallway doors burst open.

Both turned as a figure clad in ragged crimson robes stalked in, a staff in one hand. Tyros looked pale and gaunt, yet still something about him told Serene that the younger wizard hadn't yet given up the fight.

"And here is that loose end even now," mocked Valkyn. "This certainly simplifies matters."

"Your toy crumbles around you, Valkyn," Tyros declared. "The storm is against you, the citadel flies without control, and you have no source with which to power it. We have only a matter of time before it crashes!"

"Oh, it will fly for some time, my fellow mage. As long as the device itself remains intact, the power stored will keep Atriun flying until I find a new source . . . or resecure an old one."

Tyros raised the staff. "That will not happen."

"You found your staff? A useless little thing. I inspected it myself. You would have been better off stealing mine again. It might have availed you better . . . at least for a few moments."

"You know I have more than just the staff at my command." Tyros raised his empty fist, which briefly flared bright yellow, as if caught in the sun. "I have magic of my own."

Valkyn chuckled. "And I have Serene, which is all that matters."

He stretched forth his free hand, and to her horror, Serene again found herself pulled toward him. She tried to whisper a prayer, but her mouth wouldn't work. Valkyn took hold of her, cradling her shoulders as if they were once again lovers.

"My serenity," Valkyn whispered. He looked at his adversary. "You'll do nothing, of course, except drop the staff and surrender. For the price of her life, you'll give your own by returning to my device. Dear Serene will turn the storm back, so that once more it is mine to control." He frowned. "I've had enough of disruptions. Gwynned would have been the test to prove the ultimate supremacy of my design, and it still will be. No army, no dragon, can face her when she is under proper control! She will be a marvel for all to admire even as they bow to her!"

The cleric shivered. Did Valkyn understand how insane he sounded?

Likely Tyros understood that, but he nonetheless obeyed the other's commands. Dropping the staff, he held out his wrists and took a step forward. The captive mage moved with some stiffness, no doubt the results of his horrific time chained to Valkyn's arcane device.

With the wand, Valkyn drew a circle. A ring of black crystal formed in the air, a ring that floated toward Tyros's wrists.

Serene had to do something. She prayed silently to Branchala, asking him to do whatever he must to keep Tyros free.

At that moment, Castle Atriun suffered a tremendous shock wave, as if an earthquake had struck. Tyros fell forward, and Valkyn stumbled to the floor, his precious wand clattering away. Serene rolled toward the balcony, colliding with the doors there and ending up mere inches from the wand.

The tremor that had rattled the massive edifice to its foundation could not have been the result of a bolt of lightning or even a missile from the catapults below. Pushing open one of the balcony doors, Serene looked outside. At first she saw only the thick gray storm clouds that almost resembled rock. . . .

No—what the cleric saw more than resembled rock; it *was* rock.

Atriun had collided with a mountain.

Not exactly collided. Rather, the flying citadel had merely scraped along the side, but enough to send the entire castle into chaos. Outside, the gargoyles shrieked, their battle momentarily broken up. Beyond them, she could see that one of the outer walls had been completely demolished.

Bits of stone fell from above her, forcing Serene back inside. As she moved, her hand came to rest on the wand. She picked it up, startled that it should come so readily into her possession. For a moment, Serene contemplated trying to use it, thinking that at last she could teach Valkyn the folly of his evil.

"Give that to me."

Valkyn rose to one knee, gloved hand outstretched. The arresting blue eyes that had once ensnared her love now sought to trap her fear. Serene, though, had gotten past her fear of Valkyn. She held the wand out as if to return it, but as the wizard stood and reached out for it, the cleric tossed the magical artifact back over her shoulder . . . and over the balcony railing.

Lightning flashed, illuminating the sudden fury in Valkyn's visage. The hand snapped closed, and he looked over his shoulder at Tyros, who had managed to recover his balance. Both men might have come to grips, but again the citadel shook, a slow, grating tremor that sent furniture scattering and the very walls cracking.

"Your abomination will soon only be a memory, Valkyn," Tyros rasped. "One better forgotten, at that!"

"Atriun is far from a jumble of broken stone at the bottom of this mountain, Tyros." The black mage pulled his hood forward, the hood somehow larger and wider—or perhaps Valkyn somehow looked smaller. "As you shall see."

Valkyn's robes completely enveloped him, shrinking at the same time.

"No! Damn you!" Tyros threw the staff end first at the dwindling form, but it was too late. The ebony-clad wizard had faded away completely. The wooden stick struck the floor with a spark, then clattered for several seconds before coming to a rest.

"Twice now I've let him go because my reactions were too slow!" a frustrated Tyros snapped. "I will not let it happen a third time!"

"What does it matter?" Serene interjected. "Atriun is out of control. Something must have happened to the Wind Captain's Chair or its steersman!"

He nodded, his frustration at twice failing to stop Valkyn still clear. "If something has happened to the Wind Captain's Chair, then I would wager that Captain Bakal was involved."

"You think he might still be alive?" After witnessing Stone's death and learning of Rapp's, the cleric felt fearful even asking such a question.

"Perhaps, but I can't—" Again the flying citadel shook as it scraped along the side of the mountain. More cracks veined the walls, and a portion of the ceiling collapsed near

Tyros. "Valkyn can stay with his beloved monster and die with it, but we need to escape. We need the griffons."

Mention of the griffons stirred mixed emotions in Serene. The animals had long grown past the point of needing Rapp to survive, but how would they handle his death? The cleric knew that the depths of an animal's emotions could be astounding. The griffons would mourn the kender just as they would those of their family that had perished in the ill-fated journey up to the citadel.

Then it occurred to her that she and Tyros faced another dilemma. Assuming that they could find the creatures, what would happen if the griffons refused her guidance and simply abandoned the two humans? Serene had never had complete command of the griffons. Taggi might obey her, but would the others?

She would just have to find out. "I think I know where they are. Valkyn said they had been put into the animal pens under the east wing of the castle. He thought the griffons might be of some use, much like the gargoyles."

"Then we will go that direction, but it will be safer by an outside route and the pens should be easier to spot that way."

"But what about Captain Bakal?"

Tyros considered. "If he still lives, by this time, he will no doubt be searching for the griffons, too. With the citadel uncontrolled and failing, the animals are his only chance, too."

The cleric pictured Bakal trying to keep the griffons under rein and blanched. "We'd better get to them before he does. He's likely to let them loose, and if he does, they might fly off, leaving all of us to perish alongside Valkyn!"

Neither Tyros nor Serene cared much for the fact that the black wizard still ran free, but Valkyn's end appeared inevitable. With Serene leading the way, they hurried through the ominously empty corridors of the citadel. Neither shadow servants nor gargoyles were anywhere to be seen. The gargoyles were likely embroiled in battle, but surely some of the robed shadow creatures still survived. Serene clutched her medallion tightly, hoping she was prepared if she and Tyros should suddenly confront the ghoulish servants.

Twice more Castle Atriun shook as it rubbed against the peak, seemingly determined to slowly rip itself apart. As the pair reached the lower level and exited the main castle, they saw that the entire outer wall on that side had been reduced to rubble. The tower closest to the mountains had partially collapsed, and even the central tower showed worrisome cracks.

"Go past the garden," Serene urged. "The pens should be that way!"

Tyros remained strangely silent as they rushed through the wooded area, but the cleric assumed that he must be considering their odds. She herself kept glancing skyward, where the storm appeared to be lessening. Now and then gargoyles locked in aerial struggle soared past, always too swift for her to determine which side had the upper hand. She prayed to the Bard King that Stone's folk would prevail, if only for the sacrifices he had made for her.

From the wooded garden, they neared the ravaged end of the flying citadel. Serene stared at the castle with some anxiety; she hoped that no part of it had collapsed onto the pens.

Her fears seemed justified as they came across what remained of the outer corral. A portion of the exterior wall of the castle had indeed fallen onto it, crushing most of the high-fenced enclosure. Fortunately, Serene saw that the interior section still stood intact, although some rubble blocked part of the entrance. Even from this distance, the cleric could hear the roars of at least two griffons.

Near the corral, a figure rose into sight, a massive block of stone in his arms. As they watched, he hefted it to the side, then tossed it on a pile of rubble.

"Bakal!" Tyros waved as he shouted, trying to get the Ergothian's attention.

They had to venture somewhat nearer before Captain Bakal could hear them over the storm and the griffons. When he saw them, the scarred veteran gave the pair a tired, grim smile.

"Praise be to Draco Paladin!" Bakal spouted. "I was beginning to think I was the only one left alive . . . and I wasn't counting on that too much longer." He looked past them. "What about Rapp? Where's he?"

Tyros grimaced. "Rapp's dead, Bakal. He died freeing me. Valkyn killed him with hardly a care." To Serene, Tyros added, "I'm sorry . . . I wanted to tell you."

"You didn't have to. Valkyn himself had the honor of that."

A stony expression passed over the soldier's weathered features. "And I was just starting to like the little thief. . . ."

"Where are your men?"

A deeper darkness spread. "Dead. The last two were butchered by the wizard's gargoyle. I had to run from the beast before, but if I could just get him at a sword's point, I—"

"Crag's dead," Serene interjected, picking up a rock. "Stone killed him to save me . . . and then Valkyn killed Stone."

"That damned wizard—no offense, Tyros—needs to be strung up! At least General Cadrio's dead! I had that pleasure myself, up by the Wind Captain's Chair. He fell out a window while we were fighting." The captain shook his head. "Sorry to say, though, we ruined the steering mechanism during the struggle. I thought we were going to smash to pieces when we first hit that mountainside. This citadel's built to last."

"Not for much longer," Tyros informed him. "Valkyn has neither control of its flight nor the power to keep the citadel aloft much more. The storm's already abating. We need to get the griffons out and pray they will fly us to the ground!"

As they talked, Serene touched the gate leading to the griffons. She could hear the animals within, pleading to be let out. The cleric could feel their claustrophobia, their fear. Would they even acknowledge her? "If I can get inside, perhaps I can convince them to aid us."

"Let me help." Tyros inspected the lock. The cleric watched him, momentarily wishing that one of them had Rapp's skill with such things.

Raising the staff high, the wizard brought the tip down hard on the lock. Emerald sparks flared. The gate flung open, nearly striking the ragged spellcaster.

"That will do," Serene said.

She entered the animal pens, marveling at their immense size. The Solamnic lord must have kept enough livestock to survive a year-long siege.

One of the griffons noted her presence and squawked. The gargoyles had packed the forlorn animals in two of the maller pens, giving the them practically no room to spread their wings. They looked up at the cleric as she neared, eyes wary and somewhat untrusting.

"Hush, children," she cooed. "It's only me. You remember Serene, don't you? Serene, who has always tended to your wounds and scratched your heads?"

Some of the uncertainty dwindled. The largest of the surviving griffons shoved his way forward.

"And there's Taggi, first as usual." Coming up to the pen, she held out a hand. The griffon thrust his beak forward, smelling her. His eyes softened and he pushed his head near enough to have it scratched. "That's right . . ."

Her eyes more accustomed to the gloom, she could see that the creatures had been treated badly. Several had wounds and tufts of fur and feather missing. One animal lay in the back of a cage, unmoving. The cleric muttered an epithet, hoping that the griffons had been able to make some of their captors pay in kind.

"Don't you worry, now," she whispered soothingly. "I'll get you out of here."

She located the keys on a peg nearby, then quickly opened both cages. The cleric had to keep Taggi and the others from nearly bowling her over in their eagerness to be free. Serene immediately confronted the lead griffon, staring at him in the manner Rapp had whenever he had needed to tell the creature something important. How much Taggi understood, Serene couldn't say. Certainly the kender had always managed to get through.

"Listen to me, Taggi. You know I'm Rapp's friend, right?"

She nearly made a mistake mentioning the kender. Immediately the griffons looked around, seeking their friend. Serene had to work hard to regain Taggi's attention.

How had Rapp sometimes accomplished the matter? "Taggi? Do you want to go for a ride?"

Taggi blinked, then stretched his wings slightly. He gazed at Serene, as if expecting some response. She, in turn, smiled, recognizing the sign that Rapp had always received when he talked to them about taking him and his friends on a journey.

"Yes, Taggi! That's it. A ride!"

The griffons suddenly surged forward. Taggi moved to her side, trotting along with her as they left the confines of the animal pens. Serene had the pleasure of seeing the disconcerted expressions of her two companions.

"Was there ever a doubt?" she jested.

"No," returned Tyros, staring gravely in her eyes. "Just some fear."

Serene felt her face flush. She quickly turned from the tall wizard and bent down to speak with Taggi. "Now, you be gentle with these two men. They're friends of mine . . . and Rapp's."

Taggi squawked, then rubbed his beak on her side. She smiled and scratched his head for a moment.

A violent tremor ripped through the flying citadel.

Captain Bakal fell to his knees. Tyros used his staff to maintain his balance, but the wizard's face had turned ashen. Serene clutched Taggi, wondering what had happened now.

Jagged fissures appeared in the ground, some of them so near that a few of the griffons had to momentarily take to the air to avoid falling in. With a rumble, the ceiling of the chamber from which the cleric had led the animals collapsed, a cloud of dust and dirt emphasizing the totality of its destruction.

Atriun began drifting away from the mountains.

Serene felt a sense of foreboding. "What's going on?"

"The citadel is moving," a pale Tyros managed.

"Of course, but—"

"No . . ." He shook his head. "It is moving with purpose.

Its course is steady and strong. Atriun's heading back in the direction of the battle."

Bakal looked at him close. "Are you saying—"

"Yes. I don't know how, but Valkyn once again has control of the flying citadel."

Chapter 19

Bedlam in the Sky

"I want to go back!" Eclipse roared, still sulking. He would have beaten the gold dragon. Never mind that Sunfire had already been crippled before this day, and that the human atop the black had been the reason for any major successes. Eclipse felt that the victory would belong to him. He needed a victory. His mind was still fragile from the loss of his twin.

"The gold can wait!" Zander snapped. He had far too many other problems to concern himself with besides the whining of his mount. The other dragon would go nowhere. What concerned the young commander more had to do with his forces, which had become hard-pressed to maintain their ground, much less advance.

What had happened to the wizard's castle? Everything had been going well until the storm had abruptly turned against them. Then, to Zander's horror, Atriun had flown off. The last he had seen of it, it had been heading for the nearest mountains.

There had been no word from General Cadrio or, more to the point, from Valkyn. If something had happened to both of them, then everything was lost. Zander now regretted not having abandoned Cadrio and seeking out the Blue Lady. They said she could reward a good officer in many ways and, despite the chaos below, he still felt himself the best.

Zander had forced Eclipse up into the sky the moment the citadel had fled. He no longer cared about Valkyn's battle plan; if his men were to survive, he had to pull them together. With the aid of the black dragon, Zander had managed to keep them from routing, but the Ergothians had strong leaders of their own, and despite the threat of dragonfear or acid, the defenders began pushing forward.

The surviving catapults had repositioned themselves and now once again bombarded his ranks. Using Eclipse, Zander had disposed of two of the pesky machines, but he and the dragon had nearly suffered a direct hit. At the same time, the young commander had trouble trying to keep the rest of his forces under control. If Zander concentrated on the catapults, the Ergothian cavalry and foot soldiers tore through his front lines.

Things were falling apart, and even he could not put them back together without help.

"Where are you, General?" the young officer muttered. "And where are you, wizard? If one of you would just tell me what's going on, I'd be forever grateful."

"Aaah, there you are, General Zander."

Eclipse let out the nearest thing to a squawk that Zander had ever heard a dragon utter. He himself barely kept his expression in check, for in front of the pair, heedless of the lack of earth beneath his feet, stood Valkyn. Even though Zander knew that he faced an illusion, the cowled figure looked so real he expected the wizard to plummet to his death at any moment.

"What's happening, Master Valkyn? The citadel—"

The unnerving smile spread, although something about it seemed weary. "Atriun is on its way back. There have been some minor disruptions, but I have dealt with all save one." The sky blue eyes grew chilling. "And that one will be dealt with very, very soon."

A wave of relief washed over Zander. "And the battle?"

"My commendations on that, General. Excellent strategy under unexpected pressure. Maintain your actions. I will be with you shortly."

"Yes, Master Valkyn!"

The image vanished, and only then did Zander realize that the mage had called him general. So much, then, for Cadrio. Zander smiled. A field promotion.

"I see it!" Eclipse roared. "The wizard's castle comes!"

Indeed it did, but even from far away, Zander noted the

differences. Atriun had been heavily damaged on one side. One of its towers was in ruins. Gazing at the mountains from which the citadel had come, the new general suspected that he knew exactly what had caused such terrible destruction.

Yet despite the damage, the castle still flew. Only a few ominous clouds drifted along with Valkyn's creation, but Zander supposed that the wizard conserved his magic for the actual battle.

"General Zander."

This time he couldn't hide his startlement. He hadn't expected to hear from the black mage until later in the battle. He saluted. "Master Valkyn! You've need of something?"

Valkyn did not smile. What that meant, the soldier did not want to know. "A change of plans. I've immediate need of you and your beast, my general. There are some gnats about to leave my citadel . . . a woman and two—no, I suspect only *one* man! Slay the man and as many of the griffons as you need to, but capture the woman and bring her back to me."

Zander hated to leave his forces at such a crucial point, but when Valkyn spoke, it paid to obey. "As you command!"

Again the illusion vanished. Fearful of the wizard, Eclipse had already begun to bank toward Castle Atriun. Zander leaned forward, searching for griffons. He would find them. Valkyn would be proud of him.

General Zander . . .

* * * * *

Tyros stared up in the direction of the Wind Captain's Chair, then at his companions. At last he came to a decision, one not at all to his liking but necessary.

"Serene, Bakal, take the griffons and leave the citadel."

They both looked at him as if he had gone mad.

"There's no more reason to stay here, boy! This castle's going to come crashing down!"

Serene stepped up to him. "Do you think I'll leave you here alone, knowing what's happened to Rapp and Stone? If you're going to face Valkyn, I'll be at your side."

"Listen to me." He softly put a hand on Serene's shoulder, but his gaze shifted between them. "Valkyn has the citadel under some control, but unless he has something in mind I don't know of, he cannot possibly keep it from crashing. I'm afraid he might try to drop it on your people, Bakal."

"Then more the reason *I* should be going after him, not you!" the captain snarled.

"He still wields magic. Besides, the two of you have to warn Gwynned. They might be able to do something if I fail."

The cleric frowned. "I can see Bakal going to warn them, but I should stay with you!"

"No. Valkyn won't hesitate to kill even you. He might delay with me, though." Although Tyros didn't explain his last statement, they all knew what he meant. Valkyn likely still hoped to return his rival to the columns. "They'll need your help down there as a cleric, Serene. With so few healers of Mishakal about, the Bard King might be able to lend a hand."

She couldn't argue with that. While Mishakal held province over healing, even Serene could achieve some success through her god. Still, she wouldn't give up on one subject. "And what if you defeat Valkyn? How will you get off of Atriun?"

He had no answer for that.

Bakal joined in. "We'll go, Tyros, but we won't leave the area immediately. If it looks like Atriun's on its way to Gwynned, we'll fly off. But if there's a chance you're alive and need help, we'll be there!"

The mage sighed. "Then at least go now. Time is wasting!"

Serene turned and whispered something to Taggi and one of the other griffons. Bakal mounted, but before the cleric did, she suddenly rushed back to Tyros and, standing on her toes, kissed him on the cheek. Her face crimson, Serene then hurried to Taggi.

His own face feeling flushed, Tyros waved in silence as his companions flew off, then, steeling his resolve, he turned and headed back into Atriun. There was only one place

Valkyn might be at this point. With the Wind Captain's Chair destroyed, Atriun's master surely had to have gone to the chamber housing the massive crystals. Only from there could he have possibly regained control.

Those who had known Tyros in the past might have thought that he had sent the others off in order to reap the glories himself. They couldn't have been more mistaken. The events since the first attack on Gwynned had marked Tyros, opening up a part of him that he had kept locked away. He knew the danger of confronting Valkyn and intended that he face that danger alone. Leot, Rapp, and even Stone had perished at the hands of the black mage, and Tyros didn't want to lose his two remaining friends . . . especially Serene. Even if it meant sacrificing himself, he was determined to bring down his counterpart.

And in the chamber where he had been so recently chained to Valkyn's device, Tyros found the black wizard waiting for him.

"I knew you'd return," the goateed figure commented, smile in place. He stood in front of one of the columns, gloved hands crossed in front of him. "We really do think much alike."

"Forgive me if I do not take that as a compliment."

"Atriun is once more under my command. Gwynned will be crushed, and my name will go down as one of the greatest wizards of this monumental era."

The man had no compassion, no care whatsoever for others. All Valkyn concerned himself with was his magic and what he could do with it. Other lives did not matter. Valkyn would try to conquer the world not for the reasons that Ariakas had, but rather just so he could continue his monstrous experiments on a grander scale. In some ways, the world Ariakas had sought to create for his goddess would have been a blessing instead of the laboratory that the mad mage desired.

Of course, the more likely future for Valkyn would be that eventually his citadel would succumb to the might of his myriad foes, but how many more innocents would have to die before then?

"Atriun is crumbling, dying," Tyros countered. "Control of its flight will mean nothing when it falls from the sky."

The gloved hands came up, spreading in opposite directions and making Valkyn look like a scholar attempting to teach a reticent student. "But it will not fall! It will fly, and the storm will cover the heavens once again . . . now that you're here."

A sense of unease swept over Tyros, and he suddenly threw himself away from the doors.

Two fearsome forms dropped from the ceiling, nearly landing upon him with their sharp claws. Tyros rolled against a wall and then scrambled to his feet.

A pair of huge gargoyles, ember eyes flaring and jaws open wide, closed in on him. Tyros sensed something amiss about them. They not only stood taller than any of the gargoyles he had seen, but Tyros felt a strong current of magic around each.

The smiling mage extended a hand toward his demonic device. "Your place of honor awaits you again. I knew you couldn't resist coming, so I made certain that things would be fully prepared for you."

The columns had been partially repaired, and new runes of power had been etched in by magic, albeit clearly hastily. Worse yet, new chains had been set into place, this time chains that glowed from base to manacle. No simple blows from an axe or sword would free Tyros if Valkyn managed to secure him there again.

"Never again, Valkyn," Tyros retorted, his staff held before him, "but I would be glad to let you take my place if you like."

One of the gargoyles lunged. Tyros held up the staff and muttered words that would unleash one of the few spells with which he had been able to imbue it back in Gwynned. It wouldn't kill the monster, but a sleeping gargoyle could do him no harm.

Only the gargoyle did not drop. Briefly he shimmered, but that was all.

Desperate, the wizard raised the point of his staff just as

the gargoyle closed in on him. The point caught his attacker at the lower edge of the throat.

The monster collapsed, holding his throat and fighting for air. However, by then the second had also leaped forward. As he flew at Tyros, his claws grew longer, sharper, distorting into nightmarish sickles that threatened to cut the mage to ribbons.

Valkyn had enchanted the creatures, adding to their inherent magic. Small wonder he expected Tyros to fall. Yet despite their new and fearsome abilities, Tyros realized that he had one great advantage. Their master needed him alive. That meant the gargoyles had to move with caution . . . which opened them up to all sorts of weaknesses.

The macabre claws came within an inch of his face, but by then Tyros had a counterattack in motion. He muttered the words of a spell he had found useful in the days of the war, one that he had hoped to save for Valkyn but needed now.

A moist cloud, looking vaguely like cotton, formed around the oncoming monster. The gargoyle slashed, but the cloud immediately reformed where he had cut. At the same time, it continued to grow thicker, obscuring his vision.

Tyros watched with satisfaction. He had realized that to combat the creatures, he had to cast spells that did not affect them directly but rather their surroundings.

Again and again the gargoyle slashed. Tyros moved to one side and saw that his winged adversary did not turn with him. Likely now the gargoyle could see nothing but white.

The first monster had nearly recovered. Tyros called on another spell from his staff and had the satisfaction of watching the floor beneath the gargoyle's leathery feet turn icy.

Suddenly bereft of footing, the creature slipped, falling backward. Before the gargoyle could utilize his wings to right himself, Tyros used the tip of the staff to push one attacker into the other.

Unable to see who collided with him, the enshrouded gargoyle slashed out with his distorted talons. The fiendish claws tore through even the hard, enchanted hide of his comrade, leaving a gaping wound in the side of the neck. With an agonized roar, the mortally injured creature dropped to one knee and collapsed.

Unfortunately for Tyros, the magical cloud suddenly took on a fiery glow. The gargoyle within had finally realized that only magic could free him. The mage looked up at the great stone ceiling, muttered words of magic, then tapped the staff once on the floor.

The ceiling opened up, great blocks of stone dropping on the remaining gargoyle, who had just managed to refocus his baleful gaze on his prey.

Tyros stared at the rubble, making certain that the creature would not rise, then screamed as incredible pain wracked his body. A hand held him by the shoulder, a hand covered by a slim, black glove.

"They served their purpose well," came Valkyn's voice. "You should be a bit more manageable now."

The staff fell from Tyros's twitching fingers. He dropped to his knees. Where Valkyn's hand touched him, an incredible fire burned. Tyros forced his gaze up and saw that various parts of his foe's hand glowed brightly through the fiber of the glove.

He had forgotten that Valkyn didn't always need the wand. The other wizard could draw directly from the dwindling reserves of Atriun, thanks to the horrific spell he had cast on himself.

"Time to take your place, Tyros," Valkyn ordered with a smile. "Gwynned awaits."

* * * * *

Mere moments after leaving Tyros, Serene nearly had Taggi turn back. She had been a fool to let the mage go alone. He needed her help. If anyone knew Valkyn best, it was Serene.

All thought of Tyros was pushed to the back of her mind as the griffons suddenly lost all semblance of order and dropped into the wooded garden over which they had just begun to pass.

"What's going on?" Bakal shouted.

The answer became dreadfully apparent a moment later when they spotted a small, still form, arms folded, lying almost peacefully in the midst of the wooded area. Serene swallowed back tears as the griffons fluttered near the body of the only creature they had ever known as their parent.

As one, the animals let out a cry. Taggi landed, nudging Rapp's body with his beak. He squawked again, a mourning sound.

"Damned wizard," the captain muttered.

Although clerics of Branchala deemed all life sacred, there and then Serene wished that she could have been the one to face Valkyn. At the moment, the cleric felt that she had it in her to kill him.

Bakal looked at her, eyes bleak. "We can't stay here, girl."

"I know." Yet Serene hated the thought of leaving Rapp here, either to perish with Atriun or, if Valkyn triumphed, to be disposed of like garbage by her former love's pet gargoyles.

The griffons took the decision out of her hands. Taggi nudged the kender's body in the direction of the largest of the females. With talons that could have easily shredded Rapp, she gently secured the body and took to the air.

Taggi and the rest flew after her. Bakal managed to glance at the cleric just before they soared into the air, his expression one of astonishment. Both of them were amazed at the depth of devotion the griffons had for the kender.

A few battling gargoyles spun past them as they flew. Serene noticed that more of the lighter-skinned ones, Stone's folk, seemed to be airborne. Her spirits rose, and she started to think that perhaps the worst was finally over. They would locate a triumphant Tyros and abandon this citadel to it swell-deserved fate.

"Dragon!" Captain Bakal suddenly shouted.

The black form rose toward them, growing more gargantuan with each beat of his lengthy wings. Serene had forgotten about the remaining twin. That he should appear now could be no accident. Valkyn must have sent the dragon to recapture them.

An armored figure rode atop the leviathan, no doubt one of General Cadrio's aides. During her pursuit of Cadrio and the supposedly kidnapped Valkyn, she had learned somethings about the general's most zealous officers. A pair of names came to mind, but one even Valkyn had mentioned. . . and with favor. A young officer, determined and ruthless, possibly even more so than his commander, a young officer who, she recalled, had somewhat feline features, just like man atop the dragon.

Zander. Yes, Serene thought, it had to be Zander.

The great beast roared, and a sense of uncertainty filled the cleric—the first touches of dragonfear, a most potent weapon. Serene immediately prayed to the Bard King, asking for his strength. The uncertainty faded somewhat.

Nearby, Bakal, too, fought the fear. Fortunately a veteran of the war, he had learned to steel himself. After a moment of anxiety, he nodded to Serene to assure her of his readiness, then proceeded to make a spreading motion with his hands.

At first she didn't understand what he wanted, but when the captain pointed at the griffons and repeated the motion, it came to her. Bakal wanted her to scatter the animals to confuse their monstrous foe. The cleric leaned down to Taggi, hoping that once more the lead griffon would understand her request.

Branchala watched over her. Taggi cried out to the other griffons, and they suddenly darted off in every direction.

The great black paused in midair, clearly confused. However, Serene saw the soldier lean forward and shout something to his mount. The dragon's eyes narrowed, and he focused on two animals in particular . . . those that carried riders of their own.

Bakal and his griffon suddenly swooped in front of Taggi, drawing the dragon's primary attention. The ebony leviathan snapped at the soldier and his mount, then inhaled deeply. A second later, a spray of acid shot out at the pair, singeing the griffon's tail. The animal squawked in pain but continued on.

For the Ergothian captain, there would evidently be no choice of capture. Had the acid rain caught him full on, both he and the griffon would have been dead. Serene wondered what fate Valkyn had declared for her. Likely he would suffer her to live, still believing that he could manipulate her somehow. The thought disgusted her but also gave her some hope. If Valkyn did want her alive, then perhaps she could use that to help Bakal.

She had Taggi follow after the captain and his pursuers, intending to draw the dragon's attention toward her. However, as they neared, Taggi didn't try to pass the unsuspecting dragon, but rather focused his attention on the leviathan's rider.

Serene tried to make the griffon move on, but for some reason, Taggi remained fixed on Zander. The cleric held tight, disliking the thought of killing the man from behind but knowing it would be necessary.

Zander suddenly looked over his shoulder. The officer glared at her, then drew a sword and slashed at Taggi. Although the rider missed, he bought himself time to shout a command to the dragon.

The scaly beast suddenly rose up, nearly bowling over the cleric and her mount in his haste to obey.

Serene had accomplished one thing, for now the dragon concentrated on them, not the captain. Unfortunately, with the behemoth above them, the only direction Taggi could fly was down, toward the underside of the citadel.

The dragon more than kept pace, closing the gap with remarkable speed. Again Serene felt unnatural anxiety. She muttered another prayer and felt peace return. Even dragon-fear could not overwhelm the protection of the Bard King. Still, the monstrous leviathan had nearly caught up to them, and the cleric had no idea what to do.

Suddenly the sky around her filled with griffons, the rest of the pack returning to aid their brother. They swarmed back and forth, distracting her pursuers.

Enraged, the dragon unleashed another stream of acid. One griffon shrieked as a wing received a partial dousing. The animal fluttered awkwardly away, trying to shake the burning liquid from her feathers.

Bakal flew by. He gave a shout and threw something that bounced off Zander's armor. The young officer shook his sword at Bakal but kept the dragon in pursuit of the cleric.

As she neared the pitted underbelly of Atriun's island, Serene began searching for somewhere to hide. She surveyed the various crevices and openings, including what looked like the ruined corridors of underground passages, finding at last one that might serve her purposes. Serene prayed that they would reach it in time.

Hot, putrid breath warned her that the black was even nearer than she had thought. Serene glanced back at the oncoming beast, certain that he would catch them. However, just as the great talons tried to close on her, the griffon gave one more burst of speed and dived into the hole.

The dragon nearly collided with the flying citadel's island. He pulled back, roaring his fury. Great claws tore at the passage, trying to widen it.

"Come out and let this be done in a civilized manner!" the armored officer called. "You'll come to no harm, my lady!"

"You're welcome to come in and get me!"

The young officer smirked. He knew better than to try to take on the griffon at such close quarters.

With Taggi watching the outer entrance, Serene turned to investigate the interior. Much to her dismay, the tunnel she had chosen ended in a heap of rubble only a short distance inside. The rest of the passage had collapsed, likely during the raising of the castle.

She had nowhere to go but out the way she had come . . . and from where they hovered, her pursuers likely could tell that, too.

Serene had trapped herself.

* * * * *

"You can hear the roar even from here, can't you?" Valkyn asked Tyros. "You know what it means." Still down on his knees, tormented by the agony unleashed by the other wizard's touch, Tyros focused for a moment on the distant sound. Yes, he knew what it meant; the surviving dragon hunted near the citadel, and it could only be hunting his friends.

"Serene . . ." he managed to whisper.

Valkyn had the ears of an elf. "Have no fear for my dear serenity, for I've plans for her that must keep her untouched. I believe I can make use of any cleric, whoever her god, to raise my next citadel. It will truly be an inspiring experiment!"

And one likely to leave that cleric injured or dead. The thought of Serene in such straits urged Tyros to new efforts, despite his pain. His hand fumbled around and found the staff. It contained only a few spells, none of which would be effective against Valkyn, but that wasn't what the battered mage sought it for.

Summoning up what strength he had left, Tyros drew forth as much magic as he could and, mouthing the necessary spell, poured it into the staff. Valkyn didn't notice his effort, taking his sudden weakening as a sign that the crimson mage had all but given up.

Tyros, though, fought to keep conscious. When at last he could give no more to the staff, the fallen spellcaster readied himself, turning his grip ever so slightly.

He thrust the staff up, praying for the best.

Valkyn shifted to one side. The staff flew out of the red wizard's grip, sailing wide past his rival. Valkyn chuckled at Tyros's attempt. "A pitiful effort! Did you really think I wouldn't—" Chill blue eyes narrowed to slits as he noted the look of triumph creeping over Tyros's features. "What are you up to?"

Valkyn whirled and looked up.

Enchanted, the staff had not fallen to the floor but instead flew unerringly toward the nearest of the great crystalline spheres. It glowed with magical energy, all that Tyros could put into it, turning the staff into a deadly missile.

Tyros slumped to the floor, momentarily unable to do so much as lift a finger in his own defense. However, Valkyn had eyes only for his device and the missile streaming toward it. He released his grip on Tyros and reached out a desperate hand, as if attempting to cast a spell. The blink of an eye became an eternity, yet still not enough time for the master of the citadel to stop the inevitable.

The staff struck, exploding.

At first Tyros thought that he had failed, that the energies he had focused into the staff had not been enough. Then he and Valkyn saw the massive veins erupting across the immense crystal.

The entire column shook. Raw magical forces burst from the cracks, turning them into fissures.

"No!" the mage screamed. "No!"

But the power that he had sought to contain for his own dreams would be contained no longer. The golden crystal trembled . . . and burst.

The explosion ripped through the area, nearly toppling the second column. Tyros flattened himself to the floor, hoping his death would be quick and painless.

Castle Atriun shook, then lurched. Only the magical energy in the second sphere still kept the citadel functioning, but not for much longer.

A scream of nightmarish torment ripped from Valkyn's mouth. Tyros dared to look up, wondering what could cause such a cry.

Valkyn's hands blazed with pure magic, then began to burn away.

The black wizard had truly tied himself to his creation, the better to make use of its abilities. The crystals were clearly the same type as those both atop the columns and fixed to the wand. Tyros vaguely recalled an image from his earliest struggle with Valkyn, when the other mage's gloves had burned away, revealing what he had done to himself. The crystals implanted in Valkyn's hands had enabled him to cast astonishing spells, yet now they assured that the very power he had hungered for would devour him instead.

And nothing could stop it.

Valkyn's hands were no more than ash now, and yet still the magic burned away at him, twin plumes of fiery, golden light that rapidly made their way above his wrists. Valkyn clutched the stumps of his arms to himself, trying to smother what could not be smothered. At last he dropped to his knees, moaning, all trace of the mocking smile forever gone.

A menacing sound, like that of crackling ice, made Tyros recall his own imminent fate. Power still flared from the ruined crystal, but more worrisome than that were the intense web of deep fractures spreading over the remaining sphere. Without it, the citadel would definitely fall, for whatever reserves Atriun had once had surely had been drained away by now.

Forcing himself to his feet, Tyros hobbled to the doorway. He glanced behind once to see if Valkyn followed, but Valkyn no longer had any interest in him. The magic continued to eat away at the dark wizard. Already his robes were ablaze with a wicked golden fire.

A new explosion sent Tyros tumbling into the hallway. Recovering, he watched in amazement as the first column teetered. For a moment it hesitated, almost seeming to float, and then it collapsed.

Valkyn, still in agony, didn't see it tip toward him. The column fell upon the burning figure, half crushing the master of Castle Atriun.

Tyros abandoned the area, knowing that the only way to avoid sharing Valkyn's fate was to escape the castle entirely and hope that either Serene or Bakal still waited for him. He stumbled down the corridor, seeking the stairway leading up.

A new explosion rocked the citadel, sending him sprawling and dousing the mage with rubble from the ceiling.

Struggling to his feet again, Tyros peered through the clouds of dust, trying to make out the stairs. Rubble blocked part of his view, forcing him to climb over it. The stairway had to be nearby. . . .

Tyros stared in dismay. Whether or not the stairway lay

ahead no longer mattered. What remained of his path had collapsed under the weight of the falling ceiling. Tons of stone now blocked the fleeing wizard's way, and Tyros had a suspicion that some of that rubble had once been part of the very steps he sought.

His path out of Castle Atriun had been destroyed, leaving him trapped in a flying citadel that would soon fly no more.

Chapter 20

On the Wings of Victory

Atriun shook violently, sending Serene sprawling. Taggi turned, sniffing in concern. Fragments of the ceiling showered them, causing the cleric to fear that the entire castle would collapse on her. Outside, the black dragon continued to try to claw his way inside. Only the fact that they obviously wanted her alive and whole had saved her from a shower of lethal acid.

The citadel shook again. More rock showered down on the pair. Taggi howled as a large piece caught his front right paw. Serene went to the griffon's aid, freeing the paw and massaging it. The male griffon relaxed, gently licking at his bloody wound.

"Cleric!"

Zander again. Straightening, Serene went to the opening, careful to keep out of reach of the dragon's probing claws.

"What is it?"

"You'll die in there unless you surrender," the arrogant young officer pointed out. "Do so and I promise that your animals and the soldier will come to no harm."

She doubted that he would keep his word, but Zander seemed very anxious that she come out. Why became apparent a moment later as a new tremor rained down stone not only on her, but on the dragon rider and his mount as well. The great black shook his head as a particularly heavy piece struck him squarely. Zander clearly did not want to remain in this area any longer than he had to.

Serene refused to make his task any easier. "Since I doubt you'll keep that promise, I think I'll take my chances here."

"You'll die unless—" Another explosion shook the citadel, sending more rock falling. Through the dust, she saw Zander frown, then he seemed to consider something. "All right, then. Eclipse! Toss a little acid her way and see if that brings her around to surrendering."

The dragon twisted his head around. "But I might kill her!"

"Then be sure that you take careful aim, you imbecile, or you'll have the wizard to answer to!"

Eclipse inhaled, preparing to unleash a torrent of acid from which Serene knew she would not escape. She doubted that the leviathan could focus his stream so narrow that he would not burn her to death.

A quake far exceeding any previous one shook the damaged fortress. Part of the back end of the tunnel collapsed, forcing Taggi nearer to her. Serene held tight to the wall, not even daring to breathe until the shaking began to subside.

And then the flying citadel lurched.

Serene and Taggi tumbled toward the mouth of the corridor . . . and the open sky.

As she struggled to keep from falling out, the cleric saw that Zander and Eclipse also suffered. Man and monster were caught in the midst of an airborne avalanche. Great portions of both Atriun and its island poured down on the pair.

A massive rock caught Zander in the chest. The arrogant officer slipped from his seat, screaming as he futilely sought to grab hold of something. Eclipse tried to snatch him with one claw, but a section of Atriun's outer wall battered the beast. The officer vanished from sight, still screaming.

"Zander!" the dragon roared, trying to search for his lost rider and avoid the torrent of debris. Part of the perimeter wall struck Eclipse at the shoulder near the wing, spinning the dragon around. More gigantic fragments, including what looked like the top of one of the towers, nearly buried Eclipse in the sky. The rain of rubble made short, terrible work of his wings, at last ripping the membrane of one in half.

Battered, his wings ruined, Eclipse spiraled earthward, unable to control his descent.

Castle Atriun continued to dip. For a moment Serene

hung halfway out of the tunnel, her legs dangling hundreds of feet above Krynn.

Her grip at last failed her. Serene slipped out of the tunnel and into the open sky, praying to Branchala that her end would be swift.

A harsh squawk nearly deafened her. Talons suddenly sank into her shoulders.

Taggi pulled her up into the sky, managing to dodge falling debris until they finally rose to safety above the citadel.

The view she suddenly had of Atriun's death over-whelmed Serene. Most of the outer wall had either collapsed inward or fallen into the sky. Only the central tower of the castle remained standing, but it suffered from so many great cracks that the cleric knew that soon it, too, would plunge toward Ansalon. Crevices had spread all across the castle grounds, and the entire structure crackled with raw magical energy.

The gargoyles, whatever their loyalties, had fled from the frightening tableau. Atriun looked deserted. There was no sign of either Tyros or Valkyn.

She could not, *would* not, abandon Tyros. Serene had Taggi land on one of the more level portions of the dying fortress just long enough for her to climb aboard the griffon, then she urged him into the sky so that they could continue the search for the mage.

The cleric had the griffon quickly circle the outer peri-meter of the flying citadel, but still saw nothing. Tyros had to be trapped inside.

She managed to convince Taggi to enter the main castle but regretted that choice almost instantly. The immense front hall had already begun to cave in. Taggi had to back up as one column tumbled over right in front of them. Despite her desire, Serene knew that they couldn't possibly stay inside the crumbling structure. She turned the griffon around. The animal seemed more than happy to be gone from this place.

Tyros had to be in there, possibly still alive. Serene thought hard. Perhaps she could find a better way in from below. Even though the one corridor had collapsed, there were other passages. One of those might even lead her more quickly to Tyros, who likely had descended deep in the castle in order to destroy Valkyn's horrific device.

Once back below the citadel, the frantic cleric studied each opening as they passed, but most were unusable. Her hopes dwindled.

Suddenly she noticed something approaching fast. At first she thought that the dragon had recovered. Then she saw that the winged creature was not only several times smaller than a dragon, but had a rider aboard.

Captain Bakal waved her back. "Get away! It's not safe here!"

"But Tyros is still in there!"

"He can't possibly be alive!"

Serene urged Taggi on, ignoring Bakal. She had to find her way to Tyros, or else.

A flash caught her attention. Serene blinked, then saw a second flash. She steered the griffon toward it, hoping against hope.

Tyros stood at the edge of a shattered tunnel, waving feebly. The mage's robe was in tatters, and he looked so emaciated and pale that he nearly resembled one of the shadow servants. The flashes she had seen had been the last vestiges of his power, simple spells to attract someone's attention.

"Go, Taggi, go!" Only a few seconds more and Tyros would be safe.

Atriun began dropping from the sky.

Tyros seized the nearest hand hold, a jagged outcropping from the tunnel, and held on as best he could. The strain could be clearly read on his face.

The flying citadel paused again a short distance below its original elevation, but Serene knew that at any moment it might continue its death plunge, this time with no hesitations. She urged the griffon on, but although Taggi flew hard, the distance to Tyros seemed immeasurable.

At last Taggi drew close. Tyros, a look of relief etched across his worn face, reached out.

The citadel tipped. Silence seemed to enshroud it. Serene's eyes met Tyros's. Both realized what was happening.

Castle Atriun began to plummet again.

The mage reacted instinctively, leaping for the outstretched talons of the griffon even as the fortress's plunge began. Tyros missed, but Taggi dived with incredible speed, managing to get under the helpless wizard.

Tyros landed arms first across the shoulders of the griffon. Serene quickly seized the mage and dragged him aboard before he could become entangled in Taggi's wings.

A final explosion rocked Atriun even as it plunged. Mage and cleric watched in awe as the central tower sank into the main building. Golden fire burned away what remained of the wooded garden.

Already dying, Valkyn's flying citadel plummeted earthward.

* * * * *

In the depths of the collapsing edifice, Valkyn, pinned beneath the rubble, tried desperately to free himself. The magic had scored his face, leaving him a permanent, ghoulish smile. He heard the final explosion, felt the castle shudder, then watched as the cracking ceiling above finally collapsed under the weight of the upper floors.

Amidst the death throes of the flying citadel, the last scream of its creator went unnoticed.

* * * * *

Tyros, Serene, and Bakal flew after the plunging castle, hard-pressed to keep up with it.

"It's going to land in the battlefield!" Serene shouted.

Tyros had already calculated that, but what he didn't know was exactly where in the battlefield it would fall. Would Valkyn, in death, wreak still more havoc among the defenders of Gwynned?

They came within sight of the two warring forces. From

this height, the wizard had trouble identifying which side was which. Tyros was completely turned around.

Then he saw the hilly landscape to his right and knew exactly what part of the battle the citadel had been flying over.

Atriun plummeted toward Valkyn's own forces.

Tyros felt some regret for the soldiers below, whatever their allegiance. Still, nothing could be done.

Realizing just how terrible the impact would be, Tyros called, "Serene! Make Taggi fly higher again! Hurry!"

The griffon obeyed her command. Bakal's mount and the rest of the griffons followed. Even then the mage wondered if they would manage to rise high enough.

The flying citadel—and the secrets of Valkyn's spellwork that had made it such a menace—vanished the next moment in a catastrophic explosion of stone that ripped apart the former dragonarmy.

The explosion rocked the entire region. The wizard didn't doubt that the entire island felt the citadel crash and that the reverberations were heard even on the nearby mainland.

A cloud of dust and debris rose higher than the nearby hills and continued rising, swelling at the same time. An incredible burst of wind tossed the griffons about, the riders barely able to hold on. Dust filled the air, making it nearly impossible to breathe.

Small fragments bombarded Tyros and the others, but fortunately that seemed the extent of their troubles. As Serene had the griffon begin to descend again, the wizard saw that, for the invaders, the horror had not yet ended.

Rubble still rained down on the enemy forces, deadly missiles tearing apart what little remained of their lines. Countless bodies lay scattered among the debris of the fallen citadel. Entire units had been wiped out by the hurtling fragments. A rout began among the survivors.

"Look there!" Serene pointed to the west.

A massive black form, wings outspread, lay on its back some distance into what had once been part of the enemy's front. The dragon's neck and back were kinked at painful, broken angles, and the body lay half buried in stone from the castle. It was hard to say whether the fall or the destruction had killed the dragon, but it gave Tyros satisfaction to see the black beast dead.

The dust began to settle, and as it did, the Ergothians advanced, clearing out what remained of their foe. Their own lines had hardly been touched by the disaster, yet the soldiers nonetheless moved cautiously. It would take time to cover the entire field, but Tyros doubted that the defenders would find much in the way of resistance.

"It's over," Serene whispered. "It's finally over."

He held her tight, both of them overwhelmed by the devastation and their part in its making.

*   *   *   *   *

The mage now wore a crisp, clean robe, but one of white, not crimson. He had considered his choices and felt that his path would ever be the opposite of that which Valkyn had taken. The decision felt like a good one and one of which both Bakal and the cleric had approved. Tyros felt like a different man.

He and Serene had built a small cairn in the midst of the deep forest near where Rapp had raised his griffons. The two stayed there for some time, silently honoring their tiny companion. The animals mourned alongside them.

"I'll be staying with the griffons for a while, just to see them safe," Serene commented.

"And after that?"

"I don't know."

He nodded. "I must report to the Conclave, but then I'll be returning to Gwynned for a time. Bakal's superiors have requested my aid on some projects." Tyros considered. "Bakal must have spoken up for me."

The Ergothian had been promoted to the staff of Gwynned's senior general and apparently now had the ear of the commander. The promotion had required Bakal to immediately report for duty, which unfortunately had prevented him from being with Tyros and the cleric now. He had left a message saying that he hoped to see both of them before long.

"Considering what you've done for them, they should be happy to have you." Serene hesitated. "Tyros, look!"

The griffons suddenly tensed, gazing upward. Tyros heard the flutter of wings and spotted several leathery forms descending toward them.

"Gargoyles." he whispered. The creatures had disappeared before the destruction of Atriun, but Tyros had remained wary that they might yet try to fulfill their dead master's commands.

A tall, sleek creature dropped into their midst. Taggi started forward, but Serene held him back. The gargoyle hissed once at the animal, then the pupilless eyes shifted to Tyros and the cleric.

"Humanssss . . ." He went down on one knee.

Serene squinted. "I saw you with Stone after he defeated Crag, didn't I? You're one of Stone's people."

"Stone is dead. I am new leader." The gargoyle's monstrous visage took on something approaching pride. "I am Stone now. . . ."

Evidently among this group of gargoyles, the leader took the name of his predecessor. Tyros could find little fault with the first Stone's successor. He had already noted that this one spoke Common with even more fluency than their late comrade.

"You are welcome here," Tyros replied. "We owe much to the other Stone."

The horned creature shook his head. "Flock owes you, humansss. We are free. . . ."

He dropped to the ground, head bent forward. Behind him, other gargoyles descended from the trees and took up similar positions.

"I think they're paying homage," Serene finally whispered.

The new Stone lifted his head, then reached out with one clawed hand. He touched Tyros's arm once, then the cleric's. The leader even bowed his head to Taggi, then let out a short keening sound when his gaze touched upon the cairn.

"Flock friends," Stone added, finally rising.

Before either human could reply, the gargoyle suddenly shot up into the air, the rest of his band quickly following him. The gargoyles disappeared to the east, perhaps toward the forgotten province of Atriun, perhaps farther.

"That was . . . interesting," Serene finally said. "And will you be going now, too, Tyros?"

"I must. First back to the city to gather a few things, then, as I said, on to the Conclave and, after that, back to Gwynned and—"

"More glory-seeking?" Serene pressed. "The name of Tyros must be on everyone's lips now."

He couldn't hide his dismay at such a thought. "I am tired of glory, and I have seen what ambition can do. No, I thought I might find a more peaceful clime where my magic can be used to help heal the wounds of the war. Perhaps even somewhere near here."

She glanced away. "Perhaps we'll meet again soon, then."

"I would like that." Tyros truly hoped that they would. While it was too soon to say if anything long-lasting might develop between Serene and him, he thought that the potential was there. He thought the cleric acted as if she believed so, too.

Time would tell . . . and at least they had the time now.

They walked along, for the moment leaving the griffons to mourn alone. The woods felt fresh, alive, not at all like Castle Atriun.

He shivered, thinking of the fate that had claimed Leot and that had nearly befallen him as well.

Serene noticed the reaction and immediately put a comforting hand on his arm. "What is it, Tyros? What's wrong?"

The wizard didn't answer her at first, thinking of Valkyn's foul spells and dark research. The destruction of the citadel had been so complete that little remained that might relate to some curious spellcaster the methods by which to recreate yet another monstrous fortress. However, as a precaution, when Tyros returned to Gwynned, he would make it his first duty to make certain that not even a single rune had survived.

Richard A. Knaak

There could be no second Atriun.

"Nothing is wrong," Tyros finally assured her. Yes, he would make certain such a horror would not be repeated. "Just a fading memory."

And soon, if Tyros had his way, one forgotten forever.

Downfall
The Dhamon Saga
Volume One
Jean Rabe

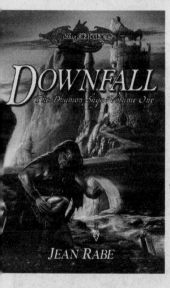

How far can a hero fall?

Far enough to lose his soul?

Dhamon Grimwulf, once a Hero of the Heart, has sunk into a bitter life of crime and squalor. Now, as the great dragon overlords of the Fifth Age coldly plot to strengthen their rule and to destroy their enemies, he must somehow find the will to redeem himself.

But perhaps it is too late.

Don't miss the beginning of Dhamon's story from Jean Rabe!

Available May 2000

Dragons of a New Age

The Dawning of a New Age
Great dragons invade Ansalon, devastating the land and dividing it among themselves.

The Day of the Tempest
The Heroes of the Heart seek the long-lost dragonlance in the snow-covered tomb of Huma.

The Eve of the Maelstrom
Dragons and humans battle for the future of Krynn at the Window to the Stars.

Serving up a generous helping of adventure!

More Leaves From the Inn of the Last Home
Edited by Margaret Weis and Tracy Hickman

Join your hosts Tika and Caramon Majere for another rollicking evening at the Inn of the Last Home. Page through this collection of recipies, kender insults, gnomish inventions, historical surveys, songs, and poetry. Pull up your chair to one of the greatest adventure sagas ever told.

Available June 2000

Bertrem's Guide to the Age of Mortals:

Everyday Life in Krynn of the Fifth Age

Bertrem the Aesthetic with assistance from Nancy Varian Berberick, Stan!, and Paul B. Thompson

Everything you always wanted to know about life in Krynn during the Fifth Age. Now Bertrem the Aesthetic (with the help of a few friends) takes you on a detailed and fascinating tour of a land torn by war and ravaged by the great dragons, but one in which ordinary people lead their lives as they have always done.

Available October 2000